COLDWAVE

V. BRICKER

BRICKER
NOBLES

First paperback edition February 2024

Cover illustration by Audrey Hotte

ISBN 978-1-963455-01-4 (paperback)

ISBN 978-1-963455-00-7 (hardcover)

ISBN 978-1-963455-02-1 (ebook)

www.brickerandnobles.com

To my ever-patient husband Rhett, who suffered through me writing on nights we had together instead of spending time with him. Your support has not gone unnoticed.

CONTENTS

ACKNOWLEDGMENTS

A lot of time, effort, and heartache from a multitude of people went into writing this book. Firstly, I would like to thank Brenna. She's the one who pushed me to write the romance novel that I inevitably trashed in favor of this book.

Next, I want to thank everyone who helped make this book possible. My beta readers: Brenna (again), Nicole, Kit, Sam, and Simona. My amazing editor Shelley, and Audrey, who did the awesome cover art. Thank you all from the bottom of my heart.

PROLOGUE

MY NAME IS SARAH FROST. A few months ago, I was just a normal high school senior living with my mom in New York. As difficult as it's been to accept what happened, it's only now that I can even begin to face and retell the strange events of last winter.

My father died when I was eight, and my mother suffered from severe absenteeism, at least when it came to being part of my life. Because of the actions of a man I once trusted, I was forced to move across the country to Seattle and live with my aunt, my dad's younger sister. It "would be good for me," or so my mom said, but it sounded like an excuse. She didn't want to have to deal with me and the trouble I brought.

She was right, but what happened was *not* my fault.

CHAPTER 1

THE DREAM WAS ALWAYS the same.

Red and blue lights flashed outside an automatic sliding door as I sat in a hospital waiting room, kicking legs that didn't yet touch the floor. The lobby was lit with dim yellow light, and it smelled of bleach. My face hurt from eyes that were puffy and swollen from crying, but I couldn't stop. A few other people were there, but their faces were blurry and indistinct. They wouldn't look at me, knowing why I was there.

A set of double doors opened to my right, and my mother walked briskly out of a long white hallway. A thin woman of average height with long, dark hair, and in the dream, she appeared younger than she was in real life. She was an impeccable dresser, but tonight she looked ragged, like a beautiful porcelain doll that had been left out in the rain. Glancing around, she spotted me and hurried over, kneeling so that she could look into my eyes. She looked tired, and her makeup, always so precise and perfect, was smeared. Tears welled in her eyes as she opened her mouth, and dread filled me in anticipation of her words.

"A car accident," Mom said in a disbelieving voice. Then she gripped both my hands and cried out, "Daddy's gone!" Sobbing, she leaned forward, burying her face in my lap and wrapping her arms around me.

I didn't wail in the dream, as I had ten years ago when my father had died. Instead, I felt empty. I already knew what came next. My mother would continue crying, and I would be led through those double doors and into a small room where my father lay. He would be unmoving and attached to many different lines and tubes leading to various beeping monitors. I would have the chance to say goodbye to a man who could no longer hear me.

As I steeled my nerves, I noticed that this version of the dream was a little different. I looked away from my mother's crumpled form, and a man was sitting next to me. He'd never been there the other times.

The man was older, with golden-blond hair streaked with gray falling to his shoulders. He looked at me, and his features blurred like the other people in the lobby, but there was something about him that made my blood run cold. Through the haze, I saw his piercing blue eyes, and they were hungry. I wanted to move away from him, but my mother pinned me there, shaking in her sorrow. The blond man raised a hand and reached toward me as I watched, trapped and unable to scream.

"Please make sure all tray tables are in the upright and locked position," recited a pleasant voice over the intercom, startling me awake. A stewardess in a black uniform walked through the aisle to make sure our seat belts were fastened, her heels thumping hollowly as she made her way down the plane.

I peeled my cheek off the window and groaned under my breath. My neck was stiff from falling asleep at that angle, and I could feel the echoes of a developing migraine. It had been a long flight, and the last I remembered, we had only been three hours in. Stretching as best I could while trying not to hit the snoozing woman next to me, I attempted to get comfortable again.

After a six-and-a-half-hour flight, we'd finally started our descent. I yawned and looked out the window. The coastline of Seattle was visible in the distance, evergreen trees scattered throughout square urban structures. Even though I had been born there, it wasn't a place I knew all that well. I didn't know what the more famous buildings were called, how to get from one place to another without GPS, what people did on weekends, and which restaurants were good. What I remembered was a reel of flashing child-hood images—cool, windy beaches, long walks in the rain, warm cups of hot chocolate, camping, and picnics in the park.

Staring down at the mist-strewn landscape made me feel dizzy. I watched as droplets of water raced each other across the window, wondering who the blue-eyed man from my dream had been. It was strange that in all the years I'd had that dream, I'd never seen him before. He frightened me, but he couldn't have been real. It was just my sleep-deprived brain adding symbolic details to an event that I'd watched a hundred times in my head. What did it mean?

Probably that I'd eaten too much fast food before getting on the plane.

One week ago, my life had been turned upside down in the course of a single evening, and since then, I'd been picking up the pieces of my shattered world. I'd had to leave everyone and everything behind. The man could have been some sort of subconscious manifestation of... what? Staying away from old blond men?

I shook my head and immediately regretted it as a dull thumping began behind my left ear. More sleep first, then thinking. It was only a dream, after all. Best not to read too much into it for now.

The sound from the engines changed as the plane approached the landing strip. My stomach always gave me fits during final descents. Landing was the part I liked least about flying, not that I did a lot of it. I don't fear heights or anything, but I don't like the feeling of my organs attempting to escape as gravity pulls me down to earth. Roller coasters aren't my thing either. Go figure.

I forcibly put the dream out of my thoughts. No matter what happened from this point forward, this was a new start for me. There was the gnawing feeling in the back of my head that I was just running away from my problems and that it was an uncomfortable comparison to what my mom did, but I tried my best to ignore it. Dad had loved Seattle, and it was about time that I stopped avoiding the memory of him, no matter how much it hurt.

Even though I didn't want to be here, for now, it was home. I would have to make the most of it.

CHAPTER 2

IT TOOK a few minutes to gather my bag from the overhead compartment, but it wasn't long before I found myself walking up the ramp into the airport. If you haven't been to the SeaTac Airport, it's a maze of different terminals, sections, and shops selling everything from jewelry to Fran's Chocolates to Seahawks jerseys. There are people with long layovers, who have time to shop, and those with short layovers, thus having to rush between gates, desperate to catch their flights. Small golden fish are inlaid into the walkway floors, which gives you something interesting to look at. It's overpriced and crowded. It's even worse around the holidays, which it was.

By following the baggage-claim signage, I eventually picked my way through the hoard of bodies and sound to the outside world. After one tram and what felt like thousands of steps later, I took a deep breath of brisk morning air and car exhaust.

Even at seven-thirty in the morning, and on a Tuesday no less, a plethora of cars were crowding into the pickup lanes. At the same time, uniformed officers waved them through, blowing their whistles at any driver who lingered too long. People walked past, triggering the automatic doors back into the airport, blasting me with the warm air from inside. They waved to cars while others loaded their luggage hurriedly into trunks to get out of the cold. It was busier here than I thought it would be, but being one of the west coast's major airports, it shouldn't have been surprising.

I shivered as a chill winter breeze blew through the tunnel-like overhang that covered the waiting zones. The weather here was colder than it had been back in New York, and the light hoodie I'd worn on the plane was not going to cut it. After a quick survey of the area, I spotted the zone numbers plastered on the support pillars. As I shivered again and moved out of the way of weary travelers exiting the airport, I pulled my phone out of my pocket, unlocked the screen, and sent a quick text message.

No checked bags. Waiting Zone 3.

After sending the message, I stuffed my hands and the phone back into my pockets, mentally kicking myself for not checking the weather before I'd left. "I thought it didn't get that cold here," I grumbled as the hot exhaust of dozens of cars left trails of white steam in the air.

It was late November, after the Thanksgiving holidays, when sane people lost their minds as the entire country got ready for Christmas. The din of honking horns was doing a number on my pending migraine, and a few people screamed at each other from car windows. It was pure chaos. I smiled. That part reminded me of the home I'd left behind.

My phone chimed, and with a bit of maneuvering, I turned it so that the top stuck out of my pocket, allowing me to read the notification without subjecting my fingers to further exposure.

Around the corner. Be there in a minute.

My breath puffed out in a long cloud of fog right before the deep rumble of an older, meatier engine reached my ears over the murmur of compact cars and SUVs. I whipped my head around, and my breath caught as a midnight-black Dodge Charger from the '60s rounded the corner. The sight of it brought back memories of warm summer days, riding around town with my grandpa, and taking the ferry across Puget Sound to go to the drive-in movie theater.

My grandparents didn't live in Washington anymore, but my heart still raced at the sight of the old Charger. It was much bigger than the little electric cars that surrounded it. The less substantial cars gave the Dodge a wide berth, and it navigated the traffic like a fish in water, smoothly pulling up to the curb in front of me.

I prefer the newer Japanese cars. They are better for the environment and get good mileage. Still, even I could appreciate the polished and lovingly cared-for relic that was Grandpa's pride and joy. It purred like a giant cat, idle and ready to pounce. I glanced around. The people near me were staring as well, and not just the ones waiting to be picked up. Even the cop, who moments ago had been directing traffic, gazed first at the Charger, then at me. It was obvious what he was thinking. *Who would risk bringing that piece of art to the airport just to pick up a kid?* I ducked my head and gave him a shy smile. Way to make an entrance, Liv.

The grumbling engine went silent with a loud snarl, and the front driver's side door opened. A beautiful woman with long, curly, dark hair emerged and stepped onto the asphalt.

She was tall, taller than most women. Even though not an inch of skin showed beneath her neck, it was easy to tell that she was powerfully built, like a fitness model in jeans, a leather jacket, and aviator sunglasses. Beneath those sunglasses, her eyes were the same bright blue as mine, and when she smiled, it was as if the morning chill was far away. It would be easy to be jealous of her beauty, but I'd missed her too much for the thought to even cross my mind. Instead, I grinned at her and glanced at the cop again. At least he wasn't staring at me anymore.

"Sarah!" my aunt gasped as she skipped to the curb in her four-inch heels, then threw her arms around me. After a moment's surprise, I wrapped my arms around her and returned the hug. It felt nice after being apart for so long. Even though I hadn't come here under the best circumstances, it was good to see her. She looked pretty much the same as when I'd last visited. Had it really been five years?

Aunt Liv let go of me and took a step back, staring at my face intently. "You're so much taller, so much more mature. You remind me of your mother." She smiled again. "Except for the eyes." Her own eyes flicked down to the hoodie and the carry-on bag I'd rolled outside. One of her perfectly shaped eyebrows lifted. "Is this all you brought?"

I felt my cheeks burn and averted my gaze. "I shipped a couple of boxes before I left. They should be here in a few days. Leaving in a rush didn't give me a lot of time to pack everything up."

She shook her head, curls bouncing around her shoulders. "Well, that's good." She glanced over at the cop. He looked like he was getting ready to come our way. One side of Liv's mouth quirked in amusement. "We'd better get going before we get in trouble." Then, turning to the cop, she grinned at him and waved, making his already red cheeks flush an even brighter scarlet. The officer stumbled as he missed a step, going back to directing traffic.

Aunt Liv put my suitcase in the Charger's trunk, and we slid into the front seats. The old car was exactly as I remembered it. Black leather seats and a larger, thinner steering wheel than any other vehicle made this century. It smelled like cedar and polish, making me inhale deeply on reflex.

However, there was one change since I'd seen it last. The dash now sported an info screen, and I could see it had a brand-new stereo, complete with Bluetooth, and a backup camera.

There wasn't a lot of talking on the way home. Well, at least not from me. Aunt Liv talked, and I stared out the window. The words she spoke did little to pull me out of my thoughts as we drove past the buildings I dimly remembered. I heard her say that my grandparents had moved to Arizona permanently, and we would have the house to ourselves, but I already knew that. At least that would be better than being at Mom's house in New York all by myself. By now, she would be on a plane to her next international destination with her latest fling. What was his name? Barry? Larry?

Not that it mattered. Mom didn't keep them around for very long.

"Do you want to talk about it, Sarah?" Liv asked, startling me out of my thoughts.

"About what?" I replied, not looking at her.

"You know what," she said, her voice dry.

I did know, but I didn't want to talk to anyone about it. At least, not yet. "No."

Aunt Liv sighed, and we rode in awkward silence for the rest of the trip. I didn't look at her, instead staring at the stores as we drove by. Eventually, I recognized the streets. Old memories sparked to life as we passed a rundown diner that my grandmother took me to on the weekends when I was a child. It was close to the house, had comfortable seats and nice people working there. If it was the same as before, their apple pie was delicious.

We pulled off the main road, and there it was. Nestled between two other houses was my grandparents' home, the house I lived in until I was nine years old—a full year after my dad died—looking just as I remembered it.

One of the great things about the Queen Anne neighborhood was that since it was built in the early 1900s, each of the houses was unique. There were no housing developments with cookie-cutter houses going up. If homes needed to be renovated, the owners had to get approval that was reviewed on a case-by-case basis, and at a great expense to their owners. My grandparents' two-story home was painted a light green, with white trim around the edges. It had been renovated a few times over the years, and the old house looked much newer than it actually was. A driveway ran along the left side to a small, detached garage. A few tall trees stood in the front yard and provided some much-needed shade to the house in the summer. Aunt Liv pulled into the driveway and parked the Charger in front of the garage.

I got out of the car and stared at the house. When my parents and I had come to live with my grandparents, the five-bedroom home was converted into two separate living spaces. We lived in the two-bedroom apartment upstairs, and my grandparents and Aunt Liv lived in the three-bedroom unit downstairs. Now, with my grandparents no longer living there, the house felt empty, the darkened windows giving the impression that the warmth that had been there before had died out.

"It will be nice having another person here," Liv said as she pulled herself out of the Charger and popped open the trunk. "It was getting a little lonely with Mom and Dad gone." She pulled my bag out and shut the trunk. Then she handed it to me as I followed her up the steps to the front door. The wood creaked under our weight, like a soft sigh. That sound was comforting. It was silly, but, to me, it was like a gentle welcome.

"You'll be in the upstairs unit. Some of your dad's old things are in the second bedroom, so you can go through them if you want to." She unlocked the door and stood aside, holding it open for me.

I stepped across the threshold and looked around at my old home. There was a staircase to the right that led to the apartment above. A long hallway to the left of the stairs stretched before me, leading to a door that opened to the backyard. A coat rack stood in the corner with one long black peacoat hanging on a hook and two umbrellas resting at the bottom. In my memories, there was a line of shoes against the wall—a testament to the life contained within these walls. Now, there was one lonesome pair of rain boots. The door on the left—just before the hallway—was the entrance to where my grandparents had once lived. Now, Aunt Liv occupied it by herself.

Liv shut the front door behind her and turned on the light, making the white walls glow in the soft yellow illumination. "I'm sure you want to rest after your flight," she said as she peeled off the leather jacket. "I put a few things in the kitchen upstairs in case you're hungry. Feel free to help yourself." She opened the door leading into her apartment, then glanced at where I was standing at the bottom of the stairs. "You're welcome to come and go as you please. I'm not your mom, so there's no curfew or anything. Just call me if you're going to be out late. You're an adult, and you can take care of yourself. All I ask is that you let me know where you are and if you need a ride. There's a house key on the table upstairs." She tapped a finger to her bottom lip in thought. "We'll get you enrolled in school before the new term starts, but there's another month or so before that needs to be done. Did your mom give you some money? I could give you some to tide you over if she didn't."

"You don't need to worry about that. I have a little in savings, and Mom said she'd send me more soon." Whenever that might be, but I didn't want to burden Aunt Liv. As soon as I could, I'd get a part-time job. Who knew? Maybe something good would come my way. If I was going to be here for a while I might as well lean into it.

A smile tugged at her lips. "Well, I'm here if you need me. I'll order dinner, and we can watch a movie later if you want to." She stared at me for a moment before saying, "Let me know if you need anything." Aunt Liv held up her phone to indicate texting her was sufficient and walked into her apartment.

As she closed the door, I stared at the landing at the top of the stairs. After my father died and my mom and I moved out, Aunt Liv had lived in the upstairs apartment to get some space from her parents. When I'd visited in the past, I stayed upstairs with her, and we spent a lot of time together. It felt more like she was an older sister than an aunt since she was so much younger than my dad. Now that she lived downstairs, I wondered if she'd left the upstairs the same as when she'd lived up there.

I carried my bag up the stairs, taking care not to let the

wheels hit the steps and scuff the wood. As my head crested the landing above, I looked around.

The living area was open to the entry below, a guardrail separating it from the stairs. Liv must have moved most of her personal stuff downstairs, leaving just the furniture, which was sparse. The same small table and chairs stood in the wood-floored kitchenette and the well-used old leather couch was in the living room, with a somewhat newer TV. The kitchenette boasted a two-burner stove, refrigerator, and microwave, all the same off-white color. A vase decorated the kitchen table with a bouquet of fresh-looking daisies, but other than that, the place was clean and empty.

I finished ascending and set my bag next to the table. The bedroom that was once my childhood bedroom was across the living room, next to the kitchenette. Its door was slightly ajar. I walked across the living room and gingerly pushed it open.

The room was tiny, just as I remembered it. A full-size bed, with a thick-looking comforter lying on top, was pushed against the far wall. The room had a walk-in closet and its own small bathroom with a shower, which you could also enter from the living room. I backed out and shut the door, staring at the door next to the landing.

When we'd lived here, it had been my parents' room and my father's office. Liv had told me some of my father's old things were in there. I vaguely remembered a large wooden desk, and a leather chair, next to my parent's bed. A weight settled in my chest as I approached the room. The memories assaulting me were overwhelming, and I was afraid of what was waiting for me behind that door. I took a deep breath, turned the doorknob, and pushed.

The room was bare except for a few cardboard boxes. They were plain, white file boxes, like those some offices used for storage. I sat on the floor in front of one and lifted the lid.

The boxes were filled with pictures. Pictures of us—my father, Mom, and me. I reached in and lifted out a small pile, then flipped through them. Some of them had my grandparents and Aunt Liv in them. Others had people that I must have met but didn't remember. The pictures were of various activities. Having a picnic in the park, swimming in the lake, and playing in the backyard. A few from a Christmas gathering, one showing a younger Aunt Liv hanging off the arm of a man with long blond hair, and me sitting on my father's lap. It was proof that we were happy once.

That was before my father died in that car accident. Tears welled in my eyes, and I didn't bother brushing them away as I picked up a picture frame with one of my dad and me. There he was, smiling at me. When I thought about him, I couldn't recall his voice or his face. The man looking at me was almost a stranger.

CHAPTER 3

"DO you think they're all right?" said a low, rumbling voice that was very familiar to me.

"I'm sure they're fine," I said with a voice that was not my own. "Liv will keep Sarah safe."

Sunshine warmed my skin, coming through the high windows in the dining area of a house that was unrecognizable. A newspaper sat on the table, with a headline reading: "Mayor Speaks Out on Woman's Mangled Body Found Earlier This Week. Third This Month."

My grandfather sat in the chair across the table. He was a man in his sixties, his dark hair peppered with gray, and fine lines showed around his mouth and eyes. He hadn't changed much in the few years since I'd last seen him, and he smiled with that same warm smile from my memories. "You're right. Liv knows what she's doing. Still..." He picked up the newspaper. "This looks bad. The Nine are losing control."

A hand brushed through my hair. Wherever I was, it was as if my awareness was trapped inside someone else's body. The next time I spoke, I recognized the voice and knew whose eyes I saw through.

"They can't lose control," my grandmother said, and despite her words, she sounded worried. "If it was that bad, they would have called us by now. They aren't having this kind of trouble in Dallas or Charleston."

My grandfather made a thoughtful sound that made me think he wasn't convinced that whoever this "Nine" was had control of what they were talking about. It didn't make sense. My grandparents lived in Phoenix now. Were they having trouble there?

He sighed. "We should ask Liv—"

"Wake up, Sarah."

With slowness that only came from sleep, I realized I was being shaken awake. I blinked my eyes open to see Aunt Liv standing over me, her hand on my shoulder. I was lying in my bed, the comforter wrapped around me to ward off the cold. Warm, golden sunlight streamed through the slats in the blinds covering the windows. It was morning. "What's wrong?" I tried to say, but it came out as a long groan.

Liv straightened, failing to hide a look of deep frustration as she stared down at me. "You need to get up, Sarah. It's past noon already."

It was *not* morning. I grunted words that were unintelligible and rolled over, intending to go back to sleep. Maybe my dreams would be normal this time.

The bed shifted as Liv sat next to me. I kept my body turned away from her and closed my eyes, pretending to be asleep again. She'd attempted to talk to me a few times over the past few days about how I was feeling regarding the move, but I didn't want to talk to her about it. It was too painful to think about, but it was the only thing on my mind. Her intentions were good, but I just wanted to be left alone. Watching TV and reading drowned it out for a while, so I'd been doing that, holed up in my little second-floor apartment.

"Sarah," she said, more gently this time. I wondered if she still had that look on her face. I didn't need her pity. "You've been here for over a week, and you haven't stepped outside at all." She sighed, and it was as if that one sound held a great sadness. "I know it's still a month out before you have to go back to school, but you should at least try to make some new friends. There are a few kids your age around the neighborhood. Hell, the light-rail station isn't too far from here either. Don't you want to explore the city at all? It's your senior year. You should be out having fun."

I rolled onto my stomach, turning my head to look at her through the blankets. I kept my silence and eyed her, willing her to leave.

Aunt Liv frowned and shook her head. "I get that you don't want to talk about Brian, but this is ridiculous, Sarah. You can't sulk up here for the rest of winter break."

Watch me, I thought, but I bit back the retort. Deep down, I knew that I couldn't stay in my room forever. I would eventually have to face the world and come to terms with my situation, but not yet. Once school started again, I would be forced to continue with my life. Aunt Liv was worried about me, but if she could help a little less, that would be great. Good intentions aside, she couldn't fix this.

After a few more moments of examining me, she stood and placed her hands on her hips. I recognized that stubborn look in her eyes and immediately knew she was up to no good. She glared at me, then spun around and headed to the stairs.

"Do you remember Jen? I invited her over for dinner. Five o'clock," Aunt Liv said over her shoulder. "I'll be cooking chicken. You need to shower if you want to eat with us. I think the smell would drive company away." Soft thumps sounded as she descended to the first floor.

Fuming, I snatched my pillow and threw it at the landing. It didn't make it that far and tumbled lamely into the living area of my small apartment. With a groan, I pulled the blanket over my head. Why did Aunt Liv have to meddle so much?

I lay face down on my bed for a few minutes before pushing myself up onto my elbows. I knew that getting out and keeping busy would be good for me, but I didn't have the will or desire to leave the apartment. Seattle was a big city, and there was plenty that would interest me here. Since I was eighteen, I could do just about anything I wanted, but the lack of motivation to get out of bed was my biggest problem.

While extracting myself from the chrysalis that was my blanket, what Liv had said sank in.

Jen was coming over. Jen had been my best friend growing up. We'd kept in touch even after Mom and I had moved to New York, emailing and messaging each other, but after a few years, we'd fallen out of touch. It was unbelievable I hadn't thought about reaching out to her myself. I'd been so wrapped up in my own misery that I'd forgotten that there was anyone who was still my friend.

As furious as I was at my aunt for forcing me to be social, I had to admit that a part of me was excited to see Jen. It would be good to catch up with her.

Pulling myself out of bed, I trundled over to the bathroom. The clothes and other miscellaneous stuff that I'd mailed from New York had already arrived, so there were warmer clothes than those I'd worn on the plane. I showered, taking my time to soak in the hot water, and dressed in an oversized sweater and fleece leggings. My mom was a fashion designer and would have screamed at me for dressing in a style she would call "messy," but she wasn't here, and it was comfortable and warm.

By the time I'd brushed my hair and finished getting ready for the day, it was already after three. Jen would be here in two hours.

Looking around the small apartment, I realized I wasn't the only messy thing. There were days-old dishes in the sink, clothes scattered around the dining table next to the vase of now-dead flowers, and socks littering the floor. If there was even the remote possibility of Jen coming up here, I needed to make my new abode look habitable.

I picked up all the clothes and threw them into the hamper located in the bathroom. Next came the kitchenette. There was no dishwasher, so any dishes would need to be washed by hand. The dead daisies went directly into the garbage.

Once I was finished, the apartment looked like it had the first night I arrived. There was nothing displayed on the walls or shelves, and I hadn't gone to the store to buy anything, so it had the look of a dwelling that was waiting for a new tenant to move in. The bare, white-washed walls had no life to them. Making this place my own would be a top priority since it was mine for the foreseeable future. I would have to go and buy a few things to decorate.

The savory aroma of rosemary and garlic pulled me out

of my thoughts. I stuck my head over the railing and looked down to the landing below. The door to Liv's apartment was ajar, and the smell of delicious cooking wafted up the stairs, making my stomach growl. Usually, my grandmother cooked when I was visiting, but since she wasn't here, that left Liv. Grandma must have taught my aunt a thing or two in the kitchen.

Dinner was a few hours off, and I wouldn't dare spoil it by eating now. The clock on the microwave read four-fifteen, still another forty-five minutes before Jen would arrive.

Tired from my sudden burst of activity, I sat on the couch and laid my head back. I'd been sleeping a lot since coming here, and it was starting to affect how I felt during the day. That would need to be fixed before it became a habit; otherwise, I would have a hard time getting up for school when I was finally enrolled.

With my eyes closed, I thought about what Aunt Liv had said. Dammit, she was right, but hell would freeze over before I'd admit that to her. Even though it was the middle of winter, the city was alive with activity. I needed to find something to do to stop thinking about Mom and New York. And Brian.

A knock at the door startled me. I hadn't realized I'd dozed off. I found myself lying on my side on the couch. A quick look out the windows told me that the sky outside was a muted violet, fading into true night. How long had I been asleep?

The murmur of voices echoed up the stairs, and Aunt Liv called, "Sarah! Jen's here!" Standing, I ran a hand through my hair, working the tangles with my fingers, and trotted over to the stairs. Leaning over the railing, I saw a young woman staring up at me.

Whoever this was, she looked little like the Jen I'd known in years past. The Jennifer Steele I remembered was a short fourteen-year-old girl with long blonde hair, who loved everything pink and Lisa Frank. This person was tall and lean, with blonde hair in a pixie cut that framed her heart-shaped face. Her pale green sweater matched her eyes, and a floor-length skirt made her legs look even longer. She wore a necklace over the sweater with a silver coin hanging from a thin, silver chain. She grinned at me, her eyes sparkling in the afternoon twilight.

"Hey, Sarah. It's been a while," she said with a wave.

I stepped down the stairs, feeling my own smile stretching across my face. "Yeah, it has. How have you been?"

She opened her mouth to respond, but Aunt Liv cut her off. "Save it for the table. The food's going to get cold." With a flick of her hair, Liv turned and walked through the doorway to her part of the house.

Jen laughed as I rolled my eyes, and we followed Liv into the downstairs unit.

I'd only been downstairs once or twice since arriving. The apartment looked similar to how my grandparents had it when they'd lived here, with well-worn but comfortable furniture and hardwood floors. The downstairs unit expanded out further than the upstairs, so the living room was twice as big as mine and could seat six or seven people comfortably. The walls here were also white, but a painting of an evergreen forest hung on the wall behind the couch, giving the room a serene quality.

A few things had changed, though. The absence of the crystal platters and bowls that my grandmother loved to collect was noticeable, and my grandfather's old guns weren't on display anymore. It was weird noticing that those little details were gone, and it made me feel less welcome in Liv's space.

There was a short hallway off the right side of the living room that led to the apartment's three bedrooms and bathrooms. To the left, between the living room and the kitchen, was a large dining table with a chandelier above. There were place settings for three, and dinner was already on the table. A baking dish with a towel under it was piled high with pieces of freshly baked chicken that made my mouth water. Roasted potatoes, asparagus, and fresh pasta were laid out in serving bowls.

With a glance at Jen, I took the seat closest to the door. Jen sat next to me, and Aunt Liv was across from us. We served ourselves, and, once our plates were filled with food, Jen smiled at me and asked, "Are you just staying for winter break?"

"No, I'll be here for a while, I think." I took a bite of a chicken leg. Perfection. "My mom's out of the country right now, and she didn't want me staying in the house alone, so I'm going to sign up at the local high school." I wasn't ready to tell her about Brian and have to explain that he was the real reason Mom sent me back here.

Jen grimaced. "That sucks, transferring during your senior year. Too bad I won't be there, but I'm sure you'll make some friends." Jen is a year older than I am, but since we'd never gone to school together, it hadn't mattered before. "You should test out. You're eighteen, right? You can get your GED."

It was an idea I'd already thought of, but I hadn't decided yet if I would do it. "There's that," I said with a mouthful of pasta. "Though if I test out, I'll have nothing going on for the rest of the school year."

She laughed. "There's plenty you can do outside of high

school! I take classes at the community college and work part-time at an art store in Capitol Hill. I'm sure I could get you a job there if you want one." She took a bite of her chicken and chewed it, her expression deep in thought. "Do you still draw, Sarah? Last time we talked, you did, but it's been a while." She smiled apologetically. "Sorry I haven't kept in touch."

"It's all right. I could have been better about that too." I leaned back in my chair, looking at my plate. "It's been a few months, but I still like to draw." I felt a little ashamed at the lie. In reality, it had been so long since I'd used a sketch pad that I hadn't even thought to pack one.

"If you want to get back into it, there are figure-drawing sessions at one of the local studios in SoDo, near Lumen Field. It would be a good place to meet some other artists too. I go once a week, and it's not that expensive, just enough to pay for the model and all. The only thing is, it's pretty intense since you'd be sketching for four hours." She grinned. "Does that sound like something you'd like to do?"

Aunt Liv cleared her throat before I could answer. Jen and I both looked at her. "Well, actually," she began, and I knew I wasn't going to like what came next. "Jen, your mom called me a few days ago to see how Sarah was doing, and she told me about those sessions. She asked if I thought Sarah would want to give them a shot." Liv took a bite of her food, avoiding my gaze. "I told her to go ahead and sign Sarah up."

"You did what?" I growled, narrowing my eyes at her.

"Would you like some dessert, Jen?" Liv asked, completely ignoring me. Jen had a concerned look on her face as Aunt Liv stood from the table and strode into the kitchen. I heard the creak of the oven as she opened it.

"I can't believe her!" I hissed low enough so that Liv couldn't hear me. "She didn't even ask me!"

"Yeah," Jen said with a nervous chuckle, "that's pretty sneaky."

I shook my head and looked at my plate, then set down my fork. I'd lost my appetite. It wasn't fair. Shouldn't someone be asked before their family signed them up for things they didn't want to do? If I wanted to get back into art, I should have been able to do it on my own terms. It was something I would have loved doing, but Liv bulldozing over my right to decide for myself made me reluctant to go along with it.

"But," Jen continued, "you should consider going. I have a few friends who go as well, and I can introduce you to the group. If I'm still the only one you know here, wouldn't it be good to meet some more people?" She watched me closely. Even though she was being casual about it, I could tell by the look in her eyes that she wanted me to say yes.

Averting my gaze, I mumbled, "I don't have any supplies."

"Oh! Don't worry about that!" she said, excitement lacing her voice. "I can give you an extra sketchbook and some pencils if you need them. Since I work at an art store, I have plenty of extras."

Jen looked so excited. How could I say no? I glared toward the kitchen. Aunt Liv planned it so I would feel too guilty not to do it. She was sneaky. "All right," I said. Ignoring the fact that I was being coerced, it did sound like fun, but that was beside the point. Even if it was good for me and she knew that I would enjoy it, Liv still should have asked me first.

At least Jen was going to be there, so it wouldn't be as

awkward as if I were going alone. I managed a smile. "It could be fun, I guess."

"That's the spirit!" Aunt Liv shouted, making me jump as she carried an apple pie in one mittened hand and a tub of vanilla ice cream in the other. "Now that that's settled, who wants some ice cream with her pie?"

CHAPTER 4

IT WAS HARD TO BELIEVE, but two days after the dinner with Jen, the weather was even colder than before. The churning gray sky threatened snow. As a result, not many people were outside, and those who were hurried to their next destination. The studio Jen had told me about was in a tall building off of King Street, just a block or two from the football stadium. The building looked similar to the ones around it, made of concrete and glass, except this one had a banner that read "COMMERCIAL SPACE FOR LEASE" in big blue letters.

Aunt Liv pulled the Charger over to the side of the road. She had stopped in a red zone, but there was nowhere to park. "Hmm..." She scrutinized the building and checked her phone. "It's the right address. Do you want me to go with you?"

"No, but thanks, Mom," I replied sarcastically. The last thing I needed was for her to play chaperone. I got out of the car and pulled my jacket a little closer as the cold air stung my cheeks.

"Call me when you need to be picked up. I have to go in

to work for a little while, but I should be finished around six," she said through the open window. I nodded and waved as the car rumbled away, then turned to the building, the sketchpad Jen had given me tucked under one arm.

I stepped over to the glass doors and peered inside. There was an attractive Asian woman at the front desk, with sleek, long black hair, high cheekbones, and dressed very sharply. She looked a few years older than me, and it was obvious that she was the receptionist.

Glancing down at my old, faded jacket, I felt self-conscious. I hadn't thought I'd needed to dress up to go to an art studio. The woman looked up from her computer screen and spotted me, smiled, and waved for me to come inside. Pulling one of the doors open, I was blasted with hot air, which thawed my face and left my skin tingling.

Inside was a long, tidy lobby with dark hardwood floors and multiple doors lining the brick walls. At the back was an elevator. Couches were spaced at a comfortable distance around small glass tables that occupied the space between the front door and the elevators. I stepped over to the reception desk, and the woman positively beamed at me. She had a welcoming smile with teeth in perfect white rows.

"Hello!" Her voice was friendly. "How can I help you?"

"Um, hi," I managed. "I'm here for the figure-drawing session." I looked around again, noting the lack of traffic through the lobby, and had doubts about the address I was given. "If this is the right place."

"It is," she said, looking at her computer screen and clicking the mouse a few times. "I can go ahead and sign you in. What's your name?"

"Sarah Frost."

"Thanks, Sarah. Let's see here..." Her eyes flicked across the screen. "Ah! Here you are." Another click of the mouse, and she looked back up. "You're good to go. Just take the elevator to the fourth floor. The model hasn't arrived yet, so they should still be setting up."

I thanked her and approached the elevator.

"Have fun!" she called after me.

After a short ride, the elevator doors opened to the fourth-floor landing, facing a heavy door that wasn't labeled. I stepped out of the elevator, but there was no signage to indicate that I'd arrived at the right place.

The woman downstairs seemed to know what was happening, so, hopefully, I wasn't about to walk in on some big corporate meeting or something. Nothing here screamed art studio. I shrugged to myself and opened the door. If this was the wrong place, maybe someone inside could tell me where I needed to go.

Twenty sets of eyes looked up at the same time. People were spread out in a large high-ceilinged room, most seated in chairs behind easels. The chatter died as they stared. A violent urge to turn around and run back to the elevator washed over me. Aunt Liv wouldn't be all the way to work yet. She could come back and get me, especially since this was her stupid idea anyway.

The loud banging of the door shutting behind me was like the breaking of a spell. Everyone returned to what they were doing, talking and setting up their easels. I let out the breath I hadn't realized that I'd been holding and spotted a few empty seats toward the back of the room. Mustering my courage, I moved over to them. Eyes followed me all the way to the empty seats. The feeling wasn't as suffocating as it had been moments before, but it still made me uneasy.

People lost interest the longer I sat there. Eventually, I felt comfortable enough to look around the room without anyone staring at me. This was definitely an art studio. It was huge and newly renovated, with canvases and sketches covering the freshly painted walls. The concrete floor had been stained, and the steel rafters shone in the natural light that poured in through the floor-to-ceiling windows. Sculptures of ears, hands, and other body parts sat on pedestals near the walls, lamps pointed at them from all sides. Photographs and magazine clippings of everything one could think of were stacked in piles next to a worktable near a section of the room that was curtained off. It looked like the space extended even further behind that curtain. Above it, I could make out the shadowed edges of a staircase that ascended into the rafters and ended with a door. It must have led to the roof.

"Hey, Sarah!" Jen slid into the seat next to me as I turned around. "Glad you could make it!" Another girl with auburn hair and brown eyes sat in the next chair and peered at me over Jen's shoulder. She looked to be the same age as we were.

"Yeah." I laughed nervously, glancing around again. "Aunt Liv wouldn't have let me bail. I'd never hear the end of it."

A few people were giving us curious looks, but Jen's face must have been familiar since most of the attendees were too absorbed in what they were doing to notice her.

"Liv's pretty intense." Jen nodded sagely and leaned back in her chair so that the person with her could see me. "This is Kat." Kat gave me a half-hearted wave, and Jen laughed. "Don't worry too much if she doesn't talk to you. She's kind of quiet."

Kat's cheeks turned bright pink, and she glared at Jen. "I'm not that quiet." Her voice was deeper than most others our age, making her seem more mature. "It's nice to meet you, Sarah," she said as she tossed some of her long hair over her shoulder and smiled.

The door opened again, and two more people walked in. "There they are!" Jen waved the two other people over. "This is Izzy and Patrick," she said as they took the two seats on the other side of me. "This is Sarah. She's an old friend of mine who just moved back to town."

Izzy was a short, petite girl who had one side of her head shaved and the other side cut at her shoulders and dyed black. She wore black lipstick, heavy eyeliner, and combat boots. There was a silver stud in her eyebrow and gauges in her ears so big that it made me wonder if the process of getting them had been painful. Overall, she looked a little intimidating, but her smile was warm and sincere. "Nice to meet you, Sarah."

I shook hands with her and Patrick, who was tall and looked to be of Asian descent. He took off his jacket and placed it on the back of his chair. Underneath, he wore a long-sleeved muscle shirt and jeans, clashing with Izzy's goth look.

Jen leaned over to talk to them around me. "Where's Tommy?"

"He's not coming today," Izzy said. "He had to babysit the gremlins."

Jen shrugged and glanced over at me. "Well, you'll meet him later. He's got a younger brother and sister he has to watch sometimes while his mom works." She grinned. "But this is the group! Well, except for Vaughn, but he's—"

The door swung open again, cutting Jen off.

A man who embodied the classic "tall, dark, and handsome" stereotype entered the room. He had shoulder-length black hair and golden skin that only came from spending many hours in the sun, which was quite a feat in Seattle.

Even from across the room, I could feel the weight of his green eyes as he gazed over the people there. His lips pulled back from straight white teeth in an impish smile as he sauntered in. He wore a black graphic T-shirt and jeans but still made them look stylish. Whoever this was, his mere presence demanded attention. Everyone stopped talking when he entered the room. I couldn't take my eyes off of him.

"—the model," Jen finished.

One of the women closer to the door jumped up and stepped in front of the man I assumed Jen had just been talking about, blocking my view. I shook my head and took a deep breath, then glanced at the others. Izzy and Jen looked a little pink in the face and intently focused on putting together their easels. The chatter started up again but was more subdued than before. Only Kat wasn't affected by Vaughn's presence. Instead, she was scowling at the woman speaking with him.

What was wrong with me? It wasn't as if I'd never seen an attractive guy before. Maybe it was because I wasn't dating anyone, and he'd caught me off guard. Right. Let's go with that.

Patrick muttered, "This always happens. I don't get it."

"He's just pretty," Jen answered, her cheeks getting even redder. She didn't look at him but continued fumbling with the easel. "They know what's coming, and I have to admit, it's still a little weird sometimes since he's one of our friends."

I didn't know what they were talking about, but I caught Jen's eye and tilted my head toward Kat, who was looking the other way. That woman talking to the model would catch fire if Kat kept looking at her like that. Jen shook her head and leaned in closer to me. "It's best to leave her alone," she whispered. "They've been friends since the third grade. She likes him and has been trying to convince him to go out with her for years, but I guess he doesn't feel the same way. It's kind of sad." She paused for a moment before continuing. "He's a nice guy, but there are a lot of rumors floating around. Vaughn used to be one of those 'bad boys,' and his guardian kicked him out last year."

A bad boy. Got it. Best to stay away from that. I'd had enough of that kind of guy for a lifetime. I stared at the sketchbook I'd placed in front of me as if my eyes could burn a hole in it, ears and neck prickling with heat. He was part of the group, wasn't he? That meant I'd have to meet him sooner or later.

Jen glanced at where Vaughn and the woman were talking and sighed. "A lot of people say he's living with an older woman, but that's not true. He's actually living in one of Carter's condos. Vaughn's a good friend, and he's been through a lot in the past few years. Sometimes, I can't help but worry about him." She shrugged a little self-consciously. "We do what we can and try to make sure that he knows we're here for him."

I looked at Vaughn thoughtfully. Jen had mentioned the name Carter, and I assumed that I would meet them later. Shaking my head, I set up my supplies. Jen had given me a few graphite pencils, a kneaded eraser, and a Ziplock bag of charcoal. The basics, but it would work well for sketching.

When I looked up again, Vaughn was standing on a table in the middle of the room. His shirt was discarded on the floor, and he was unbuttoning his pants. His gaze met mine for a brief second before I felt my face grow hot, and I looked back down at my sketchbook. Right, figure drawing. I'd forgotten what that meant. Jen's comments earlier were starting to make sense. Dammit.

"Let's get started," the woman who had been talking to Vaughn earlier said as she set a timer.

The voices of the rest of the group quieted until all that could be heard was the scratching of pencils on paper. A giggle came from beside me, and I looked over to see Jen watching me from the corner of her eye, a smile playing at the corners of her mouth. She knew that I hadn't realized that the model would be nude, and was enjoying my reaction. I made a face at her and positioned the easel to block my view of Vaughn's midsection. There, problem solved.

No one else was having any issues with Vaughn's nakedness, and they were all sketching away. I took a deep breath and let it out through my nose.

If they could do this, so could I. Just focus on safe body parts.

Before my pencil even touched the paper, the timer when off, and Vaughn changed positions. As he settled into the next pose, our gazes met again and the corner of his mouth curled, and I dropped my eyes to the sketchbook. I stared hard at the paper in front of me, trying to ignore him. He was supposed to be a bad boy, right? Was he trying to mess with me because I was new?

When I finally felt brave enough to attempt to draw him, he'd shifted his gaze and was staring off into the distance, a relaxed look on his face.

I sighed inwardly and started sketching. It was going to be a long day.

CHAPTER 5

THE TIMER WENT OFF, and I strangled the overwhelming urge to pick up the easel and throw it across the room. I'd only finished drawing Vaughn's head and had been working on his shoulder. The sketchbook Jen had given me was filling up with half-finished drawings of Vaughn's form since whenever I started getting the hang of it, he would switch poses. How was anyone supposed to draw him if he kept moving?

The woman with the timer motioned to Vaughn, and he jumped off the table. He picked up his clothes from a pile on the floor and dressed. "We have to start getting ready for the show, so that's it for today!" she called as Vaughn pulled his pants on. "Please remember that you are all invited to Carter's exhibition, and if you can make it, RSVP on the website." She set the timer down and, with a grin that was a little too wide, began chatting with Vaughn again, her cheeks turning pink.

"Show?" I asked Jen and stretched my arms above my head, leaning backward and hearing a satisfying pop from my back. Sitting for too long made my muscles ache, and we'd been here for a few hours. "Who's Carter? And what show is she talking about?"

"Carter Godfrey. He's the artist who owns the studio and is kind of the host of our art classes," Jen said as she unzipped her messenger bag to put her pencils away. "He just moved everything here from his old location off of Fourth Street, so he's throwing a housewarming party slash art show tomorrow night. There might be an auction too. Carter's pretty famous in the city. He does a lot of work for local businesses, painting murals and donating items for charity events. I'm surprised you haven't heard of him." She flipped the cover of her enormous sketch pad down, then tapped a finger to her lips in thought. "Well, he only got really popular a few years ago, so I guess you wouldn't have. Anyway, there's going to be food and drinks. Oh, and a bunch of wealthy buyers." Jen's eyes lit up, and I knew what was coming next. "You should come! Carter knows how to throw a good party," she said with that same poorly hidden anticipation that she'd had when she was over for dinner. "I went to a couple before his studio moved to the new location. He says that it's his duty to support young artists, so he invites everyone who participates in the figure-drawing sessions to his events."

"I don't know. That's a little out of my league," I said as I put my pencils away and smiled apologetically. It was obvious Jen wanted me to go, but I didn't think I was ready for as much socializing as going to a party required. "I wouldn't know what to do with myself." Pulling my phone out of my jacket pocket, I glanced at it. 5:30. The session had ended a lot earlier than it was supposed to. Aunt Liv's picture appeared as I dialed her number. It went straight to voicemail.

That was strange. I frowned at my phone and tried

dialing the number again. Voicemail. How was I supposed to call her to come get me if she had her phone off? What had she said? I was pretty sure it was that she was going to work after she dropped me off. Liv worked for the city, but did that mean that she had to have her phone off at work? "Looks like I'm taking the bus," I grumbled after the third call. There was a light-rail station close to here, but the sun had already set, and it sounded like a terrible idea to go wandering around a city I didn't know well in the dark.

"I can take you home," came a voice from above me.

To my surprise, Vaughn was leaning over my easel. His deep voice was smooth as silk. His eyes flicked around the group, and he smiled. These people were his friends; it was obvious that he felt comfortable with them around. "I'm Vaughn. My car is in the back. I'll pull it around and you can meet me—"

"No," I said without thinking.

Vaughn's eyes widened, and he looked startled.

"No," I repeated, this time conscious of my reaction. "It's all right. I'll take the light rail." Why was he even talking to me? Who went around giving rides to people they didn't even know? Serial killers, that's who. "Thanks for the offer," I said, trying to sound polite, and stood, tucking my drawing pad under my arm.

Vaughn seemed at a loss, his mouth hanging open. It took him a few seconds to come to his senses. With his looks, he probably wasn't used to being turned down on the spot. "It's not a problem. I don't have anywhere to—"

"I'm taking her home," Jen cut him off. She stood and turned her nose up at Vaughn. "You're a creeper. You haven't even been introduced yet and you're offering to give her a ride home? Do you know who does that? Serial killers," she said, echoing my thoughts exactly. She threw her arms up in exaggerated exasperation. "Who knows what you would do if you had her address?" She grinned and winked at him, then turned to me, hooking one arm in mine. "Are you ready, Sarah? Yes? Okay, then, let's go."

Vaughn looked aghast as Jen turned and dragged me toward the door. I barely had time to snatch up my bag. She was having too much fun with this. I glanced back at the surprised look on his face. He tried to cover it quickly with a friendly smile, but I still felt a little guilty. Even though I didn't want a ride from him, I hadn't intended to hurt his feelings.

"Nice to meet you, Sarah!" Vaughn called after us, amusement in his voice. I guess he was fine. Everyone was staring at us, and the attention made me want nothing more than to sink to the floor. "You'll be at the party, right?"

"We'll think about it! I'll see you guys later!" Jen called with a wave to the others, then let the door shut behind her and pressed the call button for the elevator. The metal doors slid open, and we stepped inside. Once the doors were closed again, Jen grinned at me. "That was kind of fun. Vaughn means well, but you can never be too careful." She shook her head and laughed. "You're going to be trouble, Sarah Frost."

I leaned against the wall as the elevator descended, letting out a long breath. My face felt hot, and it was a little hard to breathe. Confrontation wasn't my forte, and I felt sick to my stomach. I wasn't generally a meek person. It was just that I'd been forcing my feelings down for so long that I had difficulty dealing with the fight-or-flight response.

"Are you all right?" Jen asked, concern lacing her voice.

"Yeah, I'm fine," I lied, taking another deep breath and exhaling slowly. I'd gotten better at controlling my anxiety, but it hadn't gone away completely. It was a lingering consequence of my time in New York. I wondered if my emotions would ever go back to normal. "I'm not great with people, not anymore."

Jen looked concerned, but she could tell I didn't want to talk about it, so she dropped it. "My car's out back," she said, changing the subject.

The elevator doors opened, and we stepped into the lobby. Moving helped me get control of my body again, and the nausea subsided.

"You should look into getting a car if you have the funds. Traffic's terrible here, but probably not as bad as in New York. Buses and the light rail aren't too bad, but for me, it's the cold. I hate walking around in the cold."

The chime of a bell echoed in the lobby, and it took me a second to realize it was coming from Jen's phone.

"Hold on a sec," she said as she dug it out of her coat pocket. A look of disgust crossed her face. "Can't he at least wait until we get in the car?"

"What?"

Jen looked at me and shook her head, stashing her phone in her pocket. "Vaughn. He's asking who you are. I mean, I get that he's curious, but damn, boy, calm down." We walked by the front desk and Jen waved to the receptionist.

"You're going to be trouble," Jen repeated and shook her head, then grinned at me like it was some sort of joke.

I sighed as we walked into the freezing night. Trouble was the last thing I wanted.

Thirty minutes later, Jen pulled her silver Civic up to the curb in front of Liv's house. Lights twinkled through the windows, and the Charger was in the driveway. Aunt Liv must be home. If that was the case, why wasn't her cell phone on? She could have just gotten home and hadn't had a chance to call me back yet, but even so, it was odd.

"Looks like Liv is there," Jen said, coming to the same conclusion I had. "Well, see you later, Sarah."

I nodded and opened the door. "Thanks for the ride."

"You know," Jen continued, "you should really consider going to the party. There will be a lot of interesting people there, people with connections. They'll know about openings in the industry if you're looking for work. That's how I got my first job. Carter also pulls out a lot of stuff that he doesn't show to the public often. I think you'd like it."

Seeing some private artwork did sound interesting, but attending meant having to deal with people. That, and Vaughn would be there. Was it worth putting myself outside of my comfort zone for the chance to see some fantastic art?

It would probably be all right since Jen was going, but I wasn't sure if I wanted to go. "Maybe. I'll have to think about it."

Jen scrunched her lips together. I could tell from the way her eyes crinkled at the edges that she was trying to keep the smug smile off of it. "Okay, how about this? You think about it tonight, and tomorrow I'll come by and pick you up for dinner at six so we can talk. If you feel up to it, we'll head over to the studio after. Does that sound good?"

Jen looked so hopeful. It's not like I had anything planned tomorrow, and it was difficult to justify turning Jen down when all I would do was stew in my room all day. I could always say no to the party if I didn't feel like going after dinner, but I had the feeling that Jen was going to rope me into it no matter how I felt. If I agreed to dinner, I was going to the party. "Fine," I hedged. "Dinner wouldn't hurt."

"Great," she said, grinning at me. "See you tomorrow."

I closed the door and watched Jen drive down the street, turning onto the main road. Reconnecting with Jen had been nice, but she looked and acted so differently than what I remembered of her. I wasn't stupid. People changed over the years, and comparing Jen to her fourteen-year-old self did her a disservice. I felt a strange sense of loss for the friend who had grown up into the woman I was getting to know. I shook my head and turned to the house. Jen used to be the shy one, but now our personalities had reversed entirely. When had that happened?

My change started a few years ago, after I began seeing my now-ex-boyfriend, Brian. At the time, I had no idea what was happening to me, but eventually, I realized he was a real piece of work. It was getting more and more difficult not to blame everything on him, but it was my fault for letting it go on for as long as it did. Didn't that make me equally responsible for what happened?

The anger that had been so hot when I'd left wasn't there anymore. Mostly, I felt numb when I thought about him. He was in New York, and I was on the other side of the country. I had blocked his phone number and all the other numbers he'd used to called me from, and I hadn't told him where my grandparents lived, just that they lived in Seattle. In a metropolitan area of more than four million people, there was little chance of him ever finding me. My life with him was over, and I'd never see him again.

If I kept telling myself that, I might eventually believe it.

When I got inside, I saw that the door to Liv's apartment was open just wide enough for me to peek inside. Voices drifted through it, too clear to be coming from the

TV. I hadn't seen any other cars parked in front of the house. Seattle was a very walkable city, so it could have been that whoever it was had taken the light rail and would either do the same when leaving or have Liv give them a ride.

Curiosity got the better of me, and I leaned close to the door, listening. It wasn't eavesdropping. I was making sure I wasn't going to walk in on anything that would embarrass all of us. Liv didn't share much about her dating life, but if she had a man over, I didn't want to bother her.

The voices were so low that it was hard to make out their words at first. Then, I heard Aunt Liv's voice, smokey and rich, and the deep baritone of someone distinctly male. It sounded like they were arguing. Maybe I should ask Liv about it later. If she was arguing with her boyfriend, I didn't want to get involved. I turned to the stairs.

BAM!

The sound rang like a gunshot, echoing around the room and startling me so much that I almost lost my balance. It sounded like a solid and heavy object had hit the wall or floor. My pulse quickened, and a flash of memory overloaded my senses, the sensation of pain in my midsection as I hit the floor. I clutched my arms and willed the tears away as fear and anger warred within me and my legs shook.

My first instinct was to run and hide, but I forcibly pushed that feeling aside. What if Aunt Liv was in trouble? I would never be able to live with myself if something happened to her while I froze. The least I could do was check.

Moving before I could think about it too much, I looked around for a weapon to defend myself with. There wasn't much in the foyer, so I settled on the white polka-dotted umbrella from the coat rack and pulled out my cell phone, dialing 911 without pressing the call button. I didn't know how long it would take the police to get here, but it would be a good idea to find out what was going on first. It might not be Liv who was hurt.

That thought spurred me forward, and I pushed the door open slowly with the umbrella before creeping into the living room.

"What a bunch of assholes!" Aunt Liv shouted at whoever was with her, making me jump. The voices were coming from the kitchen, back in the breakfast nook. I'd never heard her sound so angry. She sounded okay, though, and I was inwardly relieved. Creeping forward quietly, I could see shadows moving on the wall.

Standing to the side of the door to the kitchen, I leaned around the corner and could see into the breakfast nook.

A man was standing next to the small table where my grandparents would drink coffee and read the newspaper in the mornings when they still lived here. He was tall and muscular, with short blond hair cropped close to his head. An old, jagged scar that started on his temple and ended at his jaw stood out on his otherwise smooth and clean-shaven face. His neck was thick, and the fabric of his cheap suit bulged at his biceps as he crossed his arms. He reminded me a little bit of the Incredible Hulk just before he shifted and shredded his clothes. Both he and my aunt were turned away from where I was hidden, so neither of them noticed me.

"Calm down," the man said with a sigh. He didn't sound angry, but tired and frustrated. "I don't want to believe it either, but they aren't talking. We don't have any evidence that the attacks are connected to them, and they are denying it all. It could be a rogue."

"No way. They're holding back," Liv snapped. "Just the fact that they are stonewalling us at every step is suspicious. Each one of them that comes to the city goes there first," she said more calmly. "Check it again."

"Olivia—"

Liv slammed her hands on the table, mimicking the same noise I'd heard earlier. I jumped, and the man did the same. Liv glowered at him. "Did I stutter?" she hissed. "Check. It. Again."

The man twitched violently. His face distorted into snarling anger, and a vein in his neck stood out as he clenched his jaw. The reasonable-seeming man from a few seconds ago was gone. Now, he was barely human. I gripped the handle of the umbrella more tightly. He leaned forward, hands balled into fists at his side.

In my mind, I saw those big hands reaching out and grabbing Aunt Liv. With a swallow, I prepared myself to throw the umbrella at him, trying to still my shaking arms. I wouldn't be able to make much of a difference, but it would give Aunt Liv the chance to get out. The thought of those fists swinging at me made my knees tremble even more, but I wouldn't run away while she was in danger. What the hell was Aunt Liv doing with a guy like this?

Liv didn't even flinch. Instead, she snarled right back at him. "Don't get cute with me, Will." She pushed a finger into his chest, her voice deadly serious. "I will take you down." There was a confidence in her voice that made me believe she could do what she threatened. My one-hundred-something-pound aunt would take him down, somehow. The look on Liv's face scared me. I'd never seen her look like that before.

They stared at each other for an eternity. My heart pounded in my ears, and I gripped the handle of the umbrella so hard it made my hands ache. I glanced at the apartment door, which was still open. Maybe I should slip away and call the police while they were at a standoff.

The man Liv had called Will blinked first. He shook his head and took a deep, calming breath. After another, he appeared to rein in his anger, his features smoothing into a forced calm. Then, without saying anything, he turned away from Liv and stalked out of the kitchen.

I jumped back, trying to hide before he saw me, but my shoe caught on the leg of one of the chairs at the dining table, and I lost my balance, tumbling backward with a yelp. I landed hard on my backside, sitting up as Will dashed around the corner.

He stood at the entry to the kitchen, scowling at me. He looked angrier and much bigger than before, just his shadow swallowing me whole. I clutched the umbrella. A voice in the back of my head chided that I should have called the cops. This guy was huge, and there was no way that I could take him. What had I been thinking?

There was movement behind the big man, and Aunt Liv rounded the corner as I lifted the umbrella, desperate to put anything between us. She peered at me from around Will, and her eyebrows shot up, her previous anger melting away. The large man opened his mouth to speak, but before it could leave his lips, Liv shoved him to the side. He stumbled.

"We're finished here," she said, some of the heat returning. "Come back when you have some answers." She took a step in front of Will, positioning herself between him and me with one hand on her hip.

Will glared at Liv, then with an agonizing slowness, turned his gaze on me. Those dark eyes felt like they were burrowing into my skull and dissecting my thoughts. I wanted to look away, but I was frozen under that gaze, like a scared animal about to be pounced on by a predator. If he came at me, Aunt Liv wouldn't be able to stop him.

He looked like he wanted to speak despite Liv dismissing him, but with another glance at her, he turned away and walked out of the apartment.

Moments later, the front door slammed shut.

Liv scowled in the direction Will had left. "Bastard," she muttered under her breath, then shook her head, looking down at me. Her eyes flicked to the polka-dotted umbrella, and a grin stretched across her face. Liv quickly turned away and covered her mouth, trying to turn her laugh into a cough. It wasn't successful.

I sniffed indignantly and crossed my arms, clutching the useless umbrella as my face burned. "This was all there was. See if I ever help you again," I grumbled.

"My hero," Liv teased and turned around, holding out a hand to help me up, not a trace of the laughter on her face. "But as a general rule, you shouldn't go charging into rooms with angry men, carrying nothing but an umbrella, even to help. You need to be more careful, or you could get hurt."

"Thanks, Mom," I replied flatly. "I'll take it under advisement." Back home, that comment would have earned me a scowl and a lecture from my mother, but Aunt Liv just laughed, which somehow felt even worse. I stood and brushed myself off. "What was all that about, anyway?"

Aunt Liv waved her hand, dismissing the question. "Some trouble at the office. Some difficulty in... research." She paused and scratched the back of her head. "Will's not so bad, really. Although I'll admit, that was a little over-board. I shouldn't have goaded him." She sighed again. "I owe him an apology."

I eyed Liv. That hadn't sounded like research. Research

usually involved books, looking stuff up on the internet, and talking to people. I didn't know exactly what she did, only that she worked for the city. I hadn't thought to ask. Now it seemed like a huge oversight. I'd assumed she was some sort of paper pusher. What was she doing that required her to work with a guy like that?

Liv was watching me closely, so I shrugged and handed her the umbrella. If she was working on some sort of investigation, or "research," or whatever, I doubted she would tell me anything. She wasn't exactly open about anything like that. In fact, I didn't actually know much about her social or work life at all. Our relationship had always been more about how I was doing. I had a gut feeling that pushing her wouldn't make her want to talk to me about it. It was best to act like I didn't care, then snoop around later.

"You're home early," Liv started, her tone light. "I thought you'd be gone for another hour or two. I was going to turn my phone back on once I was finished."

I plopped on the couch and rubbed my hands together, trying to help calm my nerves. "Yeah, there is some sort of party tomorrow night. The session ended early so they could start setting up. Jen brought me home."

Liv sat next to me. "How was it? Do you want to keep doing it?"

Pushing aside what had just transpired with Will, I tried to mull over Liv's question. Even considering that awkward encounter with Vaughn, it felt good to be drawing again. Going back would mean seeing him, but if Jen was his friend, maybe he wasn't so bad. It wouldn't hurt to keep attending the sessions, and it would get Aunt Liv off of my back. Jen was also going to be there, so at least I wouldn't be doing it by myself.

I nodded. "I think so."

"Good," Liv said. "I'll make sure it's paid for."

"Thanks, Aunt Liv."

Liv smiled. "I'm happy to do it. So tell me about this party," she said, eyes lighting up. "Are you going, or is it invite-only? I used to date a pretty well-known artist. He might be able to get you in."

"That's not necessary," I said. "The group that runs the sessions got invites for everyone. Jen wants to go, but I don't know if I should." My hands fidgeted with the sleeves of my shirt. I was already getting nervous thinking about it. What the hell was wrong with me? "We'll see. Jen's going to pick me up tomorrow night either way. We'll get some food and decide after that." I leaned into the couch. It smelled like cinnamon and made me think of my grandparents. Were they going to come and visit for Christmas? That would give me a chance to ask them about that weird dream. I hadn't told anyone about it yet.

Aunt Liv suddenly stood, startling me out of my thoughts. "There are a few dresses in my closet you can try on," she said, a sly smile stretching across her face. "I know you didn't pack anything nice to wear, and you'll want to look good at a function like that. You never know who you'll meet." She winked and grabbed my arm, pulling me up off the couch.

"I haven't even decided if I'm going," I complained, without putting much feeling into it, and let myself be pulled to my feet. "At least let me eat first."

At that last part, she released me. "There's some food in the fridge. I'll pick a few things that you can try on after you're finished," she said, then hurried down the hall to what had been my grandparents' bedroom.

"Make sure it's something warm!" I called after her, but

I didn't think she heard me. I shook my head and sighed. What had I gotten myself into?

As I entered the kitchen to rummage through the refrigerator, I glanced over at the small table in the breakfast nook, where Liv and Will had been arguing. A deep crack ran through the wood, right through the center. Had that been there before?

CHAPTER 6

JEN HELD up the black dress I'd just pulled out of my bag, examining its silky fabric, which all but glittered in the light. We sat at a table in the diner close to my house. My grandmother used to bring me here when I was a child, and it looked almost the same as the last time I'd been here years ago. The tables were small and clean, spaced about the room unevenly, and a small bar ran the length of the pickup window, where the kitchen was beyond. Faded pictures on the wall showed prints of Norman Rockwell paintings and classic cars. Only three of the fifteen tables were full. It was four-thirty, so we were a little early for the dinner rush.

"This is nice," she said with an approving nod.

"Liv gave it to me and told me that I should get out more," I grumbled. My aunt had made me try on four different dresses the night before. The one Jen was holding was what we'd settled on. Given the skimpy design, I realized I'd also need a coat to go with it. Maybe Jen had one I could borrow.

"That's true. You should," Jen said in a matter-of-fact tone. "She told my mom that you've only been out of the house a couple of times since you've been here." She turned the dress over and inspected the back. "I like it. You'll get a lot of attention in this." She lowered the dress and nodded to herself. "Very sexy."

"I don't want to look sexy," I growled under my breath, eyeing the dress with disgust.

Jen gave me a reproachful look. "Everyone wants to look sexy, Sarah. You just haven't figured that out yet." She winked at me and folded the dress, handing it back. "All joking aside, you'll look great in it."

"Thanks," I mumbled and sank a little lower in my seat. It wasn't too late to back out. I could walk home after dinner.

Jen rolled her eyes. "It'll be fine, Sarah. Being more noticeable means more people will want to talk to you. You could even meet some industry professionals and make some contacts. Isn't that why you're going?"

I nodded grudgingly. Jen had emphasized earlier that going to events like this was essential to getting into the art industry in Seattle. Finding a job wouldn't be the easiest thing since I had another semester of high school, but it would be good if I could have a gig lined up after graduation. I just didn't want to wear that damn dress. Aunt Liv hadn't taken no for an answer. Sometimes, she could be so difficult.

"You'll look great," Jen repeated and took a sip of her coffee. "Changing the subject, how's your mom?" She smiled at me over the rim of her cup. "We didn't really get a chance to talk much the other night with Liv looming."

"Mom's good. I think she's somewhere in Europe right now. Maybe France? She likes France." I stared out the window of the diner. We were seated at a booth across from the door to the kitchen. The sun had already set despite the early hour. The streetlight cast a harsh orange glow on the people walking by. I watched a couple holding hands cross the street as the little white man on the crosswalk signal blinked. Was it dark where Mom was? Or was it sunny? Was she enjoying herself without the responsibility of looking after a broken teenager?

"You think?"

"It's hard to keep track," I said, trying to keep the contempt from my voice. I wasn't sure if I succeeded.

That made Jen laugh. "Oh, the glamorous life. She's still in fashion, right?"

I nodded. "She does designing and marketing for a couple of different companies."

A man dressed in a black, hooded sweatshirt and jeans stopped and leaned against the wall across the street from the diner. Orange light briefly illuminated his face as he lit a cigarette. "She's gone most of the time. Even when I was around, we didn't see each other much. I was home by myself more often than not. Now, who knows if or when she'll visit."

Jen made a sound in her throat that sounded both sad and sympathetic. "I'm sorry, Sarah. That really sucks..." She trailed off as a waiter approached and set a sandwich in front of her and a bowl of soup for me. "Thanks," she said to the waiter before he went back to the kitchen. She took a couple of bites before continuing. "Have you looked into any of the colleges around here?" Jen asked, changing the subject again. "You should still be able to apply, even though it's a little late."

"No."

I stared at my soup. Back in New York, I hadn't thought of college as an option. I was too wrapped up in what my ex was doing to really consider my schooling. That was then.

Now, no one could stop me from going if I wanted to. Well, the rising cost of education could.

Asking my mother for more money was out of the question. It wasn't that she couldn't afford it, but if she didn't want me around, I didn't want to owe her anything. "I haven't thought about it too much, but a job would need to come first," I said. "My grades aren't good enough for a scholarship." Glancing out the window again, another man with a black hoodie joined the first, leaning against the wall across the street.

"It's a good thing you're going to this event. If all else fails, I could get you a job at the art store." Jen took another sip of her coffee and looked me over thoughtfully. "You know, Sarah, you're a lot quieter than I remember."

That brought my focus back to Jen. "What do you mean?"

"Well, when you would visit before, you used to tell me about New York and your friends and how fun it was. You would beg your aunt to call my mom the first day you got into town. I used to think I was the antisocial one." She laughed softly to herself. "Now, you're the one who doesn't talk much." She shrugged, and her cheeks took on a faint shade of pink. "It's not bad or anything. It's just not what I was expecting."

Jen seemed to have been thinking the same thing I had over the past few days. We'd both changed so much. Over the years, I'd learned that staying quiet was better than being yelled at, and that sticking up for myself wasn't worth the fight. It was better to suffer in silence.

Everything that had happened over the past few years had led to my banishment from the East Coast and my new residency in the Emerald City. No one other than my mom and Aunt Liv knew precisely what had happened with

Brian. Mom was there for it, and she'd told Liv when asking if I could stay with her. Should I talk to Jen about it? Would she think less of me? Would she still want to be my friend if she knew?

No, I couldn't. That was too heavy a subject for someone who didn't know the new me very well. We'd just reconnected, and I didn't want to lose that. She was the only friend I had.

I stirred my soup in nervous agitation. As I opened my mouth to break the silence, I saw that a third man had joined the two leaning on the wall across the street. My words died in my throat. This man was tall and muscular, with short-cropped blond hair and a black blazer.

Will, the one who had been arguing with Liv.

"What's wrong, Sarah?" Jen turned around in her seat to look out the window. "What is it?"

"It's him!" I hissed. Then, realizing I hadn't told her about Will visiting my house and what had transpired, I continued. "He was at my house last night when you dropped me off, arguing with my aunt. They almost got in a fight."

"Who? That blond guy? Is that her boyfriend?" She blinked. "Wait, like a fight, fight?"

"No. I mean, I don't think so, to the boyfriend part. And yes, a fight, fight. Aunt Liv said he's a co-worker and that they were arguing about a problem with his 'research,' but I overheard them talking a little. They were talking about someone stonewalling them, whatever that means. It sounded bizarre." I thought about it for a moment and came to the obvious conclusion. It didn't make me happy. "I'm pretty sure my aunt lied to me about it."

"Stonewalling?" Jen asked, sounding alarmed. "What is it that she does for work?"

I frowned. "I don't know. She says she works for the city. I'd always assumed that she had an administrative role, some sort of job that has a lot of paperwork." If that were the case, why would she be working with a guy like Will? He looked like he would be better as a bodyguard than filling out forms. What was he doing talking to those guys outside? Had they been waiting for him all this time? Did this have something to do with what he'd been researching? I had so many questions with no answers.

We continued to watch as Will gestured to a nearby alley. The two hooded men followed him and disappeared from view.

Jen leaned to the left. "Nope. Can't see them anymore. What do you think is going on?"

I shrugged. "No idea."

Jen turned to me and raised an eyebrow. "Do you want to check it out?"

I couldn't answer her. Of course I wanted to know what was going on, but Will was a big, scary guy who could crush me with one hand. Curiosity got the better of me, and I gave one sharp nod.

Seeing the look on my face, Jen dug around in her purse and left a few bills on the table. "Don't worry. If he even looks at us threateningly, we'll scream and run away," she said confidently as I stuffed the black dress back into my bag and we hurried out of the diner.

Following a strange man at night might not have been the best idea we'd had, not to mention the fact that I'd seen this same man almost lose it on my aunt the night before, but this was also for Liv's safety. Will and those guys he was talking to were pretty suspicious. If he was participating in illegal activity, it could put Liv in danger. She'd done so much for me. The least I could do was warn her if Will was up to no good.

"We need to make sure he doesn't see us," I said as we stepped into the brisk night air.

Jen shrugged on her jacket. "Duh. We'll walk by. Lots of people are walking around right now." She glanced at her phone, then put it in her pocket. "It's still pretty early. Who's to say we're not going shopping? As long as we don't stop and stare at them, they won't notice a thing."

Jen was right. There were still quite a few people walking around even though it was already dark. It looked like this was a popular part of town.

"Now, just act natural," Jen instructed. "Don't walk too slowly, but don't make it look like you're in a rush either. Normal walking speed. Oh, and keep your head facing forward. We don't want them to know that we're looking at them." She grinned, and it was obvious that she was enjoying the situation. "This is exciting!"

Exciting wasn't the word I would have used. My heart was pounding in my chest, and my sweaty palms gave away that I was more than a little afraid that Will would recognize me. A few cars passed before the traffic light turned red, and the crosswalk signal blinked. I tucked my hands in my jacket pockets, partially to keep them warm, but mainly to keep them from fidgeting. Taking a deep breath of cold winter air, I tried not to think about what we were about to do as we crossed the street.

We paused before reaching the mouth of the alley. Jen gave me a reassuring smile and stepped in front of it.

Shadows danced down the narrow space between buildings, the only illumination coming from a dim light above a back door. Trash littered the ground and collected on the sides, damp from snowfall and piled so high it was threatening to scale the walls. The men were standing near the far end. Will had his back to us. The shorter of the black-hooded men was speaking. Both of the strangers had angular faces, the deep shadows cast by the low light making their eyes look like black holes. Even though the clothes they wore were baggy, I got a distinct impression that they were strong. It was hard to see what their expressions were, but both men were focused on Will.

I watched them from the corner of my eye. I could see Will's lips moving, and the other hoodie man crossed his arms. They didn't seem to like him.

We were close to the other building when one of the hooded men glanced up, making my heart skip a beat. He watched us until the side of the building blocked our view of the alley.

"Keep going," Jen muttered under her breath.

My palms were even sweatier now, but I kept myself from rubbing them on my pants.

We walked another block before stopping in front of the wide window of a butcher's shop, a pig's head stenciled on the glass. "Okay," Jen began, "let's cross here and circle back."

"Are you serious? One of those guys saw us." I glanced over my shoulder, but no one had emerged from the alley to follow us.

"Well, my car is at the diner. How else are we going to get to the studio?"

I groaned. It would look even more suspicious if they saw us again. Worst of all, we didn't know any more than we had before. *Think, Sarah, think.* There were still a lot of people walking around. It was possible that they wouldn't be able to pick us out from the other foot traffic. It's not like we were dressed in a way that made us stick out. "All right. Let's go back."

We crossed the street and headed back to the diner. Unable to help myself, I glanced down the alley again as we passed it. The three men were gone. Maybe they'd left because of us, but maybe not. Seeing the empty alley helped to settle my trembling nerves.

Jen paused midstride when she noticed they weren't there anymore. "Hmm. I wonder where they went." She shrugged and kept walking, skipping a little to catch up with me. "That guy was pretty shady. It looked like a drug deal was going down. You should let your aunt know about this. She should stay away from him."

"He's really suspicious." There'd been a back door in the alley, so they could have gone inside the building. A few people passed us, carrying red and brown shopping bags, but there was no sign of Will or the hooded men he was talking to.

"Oh well," Jen said, looking around one last time. "Let's head to my place so we can change."

I nodded, and we walked back toward the parking lot behind the diner. We turned a corner around the building and went through a small alleyway. I spotted Jen's car at the front of the lot and stopped dead.

Will leaned against Jen's Civic, his arms folded across his chest. He looked first at Jen, then at me. He frowned and narrowed his eyes. "That was not a good idea."

I could feel my heart freeze in my chest as he glowered at me. It was like I was back on the floor of Liv's apartment, staring up at a man whose very presence screamed with imminent violence. Those eyes were like two hard stones glaring down at me.

Jen's hands darted into her purse and pulled out a black

and red canister, leveling it at Will. Pepper spray. "Back off, buddy."

He shifted his gaze to Jen and the pepper spray. Will stood straighter and opened the right side of his blazer with a calmness that indicated his ambivalence to the weapon leveled at him. It was enough for us to see the silver badge with a star in the middle, glistening in the streetlights. Large black letters that read Seattle Police were stamped on the badge. "That won't be necessary."

Jen's eyes widened, and her arm drooped a little. "Oh, you're a cop?" He nodded at the pepper spray, and, after a moment's hesitation, Jen put it in her purse.

His eyes tracked back to me. It took everything I had not to flinch away from his intense glare. "I'm not sure who you are, what Olivia told you, or why she would bring some kid into this," he said with a scowl, "but I am in the middle of an investigation. I don't think you get that. If I catch you sticking your nose into my business again, I'll arrest you. Do I make myself clear?" Jen and I both nodded. What else could we do? "Good. I'd better not see either of you again." He walked past us and paused next to me. "You can let Olivia know that I'll be watching you. If I think you're up to something, I'll report her to the Syndicate in addition to arresting you." He continued past, gravel crunching under his feet as he walked away.

His footsteps suddenly stopped. Jen and I looked at each other, then turned around. Will was already gone. There was no sign of him.

CHAPTER 7

JEN DROVE us back to her house so that we could change and I could borrow an appropriate pair of heels and a coat that looked better with the dress than the old jacket I'd had on. I slipped the tight black dress over my head, and Jen spent twenty minutes doing my makeup. When she deemed me presentable, we left for the studio, though going to a party with a bunch of strangers was the last thing I wanted to do right then. What I wanted to do was go home and demand answers from Liv.

"Maybe Liv is an undercover cop," Jen said as she drove us downtown, one finger tapping on the steering wheel. "Or maybe she's in the FBI, or the CIA, or maybe even NASA."

"NASA?" I asked with a snort. "I'm pretty sure they don't have secret agents stationed in Seattle since, you know, they deal with space."

"Hey, you never know. Liv could be part of a massive alien coverup." Jen took Exit 164 off the I-5 and waited in a long line of cars. Typical Seattle traffic. "Maybe she doesn't work for the city. She could be an undercover federal agent trying to root out political corruption."

I snorted. "This isn't a spy movie, Jen, and if she is some kind of covert agent, I don't think I really want to know what she's doing. That's her business, and I'd rather not get myself arrested." It did hurt a little that Aunt Liv hadn't told me what was going on or even what she did for work, but whatever it was, it sounded dangerous. I mean, it would have to be to justify working with Will who had just threatened to arrest me.

"What if she works for the mob or some other sort of organized crime? 'Working for the city' could be code for running drugs or being an enforcer. Or"—and Jen brightened a bit—"she is undercover like I said before and is about to bust a drug ring."

"You've been reading too many bad mystery novels. Will's a cop, remember?" I fidgeted in my seat and tried to pull the dress's neckline higher for the eight hundredth time. It was so low cut that I could see the top of my stomach between my breasts if I looked down. The dress hadn't looked so bad when Aunt Liv had forced me to take it, but now I was regretting not walking around in it more before leaving the house. My legs were exposed from the mid-thighs, ensuring that I would get frostbite, and my feet were already aching from the heels Jen had lent me. It was so far outside what I usually wore that it was laughable. I liked to wear sweaters, jeans, and comfy T-shirts. This wasn't me.

Jen glanced over at me. "Quit fidgeting, Sarah. We aren't even there yet. If you ruin your makeup, I *will* strangle you."

"Only if you can catch me after I throw these shoes at you and take off barefoot down the street." I gestured to the heels.

Jen grinned as we pulled into the parking lot next to the studio. She clicked her tongue absently as she looked around the lot. "Looks like it's going to be a walk. Go ahead and get out. I'll find parking."

The lot was full. The cars were parked in neat rows, and there were no empty spaces that I could see. "I can come with you. It shouldn't be that far."

Jen shook her head. "You can't walk in those shoes as it is," she said with a soft chuckle. "You almost tripped twice coming out of my house." She gave me a gentle shove and waved dismissively. "Just go inside. I'll only be a couple of minutes behind you."

Unable to argue with that, I shrugged and opened the door.

"See you in a bit!" Jen called behind me as I got out of the car. The Honda continued deeper into the parking lot, the red taillights disappearing as she turned down a row.

It was colder outside than it had been earlier. I avoided some of the ice that had gathered in the potholes and hurried as fast as Jen's heels would allow to the front door to the building. My teeth chattered as my legs shook. The coat I'd borrowed from Jen was thick, but since my legs were bare, it didn't help me all that much. I should have worn pants. This wasn't the 1950s. They made dress pants for women. Why couldn't I have worn those?

Warm air hit my face as I pushed open the front door, warding off the chill night air. Thank God for HVAC.

The lobby interior looked as it had the previous day, except for an A-frame sign next to the receptionist's desk reading "Please Check In." The same woman who had been there yesterday was behind the desk. She smiled at me as I walked in. "Good evening," she said in her silky voice.

"Hi." I looked around. There was no one else in the lobby. "I'm just going to wait for my friend to park."

She nodded, and I walked over and sat on one of the couches near the elevator. A few more people walked through the front door as I waited for Jen, the men dressed in pristine suits and women in blouses and skirts. They were older men and women, with gray hair and fine lines visible on their faces. Jen had mentioned that collectors would be present, and that Carter Godfrey would have pieces of art for sale. Were these some of the buyers who Jen had been talking about?

The newcomers checked in with the receptionist and headed to the elevator, chatting among themselves. They were too far away for me to make out what they were saying, but one of the women laughed, a high, tinkling sound like that of a bell. One of the men glanced over at me, an embarrassed look on his face, but continued walking with the others. I stared out the window until the elevator chimed and they piled in. Would most of the people at this party be like the ones I'd just seen? Would the only aspiring-artist types be the ones from the figure-drawing class? Black dress or no black dress, would I stick out in the midst of wealthy buyers and sharply dressed businesspeople?

I pulled at the neckline of my dress again, silently cursing Aunt Liv. This was a terrible idea.

I was beginning to wonder if I should go looking for her when Jen pulled the door open and stormed in, rubbing her arms with her hands and muttering under her breath. Her cheeks were red from the cold. I stood to meet her, wobbled, and caught myself on the arm of the couch I'd vacated. I felt a sudden, overwhelming urge to smash the stupid high heels against a wall, but that would've been childish, especially since they weren't mine.

"I had to park over by the stadium," Jen growled. "We'll have a long walk after this."

Great. Just what I needed. More chances to break my ankles slipping on ice in these high-heeled torture devices.

Jen tilted her head toward the receptionist, and I followed her over to the desk. "Hey, Ashley," she said cordially, not a hint of the seething anger from moments ago in her voice.

Ashely's bright-red lips parted in a wide smile. She could have been in a Colgate commercial. "Here for Carter's party?" she asked. I hadn't noticed it the first time I'd been to the studio since I'd felt so out of place, but her voice was surprisingly deep, though still high enough to be feminine. Sultry even.

We nodded, and Ashley looked at her computer screen. Her long nails made a loud clicking on the keyboard. "All right, Jen, you're checked in." She looked up, her large, brown eyes focused on me, her pupils contracting. It reminded me of a cat right before it pounced. "I'm sorry, but I don't remember your name."

"Sarah Frost," I said quickly, a little unnerved by her gaze.

Ashley nodded, her eyes flicking to her computer screen again. She clicked her mouse, nodded as she found my name, then smiled and said, "Let me take your coats." She hung them on a rack behind her, then handed each of us a ticket. I spotted two more racks behind those filled with more coats, mostly in black. "Enjoy the party, Sarah."

That look in her eyes made me shiver. It was somehow predatory. I swallowed and turned toward the elevator, mumbling a quick, "Thanks."

Jen followed in my wake. When we were across the

lobby and waiting for the elevator, she said in a low whisper. "I didn't know you were into women, Sarah."

"What? Oh no." I glanced over my shoulder. Ashley regarded us with normal-looking eyes. She saw me looking and smiled at me, then went back to the magazine she'd been reading earlier. I must have been imagining things. "Sorry, I was zoning out," I lied.

"It wouldn't be surprising." Jen shrugged and leaned close to me, speaking in hushed tones as the elevator opened for us. "She's stunning. People will come in off the street just to talk to her, but I think she and Carter are an item."

"Oh..." I didn't know Carter Godfrey or Ashley the receptionist, so I didn't know what to say to that, but Jen seemed to be enjoying herself and gave me a knowing smile.

The elevator doors opened when we reached the fourth-floor landing, still plain and unremarkable. The slow rhythm of a soft jazz number drifted through the closed door, muffling any sounds beyond. I'd noticed a number of bars and restaurants in the area, so thought maybe the lack of available parking was due to that and hoped that there weren't that many people inside the studio. I wrung my hands. The thought of so many bodies made me anxious. We could still leave.

Jen caught my eye and gave me a reassuring smile. "You look like a scared rabbit," she said and strode forward, gripping the door's handle. "Relax, this is going to be fun." She pulled the door open, and the sound of trumpets assaulted my ears as the music switched to a faster tune.

The dedicated workspace that was the studio of yesterday had been transformed into a chic art gallery. The lights were dimmed to the point that it was difficult to make out faces from a distance, and spotlights shone down on the tables and pedestals placed around the room, showcasing various paintings and sculptures. While the room wasn't as crowded as I'd feared it would be, it still made me feel claustrophobic. Black-clad servers weaved like skilled dancers through the masses, carrying refreshments and snacks for the guests, pausing every now and then to offer a drink or take an empty glass.

Jen scanned the crowd, then stood on her toes and waved. A few moments later, a tall man with curly black hair and caramel-colored skin emerged from the horde and smiled at us.

"Sarah, this is Tommy," Jen said once he was within earshot. "This is Sarah, my friend who recently moved here from New York."

Tommy turned his smile to me. He had a warm, friendly face. "Nice to meet you, Sarah." We shook hands, and he hugged Jen. "Izzy's lost in there somewhere. Kat, Patrick, and Vaughn are around too. Do you want a drink?" he asked me, then motioned for one of the servers to come over.

"Um, no thanks," I said as a pretty woman dressed in one of the black uniforms held out a tray of champagne flutes. "I'm underage."

"It's sparkling cider," the woman said with a chuckle. "You have to go to the bar for alcohol."

"Oh," I said and picked up a glass, feeling my face burn. Of course, they wouldn't be serving alcohol to minors.

Jen laughed and plucked a glass from the tray, thanking the woman as she turned to offer drinks to some other guests. "I'm going to go hunt down Izzy and Patrick. You should check out some of the art. Carter probably has a lot of good stuff out. Maybe you could learn something." She winked at me.

"Ha ha," I said, my tone as flat as I could make it as Jen pulled Tommy into the crowd to search for their friends.

Taking Jen's advice, I braved the crowd to look at Carter's art.

I hadn't heard of Carter Godfrey before visiting the studio yesterday. Jen's mom had set it up for me, so all I had to do before coming to the figure-drawing session had been to check the time and address. Since he was hosting the party, I'd figured I needed to familiarize myself with his art and reputation, so as to avoid awkward conversations due to my ignorance. So I'd looked him up on Google. He was a well-known local artist. He did work for businesses around Seattle, which Jen had already told me, and led workshops for the college. According to the information I found on the internet, he participated in many youth outreach programs and even had a scholarship foundation for aspiring artists. His net worth was estimated in the millions.

Most of the pieces on display were nothing like the works posted online, which were mostly the ones he did for the public, businesses or other contracted works. Those pieces were very sleek and modern. Some of the ones here were like that, but most of them were raw and rough, a completely different style from what he produced under contract. Many of the works on display were sketches of the human form in various poses, naked and clothed men and women, in different mediums. I thought I recognized Vaughn in a few of them. The drawings and paintings were beautiful, and there was an element about them that drew me in. A simple hand gesture or expression that looked natural on canvas gave the observer a glimpse of what the person was feeling, but with a complexity that would be impossible to replicate.

As I was passing a painting, a flash of blue caught my

eye. Pausing mid-step to examine it more closely, I felt my mouth drop open. It was a painting of a woman with long, dark hair that curled around her face and shoulders. She had the expression of contemplation over an important decision, gazing off from a balcony overlooking the ocean. It was done with the kind of detail and style that true masters of a brush had, and looked as if I could have reached out and touched the woman or felt the ocean breeze on my skin. It was almost as if the woman in the painting could turn and look at me at any second.

But that wasn't what shocked me. What had me unsettled was the fact that the woman in the painting could have been Aunt Liv's doppelgänger.

"Beautiful, isn't she?" said a deep voice from right behind me.

I whipped around to see a man standing a foot or so away, gazing over my shoulder. He looked to be in his mid-thirties and in great physical shape. He wore jeans with a button-down collared shirt, expensive-looking shoes, and small square glasses. His long white-blond hair was pulled back in a loose tail, and he smiled genially at me. He was handsome, and while I'd never met him before, I knew who he was in an instant from the pictures I'd seen online.

"Forgive my intrusion," said Carter Godfrey, "but I noticed your interest. She was as stunning in life as she is on canvas." He stared lovingly at the visage of Aunt Liv.

"You knew her well?" I asked with a side-long look at the painting. Liv had more secrets than I'd guessed.

Carter's smile broadened, and the look in his eyes became wistful as he recalled the memories my question evoked. "At the time I painted this, that woman was my lover. Over the years we were together, she posed for me many times." He sighed, coming back to the present as the spell his memories had cast on him broke. "But all good things must come to an end. We had conflicting obligations, and she was too proud." His eyes refocused, and he smiled sadly at the painting before turning his attention to me. "Forgive me for prattling on like a lovesick teenager. My name is Carter Godfrey. Thank you for coming to my exhibition."

CHAPTER 8

I SHOOK Carter's hand and tried to look interested, not like I wanted to turn around and run out the door, which I wanted to do very, very much. "Nice to meet you. I'm Sarah," I said, omitting my last name. "Your work is incredible."

"Sarah," Carter repeated and grinned at me. "You are too kind. I make most of my money from painting murals and marketing for businesses, but this"—he gestured around him—"is what I love to do." He chuckled, and it was smooth and so infectious that it made me smile. "These don't pay the bills, though. So tell me, how did you hear about my little party?"

"I recently signed up for the figure-drawing sessions here."

He nodded as if this made perfect sense to him. "Yes, I've been hosting those sessions for a couple of years now. It's not easy being an artist in such a big city, and the extra income helps to keep the lights on." His cadence and grin made it obvious that he was joking.

I laughed, trying to be polite and remembering what his

estimated net worth was. He didn't have any trouble keeping the lights on.

Carter's eyes focused on something behind me, and a moment later, there was a light touch on my shoulder. If Carter hadn't reacted, I'd have jumped. Vaughn was standing at my side, holding a champagne flute in one hand. His dark hair was pulled back in a short tail, and he wore a white dress shirt with the top button undone, a nice pair of jeans, and black boots. It gave him an air of professionalism that he hadn't had the day before. Not that I'd been looking at him for very long with his clothes on.

I could feel the heat rising in my cheeks as he grinned at me. "Hi, Sarah," he said with far too much enthusiasm. "Glad you could make it. I see you've met Carter, our gracious host." That last part held a touch of sarcasm.

If Carter heard it, he gave no indication. "I do what I can. The studio provides children with opportunities and education that would otherwise cost them a lot of money."

Vaughn scoffed. "Children? Most of the people who come to your workshops are in their twenties."

"Children," Carter said with an exaggerated sigh. "Still trying to find their way through life. It's my responsibility to nurture their artistic talent."

Vaughn glared at him, and Carter chuckled. It was apparent that Vaughn and Carter knew each other well, and I reminded myself that Vaughn modeled for him, after all. The way they talked to each other, their relationship was more than strictly professional.

"Hey!" Jen's voice came from behind Vaughn, and she wiggled herself between us. "Oh, I see you've met Carter and found Vaughn." She smiled at Carter, and he grinned. They shook hands. "Good to see you again," she said.

"Thank you for coming, Jennifer," he said, once again

adopting the persona of the gracious host that Vaughn had just made fun of him for.

Jen looked past Carter at the painting that we were grouped around. Her eyebrows knit together as realization crossed her face. I felt a surge of panic race up my spine, and I shook my head as she opened her mouth to speak, but the words, "Isn't that your Aunt Liv?" left her lips before she noticed me.

I glared at Jen, feeling the eyes of the two men on me. Jen flushed and smiled apologetically. With a sinking feeling in my stomach, I looked at Carter. He was studying my face with an academic interest, which made it grow hot. I didn't like being the center of attention like this.

"Sarah..." he mused as he examined me. "Yes, Livy did have a little niece." Livy? I'd never heard anyone call Aunt Liv *Livy* before. Carter leaned in a little closer, and I took a small step back. His eyes were bright, even in the dim light. "The last time I saw you, you were still living with your grandparents. Seven, maybe eight years old?" His face lit up with delight, the mask of professionalism fading away. "Has it been so long?"

Feeling self-conscious, I fiddled with the hem of my dress. I couldn't recall ever meeting him, but it sounded like he knew me from a long time ago. Most of my memories from ten years ago revolved around my father's car accident and the upheaval of my life after his death. There was no room for anything else. Carter probably meant well, but his intense gaze was making me feel anxious. I glanced at Vaughn, who was also watching me, a pensive look on his face. Did he know Liv as well?

"Vaughn," Jen said, breaking the tense silence. She smiled at him, and Vaughn finally looked away from me. "Kat is looking for you."

He grimaced and gave Jen a significant look. She frowned. They seemed to have a silent conversation before Vaughn said, "Of course she is." He smiled at me, but the smile didn't touch his eyes. "It was good to see you again, Sarah." He nodded at Carter, then turned away from us, presumably to go look for Kat.

"Carter," Jen said, giving the artist a flat look, "personal boundaries."

Carter blinked and took a step back from me, looking startled. "Sorry," he said, smiling apologetically. "I forget myself sometimes. So," he asked with a furtive glance at the painting, "how is your aunt?"

Jen put her hand to her mouth in a motion like she was going to cough but mouthed "Sorry," where Carter couldn't see her lips.

"Aunt Liv is good, I think," I said with my own uncomfortable glance at the painting. Apart from all the weird stuff that was happening, Aunt Liv did seem like she was doing okay. She'd been upset when she was talking with Will, but her attitude had completely turned around after that. Which side of what I'd seen was the true Liv?

He nodded absently, as if he was so deep in his own thoughts that I could have said anything and it wouldn't have registered. "How long have you been in Seattle, Sarah? I thought you and your mother moved to New York."

"Mom's still there. I moved back a little over a week or so ago."

That interested him, and he cocked his head to one side in a very bird-like way. "Are you here to stay?"

I gave the painting of Liv another sideways glance. Carter was nice enough, but he was also far too interested in my personal life. "For now. I don't think going back is an option for me. I'm still in high school for a few months, and

I'm not sure what I'm going to do once I graduate. The smart thing would be to start looking into college and getting a job." *Stop it, Sarah*, I chided myself. We'd just met, and I was already spilling my thoughts on him.

"A job..." Carter fished in his pocket, pulling out a business card. "You know, my agent has been hounding me about getting a new assistant. Mary, my old assistant, moved back to California, and I haven't had the heart to look for a replacement. She was so good, and I hate conducting interviews." He held the business card out to me. "I need an assistant to help around the studio part-time. Would you be interested? I'd be able to work around your school schedule, of course."

For a moment, I was speechless. Was he offering me a job?

"Why me?" The words escaped my lips before I could stop them. Offending him was the last thing I wanted to do.

Carter laughed, guessing at what I was thinking. "Sarah, if you're anything like the girl I remember, I know you'll do a good job. If I can help someone who just came to town, why not?" Then he smiled slyly. "I'm also not above doing favors for Livy. Maybe I'll even get to see her sometime if you come work for me."

Somewhat reluctantly, I took the card, feeling like it would've been rude not to. This was a little too convenient for my tastes. I'd met a semi-famous artist who used to date Liv, and he just happened to have an opening when I mentioned off-hand that I'd be looking for work? Carter didn't seem like the type of person to be offering jobs to random people like that, but I did just meet him ten minutes ago, so who knew? Maybe he did this all the time.

"My personal number is on the card. Think about it and give me a call." He smiled at me the same way movie stars smile at their fans and car salesmen smile at potential buyers. "It may not be the most glamorous job, but I offer benefits and pay well. I'll try not to work you too hard." His eyes flicked over my shoulder, and he gave an exaggerated sigh. "If you'll excuse me, I need to go and mingle with my other guests. It was great to see you, Sarah, Jennifer." He nodded at Jen and drifted off to talk to another group of people who'd been standing near us, the group of collectors I'd seen in the lobby.

When I looked, Jen was staring at me, a bewildered expression on her face. "What just happened?"

"I didn't do anything," I grumbled and stuffed the business card into my purse. I longed to throw my hands into the air in exasperation but refrained from doing so. It could wait until I got home.

Jen snorted. "Of course you didn't do anything. Carter doesn't think before he acts sometimes." She looked at the painting. "I didn't know your aunt had dated him."

"Welcome to the club," I said grumpily. "I don't remember him at all, but a lot was going on back then."

Realization washed across her face. "Oh... of course you wouldn't remember some random guy that Liv was dating." She glared at the back of Carter's head. "Honestly, Carter," Jen said in an undertone that only I could hear. "How thoughtless."

Carter hadn't noticed Jen's stare and laughed at whatever the man he was talking to said. He did act like a nice person. A little forward, but nice. I didn't blame him for bringing up my past. It was the one thing we had in common, even if I didn't remember meeting him before. How was he supposed to know that I was still coming to terms with the death of my father? Being back here made me feel things that I hadn't in years.

"Are you all right?" Jen asked as she stepped closer to me.

Had someone cranked up the heat? "Yeah, I think I need some air." My eyes passed over the crowd, focusing on the stairs to my right that led to the roof. It would be a lot easier to escape there than going back down the elevator to the lobby that Ashley was watching over like a silent sentinel, guarding access to the upper floors. "Just give me a few minutes," I said as I pointed at the stairs.

Jen frowned but nodded. I knew she was worried about me, and now she was stuck watching over me instead of having fun with her friends. She could relax a little if I was out of the way. I climbed the stairs with some trouble—damn these heels—and pushed the door open. Hot air rushed past me as I stepped into the frigid night air and closed the door with a soft *click* behind me.

The roof was adorned with wicker chairs and tables spaced all over the rooftop, umbrellas open over them in case it rained. The area was lit by strings of bulbs that hung from the entry to poles near the guardrail. Plexiglass barriers lined the edge of the rooftop under the railing. Between some of the taller buildings, you could see Puget Sound. I hadn't realized how close to the water the studio was. It must be delightful to sit here in the summer, but it was the middle of winter and freezing.

I rubbed my upper arms with my hands and shivered. Why had I checked my coat in the lobby? I blew out a puff of steam. Coming here tonight had been a mistake. There was no way that I was ready to face a room full of strangers. I'd come out hoping to have a good time and look at some art, even if reluctantly, and now, Aunt Liv's ex was trying to get me to work for him. He didn't give me the creeps, so that was a plus. Working for him would allow me to save some money before summer came around. If I accepted this job, how would I tell Aunt Liv? Would she be mad?

What a mess. Next time, I'll stay home.

I picked my way to one of the chairs out of sight of the door, careful not to slip on the slick cement surface, and pulled my phone out. There was a notification on the screen, a missed call from Aunt Liv. I tapped her name to return the call.

Aunt Liv picked up after only one ring. "Hello?" Liv sounded flustered, and there were other voices in the background.

"Hey, Aunt Liv. Is everything okay?"

"Oh yeah," she said with a laugh that I was sure was fake. "I just got to the office. How's the party?"

"Stressful and socially awkward."

She laughed for real that time. "You'll get used to it." There was a loud banging in the background. "What the f— Ah, I have to go. I'll see you at home." She hung up before I could say anything.

I stared at my phone. What the hell had happened? Wasn't it a little late for Liv to be in the office?

Just as I was about to stand and go back inside, the door to the roof creaked open. Voices drifted to where I was sitting, and I realized that I recognized them.

"No, I can't. You know that," Vaughn said, sounding frustrated.

I barely stopped a groan from escaping my lips. Of course, when I wanted to get away from everyone, Vaughn would come up here. I glanced at that side of the deck, but I couldn't quite see them. They must have been in front of the door.

"It's not that you can't, it's that you won't." It was Kat.

She let out a bitter laugh. "Even Marius thinks it's a good match."

"I don't care what Marius thinks," Vaughn growled. "Who I date is none of his business."

Oh boy, I really did *not* need to be here for this. Maybe there was another exit, or I could sneak to the door when they moved away from it.

But my life never worked that way. As I went to stand, one of those stupid heels caught on the leg of the chair, and I went tumbling to the ground, flipping the chair, which knocked into one of the tables and made enough noise to wake the dead.

As I tried to pick myself up off the ground, Vaughn was suddenly there next to me, helping me to my feet. "Are you all right?" he asked.

"Yes," I said, flustered and embarrassed. "I was getting up to leave. Sorry, I didn't mean to interrupt."

"It's okay," he said as he brushed off my purse and handed it to me. "That conversation is over anyway."

Kat glared at me, fire in her eyes. If looks could kill, my ashes would already be drifting away in the breeze. I started to apologize to her, but before I could get a word out, she turned on her heel and stomped off, slamming the door behind her.

Great. Now she hated me. I should go crawl into a hole for the next year or so. It would make everyone's life easier.

Vaughn frowned after her. "I'm sorry about that. She doesn't take rejection well."

My mouth moved before I could stop it. "You think anyone does? No one likes being rejected, Vaughn."

He looked a little hurt and shocked by my words. Way to go on making friends, Sarah. There was no way that I was going to follow Kat into the studio. For all I knew, she was waiting behind the door to push me down the stairs. So I sat back down in the chair that we'd just righted. "Sorry, it's not my place to judge. I don't know anything about the two of you."

Vaughn sat in the chair next to me and put his head in his hands. Now that Kat was gone, he looked vulnerable. Which was strange. I mean, I'd seen him naked. You don't get more vulnerable than that. "It's all right. It probably looks pretty bad from the outside." He leaned back in the chair. "Kat and I have known each other since we were kids. We grew up together, and I love her, but as a sister. She doesn't understand that. She thinks that if we start dating, I'll come around." He grimaced. "It's complicated."

"She really likes you," I said, remembering how she looked at him during the figure-drawing session the day before.

"I know," he said, and he sounded miserable. It was clear that he cared about her and didn't want to see her hurt, but in a situation like that, everyone involved gets hurt.

I sighed. This wasn't any of my business, but I felt bad for Vaughn. There was no easy way out of this for him. He abruptly turned his head to the left, looking past me and toward the roof entrance. I looked over to where he was star-ing, but I didn't see anything except the other tables and beyond that, the tops and sides of other buildings. I turned back to him. "Is something wrong?"

"No, I just thought I... Never mind." He shrugged and looked at me, his deep-green eyes meeting mine. "You're new to Seattle, right? Jen said you moved here from New York. Did you like it there?" He was obviously trying to change the subject.

It was my turn to shrug. "It was okay. Like any other big city." I wasn't sure I wanted to talk to Vaughn, but like

Carter, he didn't strike me as a bad guy. He hung out with Jen's group, after all, and she wouldn't be hanging around him if he wasn't a good person, bad boy rumors aside. I could see how he would be reluctant to talk about his relationship with Kat to the others if they were all friends. There was a good chance that I'd be seeing him around, so I should at least give him the benefit of the doubt.

"Is your aunt nice?" he asked as I was lost in my thoughts.

"What? Why?" I asked, not sure why he cared.

His cheeks turned pink when they had otherwise looked normal, even in the freezing night air. "I mean, I've heard a lot about her, so I was just wondering... You like her and all, right?"

Geez, did everyone know Aunt Liv? Was she famous? I narrowed my eyes at him. There was no way she'd been with Vaughn too. He looked like he was my age. "She can be a pain sometimes, but she's generally a nice person."

He let out a nervous laugh. "That's good. I've heard Carter talk about her. He made her sound a little difficult, if you can read between his poetic nonsense." The look I gave him must have made him uncomfortable because he quickly looked down at his hands. "Sorry, I'm sure you don't want to talk about your aunt's personal life. Why did you decide to move here?" His eyes met mine.

I looked away first. I wasn't going to explain to Vaughn, whom I'd just met, the reason Mom had forced me to move in with Aunt Liv. "I needed a change of scenery," I said evasively. With any luck, he would leave it at that.

"I feel that way sometimes too." That made me look at him. Vaughn was staring off into the distance, into the glittering city lights of downtown Seattle. He looked sad, like he was thinking about some old hurt that was still raw. "My family can be so stressful sometimes that I tell myself I'm going to pack up and leave them all behind me, consequences be damned." He gave me a small smile as our eyes met again. "I'm too much of a coward to do that. I love this city, I love my friends, and I love what I do."

"You mean, posing naked in front of a bunch of strangers?"

Vaughn laughed, really laughed, and I couldn't help but smile right along with him. "That's not all I do, Sarah. I do other gigs."

"I don't want to know what else you do," I said but gave him a smile to show him that I was joking.

He grinned at me. "It's nice to be able to talk to someone who's not connected to any of my family drama. The others," he said, and I knew he meant the rest of Jen's group, "already know about a lot of what goes on through Kat and me, so it's kind of old news to them. It feels good just to talk about it and not get a million suggestions on how to fix things." He scratched the back of his head with one hand. It looked like a nervous gesture. "What I'm trying to say is that I'd like to get to know you better, if that's all right."

I watched him as he waited for my answer. It didn't seem like he had an ulterior motive, but, since I would be seeing him around anyway, it might be best to start things on the right foot. "I'm not looking for a boyfriend, if that's what you're getting at, but it would be nice to have someone other than Jen to talk to."

He smiled at me, and it reminded me of Carter's, warm and genuine. "Tommy and I are going to get dinner on Friday. Would you like to come? You can invite Jen and her girlfriend too."

The invitation surprised me. "We just met, and you're asking me out? Isn't that a little fast?"

Vaughn rolled his eyes dramatically. I thought he overdid it a bit, but what do I know? "I heard what you said, Sarah. It's just dinner. I'm not looking for a girlfriend either."

I pretended to mull it over before answering. "Fine, I'll ask Jen, but I'm only coming if she does too."

"Great. Let me see your phone."

By reflex, I moved my bag away from him. "Why?"

"So I can put my number in it. I have an app that will transfer my contact info to your phone via Bluetooth." He pulled out his phone. "Make sure your Bluetooth is enabled and accept when my phone connects."

I pulled my phone out and held it next to his. A notification popped up in less than a second. *Transfer contact info with Vaughn V.?* I tapped the accept button on my screen, and another message popped up. *Success!*

"Text me when you decide if you want to go or not. It's a Thai place in Capitol Hill, and it's pretty good." Vaughn put his phone in his pocket and stood. "I'd better get back inside. Carter will throw a fit if I don't mingle with his guests a little." He held out his hand to me. "Do you want to go back too? I'm sure Jen is looking for you, and if you stay out here without a jacket, you're going to get sick."

After hesitating for a moment, I took his hand and let him pull me to my feet. It was too cold to be out here anyway.

CHAPTER 9

FOOTSTEPS ECHOED on the wet cobblestone street as I ran, the cold air burning my lungs, and my muscles ached from exertion. Even in the darkness of the cloudy, starless night, the streetlights illuminated my way, their yellow light reflecting in puddles of water that gathered between the road and the sidewalk. There were few lights on inside the buildings surrounding me, and I knew instinctively that it was too late for regular people to be awake. Rounding a corner, I stopped to catch my breath and look around.

Like the previous dream I'd had, I was a spectator in the mind of whoever owned this body. I didn't know where I was, but I was certain that it was not Seattle. The buildings were too old and in a style too different, with several stories of long, rectangular windows. They were made of brick, and the area smelled like wet stone. Wherever I was, it was cold here, just as cold as Seattle, with dark clouds above that blocked out the moon and stars. Frost crept in at the edges of the pooling water around me.

If this was a place that I had never visited before, how was I dreaming of it?

"Damn," said a feminine voice that held the touch of an accent I couldn't place from the one word. The person who owned this body jogged to the end of the building and turned down an alley that was even darker than the street she'd come from. After taking a few steps, she glanced behind her to ensure no one was watching and pulled out a cell phone.

Almost as if she foresaw it, the phone began to vibrate.

"I lost him," she said as she answered the phone, and I finally pinned her accent as British.

"That's unfortunate," said a male voice. "Do you know where he went, Ava?"

"If I knew that, I wouldn't have lost him," Ava snapped. "He was heading down Wharfdale when he spotted me." There was a rustle behind me, and she whipped around, but it was just a breeze coming through the alley and tossing around an empty paper coffee cup. Ava looked around nervously again, but if she saw anything, I couldn't spot it. It was so dark. Why hadn't she pulled out a flashlight? "He couldn't have gotten far. I'll find him."

"You should come back to headquarters," the man on the phone said. "If he's already spotted you, there's no use trying to hunt him down."

Ava grunted in frustration but took a few deep breaths. "Fine." I had the impression that Ava had needed a few moments to gather in her anger at the person on the other end of the line. "I'll head over to King's Cross and catch the next train."

King's Cross? As in King's Cross Station in central London? How the hell did I end up here? The last time I'd had one of these dreams, I'd been in the body of someone I knew, but I didn't have any family in London, did I?

Ava stepped onto the street and went back the way

she'd come, walking with a slow, casual pace. I caught a glimpse of her in a dark storefront window. Tall and lean, with straw-colored hair that was pulled back into a no-nonsense tail. There was a hard edge about her face, the kind you saw in people who'd had a tough life. I didn't know who this Ava person was, but she looked like she could take care of herself.

There was a scuffing sound that came from the direction Ava was heading. She froze, listening hard, then reached into her jacket and pulled out a black handgun. Weren't guns illegal in the UK? She peered down the street, but like her, I didn't see anything that looked out of the ordinary. After a few moments, Ava relaxed and stepped onto the sidewalk, moving to put away her gun.

A snarling growl came from behind her, and a white-hot flash of pain radiated throughout my body before I started awake, lying in my bed again. I sat up, my entire body shaking as a bead of sweat ran down my back. With trembling hands, I checked myself over, looking for any injuries, but found none. It had only been a dream. Why was I having dreams like this, and the one before with my grandmother?

I lay back down to try and sleep again but stayed awake in bed most of the night, afraid of what I'd see if I closed my eyes.

CHAPTER 10

AT SIX O'CLOCK ON Friday evening, I found myself walking along East Pine Street in the Capitol Hill district. Capitol Hill was arguably the most vibrant part of the city, with bars and coffee shops on every street corner. I'd taken the light rail over from Aunt Liv's house. It had been a quick trip since the two parts of the city were close to each other. It was already dark outside, and snow drifted through the air. It didn't snow that much in Seattle, not like it did in New York anyway, so the city's residents lost their minds when it did.

Traffic was at a dead stop, and every few seconds, a horn blared. Even on the sidewalk, there were a lot of pedestrians hurrying to get indoors. Most of the people around me looked a couple of years older, like they could be in college or starting their careers. There were lots of piercings and hair in more colors than you could imagine. It was all fascinating, but it was rude to stare, so I kept my focus on the street ahead of me.

I followed the GPS on my phone past a park, then up a few more blocks to a place called *Thai For Me*, where I was to meet Vaughn, Tommy, and Jen. The name was supposed to be funny. I rolled my eyes, as I had when Vaughn had first texted it to me, and waited at the crosswalk. The greater Seattle area was full of restaurants with ironic-sounding names, so I hadn't dismissed it as a joke. Google showed me that the place had about a thousand four-star reviews, so I was hoping for some good, hot food.

The restaurant windows were fogged over. Opening the door, I was hit with the delicious smell of cooking meat, garlic, and basil. It was a small place, with about twelve tables, and all of them were occupied. It was a seat-yourself kind of place, with a counter where you placed your order. A smiling woman, her shiny black hair in a bun, stood behind the counter and greeted me when I walked in. I smiled back at her, then looked around until my eyes fell on Vaughn. He was sitting by himself at a larger table at the back of the restaurant, staring at his phone.

He looked up as I approached, and stood to greet me. "Hey!" he said with a grin. The couple at the table next to us glanced over but quickly went back to their conversation. They seemed to be in some sort of intense discussion.

"Hi! Is Tommy not here yet?" I peeled off my heavy winter jacket and scarf, draping them on the back of my chair before sitting, my back to the restaurant's door. Not my favorite place. I liked to be able to see the exit, but the only other option was to sit next to Vaughn. I closed my eyes and took in a deep breath, my stomach giving an antici-patory rumble. "This place smells wonderful."

"I told you it was pretty good," he said as he retook his seat. "And no, obviously Tommy hasn't gotten here yet. Jen didn't come with you?"

"*Obviously* not," I said with mock scorn. "She had errands to run before this and said she'd be a little late." It was nice and warm at the table Vaughn had chosen and far enough away from the front door that I didn't feel the rush of cold air when it opened and closed. "She should be here soon, though."

"So," Vaughn began, "thanks for meeting up with me. I wasn't sure if you were actually going to come." That made two of us. He smiled at me, and by the way his hands were fidgeting, I could tell that he was fishing for conversation topics. "Are you doing anything for the holidays?"

Good question. I kept forgetting that Christmas was just two weeks away. "No, I don't think so. I would usually spend Christmas with my mom, but she's... somewhere. She travels a lot. Aunt Liv hasn't said anything, so I'm pretty sure I'll just be sleeping in and hanging around the house that day." After saying it, I realized how sad it sounded. It had been years since Mom and I had done anything for Christmas together. She'd tried to keep up with it for a while, but after Dad's death, she buried herself in her work. She would drink wine and watch the Hallmark Channel while I made sure she had enough water to keep the hangover mild. Fun times.

"It's okay," I said at his concerned expression. "I prefer it being low-key. What about you? Do you have any plans?"

"Well," Vaughn said, looking at me with a sheepish expression. It was his turn to be uncomfortable. "I have some family in Portland that I'll go visit for New Year's. I don't see them often, and Carter isn't doing a Christmas event this year, so I'll have some free time." He blinked as if he had just remembered something. "Didn't Carter offer you a job?"

"How did you know that?"

"How do you think?" he asked with one eyebrow raised.

"He told me. I'm not only a model for Carter. I'm also his friend."

Damn. They did seem close when I saw them together before. "Well, I haven't accepted yet. I don't know if I will."

"Why not?"

I shrugged. "I don't know Carter well, and being his assistant sounds a little... personal. Plus, I don't think he's doing this out of the goodness of his heart or anything. I'm pretty sure he just wants an excuse to talk to my aunt."

The woman I'd seen behind the counter moved past my chair and set two plates of steaming golden-brown noodles in front of the men next to us, confirmed their orders, then made her way to the kitchen. I could feel my mouth watering as I shot their food covert glances.

"Maybe we should order," Vaughn said, catching my hungry expression. "Jen and Tommy can order what they want whenever they get here."

I left my jacket, which was so old I doubted anyone would steal it, on the back of the chair as we got up to take a better look at the menu that was hanging over the front counter. After a quick glance over the dishes, I ordered curry, Vaughn ordered a noodle dish, and we took our number cards and returned to our table. I glanced at my phone. No calls or texts from Jen yet, and it was already a quarter past six. It was getting late, but I hadn't been hanging out with her long enough to know if that was normal or not. In any case, it made me feel uneasy.

Vaughn also looked down at his phone. He frowned. "It looks like Tommy's not going to be able to make it. He got called into work."

"Oh." I didn't know what else to say. Not knowing Tommy well, I wasn't disappointed that he couldn't make it.

It just meant that I was alone with Vaughn for longer, but Jen would be here soon, right?

As that thought crossed my mind, my phone rang.

"Hey, Sarah," Jen said when I answered. "I'm so sorry, but something came up, and I can't make it."

My stomach did a backflip as my eyes flicked up nervously to meet Vaughn's. "I– Is everything okay?" I managed, hearing a note of panic in my voice. Had he noticed?

"Yeah, I'm okay. I'll tell you about it later. I'm sorry, Sarah, but I have to go."

The muttered "Bye" had barely left my lips when the phone beeped, signaling the end of the call. "Jen isn't coming either," I said as I put my phone in my pocket. My voice sounded much steadier than I felt. Being in a group of people was one thing, but having to hang out with Vaughn, the "bad boy," by myself?

"Is Jen all right?" Vaughn asked cautiously.

"I think so. She didn't say what was going on." I smiled at him. It wasn't his fault that I had issues, and I didn't want him to worry or blame himself. Rumors aside, he could be a decent person, but we'd just met, and he still made me nervous. Not in an "oh, he's cute" kind of way. More like, "run and hide."

"Pad kee mao and Massaman curry?"

I jumped as the server set two dishes on the table between us and took our number cards. I'd been so absorbed in Jen's cancellation that I hadn't even heard her approach.

Vaughn thanked her as she walked away, then looked at his food, brows furrowed in thought. "We can take it to go if you want. My car's parked down the street, and I can drive you home."

I glanced down at my own bowl and mentally kicked

myself. He'd noticed my nervousness at being here alone with him and was trying to be considerate. There was no need to rush out on him. I could leave once we finished eating. It was a public setting, and there was no need to ruin this perfectly good meal. "No, it's fine. I'm starving." As if to punctuate my words, my stomach growled.

Vaughn smiled and picked up his chopsticks. "Good. Me too."

It wasn't long before my spoon clattered into the empty bowl, and I leaned back in my chair, stomach full enough to be satiated, but not so much that it was uncomfortable. If nothing else, I was glad Vaughn had introduced me to this restaurant. The food was good enough that I would be coming here again. Vaughn wasn't unpleasant to talk to either. As we ate, he'd asked me about school, my family, and if I'd liked Carter's show. That last line of questioning reminded me of Carter's job offer. I was still on the fence about taking it and how much it would complicate my life to be working for Aunt Liv's old lover.

"So back to Carter's job offer. It could be a great opportunity," Vaughn said.

"I don't know. Being his personal assistant..." I said as Vaughn was still eating his noodles. With the peppers mixed in, it looked spicy. "He doesn't even know me. Why would he offer a job like that to someone he just met?"

"He's been looking for a new assistant for a while," he said before taking a long drink of water. "Carter's getting a lot more contracts than he used to. And he does know you. He just hasn't seen you in a while." Vaughn set his chopsticks across the plate, wiping a few beads of sweat off of his forehead and admitting defeat.

"Well, *I* don't remember *him*," I said stubbornly. "Even if he remembers me from however many years ago, he's basically a stranger to me. How can I trust that he won't do something shady?"

He laughed. "I work for him," Vaughn reminded me. "He's a kind person, more kind than he has any reason to be. He gave me a job when no one else wanted to hire a high-school dropout. Modeling is way better than any other offers I had, and it pays pretty well even though it's part-time."

We sat in silence as I thought about what it would mean to become Carter's assistant. It would be nice to have my own money and get some work experience, which I was sure I would need after school ended. It would also help pay for college, but I'd just met Carter and wasn't sure if I even liked him yet. Working for him meant we'd be alone together for long periods of time.

I looked up from my food, and Vaughn had steepled his hands in front of himself and was looking intently at me. "Why is it that you don't want to be around me? Do I make you that uncomfortable?"

The question caught me off guard. Had my discomfort been that obvious? "I'm here, aren't I?" I asked, my tone defensive, then took a deep breath to calm myself. "Sorry, it's not you." I considered my next words carefully. It was weird, but I liked Vaughn. Talking about my problems was not my strong suit, but I needed to try. "I left New York in part due to a bad relationship, and I'm still trying to work through it. Being around new people makes me uncomfortable. You're one of Jen's friends, but I don't know you, Vaughn. Jen says you're a good person, but she also said you had a reputation for being a 'bad boy.'"

Vaughn stared at me in silence, his eyes searching my face. After a moment, he said, "We should get going. There are people waiting for a table."

Nodding, I grabbed my jacket and purse. He didn't look angry, but he must have been if he wanted to leave so abruptly. Maybe it was the bad-boy comment. He'd probably heard that a lot.

We made our way into the cold night. Traffic was still as bad as ever, but there were fewer people on the sidewalks now. The after-work foot traffic had abated as people reached their destinations and stayed inside, unwilling to brave the chilly, snowy night.

I took a deep breath and sighed as I felt the stinging chill in my cheeks.

"Do you want a ride?" he asked, as a breeze ruffled his hair.

"No, but thanks." Patting my stomach, I attempted to make a joke. "I need the walk after that meal."

"Come on," Vaughn said with a chuckle, "I'll walk you to the station then."

We walked in silence, turning onto Broadway and heading toward the Capitol Hill light-rail station. It wasn't perfectly quiet. Seattle is much too big of a city to be completely devoid of sound at any time of day. People laughed, car horns still blared, and the sound of a steady rush of feet on concrete filled the space around us, but we didn't speak.

Why did I open my big, fat mouth? No one wants to hear that their friends are talking about them behind their back. The tension was so thick between us that it permeated the air and made my skin crawl. I couldn't take it anymore.

"I'm sorry," I finally said, breaking the silence. "I didn't mean to upset you, but, if it makes you feel better, Jen also mentioned that those rumors were just that, rumors. She was letting me know who you were, that's all."

Vaughn shrugged. "No, I'm the one who should be

sorry." He looked frustrated but still smiled. "I have a reputation for being a bad boy because honestly, I was one. I acted out, I shoplifted, drank, and I was kicked out of school right before I graduated. I was eighteen, so my guardian didn't bother looking for another one to enroll me in." Vaughn looked a little embarrassed. "My point is, I know what kind of reputation I have, but the last two years have been rough, and I'm not that guy anymore."

"Rough?" Damn it. Now I was curious.

"Well, I was..." He trailed off and glanced down at the ground before meeting my eyes. "I used to be in the foster-care system and technically aged out when I turned eighteen. My guardian was going to let me stay on at his place, but when I got kicked out of school, he booted me to the curb." Vaughn screwed up his face into a stern expression, complete with a disapproving scowl. "'If you want to act like a badass, you should be able to make it on your own too.' That's what he said to me."

"That's a little harsh," I said as I stepped out of the way of a woman walking in the opposite direction.

"Looking back, I think it was necessary. It really forced me to examine my life and think about the bad choices I'd made and how I wanted to live my life moving forward. Sleeping in my car wasn't much fun, and I worked a few odd jobs to get money for food. Summer wasn't too bad. It was almost like camping. It got worse last winter."

In my mind, I could see Vaughn huddled in the back seat of a small sedan, trying to keep warm while frost coated the windows. It must have been hard on him. I don't think I could have done it.

Vaughn smiled a little, as if he recalled a fond memory. "Then I met Carter. I'd heard of him before and had hung out at his studio once or twice with Kat, but I'd never talked to him. 'You have great bone structure,' he'd said to me. 'I could use you in this piece I'm working on,' and, just like that, he plucked me off the street and set me up in the back room of his old studio. He bought a mini-fridge and kept groceries in it, and he paid me to model for him and help him out." Vaughn chuckled. "You could say I was his first assistant. Now I get paid for modeling for the figure-drawing sessions and helping him with his shows. He even convinced my guardian to reconcile with me. On top of that, he's letting me live at one of his properties. He has been a good friend."

Red and blue lights from police cars flashed ahead of us, but there were too many people on the sidewalk to see where exactly they were coming from. A car must have gotten pulled over.

"That's why I feel comfortable assuring you that Carter is a good person," he continued. "I don't think I would have done what he did if the situation had been reversed." He looked over at me and blew out a breath that steamed in the night air. "I'm not going to tell you that you should or shouldn't work for him—that's for you to decide—but I can tell that his offer is genuine. He's not trying to pull something over on you if that's what you're worried about."

The flashing lights grew steadily closer. I stared ahead, not knowing what to say. I should take Carter up on his offer. Maybe it would help me come out of my shell, and maybe, just maybe, it could even help me get back to where I used to be—confident and happy.

I was so absorbed in this thought that I didn't realize Vaughn had stopped walking until I was a few steps ahead of him. He stood in the middle of the sidewalk, staring at the police cars and a large crowd of people in front of us.

His eyes looked funny, out of focus. His pupils were dilated, and he had a far-off look on his face.

"Are you okay, Vaughn?"

"No," he said, his voice a tense whisper. He swallowed hard and closed his eyes. When he opened them, they looked normal again. "We need to get out of here."

CHAPTER 11

"WHY? WHAT'S GOING ON?" I asked, feeling my eyebrows climb my forehead. I glanced at the crowd. Most had their backs to us, and I couldn't see what was past them. There must have been some sort of spectacle on the sidewalk. There were too many people standing around for it to be a pulled-over car as I had originally assumed.

Vaughn seemed to come out of a daze and shook his head. "I'm sorry. I was thinking about something else." He sounded less anxious to leave, now staring intently at the people gathered in front of us. A few of them moved, and I spotted an officer standing near the mouth of an alley. By the way he moved his hands in a shooing gesture, it looked like he was asking the people to leave. Vaughn gave me a faint smile. "Maybe we should go around?"

We moved as close as we could to the edge of the sidewalk without being in the street. At the officer's words, a few people started peeling off from the gathering and continuing on their way. As we passed, I peered down the alley. Through the gaps created by the departed onlookers, I could see four officers, including the one attempting to keep the public back. There was one other person, not in a Seattle Police Department uniform, who caught my eye. He was a tall, muscular man who looked familiar.

Will. The same Will who had been at my house and had threatened me in the parking lot was standing over an indistinguishable lump on the ground. It was too dark to tell what it was, but Will crouched down and shined a light on the form, giving me a quick glimpse of a lumpy red mass and—was that a *hand*? It wasn't easy to see the details from this distance, but I was pretty sure that had been fingers that I'd seen illuminated by Will's flashlight. After a moment of examining it, he stood and said something to one of the uniformed officers.

Vaughn, who had taken a few more steps before stopping, looked at me before glancing down the alley. "Sarah, are you all right? Why did you stop?"

I hadn't realized I'd stopped walking. "That guy," I hissed. "That man was at my house. He's a detective, or so he said." Out of the corner of my eye, I saw Vaughn stiffen.

"We should go," he said, the tension back in his voice. "We shouldn't be here, Sarah."

I ignored him and continued looking as more people cleared away. I'd seen enough cop shows to know what an active crime scene looked like. "What is going on?" As I whispered the words, Will's head whipped around, and our eyes met. I took an involuntary step back as he turned and hurried our way.

The scar on Will's face was ghostly white in the harsh light of the streetlamps as he loomed closer, his face twisted in tightly controlled rage. I had a sudden urge to run, but I tried to stand my ground. The look on his face could curdle milk, but I hadn't done anything wrong. I wasn't going to let him scare me off for the third time, even if he was twice my size. He wouldn't try anything with all these cops around, would he?

Vaughn smiled at Will, but it looked forced. He waved as Will pointed to us and motioned for us to come forward.

My heart leapt into my throat. I gave Vaughn a sidelong look, then wove through the few remaining people and past the uniformed officer, who gave me a curt nod. Vaughn followed close behind. I stopped a few steps from Will, staring into his eyes defiantly. He scared me, but he didn't need to know that.

He met my gaze with a glower of his own, then turned and walked away from the crowd, motioning for us to follow. He took us near the mouth of the alley, right in front of the police tape, before he whirled around.

"What the hell are you doing here?" Will growled. We were far enough from the group of people and the other officers that it would be difficult for them to hear him.

"Hi, Will," Vaughn said coldly. "Nice to see you too."

Will's eyes flicked over to Vaughn, and his scowl deepened. I tried to keep my eyes on the looming threat rather than glance at Vaughn. Did they know each other?

"Why are you here?" he asked again.

Before I could open my mouth to tell Will that what we were doing was none of his business, thank you very much, Vaughn said, "Having dinner. Is that illegal now?" This time, I did give Vaughn a sidelong look. He looked angry, too, his expression telling me that he had dealt with Will before. What the hell was going on?

Will flushed at Vaughn's words. I could see the rage on his face again. It was just like when he'd been talking to Liv in our kitchen. He looked down his nose at Vaughn, which was impressive since Will was a few inches shorter, and he looked like he was about to tear Vaughn's head off. Instead of yelling, he did something that surprised me.

He closed his eyes and sighed, visibly trying to rein in his emotions. When he spoke, his voice was much calmer than it had been moments ago. "It's quite a coincidence that I would be called out to examine a body right before the two of you show up," Will said in a low growl that held a fraction of the heat it previously had. "Some would call that suspicious."

"Body?" I asked in a high squeak. I felt my blood run cold as I glanced down the alleyway to the shape on the ground, now covered by a tarp. The memory of the lumpy red mass that Will's flashlight illuminated and the hand that, now that I thought about it, wasn't attached to an arm, made my stomach turn.

A look of confusion passed over Will as he examined my expression. He was surprised by my reaction. "Olivia didn't send you?"

The question tore my eyes away from the tarp. "Send me? Why would she—"

"I told you I would arrest you if you interfered with my investigation," he said over me, the anger starting to return to his voice. One of the other officers looked over at us, and I saw him rest a palm on the grip of his sidearm. "I should haul you to the station for obstruction—"

"Sarah is Olivia Frost's niece, Will," Vaughn said as he interposed himself between the blond man and me. "She's not trying to interfere with anything. We went to dinner, and I happened to be walking her to the rail station." His voice had lost the earlier coolness and just sounded tired. "We're bystanders. We don't know anything about what is happening. Sarah isn't a part of this."

What did he mean by that? Was Aunt Liv involved with whatever Will was investigating? "What is Liv—?"

"It doesn't concern you," Will snapped.

I glared at him around Vaughn. I was getting tired of being interrupted. "Oh, so now you decide I have nothing to do with it? Well, guess what. It does *concern me* when you show up at my house and my aunt has to threaten you to get you to leave."

A sheepish look crossed his face, and he took a step back from Vaughn and me. "I... that was a mistake. Olivia knows how to get under my skin. She never listens." He shook his head and ran a hand through his hair. "You should go home, Miss Frost. It's dangerous to be out at night these days."

I stuck my hands in my jacket pockets and sidestepped Vaughn. They were shaking, and I didn't want either of them to see. Mustering my courage, I threw Will my best Aunt Liv glare. "I can take care of myself, Officer Will, or whoever you are. I noticed that you're not telling *him* to go home," I said as I nodded toward Vaughn.

Will's eyes slid over to Vaughn. "He doesn't need protection. You do. You're in over your head, *girl*." He emphasized the last word, making it an insult. "You have no idea about what is going on around you, and it's best that it stays that way. I can't believe Olivia let you stay with her in the middle of all this. She should know better than to let outsiders get involved."

"Will!" Vaughn whispered harshly, throwing a look at the detective. "Sarah isn't a part of this," he repeated.

My temper flared, and I couldn't contain it. "A part of what?!" I shouted, drawing the attention of both the other officers and the onlookers. I didn't care. I'd had enough of being afraid, and I'd had enough of being treated like a child who couldn't take care of herself. Now I was just angry.

Vaughn and Will both looked startled. To be honest, I was a little surprised myself. "I don't know why you are BOTH treating me like I'm some sort of idiot, but if my aunt is doing something dangerous, I will absolutely be involved." I glowered at Vaughn. "You say you want to be my friend, but you're hiding something from me that could hurt my family? Friends don't do that."

Vaughn looked at his shoes, guilt plain on his face, and I felt heat creep up my neck, realizing that the people there, cops and looky-loos alike, were staring at me. I kept up the glare anyway, refusing to back down from the two men. I would not be painted as some weak little girl, not this time.

Will recovered the quickest. Being a cop, he had to be used to people yelling at him. He shook his head. "You don't understand." Contrary to his earlier heat, his voice was surprisingly sympathetic, and his expression was one of concern. It was fake. The act probably worked on most people, but my mother had used the same expression on me too many times. "It's best if you go home, Miss Frost. This is nothing for you to worry about."

Rather than mollify me, his suggestion made me more upset. "Fine," I said hotly and whirled around, walking with fury over to the street. The cop keeping the onlookers back moved to block me, but Will must have signaled that it was okay for me to leave because a moment later, the man nodded and let me through. After I cleared the crowd, I pulled out my phone, tapped on the neon pink Rideshare app, and ordered a pickup.

I heard quick footfalls behind me and turned to see Vaughn jogging to catch up.

"Sarah—" he began, but I held up my hand to stop him.

"Save it," I said coolly. Anger still bubbled within me, and I fought to keep it from bursting out again. Did he think

I was stupid? Did he think that I wouldn't notice when strange things were going on around me?

"Something is going on with that guy"—I pointed at Will—"and my aunt, something dangerous, and somehow dead bodies are involved. You know about it, but you don't think I should know. Does that about sum it up, Vaughn?" I wasn't able to keep the accusation from my voice.

Vaughn wasn't cowed. He looked surprised at first, but I could see his own temper rising in the set of his brows. He glanced around, but no one was passing us at the moment or paying attention to us. "It is dangerous, Sarah. You don't under—"

"Don't tell me I don't understand," I growled. "You don't know me. You have no idea what I've been through." I glared at him. "If my aunt is in danger, I need to know what is going on, and you have no right to keep it from me."

Vaughn seemed at a loss for words. We stood there looking at each other for another minute before a black Prius with a sticker in the front window that matched the app I'd used pulled to the curb beside me. I waved to the driver. "That's my ride. I'll see you later, Vaughn." Without waiting for him to reply, I opened the passenger-side back door and slid into the car. I glanced at Vaughn, but he'd turned away and was walking back toward the scene. Back to where Will was standing. Will, who was watching the Prius.

As I sat in the warm, comfortable sedan, I looked out the window. The flashing lights of the police cars reflected off the snow, a pulsing red glow that seemed almost alive. I needed to find out what the hell my Aunt Liv was involved in, and I needed to do it soon.

CHAPTER 12

OVER THE NEXT FEW DAYS, I watched Aunt Liv closely, looking for signs of anything amiss. During dinner those nights, when there was the highest chance of us eating together, I asked about how her work was going. Her replies were usually some variation of "fine," and by the fourth day, I could tell that she was starting to get suspicious. By Wednesday, she'd started ignoring my questions completely.

"Why don't you get out of the house?" she suggested in a huff. "It's been a few days. What about those figure-drawing sessions? Isn't there another one this week?" We were sitting together in the living room after having leftover take-out Korean food for breakfast, the boxes still littering the coffee table. The TV was on, and a young newscaster was gesturing animatedly with his hands as he spoke, but Liv had the volume too low to hear what he was saying.

"We're breaking for the holidays." I'd gotten the email informing everyone of the break yesterday. To be honest, I was more than a little relieved that I wouldn't have to see Vaughn again for a couple of weeks.

Liv's question reminded me of Carter's offer. I hadn't

called him yet, and his card was hidden in the dresser upstairs. I wondered what Aunt Liv would think of me working at the studio, though she didn't need to know who I'd be working for, not yet anyway. "I did get a job offer while I was at that party last week. I forgot to tell you about it."

Aunt Liv, who'd been sipping a steaming mug of coffee and reading on her phone looked up. "A job offer?" she asked. "Doing what?"

"The artist that owns the studio wants me to be his assistant," I said, not mentioning what the name of said artist was. I still hadn't told her that I'd met Carter, her ex. Now that I thought about it, Aunt Liv hadn't mentioned any of her boyfriends before. Had she and Carter really dated at some point? He could have been exaggerating about their relationship. My curiosity got the better of me, and I asked, "Do you know who Carter Godfrey is?"

After an initial look of shock, her features fell into a neutral mask. Oh yes, Liv knew him all right.

"Is he the one who offered you the job?" she asked flatly, narrowing her eyes.

"The job offer was from the artist that owns the studio," I repeated, trying not to outright lie. "I met Carter at the party. He mentioned you, so I just wondered if you knew him." Liv eyed me suspiciously, and I continued on before I gave myself away. "Anyway, it seems like a pretty good gig, and I can work in the evenings when school starts again."

She leaned back into the couch. "Yes, I know Carter," she said, her voice quiet. There was a far-off look in her eyes, like she was recalling a memory from a long time ago. It was the same look that Carter had when thinking about Liv. After a moment, she shook her head and focused on me again. "It sounds like you've made your decision if you're already working it into your school schedule."

Had I decided to take the job? As Liv took another sip of her coffee, I thought about it and found that I did want to do it, not just for the money but because I was curious about Carter. Maybe he could give me some of the information I needed.

"I guess so." I smiled at Liv. "At least I'll be getting out of the house."

I hugged Aunt Liv to the warnings of "Coffee, coffee!" and dashed up the stairs. I'd been getting nowhere at home with Liv, but if Carter knew her well, he'd have some idea of what she was doing and who exactly Will was.

I dug Carter's card out of my sock drawer and called the number. He picked up on the second ring.

"Carter Godfrey." The voice was brisk and crisp, much different from the friendly tone he'd had at the exhibition.

"Um, hi," I said, suddenly unsure of what to say. "This is Sarah Frost. We met at the studio," I added, in case he'd forgotten who I was.

"Sarah!" His voice warmed considerably. "I was wondering if you'd be giving me a call. Have you given any thought to my offer? I'm still looking for an assistant."

Straight to the point. "Yes. I'm very interested." I could hear my mom's voice in my head, telling me to get more information before agreeing to anything. Mom worked in the fashion industry and was a ruthless negotiator. It was hard to remember what I'd heard her say in the past when talking to clients. She'd brought work home a lot, so over the years I'd learned to tune it out. "Can we talk a little more about compensation and what exactly I'll be doing as your assistant?"

We spent a while going over the details. The pay was

good, and the hours were reasonable, a little over twenty-five a week. That would still be manageable once I started school in January. It was part-time, but it would give me a good head start on saving for a car and college.

He invited me to come by the studio after lunch and said that it could be my first day. It seemed a little fast to get the job stuff settled, but it wasn't like I had anything else going on. By the time I hung up the phone, I was smiling. Carter's upbeat attitude was infectious. I'd have to think of a way to broach the subject of my aunt with him so that he wouldn't get suspicious. Better save it for another time. I didn't want to get into trouble for being nosey on my first day, no matter how much the questions nagged at me.

I picked a nice blouse and some jeans, then showered and put on a little bit of eyeshadow and lip gloss. Glancing at myself in the mirror, I put on a pair of small, rose-shaped earrings. With the makeup and nice clothes, I would go as far as to say that I was on the low end of pretty, with my long brown hair, blue eyes, and pale skin. The person looking back at me in the mirror looked like a professional, but not gorgeous like Aunt Liv, who could have modeled if she wanted to. Sarah Frost, all grown up.

Liv *had* modeled. I remembered the painting of her that had been on display at Carter's show.

The door to Liv's apartment was open when I left, and I heard the sound of the newscaster on the TV again. "Another young woman has gone missing in the Seattle area. Christine Thomson lived by herself in Ballard and was reported missing by co-workers when she missed two of her shifts at a local diner."

I popped my head in the door. "I'm heading out. My new boss is going to show me what I'll be doing at the studio."

Aunt Liv was sitting on the couch, watching the TV with an intensity I didn't see her show often. She looked troubled. Was it because of the missing woman? She nodded her head absently and said, "Be careful. Call me if you need a ride home or anything."

I assured her I would and walked out the front door.

It was another crisp, cold day as I walked down the street to the light-rail station. The sun was hidden behind gray clouds, but at least it wasn't snowing. Seattle is a bustling city, even in the wintertime. True to form, when I stepped off the light rail at the International District station, the sidewalks were full of people. I could smell the various East Asian cuisines mingling in the air, making my mouth water. With great willpower, I turned away from the inviting scents and headed off toward Lumen Field.

It took me about ten minutes to walk across the giant parking lot that surrounds the stadium where the Seahawks play to S. King Street. Ashley was behind the front desk again, and she waved me over as I removed my jacket.

"Hi, Sarah! I heard that you're Carter's new assistant." She beamed at me, talking excitedly. News traveled fast. I wondered if she remembered me from the previous two times I'd been here or if it was just her job to be that personable. She reached into a drawer and pulled out a white plastic square and a lanyard with a key on it, then held them out for me. "These are for you. The badge will get you into the building after hours, and the key is for Carter's studio. You'll have to swipe the card to get outside as well. You're on the list for authorized access now, so building security won't bother you. I just need your driver's license and your Social Security card to scan in for Carter."

I took the key and badge from Ashley and dug in my purse until I found the items she'd asked for. "Do you usually process new employees?" I asked as I handed her the documents.

She laughed, and it sounded genuinely amused. "Only for Carter. He hates dealing with paperwork." Ashley scanned my items, then gave them back to me. "He emails me the documents, and I do the rest. He's a pretty smart guy, but he'd be lost without me. Though, I guess you'll be doing his paperwork from now on. Please sign this. It's the official offer."

Ashley placed the document and a pen on the counter. I skimmed it over, seeing my name and Carter's, along with the title of *administrative assistant* and a per-hour rate that made me blink. It was more than he'd stated on the phone. Should I say something about it? I glanced at Ashley, but she just smiled at me, so I grabbed the pen and signed.

"Great! You're all set!" She took the document and placed it in a folder labeled Sarah Frost. As I murmured a hurried thanks and turned toward the elevators, she said, "It will be nice having you around. Good luck, Sarah."

I waved at her and stepped onto the elevator. Ashley seemed lovely. I wondered if she and Carter were a couple, like Jen had said. It wouldn't surprise me.

When the elevator doors slid open again, the door on the studio's landing was propped open with a small metal trash can. I stuck my head inside and glanced around before a booming "Sarah!" made me jump. Carter was walking down the staircase that led to the roof, the place where Vaughn and I exchanged numbers just last week.

"Welcome, welcome!" he said enthusiastically as he approached. "Did Ashley give you everything you need?" When I nodded, he grinned. "Excellent. I don't know what I'd do without her."

That made me smile. Ashley had said the same thing.

"Thank you for the opportunity," I said. "I'm looking forward to working with you, but I think there was a mistake on the paperwork. The pay was different from what we'd agreed on earlier."

"Oh yes. After thinking about it more, I increased it a little since I'm not the easiest person to work with. You may not be thanking me in a couple of weeks. Hopefully, the great pay keeps you around." He gave a sheepish look that somehow fit on his handsome face and gestured for me to follow.

The studio looked different from the two times I'd been there before, at the exhibition or even during the figure-drawing session. The chairs and tables were gone, replaced with a nice area rug, two couches, two chairs, and a coffee table. It looked like an office reception area. Near the windows in the back, a tarp was taped to the floor, and the largest easel I'd ever seen stood empty with clear plastic bins surrounding it. Behind the stairs that led to the roof was a kitchen I hadn't noticed before and another door. Carter led me to the kitchen and pulled out a stool so that I could sit at the bar.

"This is how it normally looks during the week," he said as he watched me look around the room. "That door"—he indicated the one to the left of the refrigerator—"leads to a set of bedrooms. I sleep here sometimes if I'm working on a project late into the night. I keep a few changes of clothes here, and there's even a shower. You won't need to stay here though," he said when he saw the look on my face. "You're still in high school, so I'll try not to keep you too late, but if that ever happens, there's another room with a futon you can use. Feel free to bring an overnight bag to keep here just in case."

"What would I be doing that would keep me here so

late?" I asked, not sure how I felt about being asked to stay at the studio overnight.

Carter scratched his chin and frowned a little in thought. "Well, you'll be doing the normal administrative stuff for me. Answering emails, communicating with buyers, setting appointments with some of the galleries around town, stuff like that. Sometimes, you'll need to be here when clients pick up pieces, either for a show or to purchase. I'll have you doing other things as well. If I have a deadline, I may need an extra pair of hands. That's usually when the late nights happen." He gestured at the empty easel. "I like my employees to learn while they're employed by me, so I'll be showing you some of my techniques, and I'll even have you do some simple tasks on my work."

"Really? What kind of stuff would I be doing to help you with your work?"

He waved a hand vaguely, and his brows knit together, like he was trying to come up with the right words. "It will vary depending on what we are working on. I might have you whitewash a surface for me or block in colors on a canvas. Occasionally, I'll send you into the city to take pictures or draw sketches of a building from different angles if I'm including it in some work." He shrugged, smiling. "I'm afraid I can't be more specific than that."

I absorbed what he'd said and nodded. That didn't sound too bad. Some of it actually sounded like fun.

"To answer your original question, I have no idea. We'll just have to see what it is when we get there." He grinned a boyish smile that was mischievous, and it made him look years younger. "Anyway, let me give you a tour."

Carter showed me around the studio, explaining that I was welcome to use the refrigerator and microwave, then opened the door that led out of the kitchen and into a little hallway with three doors. He showed me where the bathroom was and the room with the futon that I could use, then ushered me back into the main room. He pointed out the storage area, where he kept his supplies along with the chairs and easels for the figure-drawing sessions.

"I'll need you to be here an hour before the sessions to let everyone in. Kari is the woman who organizes those, so she'll be the first one here. You'll need to help her set up. Ashley collects the fees, so you don't need to worry about that. If I don't have you working on anything those days, you're more than welcome to participate. I'll be paying you for all those hours anyway since you'll need to lock up after them. Oh!" He clapped his hands together. "I'll make sure to have your fees refunded as well." He grinned at me, and I couldn't help but smile back. There was something about Carter that I really liked despite this being only the second time we'd met.

Normally, I didn't like being alone with people I didn't know well, but Carter was so welcoming that it felt like we'd been friends for years. Staying late at the studio with my boss might be a little uncomfortable, but I could always call Aunt Liv to come get me if I needed it. There was no way I was going to walk to the light-rail station in the middle of the night. That settled it—getting a car would be my first priority.

Carter walked me through creating my email on the laptop that had been lying on the counter, which I found out was my new work computer. A brand-new MacBook Air. He sent me an invite to his calendar and showed me what events I would be expected to attend with him. Which was all of them. He also gave me a credit card for expenses. He had me sign a form agreeing to only use it for purchases that he authorized. I took notes as he talked, and by the time we were finished, it was almost five.

I glanced out the window. As expected, it was dark already.

"I'll call you a ride," Carter said, whipping out his phone.

"It's okay. I can take the light rail. It's not too late." I pulled my own phone out and saw that I had a message from Vaughn. I put the phone back in my pocket.

"Nonsense," he mumbled. "Your aunt would flay the skin from my bones if I sent you out walking the streets at night."

He continued tapping on his phone as I considered my next words carefully. I smoothed my face out into a neutral mask. Contrary to what he and Liv thought, I didn't need constant supervision. However, contradicting him this early in my employment seemed like a bad idea. Since we were waiting anyway, this was the perfect opening to ask about Liv. "You dated my aunt, right? How did you meet her?"

He looked up from his phone, his expression unreadable. "We've known each other for a long time, but Livy and I didn't start dating until she was in college. By then, I was friends with your mom and Dave, your father. He introduced me to her."

And with those few words, it felt as if time had stopped. Carter had known my father before he'd died. My mother never wanted to talk about him, so I knew precious little about the man he was. Liv had told me some things, but in the years between his death and now, I hadn't been brave enough to ask her the really important questions. Now I had a million more. "Oh, I didn't know that," was all I managed, my throat suddenly dry.

Carter watched me, then reached out and squeezed my

shoulder. "The car will be here in a few minutes. Why don't I walk you out?"

I nodded, feeling a little numb as we walked toward the elevators. "Were you good friends?" my mouth asked before I thought about it. Did I really want to drag this up after all these years?

The sympathetic look he gave me made me want to kick myself. "Yes, he was my best friend and a very good man. He cared a lot about you and your mom." He pushed the button to call the elevator, then we stepped inside as the doors slid open. Carter let out a long sigh and scratched at his chin. "Dave loved clam chowder—it was his favorite— and sushi. He hated carrot cake with a passion and was allergic to bananas. The day before he asked your mom to marry him, he was so nervous that he drank half a bottle of whisky without realizing it, and tried to climb the side of her parents' house to serenade her. He fell and injured himself, of course, and your parents ended up getting engaged at the hospital." Carter grinned as we stepped into the lobby.

The reception desk was empty, but the lights were still on. My heart felt heavy in my chest, and try as I might, I couldn't keep my eyes from watering. Hearing Carter talk about my dad with such fondness in his voice was so different from what I was used to. Mom drank too much when his name came up, so over the years, I'd stopped asking. The only people who talked about him like that were my grandparents, and it had been a while since I'd last seen them.

"Once you were born, your dad's focus turned to you and your mom, and rightly so. As a result, we drifted apart for a while, but once you were two or three, I reached out. I was having a hard time making my own way, and your father was there for me." Carter looked up as a car pulled to the curb outside. "I think that's your ride." He nodded at me, the smile still on his lips, but the expression faded as he got a look at my face. "Sarah? Are you all right?"

"I'm fine," I tried to say, but my voice cracked on the word "fine." I cleared my throat. "We don't talk about my father much. I didn't know all those things about him."

"Well, if you want to talk about him more, I'm happy to oblige," he said, his voice gentle. "There was a lot of sadness and heartache surrounding his death, but he would want us to remember the happiness his presence brought." Carter placed a hand on my shoulder and squeezed. "I know that you haven't seen me in a long time and I'm practically a stranger, but if you ever need to talk about Dave or anything else, I'm willing to listen. Livy can be a little much sometimes. I remember that clearly enough."

I returned Carter's smile, not trusting myself to speak. The goal had been to ask him about Aunt Liv, but hearing him talk about my father, all I wanted to do was ask Carter more about him.

As if he could read my thoughts, Carter said, "We'll talk more about Dave another time, Sarah. You need to get home." Before I knew it, he was leading me out the front door to the car that was waiting for me.

CHAPTER 13

"SOMETHING WEIRD IS GOING ON," I said to Jen as she perused the shelves at the local library. We'd met up a few minutes ago. She'd answered the phone sleepily when I'd called her, even though it had been close to noon, and agreed to meet me at the library that afternoon. I looked around, making sure that there wasn't anyone listening to us. There weren't a whole lot of people there on a Thursday afternoon. Still, there were a few younger people who looked like college students and a mother with a boy around ten years old in the children's section.

"We already knew that," she said as she lifted a small book off the shelf. We were standing in the Young Adult section, which was devoid of other browsers. "Why did you want me to meet you here?"

"I thought you wanted to know what she's up to," I said.

"Yes, but we already know something weird is going on," she said with a concerned smile. Clearly seeing my disappointment in her lack of engagement, she continued with, "Don't look at me like that. I'm just telling it like it is. Honestly, you're a little obsessed, Sarah. Why don't you ask your aunt who that guy is," she said, referring to Will, "and where they work?"

"I did," I said as my eyes glided over book titles, not looking for anything in particular.

"You did?" Jen asked. Her tone suggested that she didn't believe me.

"Well," I hedged, "not in so many words. I asked Liv a lot of pointed questions that would lead to where she works and what she does. You know, without giving away what I was doing, but she's been dodging them."

Jen snorted. "That's because she saw right through you. You're not exactly subtle." She put the book back and turned to face me. "It's weird that she won't say where she works, but I doubt she'd be doing anything dangerous. Maybe she works at the police station since that Will guy is an officer. Like I suggested before, she could be undercover."

That sounded like the plot of some mystery novel. "Don't undercover cops fake their own death before joining the mob?" I asked sarcastically, and Jen giggled. "My gut tells me Will is the key to all this. I think he's a detective," I mused. "He was at that crime scene and wasn't wearing a uniform like the other cops. That means he's not a regular officer, right? He must be different."

"Crime scene?" Jen asked sharply. "What crime scene?"

I hadn't seen Jen since last Friday. The events of that night weren't something you could explain over text messages, or even the phone. I quietly told her about getting dinner with Vaughn and running into Will, but glossed over what happened after talking to him, how I'd left Vaughn on the sidewalk. Jen wouldn't be too happy with me for ditching him like that.

Jen looked aghast. "He thought you were involved with that poor woman's death?"

"Woman? What woman?"

"Sarah," she began, shaking her head. "Where have you been? It's been all over the news." She sighed as I stared at her blankly, but I started to recall hearing the newscaster on Liv's TV talking about missing women and the newspaper headline from my dream with my grandparents. "There have been a few disappearances, and four bodies have been discovered so far, all of them looking like they've been mauled by animals." Jen let out a shaky breath before continuing. "I mean, it happens sometimes. Hikers will get attacked by a bear or a mountain lion, but not in the city."

"So there's some sort of wild animal going around mauling people? In the middle of Seattle?" I asked, incredulous. "That makes no sense."

Jen grimaced. "I know. The police speculate that the real killer is using animals to hide the actual cause of death and then dumping the bodies, but why would they dump them in the city? Why wouldn't they leave the bodies in the woods where it would take days or weeks to find? Or bury them if they're already out there. It's stupid, really. It's like the killer is taunting the police."

It suddenly felt a lot colder in the quiet library as we stood there in silence, considering the gruesome murders. Most people assume that being in a group makes them less likely to come to harm. As the old saying goes, there's safety in numbers. For most, that's true. Sure, people still die in car accidents, sickness, and crime, but in general, we're safer with others than if we were going at it alone in the wilderness. Because of that, there is something so gut-wrenchingly sickening at the thought of a person taking another's life just because they can. With four women dead, whoever was doing this wasn't acting in a fit of passion or in self-defense. This was a serial killer with no justifiable reason to kill, or at least, not one that the rest of us would call acceptable.

I was no stranger to violent crime. New York City was far from the safest place in the world, but I'd avoided being a victim. For the most part anyway. But the real question that I couldn't figure out was how Aunt Liv was involved in all this. Could she be trying to find out who this killer was?

Jen cleared her throat. "How's working with Carter?" she asked in a let's-not-talk-about-this-anymore tone of voice. "You started working for him a few days ago, right?"

"Yeah. It's okay. For right now, he has me answering emails and picking up coffee. Once I've been there for a while, I'll be helping him with his projects. Oh, that reminds me." I pulled out my phone and looked at the text I'd received earlier that day. "I need to buy a couple of canvases for him before I go in tomorrow. I know you aren't working today, but can we go by the art store later?"

Jen nodded, and we made our way over to a row of computers for public use. "Back to my original question," Jen said as she sat in the chair next to me. "Why did you want me to meet you here?"

I tapped in the numbers from my library card, and the screen unlocked. "I didn't want to look into this at home. Aunt Liv might be upset if she found out." Call me paranoid, but I had the feeling that she wouldn't like me digging around. "The only computer I have right now is the one Carter gave me, and I don't want to use it for this just in case he has monitoring software installed. Also, I like the library. It's quiet."

Jen stared at me hard. "You could just use your phone, you know."

That was true, but, somehow, it felt better using a

device that Liv didn't have access to, and I told Jen as much. She just rolled her eyes at me and checked her email.

Opening the web browser, I started off by searching for information on the missing women Jen had mentioned. It wasn't hard to find. The situation had made national news. By glancing through a few articles, I learned that the four women who had been found so far had all lived close to the city. One from the Lake Union area, another from Renton, and two from Everett, all within the small collection of cities that made up the greater Seattle area. It wasn't uncommon for people from all around Puget Sound to commute into the city. Housing was crazy expensive, so many people lived where it was more reasonable, trading convenience for a property that wasn't over seven figures. Living in Queen Anne, a neighborhood in Seattle, had only been possible because the house that my aunt and I lived in was owned by my grandparents, who had bought it in the '90s.

Everett was north of Seattle, with a light-rail station for commuters. Renton was to the southeast, and Lake Union was another neighborhood like Queen Anne. If the killer was operating within an hour or so of those locations, they had a vast area to choose from. Since it was so big, the police were having difficulty pinpointing why these specific women were targeted. Other than being in their twenties, they didn't cross paths professionally, so nothing tied them to one another.

The rest of the articles repeated what Jen had said. Multiple women had gone missing, and so far, four bodies had turned up, appearing to have been mauled by some sort of animal with enormous teeth. The authorities weren't sure what type of animal it was yet. They were saying that the wounds were consistent with canine teeth but of a slightly different and much larger variety than any species native to the area.

"Sarah, are you listening?"

I jumped, having been immersed in the report I'd been reading. "Sorry, what is it?"

"I said that we should get going soon if you want to make it to the store to get those supplies." She frowned at my expression. "Are you all right, Sarah?"

It took a lot of willpower for me to shove the images of the missing and dead women out of my mind. Making Jen worry about me wouldn't help matters, so I tried to smile at her. "I'm fine, just trying to figure this all out."

My smile must not have been convincing because her brows furrowed, but she didn't press. I closed the web browser and logged off the computer. I could always look into this more later. Now that I knew it was national news, it wouldn't be weird for me to look this up at home. If Liv asked what I was doing, I would just tell her that I'd seen it on TV and wanted to learn more about it in case there were areas of town I needed to avoid. Those missing women might have been somehow connected to Will and my aunt, and I was going to find out how.

After the library, we went to the art-supply store Jen worked at to get the items Carter had asked for. I used the credit card he'd given me for the first time. It felt strange using it, and I was sure that the clerk was going to question me—there was no way I looked the part of a high-profile assistant—but he didn't. I took a picture of the receipt and then stuffed it in the bag with the rest of the supplies, planning to email it to Carter later.

The next stop was the grocery store, a little Italian

market and deli near Jen's house. She picked out a few things as I browsed around drooling over the various pasta dishes for purchase behind the deli counter.

By the time we finished shopping, the sun was already setting. The early days were aggravating sometimes, but the trade-off of a 3:30 sunset in the winter was a day that lasted until 9:00 or 10:00 in the evening during the summer months. Jen promised to make dinner as she dragged me away from the delicacies of the market and drove us to her house.

Less than thirty minutes later, I found myself sitting on a stool at the counter as Jen worked in the kitchen, prepping the food she'd bought. Jen lived with her mother in a small three-bedroom house that wasn't too far from Lake Union. It didn't look like much from the outside, but the inside had been renovated in recent years; it didn't look the way that I remembered it at all. The countertops that had been tile were granite now, and all the appliances were a brushed stainless steel. The carpet in the living and dining rooms had been replaced with hardwood, and bronze light fixtures had replaced the old ceiling lights. Even with the changes, it was warm and inviting and smelled like herbs and fresh-baked bread—a house that had seen many home-cooked meals.

Jen's house had been a safe haven for me when I was little. A place away from my grandparents, Liv, and my mom, and the memories of my father that permeated the old house in Queen Anne. My mother had tried to make it work at first, and she made it a year before we packed up and moved. I didn't blame her for that. I loved my grandparents' house, but it was a constant reminder of a happiness that was forever gone. Here, I hadn't had the tragedy that had broken my family apart shoved in my face every day through pictures and unspoken words. I didn't have to feel guilty about wanting to be away from the family that my mother had left behind.

I watched Jen. She had actually put on a flowery apron, and I was trying to hide my smile behind my hand. It was adorable. I mean, it even had lace at the edges. I didn't know they made those anymore. "Why weren't you able to make it on Friday? You said you'd tell me about it later."

Jen pressed her lips together as she pulled a small package wrapped in brown paper from the shopping bag. Her eyes narrowed as she set it on the counter, and it was a few moments before she answered me, busying herself with unwrapping the chunk of beef she'd purchased. "I got into a fight with Stella that night."

When she didn't continue, I said, "Okay… why?"

She pulled a cutting board out of the cabinet and slammed it down on the counter. I winced at the noise. "Sorry," Jen mumbled and sighed. "It's just that we've been dating for a while now, and I want her to meet my family, but she says she's not ready to take that step." She placed the meat on the cutting board, then drew a knife from the knife block next to the stove. "I want to respect her boundaries, but I also want to move forward with our relationship." She was cutting the meat with vigor. "I mean, we've been dating for over a year!" she said with sudden heat. "We should know if our relationship is going anywhere."

"Maybe she needs more time," I said as I propped my elbow on the bar, watching Jen. She looked distraught, and I wanted to help her, but my own relationships had been a mess. Given my track record, I was probably the wrong person to come to for this sort of thing. "I know I'm not really the one to give relationship advice, but you're still together, right? Did you come to some sort of compromise?"

She let out a heavy sigh again. "We're going to talk about it later and—shit!" Jen hissed as the knife clattered to the ground. She reached for the towel that was hanging on the stove as blood dripped to the floor.

"Jen!" I jumped up from the stool, almost tripping. "Are you all right?"

"I cut myself," she said as she wrapped her hand in the towel. Blood was dripping down her arm. "Mom's going to kill me."

"Don't be ridiculous. I doubt she'll care as long as you're okay." I knew Jen's mom, Amanda, and she wasn't the type to get upset over this. Jen struggled to wrap her hand, so I took the towel and helped her, examining the wound. It was pretty deep. She'd almost sliced part of her finger off. "I think I should take you to the hospital."

She grimaced but didn't argue. The blood was already starting to soak through the towel. "Yeah, okay. My keys are in my purse. Let me get a bag for this."

She wrapped a plastic bag around her towel-wrapped hand and secured it with a rubber band as I fished her keys from her purse. Once we were out of the house, I locked the door and helped her down the steps and into her Civic.

Jen's house wasn't too far from Aunt Liv's, but I still wasn't that familiar with the area. I asked her what the closest medical facility was, and she said the Virginia Mason Emergency Department in downtown Seattle and pointed me in the right direction. Not having my own car yet, I hadn't driven anywhere in Seattle, but, luckily, it was after rush hour traffic, so at least we weren't bumper to bumper. Jen was calm during the ride. I glanced over every few seconds to make sure she was still awake, but she gave me directions and seemed alert. My body wanted to go into panic mode and speed down the freeway, but I somehow managed only ten miles an hour over the speed limit.

"Can you walk?" I asked as we pulled up to the emergency entrance. "Should I get you a wheelchair?" I tried to locate the button for the hazard lights. You'd think it would be easy, but in the dark, it wasn't obvious.

"I'm fine, Sarah," she said as she opened the door with her right hand, her left still securely wrapped in the plastic bag. I guess she didn't want to get blood all over her car. "I'll meet you inside, okay?" She shut the door, and I watched with apprehension until she disappeared beyond the automatic emergency-entrance doors.

It must have been a slow night because I was able to find a parking spot right up front. I rushed in the door carrying both my and Jen's bags. An older woman sat at the reception desk. She didn't look at me as I entered but continued typing away at her computer. Jen was seated in a padded chair to the right of the desk and waved me over.

"They haven't seen you yet?" I asked in a quiet voice as I sat in the chair next to her. There were a couple of other people in the waiting room, but none of them had a plastic bag tied around their hand, so you'd think she would have been able to get their attention.

"Of course not," she said with a roll of her eyes. "It's not like I'm bleeding out."

I eyed the bag pointedly, which had a small pool of blood at the bottom of it.

"Okay, I've lost a little blood," she amended. "I'm sure I'll get called soon."

Just as she said it, the door next to the reception desk opened. "Jennifer Steele!" called a man in scrubs.

Jen raised her uninjured hand, and we followed the orderly through the door and into a larger area that was the intersection of a few hallways. There was a nurses' station in the center of the room, and curtains lined the walls, hiding small alcoves behind them. He led us to one of the curtains. Behind it was a tiny room with an examination table, two chairs, and a computer. He asked Jen to sit on the exam table and unwrapped the plastic bag from her hand, throwing it in a red bin marked "Hazardous Waste." He asked her a few pointed questions, and Jen explained how she cut herself while he took off the towel and cleaned some of the blood. He nodded as she talked and, when he was done, he wrapped the wound again with some clean gauze, then pulled his gloves off and jotted a few notes on a clipboard.

"The doctor will be with you in a couple of minutes," he said as if he'd said it a million times that night. "Are you in pain? I can get you some Tylenol."

"Yes to the pain," Jen said, scowling at the orderly, "but I think this is going to take more than some Tylenol."

The man smiled apologetically. "I can't give you anything stronger until the doctor sees you. It will be a few minutes," he repeated and left through the curtain.

Jen made a face at him as he left and lay back on the table. She gave me a watery smile. "It really hurt when he unwrapped it." She closed her eyes. "Dammit. I should have been more careful."

"It was an accident," I said, trying to console her. "Don't blame yourself for this, Jen." I took her uninjured hand and squeezed it. Just being at the hospital, minutes away from the care of a doctor, made me feel much calmer than I'd been in the car. "You'll be okay."

She smiled at me and squeezed my hand in return. "Thanks, Sarah. I promise I'll make up for bailing on you last Friday. Next time, we'll get sushi."

I chewed at my bottom lip. "I don't think there's going to be a next time. Vaughn looked pretty hurt when I left."

Jen snorted softly. "Yeah, I've been hearing about it all week."

"You... you have?" Had Vaughn already talked to Jen? It shouldn't have been so surprising, but dammit, I didn't want to cause trouble with her friends.

Jen pursed her lips in annoyance. "Kat called me over the weekend saying Vaughn wasn't acting like himself. She was furious when she found out it was just you and Vaughn at dinner Friday, but don't worry about her," she said quickly, seeing the look on my face. "Kat needs to accept that he sees her as nothing more than a sister. He's free to date whoever he wants to."

"I don't want to date him," I said firmly.

She winced. "Yeah, I know. Vaughn can be moody all he wants, but he overstepped. You shouldn't apologize to him, but you should let him know you don't hate him." She squeezed my hand again.

Before I nodded in agreement, a thought struck me, and I narrowed my eyes at her. If she already knew all the details about what had happened on Friday and that Vaughn thought I hated him, Kat probably wasn't her only source. "You've been talking to Vaughn about me, haven't you?"

She flashed me a wicked smile as the doctor moved the curtain aside.

The doctor was a younger man who looked to be in his late twenties, with blond hair and wearing a white knee-length coat. He introduced himself as Dr. Jacobs and asked Jen to explain what happened again. As Jen spoke, the doctor examined her hand. He gave her a shot to numb the area and started cleaning it with gauze he'd dipped in some sort of solution that smelled bad. She let out a long breath as the anesthetic kicked in.

"This is pretty deep. It looks like you just missed the tendon," he said, not looking up from his work. "After I clean this up, we'll get you some stitches and some antibiotics so this doesn't get infected."

I felt my stomach lurch and turned my head away. It would probably be bad to throw up on an open wound.

"Miss," the doctor said, and it took me a moment to realize he was talking to me. "Would you like to step out for a moment? You're looking a little pale."

"It's okay, Sarah. I feel fine now." She smiled at me. "Can you call my mom, though? You can use my phone, since I'm sure you don't have her cell number. I don't want her to come home and find blood all over her kitchen and me missing."

I took a deep breath through my nose and nodded. Then I went out into the main area, close to where the nurses' station was. I wasn't sure if I could use a cell phone in here. On TV shows, they never allowed people to use them around medical equipment, but I wasn't sure if that was true outside of medical dramas. So I approached the station in the middle of the ER.

A few people were behind the counter, and a matronly nurse looked at me from where she was seated and smiled. Her name badge read KATHY ROBERTS in bold letters. "Yes, dear?"

"Do you know where I could find a bathroom?" My stomach flipped again. "And maybe a place to get some snacks?" Eating usually helped to calm my stomach.

"Of course," she said with a knowing nod. Kathy pointed down a hallway to the left. "The bathroom is right down there, past the vending machines."

I nodded my thanks to her and started to walk away, but remembered I had to call Jen's mom.

"I'm sorry to bother you again, but can you tell me if I'm allowed to use a cell phone in here?"

The nurse smiled and said, "We prefer people refrain from using them in this immediate area, but it's fine to use them down near those vending machines."

I nodded my thanks again and walked briskly down the hallway. A few doctors and nurses were going in and out of curtained-off areas, but none of them gave me a second glance as I rushed by. I saw glimpses of the various people beyond the curtains, but I didn't linger long enough to get a good look. Most of the rooms were empty, confirming my suspicion that we had been lucky enough to come on one of the slower nights.

Once I found the bathroom, I hurried over to the sink, splashed my face with water, and took a few deep breaths. The sight of blood didn't usually affect me like this, but the cut had been so deep that I could clearly see the different layers of her skin. I'm sure I learned the name of each in biology, but it's not information I cared to retain. I let out one long breath and dried my face with a paper towel. I needed to pull myself together. Jen was the one who was hurt, not me.

After taking a minute to collect myself, I pulled out Jen's phone and went back into the hallway. I found her mom's number easily enough, and as soon as the line rang, she picked up.

"Jen?" she asked tentatively, "are you okay?"

"Hi, Mrs. Steele. It's Sarah." I frowned, thinking about my words. "Jen is fine, but she cut herself with the kitchen knife earlier, so we're at the emergency room. The doctor said she would need some stitches."

"Cut herself?" Amanda's voice was remarkably calm after just being informed that her daughter was injured. I heard a long sigh, and she continued before I could answer. "Thank you for calling me, Sarah. I was about to leave work, so I'll head over to the hospital."

I told her which one we'd come to, and she thanked me again before hanging up. Jen's mother worked in north Seattle, so it would take her a while to get to Virginia Mason.

Next was the vending machines. Now that the crisis was over and my stomach had stopped trying to climb out of my throat, it was angrily protesting the missed dinner Jen had attempted to make. The machine was full of the type of food that was easy to eat and of little nutritional value, but it would do for now. I paid for two bags of chips and a bottle of water, then headed back toward Jen's little alcove.

Out of the corner of my eye, there was a flash of dark brown hair. I turned and saw a familiar woman walking away from me down another hallway, deep in conversation with a doctor. It couldn't be... Was that Aunt Liv?

CHAPTER 14

I STOOD in the middle of the emergency room, staring at Aunt Liv's retreating form. Hospital staff walked around me, giving me odd looks, but I barely registered their presence. What was she doing here? Had Jen's mom called her and asked her to come to check on us? That didn't seem likely, since the call had ended just a few minutes ago. If she wasn't here because of Jen, why was she here?

Liv and the man in the white coat turned a corner and disappeared from view. In that moment, I decided to hurry down the hallway after them. Jen wasn't going anywhere anytime soon. She could wait a few extra minutes. This was my chance to find some sort of clue as to what was going on with Liv. I wanted answers, and I wasn't going to find them standing around doing nothing.

I hurried down the hallway to the corner where I'd seen Aunt Liv go. Carefully, I leaned around it to peer down another hallway. The emergency department must have been huge to have so many hallways. That, or I was going in a big circle.

Liv was alone now, standing in front of one of the

curtained-off rooms. She looked to be deep in thought. After a few moments, she pulled back the curtain and entered the little alcove.

My mind raced as I waited for her to reemerge. Was she visiting a patient? Anyone admitted to the emergency room wouldn't have been here very long, a few hours at the most. Once the doctors assessed a person's condition, they moved them to another part of the hospital if they needed more care. She could have been visiting a friend who had been injured like Jen, but I didn't know much about Liv's personal life outside of what I saw at home. The person she was seeing could also be someone she worked with.

I felt my stomach lurch again. It could be Will who was behind that curtain. Will was the last person I wanted to run into, but if he was injured, that was bad. As I started to think about going back to Jen's room, Liv emerged from the alcove and turned in my direction.

I jumped out of sight. Had Aunt Liv seen me?

In a panic, I dashed over to the nearest alcove and slipped inside and jerked the curtain closed behind me. I sat in the chair by the hospital bed and pulled my knees to my chest so that my feet wouldn't be visible. The potato-chip bags crinkled loudly in my hands, and I cursed under my breath as I tossed them onto the bed and listened intently.

What must have been a few seconds later, but felt to me like an eternity, I heard the soft thump of heeled boots on tiled floors. Familiar boots passed under the curtain, and I watched as they moved away from me, my heart pounding in my ears. Liv's boots paused, and I thought briefly about jumping over the hospital bed and ducking behind it, but a moment later, she continued past.

I counted to one hundred, then nudged the curtain aside so that I could see into the hallway. A man in scrubs hurried about, but Liv was nowhere to be seen. Grabbing the chip bags and stuffing them and the bottle of water into the pockets of my jacket, I slowly edged into the hallway and over to the alcove that Liv had gone into. After a quick glance over my shoulder to make sure no one was paying attention to me, I slipped inside.

The room was dim, the lights within having been turned low, which is nice for the patient. Monitors beeped softly, and I could smell the iodine used to treat the wounds of the woman lying on the hospital bed.

She lay on her back, her chest rising and falling as she breathed. Her arms and neck were wrapped in white bandages, and I guessed she had more injuries that I couldn't see under the blanket that covered her. Her long blonde hair was messy, and I could see dirt and leaves tangled in it. I spotted a clear plastic bag beside her bed. Inside I could see what I presumed were her clothes. They were torn and dirty. When I looked more closely at her, I could see she wore a hospital gown.

The multiple bandages I could see and the condition of her clothes told me she definitely had more injuries that I couldn't see. But her face, which had no bandages, made me both angry and sick. One of her eyes was swollen shut. Her nose looked like it had been broken, and there were multiple lacerations on her cheeks and forehead. One cut ran the entire length of her face, starting at her forehead, going through the eyebrow and just missing the other eye, and ending at her chin. She looked like she'd been through hell, or a horrible car accident.

The woman's good eye flicked to me as I entered, and I stood there in awkward silence, searching for a reason as to why I was there.

"Hi," I said finally. "I'm with Olivia." When she didn't say anything, I added, "The woman who was just in here."

She sighed and looked back at the curtain. "Ah, yes," she said, voice hoarse. "She said she had some questions for me."

A tear fell down her cheek, and I felt guilty about what I was about to do. I should have just let her rest, but the idea of Liv lying there on the hospital bed covered in the same wounds spurred me on. I took a few steps forward and stopped next to the bed. "I'm sorry. You look like you're in a lot of pain, but can you tell me what happened to you?"

She closed her eye and her head moved in a slight nod, making her wince. She took a few deep breaths before she spoke. "Like I told your partner, I had just gotten off work and was walking to the bus stop when I noticed someone following me. My office is off Pike Street, but it's a little way to the pickup spot that I use to get home. It was dark, so I couldn't see his face, but I assumed that he was taking the same line as I was." As she opened her eye again, another tear ran down her cheek. "After a block or so, I got the feeling that he wasn't another commuter. I could feel his eyes on my back, and I didn't want to turn around and see him staring at me, you know, so I walked a little faster. There weren't any other people on the street since it was a little later than normal, but I knew that there would be some soon if I just kept going." I could hear the desperation in her voice.

"Right after I thought that, he grabbed my arm." Her voice broke as she continued. "I— I didn't know he'd been that close to me. I thought he was still pretty far back, but he must have moved closer when I wasn't paying attention." She took a few deep breaths to calm herself before she spoke again. My conscience screamed at me as she relived her assault. Hadn't she been through enough? Why was I doing this to her? "I was going to fight him. I should have fought him, right?" She let out a laugh, and it sounded hollow and bitter. "But when I looked into his eyes... It was weird. It was like I knew him, but I couldn't place his face. I didn't do anything!" Anger and frustration laced her voice, and more tears spilled from her good eye. She raised a bandaged arm to push her tangled hair out of her face, wincing as she accidently bumped the laceration down the side. "I didn't even try to get away from him as he pulled me behind a building. It was dark, and my head felt fuzzy, like he'd drugged me, but he hadn't given me anything." The woman looked at me, her eyes pleading for my understanding. "I sound crazy, don't I?"

I shook my head, not daring to say anything. White-hot anger pulsed through me. Standing here, seeing this woman's pain and suffering, made me want to help in any way that I could. How could someone hurt another person like this? Worse, she was blaming herself for not fighting back when she was the one being assaulted. I knew how that felt, internalizing what other people did to you, but I also knew that this was not her fault.

Some of what I'd been feeling must have shown on my face because the woman continued her story hurriedly. "He pinned me against a wall and leaned in close. I don't remember much of what happened after that. Just pain. So much pain. When I came to, it must not have been too much later. It was dark and cold, and I hurt everywhere. A police officer was standing over me with a flashlight, saying that it would be okay and that she'd called an ambulance. Sargent Larson, I think. She said I looked like I'd been attacked by an animal, but I can't remember seeing anything besides that man. I— I'm sorry, I can't remember anything else." More tears.

"It's not your fault," I said hotly. She was still blaming herself, even for not being able to remember the details. For all she knew, the man who'd attacked her could have knocked her out. "None of this is your fault."

The sound of a clearing throat behind me made me jump so fast I almost lost my balance. I whirled around to find Aunt Liv standing inside the curtain, leaning one shoulder against the wall.

The glare that Liv threw my way froze the blood in my veins. She stepped over to the injured woman. "I'm sorry, Kendra, but thank you for telling us this." She reached into her pocket and pulled out a sleek white business card. "If you think of anything else, please give me a call. This number will go to my personal phone." Kendra nodded, and Liv placed the business card on the table next to the bed. She turned around, throwing me another glare, and when she spoke again, her voice was cold as ice. "Let's go."

I didn't argue and followed her without a word into the hallway. She walked briskly, leaving me hurrying to keep up with her. As we neared the doors that led into the waiting room, I finally found the courage to speak.

"Wait! Jen's here. I need to go back to her room. She's waiting for me."

Liv paused and looked at me. Her expression softened marginally. "Is she all right?" she asked.

"She cut herself pretty badly. She's over this way." I led Liv back to where I'd left Jen, her freshly bandaged hand lying across her stomach.

She looked at us as we approached, and her mouth opened in surprise. "Liv? What are you doing here? Did Sarah call you?"

"No, I—"

"Yes, she did," Liv said, cutting me off. "I was already in the area. Are you doing okay? Do you need anything?"

Jen gave me a sideways glance. She wasn't stupid. She knew that Liv couldn't have gotten here so soon, but she didn't point that out. Jen was much smarter than I was. "I'm sorry you had to come out here for nothing. It was just a cut. I'm fine, really. A couple of stitches, and I'll be good as new."

"I called your mom," I told her as I put her cell phone by her bed and pulled a bag of chips and the bottle of water out of my jacket pocket. "Here. I thought you might be hungry since we missed dinner."

She took the food with a grateful smile. "Thanks. I'll make dinner for you next time without cutting myself. Promise."

"Don't worry about it," I said with a glance at Liv. "Your mom is on the way."

"Great," Jen groaned.

Liv reached over and placed a hand on her shoulder. "I'm sure Amanda won't give you too much grief. Do you mind if I take Sarah home? I have a couple of things I need to talk to her about."

"Sure." Jen gave me a knowing look. "They only gave me a local anesthetic, so I'll be able to drive my car with my good hand. I'll text you when I get home."

I nodded and followed Aunt Liv back through the doors to the waiting room. "Aunt Liv—"

"Wait until we get in the car," she said as we left the hospital. She didn't look as angry as before, but I didn't want to push my luck. We walked in awkward silence through the parking lot until we reached the Charger, then Liv unlocked the doors, and we slid inside.

"What," she began as she put the keys into the ignition, the Charger starting with a rumble like the purr of a giant beast, "did you think you were doing?" Her voice was low and flat, and anyone who knew her would know how angry she was.

There weren't any good answers to her question. Telling her that I'd been following her to try to find out what she and Will were investigating was not a good idea. In hindsight, questioning Kendra had been an even worse one. I played dumb. "You mean taking Jen to the hospital? She was injured. What was I supposed to—"

Liv slammed her hand on the steering wheel, and I jumped. "Dammit, Sarah! This isn't a game! There are real consequences to your actions!" She took a deep breath and rubbed her temples with two fingers. When she spoke again, she was considerably calmer. "Look, I know things have been a little weird, but you can't insert yourself into things you know nothing about. What I do is dangerous, and snooping around can make you a target."

"If you'd just tell me what you were doing, I wouldn't have to try and figure it out on my own." Before she had a chance to retort, I blurted the questions that had been chasing each other around in my head. "Do you work for the police? Are you investigating the murders of those women who have been on the news? Is Will a detective? Is he your partner?"

Liv grimaced and turned her attention to the cars around us as she pulled out of the parking space.

"No, I don't work for the police," she said, evading my other questions. The look on her face was not a happy one, and that made me think that my questions were hitting close to the target.

"But you work for the city, right?" I jumped in when she

paused. "So, you are helping them somehow. Are you a bounty hunter?"

Liv growled. "Sarah, it really is better if you don't know what I do. Nothing good can come of it." Her jaw worked a few times before adding, "I promised your mother I would keep you out of this."

My mother was also in on this? I sat in the passenger seat, feeling shocked and angry. She never cared to notice what was going on in my life before, so why did she want to meddle now? What right did she have?

"Listen," Liv continued, "there's a lot that you don't know, things that you don't need to know, and people who could make trouble for you if you did know. I don't want that kind of attention on you, Sarah. You deserve the chance to have a normal life."

I felt my anger bubble up as I turned on Liv. "I'm not a child that you need to protect!" Despite how I was feeling, I tried to rein in my emotions, with little success. "I'm an adult, and I can decide for myself. Just tell me what you are doing with Will and why you're being so secretive about it."

The leather of the steering wheel creaked as Liv gripped it. She waited for a car to pass before turning right onto Madison Street. "You say you're not a child, but you can't even talk about why you left New York," she hissed. "If you aren't ready to open up about Brian, there's no way you are ready for this."

Something inside me snapped. "Stop the car," I said, my voice surprisingly calm for everything I was feeling.

"What?"

"I said STOP THE CAR!" I shouted the last three words as the hurt and anger washed over me in a wave. Making sure I had my purse, I popped the lock on the door and reached for the handle.

"Hold on!" Liv said in a panic. "Let me pull over."

She guided the car to the curb, and I jumped out. Then I turned and walked in the opposite direction we'd been driving.

"Where are you going?!" Liv called out her window at my back, but I ignored her.

Too angry to think straight, I left the image of Liv's worried face behind me as I walked off into the night.

CHAPTER 15

IT WAS STARTING to get late as I walked around aimlessly in the cold Seattle night. Flecks of snow drifted through the air, and cars passed me by, their exhaust fogging behind them. I didn't know where I was going, but I turned down familiar streets and kept a brisk pace to keep myself warm. My anger had yet to cool. I was still seething about what Aunt Liv had said to me. It didn't matter if she was right, that this situation was too dangerous for me. What mattered was that she hadn't even given me the chance to decide that for myself. Contrary to what she and Mom thought, I didn't need to be lied to, and I hated that they had taken away any choice I had in this.

Aunt Liv was working for some sort of government organization investigating the disappearances and murders; of that I was sure now. Will had to be her liaison with the local police. That was why they were working together. If she'd come out and said that, I'd have dropped the entire thing. I didn't want to get into any trouble with the police or whatever acronymic agency Liv worked for, but she was in danger while she worked on this investigation, and that was information that I deserved to know. The last thing I wanted was to wake up someday with a knock at the door and a man in a black suit and sunglasses telling me that my aunt had been killed on the job. *Your aunt served our country well. Sorry for your loss, and here, take this medal to remember her by.*

A tear slid down my cheek, and I wiped it away hurriedly. I'd had enough death in my life. I didn't want something like that to happen again.

After twenty minutes or so, I started seeing buildings that I recognized. A glance at a street sign told me I was on James Street and heading toward 1st Avenue. This was close to the light-rail station by the studio. I had my keycard to get in after hours, so I walked that way. There was no work I needed to do for Carter, but I could call a car to pick me up there and wait in the warm lobby until it arrived.

The thought of facing Aunt Liv made me grimace, but in light of the disappearances, it wasn't safe to be out too late. There weren't many people out and about, but I could see people going in and out of the restaurants and bars in Occidental Square, a popular nighttime hangout area. I glanced at my phone. 8:30 p.m.

Within ten minutes, I was standing in front of the glass doors of the building that housed Carter's studio. There were a few lights on, giving the reception area an ambient glow. No one was at the front desk, but that didn't surprise me. Ashley must have gone home hours ago.

I swiped my card on the reader, and the little red light turned green. It was nice and warm in the lobby, and I slid into one of the couches near the elevator. The front door clicked again as it locked, and I let out a sigh as the feeling returned to my face.

As soon as I sat down, my phone vibrated in my pocket.

I pulled it out, expecting Aunt Liv's picture to be on the screen, but it flashed with Carter's name and number. "Hello?" I answered, glancing around.

"Hi, Sarah," he said, sounding far too energetic. "I just got a ping that you used your keycard to get into the building. Are you on your way up to the studio?"

I felt heat creep up my neck. Of course, Carter would have a way to track the keycard usage. "Not exactly. I'm in the lobby. Sorry, I just needed a place to get warm for a few minutes. I'll get going."

"No, it's all right. I'm glad you thought to come here." There was a shuffling sound on the other side of the phone. "I'm actually here working. Why don't you come on up?"

"Oh, all right." We hung up, and I headed over to the elevator. It wasn't that late, but I wondered what he might be working on? There hadn't been anything on his calendar. I didn't have the supplies I'd bought for him today, having left them at Jen's house in our rush to get to the hospital. Hopefully, he didn't need them now.

When I entered the studio, Carter was in the corner, by the large easel I'd seen before. He wore his long blond hair pulled back in a bun and a white apron spattered with different colors of paint. He turned to me and waved as I walked in, a green smear of paint on the back of his hand and forehead. Heavy metal blared out of a speaker next to the canvas he was working on. He was swaying in time with the beat.

I stifled a laugh at the ridiculousness of it all and headed to the kitchen to get Carter a towel. He seemed not to have noticed how much paint he'd spilled on himself.

"Thanks," he said as he took the towel. "I'm surprised you're in the area so late. There's not much to do around here besides eat, and you wouldn't be able to get into any of the bars."

Scratching the back of my head, I glanced away, embarrassed by the turn the night had taken and how I'd ended up at the studio. "Well, I walked here from the hospital." I told Carter what had happened to Jen and how I'd met Aunt Liv at the hospital, how we'd argued in the car, and I ended up here. I kept most of my descriptions vague, not telling him what Liv was doing at the ER and what we fought about. He didn't ask any questions about the omitted details.

"So here I am. I was going to get a car to take me home, but then you called." I looked at the canvas he was working on. So far, it was a green background and a few blocked-out shapes. "You didn't tell me you were going to be working late tonight."

"It happens sometimes. I lose track of time, and the next thing I know, the sun is rising." He took off the apron and folded his arms. Having wiped some of the paint off while I talked, the danger of smearing paint everywhere again was minimal. "I'm not trying to pry, but I'm surprised Liv let you walk here by yourself. I won't tell you what to do, but it's not safe around the city at night right now."

As I thought about being followed by a faceless man like what poor Kendra had described, a chill went down my spine. I had been so mad, I hadn't thought about the consequences before getting out of the Charger. "I know. It wasn't the smartest decision." That made me think about what Aunt Liv had said. Looking into Carter's kind, blue eyes spurred on my next words. "Can I talk to you about something?"

"Of course," he said and gestured over to the couch. When I sat down, he sat across from me in the armchair. "What's on your mind?"

Liv thought that I needed to talk to someone about Brian. Why couldn't that be Carter? I hadn't known him for long, but he seemed to be a good listener. He'd been so kind when he'd talked about my father, and I had an instinct that he would understand how I was feeling.

Was I really going to open up to someone I barely knew? But that was the beauty of it. Carter's ignorance of the situation also meant that he was unbiased. I didn't think I was putting my job at risk by telling him, and maybe an outside perspective was exactly what I needed to hear.

"We don't know each other that well," I began, trying to find my courage, "but I think I need to talk about this, and you'll have an outside perspective." Carter nodded but remained silent, allowing me to gather my thoughts. "There's a reason I came to Seattle." I took a deep breath to calm my nerves and started to tell my story.

"I'd met Brian through Kelly, a friend of mine from high school. He didn't go to the same school I did, but he lived close enough that we could see each other whenever we wanted. Being only a year older than me, we went through many of the typical teenage life experiences together, which brought us closer. He was the one who taught me how to drive, and we helped each other with homework a lot. Mom wasn't a huge fan of his because he'd gotten into trouble a few times, but she wasn't there much. She was just happy to have someone who could be around while she was on business trips.

"Things were good when we first started dating. It wasn't until after he graduated that things started to get bad. Brian and his father had struggled with money, so he got a job at the auto shop near his apartment as soon as he was out of school. He desperately wanted to get out of his living situation. His dad was drunk more often than not, living off the insurance money he'd gotten after Brian's mother had died a few years before I'd met him.

"We'd been together for two years when he started working at the shop. Brian hadn't always been the happiest person, but after he started working there, while I was still studying and trying to cope with high school, he became even... less happy. There were more brooding silences and pointed looks than normal. Brian had always been overprotective of me, but he started getting angry when I hung out with other people. He slowly drove all my friends away. I didn't know what was happening or why he got so upset, and I didn't realize that he was isolating me until it was too late.

"He'd hurt me before, a few bruises here and there with hurried apologies of 'I didn't mean to grab so hard' or 'I don't know my own strength, and you're so fragile.' I'd thought things would calm down with him once he got his own place, that he'd return to the person I'd fallen in love with when we'd first met, but his moods only got worse. He worked a lot of overtime at the shop to afford to keep living in the city. Sometimes, he would disappear, and I wouldn't hear from him for a few days."

"Disappear?" Carter interrupted me. "What do you mean?"

I shrugged. "He wouldn't reply to any of my texts. When I'd call his phone, it would go to voicemail. I'd drive by the shop when I couldn't get ahold of him, but it would be closed, then a few days later, it would reopen, and he'd be there as though nothing happened. It was weird."

"How often did he disappear?"

I thought about it. It seemed like the shop was closed a lot. "Maybe once a month."

Carter made a thoughtful noise but asked no other questions, so I continued.

"Brian's moods became blacker as time went on. He asked me to move in with him, but I was still in high school. I told him my mom said no since I was underage, but that wasn't exactly true. She didn't want me moving in with him, but it was more that I was afraid of him, afraid of his moods, afraid of his touch, and afraid of what he was becoming. I was terrified he would find out that I was lying to him, that I'd never asked my mom about living with him.

"There was no one I could confide in. Mom was gone most of the time, and I didn't have any other friends to turn to anymore. I could have called Aunt Liv, but she was far away, and what would she think of me? Running to her with all my problems? It would be pathetic.

"So I lied and pretended that I was fine, that I didn't have bruises, and that I didn't have fantasies of packing my bags and driving as far as I could to get away from him and my absentee mother, who was too busy to protect me.

"One night, a few days after I'd turned eighteen, there was a loud knocking on the front door of our apartment. I looked up from the magazine I'd been reading, one of the many fashion magazines that were always scattered around the living room. Who could that be? I wondered as I trotted toward the door.

"Our building was on the upper west side and over-looked Central Park. Between the area's general price tag and building security, I didn't think twice about checking to see who it was. I opened the door and was surprised to see Brian standing there, a bouquet of flowers in one hand and a grin on his face.

"I was truly in shock. I hadn't heard from him in a few

days. He had pulled one of his disappearing acts again. 'What are you doing here?' I asked.

"He stepped forward and wrapped his arms around me in an embrace that I had to stop myself from cringing away from. 'What do you think? Happy birthday!' He pulled back and pushed the flowers into my hands, then moved past me and into the apartment, going straight into the kitchen and opening the refrigerator.

"I closed the door behind him mostly by reflex and stared at him incredulously. I asked him where he'd been, and explained I'd been trying to call him for the past few days. When he turned back to me, he had a jug of milk in one hand. He casually said, 'I just needed to go out of town for a little bit.' He took a long drink straight from the jug, then asked, 'What's the big deal? It's not like I missed anything.'

"'You missed my birthday, for one thing,' I told him. I remember folding my arms and hearing the plastic wrap of the flowers crinkling. There was no way I was going to let it go this time. I pushed, looking for answers. 'Where do you keep disappearing to, and why is your work closed when you're gone? It's not like you're the only person who works there. Where does everybody else keep going?'

"I guess I went too far. His expression changed, and he set the jug on the counter, approaching me like a predator stalking its prey. 'Drop it, Sarah,' he growled. 'It's none of your business what goes on at the garage or where I'm going.'

"I wanted to control my own rage, but it was hard. 'None of my business?!' I yelled. I could hear my voice getting louder, but I didn't care. I went on a tirade. 'Of course, it's *my* business when *my* boyfriend vanishes without a word. What do you think I'm going to do? Just sit here quietly and wait for you to get back? What is going on, Brian? Are you seeing someone else? If you want to end it, tell me.'

"At this point, I was panting, and my eyes were full of tears. I felt betrayed by his actions. How could he not trust me after everything we had been through together? If he was seeing someone else, it would hurt me, but I preferred to know about it rather than be kept in the dark. Despite everything, I didn't have anyone else besides him, and I wanted the truth from his own lips. I tried to calm down. 'Just tell me what is going on. Are your coworkers helping you cover up an affair?'

"Brian's face turned red at that moment, and I knew I'd made a mistake. A vein was popping out of his forehead. I didn't remember ever seeing him look so angry before. When he spoke, it was through clenched teeth. 'It's none of your business,' he repeated, his voice deadly low. 'You accuse me of wanting to end it? You're the one who refuses to move in with me!'

"I flinched back from him as he shouted that last part and tried to explain. As I spoke, I took a few steps away from him. 'I told you, my mom said I'm underage and—'

"He snarled in rage and kicked the couch, knocking it over and causing it to slide a few feet across the floor, then started ranting. 'I can tell that you're lying! You don't want to be with me!' He closed the distance between us in a flash, looming over me, then spat, 'Daryl was right about you.'

"I knew Daryl was his boss and wondered what he had to do with this. At that point, Brian raised a hand, and I ducked, but he grabbed my arm and held me in place. 'You just need convincing. You'll be happy if you give it a chance.' His tone was soft, but kind of maniacal. The sheer power behind it left me reeling.

"'Brian, let go of me,' I said softly. I didn't dare pull away from him or raise my voice. It was like trying to calm a wild animal. Over the years, I'd gotten good at talking him down when he got like this, but this time was different.

"His grip tightened, and pain lanced up my arm. With a jerk, he threw me to the floor, my shoulder hitting hard on the polished wood. I cried out in pain, and the bouquet fell to the floor, petals scattering. He knelt next to me and pushed some of the hair out of my face. 'Don't touch me!' I hissed and crawled away from him. His strike came so quickly, I never saw it coming. One second, I was pushing myself across the floor, and the next, I was curled into a ball, holding my stomach and trying not to vomit, painful tears running down my face.

"He reached down and picked me up like I weighed no more than a child, leaving the flowers where they'd fallen. In a voice I barely recognized, he said, 'It's going to be okay, Sarah. You'll understand soon.' I was too terrified to speak. Wherever Brian was planning to go next, he was taking me with him.

"Right before he reached the door, there was a click, and the lock turned. My heart leapt into my throat as the door opened and my mother and her new boyfriend stared at us. Mom's eyes flicked over me, and her face went white.

"I couldn't believe she was there. 'Brian,' she said, her voice low and dangerous. 'Put my daughter down.' Brian set his jaw stubbornly and said, 'We were just leaving,' then tried to move past them. Mom stepped into his path, causing him to stop. 'PUT HER DOWN!' she screeched, looking ready to lunge at him.

"Mom's words prompted her boyfriend into action. He pulled my mom behind him and told her to call the police, then turned to face Brian and told him to put me down. He tried to convince him there was no need for this to escalate any further. His eyes flicked to my face, then back to Brian. 'She clearly doesn't want to go with you, so walk away.'

"I watched Mom as she took her phone out of her purse and stepped into the hall, then glanced at Brian. I was still too shocked and scared to say anything, but I could see Brian thinking furiously, weighing his options. The vein on his forehead was still prominent, a sign of the roiling anger under his barely controlled facade.

"Brian had never met my mom's boyfriend and lashed out, saying, 'How do *you* know that she doesn't want to leave with me? You're just Anabelle's latest fling. You don't know anything about us.' Not knowing this guy at all, I had no idea how he would react to Brian. But, staying calm, the guy—I can't remember his name at the moment—said, 'I know enough to tell that she's scared.' Brian's remarks didn't seem to faze him. 'If she wants to leave with you, it needs to be on her terms. Not yours. Put her down and go. You can talk later.' His words surprised me. He was so calm in the face of Brian's anger.

"My heart pounded in my ears as I watched several different emotions flicker over Brian's face. The anger was still there, but there was also uncertainty and fear mixed in. I was sure he was afraid of what would happen with the police, who were surely on their way. He opened his mouth, but I found my voice—the pain in my stomach finally subsiding. 'Brian,' I said, trying to keep my voice from shaking. 'It's okay, we can talk later.'

"Relief washed over his face as he looked at me, and he actually smiled, making my stomach turn. 'You understand?' he asked, his voice full of hope. I nodded, having no idea what he was talking about but willing to say anything to get away from him at this point.

"He set me down much more gently than he'd picked me up, like I was a fragile doll that could easily break, and helped me get steady on my feet. He kissed my forehead, sending a chill down my spine, and nodded at Mom's boyfriend—Jerry! That was his name. He walked past him and out the door. They let him leave.

"Mom and Jerry set the couch in its proper place and helped me sit. When the police got there, they questioned me for about fifteen minutes, taking my statement and Jerry's, then promising to be in touch once they talked to Brian.

"I heard the policewoman whispering to my mom at the door, not knowing that I could hear them from the couch. She explained that Brian hadn't actually kidnapped me, and he let me go willingly. She said she thought they could take him in on assault, but that I'd have to testify.

"Reliving the events in front of a judge and jury didn't sound like fun to me. My mom told her she'd talk to me about it and asked her to just do what they could.

"After seeing the officer out, Mom sat next to me while Jerry made us tea in the kitchen. That's when she told me her big idea... That since she traveled a lot, I should move

back to Seattle and live with Aunt Liv..."

I sank back into Carter's sofa. "The next week, I was on a plane to Seattle. New phone number. New city. New home. Mom's off in Europe somewhere, and I'm stuck here."

"I'm sorry that happened to you," Carter said and reached over to put a hand on my shoulder. "For what it's worth, I think you made the right decision in coming here. Sometimes, we all need a fresh start."

That was all he said. No "that's so terrible" or "let's talk to a lawyer" or anything like that. Bad things happened to people sometimes. It was how life was. Mom and Liv only wanted to fix things, but this couldn't be fixed. The damage had already been done.

I had to admit that Liv had been right. Talking about what had happened with Brian did make me feel better for some reason. Nothing had changed. I was still stuck in Seattle, but having Carter listen to me and not try to fix my problems made me feel like I could begin to put it behind me. I'd had my reservations about Carter at first, and while it had only been just over a week since we'd met, I was glad that he'd asked me to be his assistant.

"Thanks," I mumbled, wiping a tear off my cheek. "I'll be okay. I just need some time to adjust."

He nodded as if what I'd said was very wise and glanced at his watch. "Would you like a ride home, Sarah? It's already almost midnight."

I started. While telling my story, I'd lost track of time. "I don't want to be a bother. I can still call a car myself."

He waved a hand in the air as if waving away my concerns. "It's no problem. To be honest, I should get home soon anyway. Bree is going to be wondering where I am by now." Carter grinned at the confused look on my face. "Bree is my cat."

"Oh!" I said, feeling dumb. "I didn't know you had a cat."

Carter let out a chuckle. "Most people are surprised. I guess they think I'm more of a dog person." He grinned as if that were the funniest joke in the world, then grabbed his keys and a jacket off the counter. "Come on, let's get going."

Even though I'd texted Aunt Liv that I was getting a ride home and not to wait up, she was outside on the front porch when Carter pulled his BMW next to the house. She watched the car pull up, and I felt my stomach plummet. The scowl on her face was visible from the street. She stood and walked down the steps to meet us.

"Oh dear," Carter said, noticing the same thing I had. "She doesn't look happy. I don't suppose you told her I was your new boss." I shook my head, and he sighed. "Better get this over with." He turned the car off and opened his door.

Talking to Liv did not sound like fun after the argument we'd had earlier, but I followed Carter's lead and got out of the car.

Liv stopped a few feet from us. "Carter," she began coldly. "Why am I not surprised? When Sarah told me she'd gotten a job offer, I thought, *Wow, that's lucky*, but I should have known you'd try to weasel your way back into our lives."

I felt my mouth fall open. I'd never seen her be so rude to anyone. Well, maybe to Will, but he was an asshole.

Carter held his hands up in a placating manner. "I needed an assistant, Livy. Sarah came at the perfect time. She came to my studio, not the other way around."

"If I had known you were the one hosting those figure-drawing sessions, I wouldn't have signed her up," she scoffed. "You only asked her to be your assistant to get to me."

"Aunt Liv, that's enough!" I could feel my face getting hot. "Carter's my boss. You shouldn't be so rude to him." I didn't care what kind of history they had. If she kept talking to him like that, she'd get me fired. "The choice to work for him was mine. If you want someone to blame, I'm right here." Before she had a chance to reply, I turned to Carter. "Thank you for the ride home. I left the supplies I got for you at Jen's, but I'll swing by her house to get them on my way to work tomorrow."

Liv looked back and forth between us and sighed. Without another word, she turned around and went up the steps and into the house.

Carter flashed me a grin and winked, then started back toward his car. "I'll see you tomorrow, Sarah."

As I watched him leave, a thought occurred to me. "Carter, before you go, I have a question for you."

He stopped mid-step and looked over his shoulder. "Yes, what is it?"

I took a deep breath. It was now or never. "Do you know what Aunt Liv is up to? She's working with a guy named Will, and they're investigating the disappearances and murders that have been happening around the city lately. She won't tell me anything about it. Do you know who she's been working for?"

Carter regarded me with those cool blue eyes before looking away. "Yes," he said, his voice soft. "To both questions." He held out a hand to forestall the barrage that was about to leave my mouth. "But it's not my secret to tell. Goodnight, Sarah."

CHAPTER 16

THINGS HAD BEEN quiet over the holidays. Having time off from my job and no drawing sessions, I had nothing to do and nowhere to go. The Christmas holidays had been uneventful for me. Liv had made a roast, Mom and my grandparents had called, and after that we'd lain around in a food-coma stupor and watched Hallmark movies. Things still weren't great between Liv and me after the whole Carter thing, but we'd learned to share space in somewhat comfortable silence.

My phone ringing broke that silence. It was Jen. "I looked up Kendra, the woman you talked to at the hospital," she said when I answered my phone. "Her full name is Kendra Thompson. She's a systems admin and works for a small advertising agency on Pike Street. Twenty-six years old and lives alone. She commutes into the city from Bellevue using the East Gate Park and Ride, so we can assume she lives near there."

I blinked and glanced over at Aunt Liv. She was reading a book at the table while I watched TV. Making an excuse about needing to get my sketchbook from my room, I went upstairs where she wouldn't be able to hear me. "How did you find all that out?" I asked once I was out of earshot.

"It wasn't hard," Jen said, and I could hear the satisfaction in her voice. "I *investigated*."

I rolled my eyes but couldn't hold back a smile. From her tone, she was fishing for a compliment. "Yes, you are incredibly smart and talented."

"And beautiful," Jen added.

"And beautiful," I confirmed. "There is no peer to your talents and beauty. People fall to their knees in the street, awed by your glorious deeds. Happy?"

"Ecstatic," she said, a smug note in her voice. "It took a little longer than I thought it would, and I had a lot of family stuff going on over Christmas, but there are some inconsistencies I noticed between her story and what I dug up. You said she was attacked by a man, right?"

"Yeah, that's what she told me."

"Well, articles I've found say she was mauled by an animal, like the other women who were attacked."

I racked my brain, trying to remember what Kendra had said. "She definitely said that she was followed and attacked on the way to her bus stop by a person, not an animal, but she did say that after he grabbed her, she couldn't remember what happened to her. Maybe he drugged her."

"He could have sprayed her with something. I've heard of some aerosol drugs that can knock a person out, but she was found in an alley not far from where her bus stop was. He would've had to have the animal with him, and that's the type of thing people would notice," she said.

"Are you sure it was an animal attack?" I asked, remembering Kendra's bandaged neck and arms.

"Well," Jen hedged, "all I have to go on is what I can find online and a few notes from her medical file. The doctor wrote that it looked like canine bite marks and to test her for rabies."

"Medical file? How the hell did you get that?" Jen worked at an art store, not the hospital. She didn't even know about Kendra until after she'd gotten out of the emergency room.

"Oh, Sarah," her voice was smug again. "I used to date one of the nurses there. After you texted me about what happened, I went to talk to my ex. Lucky for me, the file was at the nurses' station, so when no one was looking, I snapped a few pictures with my phone. I didn't get much, but it was enough."

I laughed. "Isn't that illegal?"

"Only if we get caught. This is for the greater good!" She sounded exasperated. "You're the one who asked me to find out everything I could about what happened to Kendra."

I pressed my thumb and forefinger to the bridge of my nose. "You can be scary sometimes."

"I prefer 'resourceful.' Anyway, it sounds like the doctors think that she was attacked by a large dog, but I don't know. Gina, that's my ex, said that she's still in intensive care. She's been there over a week." Jen paused, and it sounded like she was shuffling papers around. "I don't think they're going to discharge her anytime soon. The police aren't sure if it's connected to the other attacks since they're working under the assumption that the bodies were mauled after the victims were already dead."

A twinge in the back of my neck signaled the oncoming headache. This was too much to take in. "What does this have to do with Aunt Liv? How is she involved with this? Why would she be involved with this?"

"Oh, I've got some information on that."

"Why didn't you lead with that?!" I hissed into the phone, trying to keep my voice down.

Jen laughed. "Calm down. It's not much. I called the police precinct and asked for Will. They were able to figure out who I was talking about after describing him. Anyway, I told them that he was talking to me the other day about that case on Broadway, you know, the one you saw when you went out with Vaughn, and that I remembered something that he should know."

"Jen," I groaned. "You're going to get into trouble with the police."

"It'll be fine, Sarah. I'm not going to lie about anything for the investigation," she said dismissively. "I just wanted to find out what department he worked for, and I did. He works for the Office of Intergovernmental Relations, not homicide."

"What? He's not a detective?" That didn't make any sense. Why was he investigating the murders then?

"I didn't say that," Jen clarified. "I don't know how the—what would it be—the OIR is set up, so he still could be, but it's strange that he'd be working with Liv if she's investigating Kendra's attack, isn't it? Assault and murder would be out of his jurisdiction, right?"

We both fell silent, thinking about what this new information could mean. Why was Will working on this case if he wasn't in homicide? Was Aunt Liv a member of some government agency assisting the police? If so, why would she keep that from me? Why was she interviewing Kendra at the hospital? There were so many questions with no answers.

I heard the door to Liv's downstairs apartment open. "I should get going," I said quickly. "Figure-drawing sessions start back up today, and I need to be there to help set up."

"Oh right. I'll be there today too." Jen sighed. "There's something else you should know. Kat is on the warpath."

"Kat? About what?" She'd been out of touch over the holidays. "Is everything okay?"

Jen sighed even louder. "It's about Vaughn. You had that argument with him, and he was upset over it. He didn't tell her what happened, but she heard about it because, of course, and now she's upset with you."

I blinked. "You've got to be kidding me! It wasn't an argument. I told him off because I don't appreciate him trying to speak for me."

"I know, Sarah. It's stupid. She's not even dating Vaughn, and she obsesses over things that have nothing to do with her." Jen sounded annoyed. "It's not like her to be vindictive, but keep an eye out all the same."

Remembering the look of pure hatred Kat had given me on the rooftop the night of Carter's party, watching out for Kat was a good idea. I groaned. Great, another thing to worry about.

I arrived at the studio around noon, an hour before the figure-drawing session was scheduled to start. Since I'd been working for Carter for a few weeks, I mostly knew what I was doing.

Working also meant Aunt Liv had stopped bugging me about getting out of the house. She pretended that the night at the hospital never happened and didn't want to talk about the fact that I was working for her ex, which was fine by me. The last thing that I wanted was that awkward conversation. I didn't bother asking Liv about Kendra either since I knew she wouldn't tell me anything. So in general, we didn't talk much.

Things around the city had been hectic leading up to Christmas. Harried shoppers had filled the streets en mass in a last-minute holiday surge. After the holiday, the city slowed to the point of cozy sluggishness as it was covered in a blanket of crisp white snow. Most of that snow had melted in the last few days, and I, for one, was glad that things were starting to return to normal.

I was happy that the figure-drawing sessions were on again. It was a nice break from the admin work that Carter had me doing. He would sometimes have me go get supplies for him or bring lunch, but most of what I did was answer emails and enter expenses. Who knew being a professional artist would require so much paperwork?

The one person I didn't want to see was Vaughn. I would have to see him again eventually since he also worked for Carter, but I would put that off for as long as possible.

When I got to the studio, it took about thirty minutes to arrange the chairs and easels into some semblance of order. The model for today would be Sheila. It wasn't always the same person since the models rotated, making it so that there was a different one each week. While Vaughn was the model that was here most often, Carter hired five others for both this and his other work. I had their schedules on my computer and knew I wouldn't have to see Vaughn for another week.

Sheila knew what she was doing, so I let her get everything ready and stayed out of the way. People started to trickle in as it got closer to the starting time, and I saw Jen, Izzy, and Tommy find seats toward the back. I waved and grabbed a chair, dragging it over to join them.

Before I could reach the others, the studio door slammed closed behind me, making me jump. I dropped the chair and turned around to see Kat stomping straight at me, auburn hair flowing behind her and her expression furious. I braced myself for the explosion.

"I don't know who you think you are"—Kat growled when she reached me; I had the feeling that she wanted to jump at me— "but you need to back off. Vaughn is *mine*." Her brown eyes flashed in anger, and I swear I saw the pupils narrow.

I took a couple of steps back, my surprise wearing off and being replaced with anger. My annoyance with Vaughn aside, he was still a nice person who didn't deserve to be treated like an item to be possessed.

"Because he's a thing that you can own, right?" I snapped. "You can't just lay a claim to him without his say." It was ridiculous that Kat was trying to scare away any woman he wanted to be friends with. As I spoke, I kept my voice as low as possible so as not to cause a scene. "How dare you come to my place of work and try to pick a fight with me."

A low noise came from Kat's throat, and it took me a moment to realize she was actually growling at me. "You're new, so I'll give you a warning. Don't mess with me. If you're in my way. I'll remove you."

There was no doubt about it. Kat was threatening me. Good thing most of the attendees hadn't arrived yet, because I wanted to slap her. If she had cared to ask me in the first place, she'd know that I had no interest in Vaughn. He wasn't even really my friend, not yet.

We were so absorbed in the altercation that neither of us noticed that Jen had joined us until she spoke.

"That's enough, Kat!" Jen hissed. "You don't even know Sarah, and you are literally attacking her over nothing. Vaughn is an adult, and he is not your boyfriend. Even if he were, he can hang out with whomever he pleases and doesn't need your permission. He made an ass of himself, and Sarah set him straight. End of story." Jen stepped between us, looking angrier than I had ever seen her. Kat was forced to take a step back. "Sarah doesn't need me to fight her battles for her, but I'm not going to let you treat my friend like this. Kat, get over it. You've been after Vaughn for years, and he's not interested."

Kat looked shocked, with her cheeks flushed pink and her mouth hanging open. She made a few sounds but seemed at a loss for words.

Jen didn't give her a chance to respond. "Come on, Sarah." She turned and paused, throwing a glance at Kat over her shoulder. "I love you, but you need to think about how you're making the people around you feel. If you care about any of us, you'll think before you say anything you'll regret." She walked away.

Not daring to glance at Kat, I followed Jen.

By the time I caught up with her, she was at the back of the studio. There were tears in her eyes, but her face was set in a determined frown. "Sometimes, I just want to strangle her!" she hissed under her breath. Jen looked back over at Kat, and her expression cooled. "Was I too harsh?" she whispered.

I thought about it. My gut reaction was that it wasn't too much, but that didn't feel quite right. There was more to the situation that I just didn't understand, and I didn't know Kat very well. "I can't answer that for you. I don't know enough about your relationship." Acting on instinct, I hugged her, and she hugged me back. "Thank you for defending me, though. I hope I didn't damage your friendship."

Jen sniffed as she pulled back. "Don't worry about that.

If I can't tell her when she's being dumb, are we really friends?"

"No, I guess not."

That didn't make me feel any better, but she didn't seem to want to talk about it anymore. *Way to go, Sarah. You've been here less than a month, and you're already causing trouble for your friends.* I hoped that they could talk it out later, but it was out of my hands. I would have to trust that Jen could mend their friendship and that Kat wouldn't be too stubborn about it.

A few more people walked in the door, and I recognized Kari, the woman who ran the sessions. I glanced over at Kat, but she had gone to sit with Izzy and Tommy, her back to me. A few people gave us surreptitious glances. I sighed. There went my chance to make new friends. "We should get seats. The session will be starting soon."

"One second," Jen said seriously. "I was going to talk to you about this later, but my girlfriend is going to meet us here after we're done."

That surprised me. I hadn't met Jen's girlfriend before. Weren't they in a rough patch? "Why?" I asked. "Is everything okay?"

"Yes, but she wants to talk to both of us. She said she had some information about one of the victims."

CHAPTER 17

STELLA, Jen's girlfriend, was an absolutely gorgeous woman. She had darkly tanned skin and long, thick black hair that she wore down in long locks. She was also half a head taller than me and had stunning green-brown eyes in her heart-shaped face. Standing next to Jen, who, as usual, was dressed in stylish comfort, they looked like they should have been on the cover of a magazine. It made me feel a little self-conscious about the hoodie and old jeans I was wearing.

I'm not Frankenstein's monster or anything, but sometimes it was tiring being surrounded by so many beautiful people. Aunt Liv, Jen, and now Stella. Hell, even Vaughn was prettier than I was. Sometimes it was too much.

"It's nice to finally meet you, Sarah." Her voice was deeper than expected, and she held out a hand in greeting. "I've heard so much about you."

I took her outstretched hand and shook it. "Nice to meet you too."

Stella smiled, and it made her look even prettier. Jen put a possessive arm around her waist and grinned. Her cheeks were slightly pink. "Shall we get going? There's a dim sum place not too far from here that is pretty good. It shouldn't be too busy right now."

My stomach rumbled at the thought. "That sounds like heaven. Give me a few minutes to lock up. I'll meet you downstairs."

Jen and Stella left the studio as I started stacking the chairs. I didn't have to worry about Kat approaching me again. She'd bolted right after the session ended. I still felt terrible about having an argument with her at work. Would Carter get upset about it? There wasn't any way I could have avoided it since she was the one who'd approached me, but that didn't mean I wouldn't be blamed for it. I sighed as I put the last of the easels away. At least there hadn't been many people here when it happened. With any luck, Carter wouldn't hear about it.

I paid Sheila with the check Carter had left for her and locked the studio. Jen and Stella were waiting for me downstairs, and we waved to Ashley at the front desk as we left.

We walked past the stadium and into the International District. It was the beginning of the afternoon commuting rush, so the restaurant was only about half full when we got there. Jen asked for a table in the back, and the waitress seated us in a secluded corner near the windows.

Once our drink orders were in, Stella pulled a computer tablet out of her bag. "Jen has been keeping me apprised of what you two have found out about the murders happening around the city. I have been keeping tabs on it as well. It's part of a personal project." The confusion must have shown on my face because she smiled and added, "I'm a journalism major, and I like to keep track of current events." She tapped on the tablet a few times, then turned it so that I could see the screen. There were pictures of five different women. Kendra was one of them and looking in much better shape than when I'd seen her. "These are the women who have been attacked."

"As you know, all but Kendra have been killed." She tapped the screen, and a list appeared. "There are a few things that these women have in common. They were in their mid to late twenties, commuted into and around the city by bus, and even looked a little similar.

"The problem is that since they were from all different parts of the Seattle area, it's hard to narrow down where the killer is hunting with any precision and what the pattern is with his victims." Stella tapped the screen again, and a map of the area came up. There were a few green and red dots in different areas. "The red dots are where the victims were found, or in Kendra's case, where the attack happened. The green dots are where the women lived. From what I've been able to gather, most of these women were abducted on their evening commutes, and Kendra's story confirms that theory." She sat back in her chair as the waitress came with our drinks and took food orders.

Once the waitress was gone, Stella put the tablet in her bag. "There's one other connection that I think needs to be explored." She pulled out a folded piece of yellow paper, a flyer with the name Tombstone on it, along with LADIES NIGHT printed in big, bold letters.

"What's this?" I asked, looking over the flyer. "It's an advertisement for some club downtown."

"Yeah," Jen said. "Tombstone is in Capitol Hill. It's an eighteen-and-older club that's known for being kind of shady. They were busted last year for serving alcohol to minors."

Stella nodded. "I'm a second-year student at the University of Washington. I asked around and found another student who knows Kendra. She told me that they went to this club a few times before Kendra was attacked. Not only that, but she said they saw Alissa Sanders there, another one of the victims. Both women went to UW." She pronounced the W as just dub. "But none of the others did. This could be a connection between them."

Will's angry face came to mind. "Have you told the police this? They can do a lot more than we can with this information."

"They already know," Stella said. "My classmate told them before I talked to her." She put the flyer back into her pocket. "They've probably already gone to Tombstone and asked around about Kendra and Alissa, but I have a feeling that the owner wouldn't say much. The club already has a lot of bad publicity, and I'd bet that the people who go there won't talk to the police. I've known a few people who've bought drugs there, so no one is going to want to go anywhere near law enforcement."

"Wait, let me get this straight," I said, holding up my hands. "Are you saying that *we* should go to Tombstone? A couple of teenage girls going to a club to investigate the murder of five women?"

They both nodded.

"Are you insane?!" I shouted. I couldn't help myself.

Jen made a shushing motion and looked around. "Calm down, Sarah. We don't want to make a scene."

"This is a joke, right? I have to assume that this is a joke because otherwise, I can only assume you're both delusional." I ran a hand through my hair. "Let's say that we do this. How would we even know what to look for? We don't even have a description of what this guy looks like, and if he is there, we could become targets ourselves."

"Well," Stella began with a sideways look at Jen, "you don't fit the profile, but..."

I looked back and forth between them and felt anger rising as I realized what Stella was alluding to. "No way," I growled. "Jen, you can't use yourself as bait!"

Jen smiled, but it looked a little sickly. "Don't worry. I don't have a bus commute. Meaning that while I look like his type, I don't fit his pattern." Her eyes suddenly blazed, and her mouth set in grim determination. "If I can do anything to help put this monster behind bars, I'll do it. I hate having to worry about my friends, scared that one day it will be their faces I see on the news, their funerals that I'll have to attend. I'm doing this with or without you, Sarah."

Stella placed a hand on Jen's shoulder, her expression concerned. "We may not be able to find anything else out. This might be a waste of time, but we have to try," she pleaded, meeting my eyes. "We have to do something." She echoed Jen's words.

Their expressions reminded me of how helpless I'd felt after leaving New York, when I'd first come here. I'd felt like everything was outside my control. In a way, it had been, and I'd hated it. It was easy to understand how Jen and Stella were feeling, but what they were planning on doing was dangerous. Even if they were wrong about the killer using Tombstone to find their victims, going to this club didn't sound safe, but they seemed dead set on going with or without me. If only there was a way to mitigate the risk...

"Why don't we ask Vaughn to come with us?" I heard the words leave my mouth before I could stop them.

They both stared at me with surprised looks as I flushed. "Well," I started, trying to reason it out to them as well as to myself. Stupid mouth. "If we're going to do this, it would be better to have more people than just the three of us, and I think having him there would offer us some protection if things do go south. He'd be much better in a fight than I'd be."

Jen nodded. It didn't need to be said that men were less likely to be targets of assault than women in these places and that he could have our backs. It sucks that the world works that way, but we needed to do what we could to keep ourselves safe as women.

"What about Kat?" Jen asked.

I felt my eyes narrow. "What about her?"

"Not that it matters, but she'll be upset again if she finds out that you're hanging out with Vaughn." Next to her, Stella looked annoyed, like this was a subject they'd spoken of often, but she didn't add to Jen's comment.

"Screw Kat," I said hotly. "She can deal with it, as you said. He's not her boyfriend. This isn't a date, and even if it were, it's none of her business."

Jen frowned and looked down at her tea, then back at me, looking like she had a question on her lips.

I don't know what expression I had on my face, but it was enough to make Jen look away again. "I'm sorry, I don't mean to pry, but this whole thing between Vaughn and Kat seems to push your buttons. If it triggers some bad memories for you, I apologize. I shouldn't even talk to you about them. I'm just worried for them both," she said.

I took a few deep breaths to regain control of my anger. Was the reason that I'd been so upset about Kat's behavior over Vaughn because it reminded me of the abuse I'd suffered from Brian? Vaughn didn't appear to be suffering as I'd been, but that didn't mean it wasn't happening. "It's all right. You're just concerned for your friends. I'm not upset that you brought it up, and I think you might be right."

There was an awkward silence as the waitress brought our food and set it on the table. She must have felt the tension because she murmured a quick "Let me know if you need anything" before scurrying away.

"I think Vaughn coming with us is a great idea. He can keep an eye out in case we run into any trouble," Stella said, her attempt to direct the conversation away from Kat and Jen's idea, not being subtle at all. "We should do it Friday night."

"That soon?" Jen blurted out, her eyes wide in the surprise that I'd felt. "We don't even have a concrete plan."

"The longer we wait, the greater the chance that the killer is going to strike again. If there is information to be found at Tombstone, we need to get it now so that the police can look into it," Stella argued.

"Will would look into anything that we find, I'm sure of it." And as I said it, I had complete confidence in my words. Will seemed deadly serious about finding the killer, and a lead was a lead, even if it came from a bunch of teenagers who he'd threatened and warned to stay out of it.

Jen must have filled Stella in on who Will was, because she nodded. "Great, so Friday then?" She looked at us hopefully.

"I work Friday," Jen said. "But these kinds of clubs don't get going until late anyway, so it should be fine." She didn't look happy about it, even though she and Stella were the ones who'd come up with the idea. Maybe the fact that her half-baked plan was actually happening was throwing her off.

We agreed to meet at Tombstone at 11:00 p.m. on Friday night. Jen would ask Vaughn to join us to infiltrate one of the city's most notorious nightclubs. I was already mentally preparing myself to either ask Liv if I could borrow a dress, which would involve a subsequent awkward conversation about why I needed it, or brave the snowy Seattle streets to buy my own.

As we ate our food, I had the feeling that we were getting into something we were in no way prepared for and that nothing good would come of it.

CHAPTER 18

"I'M NOT sure that this is the smartest idea," Vaughn said as he turned into a parking lot near Tombstone. "This place is kind of sketchy." Since out of the four of us, only Jen and Vaughn had cars, Jen had gone to get Stella, which meant I was stuck with Vaughn. He'd picked me up in his newer Mazda 3, and we'd sat in awkward silence the first couple of miles until he turned on the radio. I'd already forgiven him for his misstep a few weeks ago, but he wasn't quite off the hook yet since he hadn't apologized.

"I've heard," I said. Vaughn found a parking space and backed into it. "Try telling that to Jen."

He frowned. "I did. She said, 'Life is about taking risks.'" He imitated her in a high-pitched voice that made me smile. "Then she told me that what she did was none of my business."

"Sounds like Jen."

"Yeah, it does." He put the car in park and glanced over at me. It looked like he had something else on his mind.

"What is it, Vaughn?" I asked. "Better spit it out before we go inside."

He let out a long sigh. "Look," he began, "it took me a while to figure out why you'd been upset with me, and I'm sorry for speaking over you before. I'm so used to the stupid dominance games and gender roles I used to deal with at my guardian's house that, sometimes, I don't realize I'm doing it. You don't need me to defend you against Will, or anyone else, and you can speak for yourself." Vaughn closed his eyes and took a deep breath, his cheeks flushing. "You didn't want or need me to step in for you. It wasn't my place, especially since our friendship is still in its initial stages."

"Is it?" I asked, trying to keep the grin off my face. The way he was trying so hard to be considerate of my feelings... It was cute, okay? I may not have been interested in Vaughn in a romantic sense, but I can recognize cute when I see it.

He looked stricken by my words. His green eyes widened, and I could see a freaking pout on his lips. "Do you not want to be friends anymore?"

I laughed at the look on his face. "Of course I still want to be friends," I said. "Thank you for apologizing. It might look like a small mistake to some people, but I'm trying to take back control of my life, so to me, it's a big deal."

Vaughn nodded. "I can understand wanting that control over your life. It's been a rough year for me too."

That reminded me of what he'd told me before, how he'd been homeless for a while. "Yeah, it's a lot of work, but I'll get there." Since we were talking now, I figured it was as good a time as any to ask him. "Vaughn, how do you know Will, and how did you know that he was talking about my Aunt Liv? I don't remember telling you that I'd met him before." Maybe I could get some of the information I was looking for out of him. He knew Will, and I was betting he knew why the man was investigating these murders while working for the Office of Intergovernmental Relations. Hell, he could even know why Will was working with Aunt Liv in the first place.

Vaughn went suddenly still right in the middle of unbuckling his seatbelt. He looked over at me, his expression wary. "Will is someone I know through my guardian," he said, "and I wasn't sure it was the same Olivia that he knows. I just guessed."

I could tell he was lying. "Friends don't lie to each other, Vaughn."

A pained look crossed his face, and he finished unbuckling himself. "I'm sorry, Sarah. I want to tell you, but it could put your aunt or Will in harm's way if people know what they're doing."

"I'm not 'people.' I'm her family."

He turned in his seat to look at me, and I saw sadness in his eyes. "I know, and that makes it even harder. Have you asked her about it?"

It was my turn to sigh. "Yes, but she won't tell me anything. She doesn't trust me with the truth."

He was silent for a moment before he spoke again. "As much as you want to know, shouldn't it be her choice to share her business with you? You're right. She's your family. So shouldn't you hear it from her?"

Dammit, he was right. It should be Liv's choice to tell me what she was doing that seemed so dangerous. With all the talk of taking control of my life, it wouldn't be fair if I took the choice of coming to me away from her. At least this proved that there was something she was hiding from me. Carter had said as much when I'd asked him, and now I had another source that was saying the same thing.

"Okay, okay," I said, trying to cool the anger that had flared up. "I'll give her some time to talk to me, but I'm not going to wait forever. If I have to find out for myself, I will."

I fingered the wristlet that held my ID card and some money. *Time to get your game face on, Sarah.* "Back to tonight—how much did Jen tell you about what we are doing?"

"Just the basics. Kendra Thompson and Alissa Sanders were seen at Tombstone by a mutual friend of Stella's before the attacks. We're going in to find out if anyone knows any information about them or the killer so that we can turn it over to the police. Simple, but stupid and dangerous. What if the killer gets wind that you three are asking about him? What if he targets one of you because you're snooping around?"

"What about you?" I countered. "You could be targeted too. Just because he's only killed women so far doesn't mean he won't make an exception for you."

He frowned. "That's true, but—"

"Don't patronize me by saying you can take care of yourself or some other masculine B.S," I said with a sigh.

Vaughn smiled. "Fine, I won't *say* it." I threw him my dirtiest glare. "You're right," he continued. "I shouldn't be there either. None of us should be, but you want to help, and I can understand that." He reached into the back seat and grabbed his jacket. "Shall we?"

We paid for parking, then hurried across the street to the entrance to Tombstone. It was a large white building wedged between a cafe and a restaurant. Both of which were closed. There was a small line to get in, seven people, and once we got in line, I spotted Jen and Stella approaching from down the street. I waved at them, and they waved back.

"Hi, Vaughn!" Stella said breathlessly once they were within earshot. "I haven't seen you in a while."

Vaughn smiled and gave her a one-armed hug. "I've

been busy with the holidays and all, but things should be calming down now that they're over." He blinked and looked at their outfits. "You take this being bait thing seriously, don't you?"

Under their long jackets, Jen and Stella were both wearing tight dresses that barely covered their butts. They looked like they'd come from some boutique shop, akin to a Victoria's Secret or some other store that sold clothing with very little fabric. Jen's was black and Stella's a dark blue, and both were sleeveless, showing off their curves in ways that caught the eye. Pair that with the five-inch stilettos they were wearing, and they definitely looked ready for a night on the town.

"Wow, aren't you cold?" was all I could say as I shivered in my own coat. I was dressed in a knee-length, long-sleeved black dress that I'd purchased the day before. It was form-fitting, but I wouldn't have to peel it off later, unlike their dresses. And because I wasn't a crazy person, I was also wearing fleece tights and flats so that I didn't freeze to death.

Jen flashed me a wicked grin. "Very much so, but sometimes beauty is painful."

The line went quickly, and we were inside the building with its welcoming central heat within a few minutes. Music with a lot of bass blasted over the speakers, making it hard to hear anything else. Jen and Stella showed the tall man in the black-leather trench coat their IDs, and he directed them with a hand to a small table where a shorter woman with bright-pink hair was checking in coats.

When Vaughn handed the man his ID, he stared at him, not even glancing down at the card, and said, "You shouldn't be here." The glare he gave Vaughn gave me chills.

"I'm not looking for trouble," Vaughn replied. "We're just here to have some fun, that's all."

The man was silent for a long moment, and I thought he would tell us to leave, but then he nodded sharply. "Have a good time," he said and handed back Vaughn's ID. For some reason, the words sounded like a threat.

I raised an eyebrow at Vaughn, but he waved it away. He looked visibly shaken, even though he was trying to smile through it.

"Please make sure the pockets are empty. We are not responsible for any items that go missing!" the woman with the pink hair shouted as she held out a hand for my coat. I checked the pockets before handing it to her. Taking it with a smile and a nod, she handed me a claim ticket before saying, "Have fun!"

After checking everything in, the four of us huddled together at one of the tables lining the walls. Now that we were inside, I was able to take a good look around at the place. For being a club with a less-than-sterling reputation, Tombstone was fairly clean and well taken care of.

The floor and walls were painted black, and the leather couches placed next to the tables that lined the room carried the color scheme. There was a stage on the back wall where a few women dressed like Jen and Stella were dancing. Next to the stage was the DJ's table, a man looking to be our age wearing headphones and nodding along with the beat. A small crowd of people dressed in all-black leather were on the dance floor, but few of them were dancing. From the looks of it, most of them were standing in groups talking, which seemed impossible given the volume of the music. To the right of the bar, a staircase led to a second-story loft that overlooked the first floor. I couldn't see what was happening in the loft, but people were walking up and down the stairs, so it must have been open to the public.

Jen leaned in close so that I could hear her. "Stella and I are going upstairs. Can you and Vaughn see what you can find out down here?" I nodded, and she smiled at me. "Don't look so scared. You should still try to enjoy yourself. There might be nothing here to find, so don't let the night be a complete waste. Jen patted me on the shoulder, then she and Stella made their way across the dance floor to the stairs.

I watched them go, and a small bundle of fear knotted in my stomach. I was regretting coming here. This was not a good idea. Why did I agree to this?

"They'll be all right," Vaughn said, speaking loudly to be heard over the music. "Do you want something to drink? I can get you a soda or water."

"A Coke would be nice." I looked around at the people. They weren't looking at me, but a few women were staring at Vaughn. "I guess I should start asking about Kendra."

He looked around, too, a small frown on his face. "Stay here for a minute. I'll get us some drinks, and then we can ask questions. If you don't mind, I'd like to stick together when we do that."

I nodded. That sounded like a good plan. Talking to strangers wasn't my forte, so having Vaughn there with me would make it easier. People would actually want to talk to him. Maybe we could get some information from the women who were staring.

Vaughn made his way over to the bar while I picked one of the sofas to sit and wait. I felt a trickle of sweat run down my back. I should have worn a different outfit. While it was freezing outside, Tombstone was hotter than I'd expected. Jen and Stella had had the right idea. Granted, I'd never been to a nightclub before, so I hadn't known what to expect. There was a lull in the music, and the noise of dozens of voices filled my ears.

"I haven't seen you here before," said a deep voice above me.

I looked up to see a man standing on the other side of the table. He had black hair and a long, thin face, looking to be in his late twenties. His skin was pale, but he was wearing a lot of black eyeliner and had on a fishnet shirt with nothing under it. I could see his muscles working as he sat on the other end of the sofa. I tried not to stare and glanced toward the bar.

"My name is Santo. It's nice to meet you," he said, and I could hear the smugness in his voice. He must have caught me looking. Oops.

"Hi..." I searched the area around the bar, but didn't see Vaughn anywhere. Where did he go? "My name's Sarah," I said absently, still trying not to look at him.

"Is it your first time here, Sarah?" He smiled, and his teeth were all white and straight. Dentists here must make a killing. "It can be a little overwhelming the first time," he said, his voice full of implications.

Gross. "I'm fine, thanks." I pressed into my end of the couch. This guy was giving me the creeps. It was obvious that I was way younger than him, and he was hitting on me? His face had predator written all over it. *You're here for a reason, Sarah.* I told myself. *Get to sleuthing!* "So, uh, Santo, right?" I began awkwardly. "Do you come here often?"

The music started playing again, but this melody was quieter than what had been blasting through the room before. I could hear myself think.

Santo leaned back into the sofa. "Often enough. Is there something you want to know about Tombstone? Would you like me to show you around?" He bit his bottom lip, and I had to beat down the urge to roll my eyes. Did that really work on other women?

"No, but I do have a question for you," I fidgeted with the hem of my dress, and his eyes followed my hands. "I have some friends who've come here before, and one of them was hurt recently. Maybe she met someone here she shouldn't have."

"The city can be a dangerous place," he said in a lazy drawl, still watching my fingers.

"Her name is Kendra. Kendra Thompson. Do you know her?" I asked, trying to make the question sound casual.

Santo had been reaching to brush back some of his hair when he froze, a reaction to the name. He stared at me, his expression falling into a neutral mask. Oh yes, he knew who Kendra was.

It took him a few seconds to recover, and his eyes narrowed. "Who do you—"

"Santo," Vaughn said as he stepped up to where we were sitting. "Why am I not surprised to see you here?" He set the Coke in front of me.

"Vaughn," Santo said with a dismissive wave of his hand. His posture relaxed into the smugness he had been exuding earlier. "*You're* not supposed to be here. I'm surprised they let you in."

"They made an exception." Vaughn sneered. It was clear that he did *not* like Santo. I made a note to myself to ask him later why he wasn't supposed to be at this club. "Do you know anything about Kendra or not? I'm not going to waste my time with your stupid games." I tried to catch Vaughn's attention, but he either didn't see my look or ignored me.

Santo glared at Vaughn. "What's in it for me?"

"How about I let you leave here with all of your limbs intact?" Vaughn growled.

"Whoa! Vaughn, back off," I said and glared at him. I didn't know what kind of relationship they had, but we weren't going to get any information out of this guy if Vaughn kept threatening him. Thinking fast, I picked up my glass, chugged the soda, and held it out to Vaughn. "I'd like another Coke, please."

Vaughn frowned and opened his mouth to speak, but I waved it off with a hand. "Vaughn, go take a minute to cool off. Remember why we're here? We need to focus, and, right now, you're the problem."

We stared at each other for a long moment, but I wasn't going to back down. He growled and took the glass out of my hand, then threw another glare at Santo. "Don't get any funny ideas. I'll be back in a minute." Vaughn turned and made his way over to the bar again.

I shook my head and glanced over at Santo, who was still on the other end of the couch. He was staring at me, a pensive look on his face. "What?" I asked and wiped at my face with the back of my hand. "Did I spill soda on myself?"

He ignored the question. "*You're* the one who has Katherine agitated." Santo nodded to himself and grinned. "She's all hot and bothered by your sudden appearance in Vaughn's life. I can see why she's worried."

Geez, did the entire city know about the fight I'd had with Kat? My ears felt like they were burning. "Kat can mind her own business, and I'm not here to talk about that. I want to know about Kendra or Alissa." I thought it was best to be direct with Santo since Vaughn had already blown any ounce of secrecy we'd had. "Is there anything you can tell me about who might have met up with them? Or if anyone had taken an interest in them?"

His eyes flicked over to the stairs. I followed his gaze. There were a couple of people close to the staircase, two women and a tall man with blond hair and a black tank top. The man noticed us staring, grinned, and gestured to the two women. The three of them ascended the staircase. Was Santo thinking of fleeing to the loft?

Santo let out a deep breath, drawing my attention back to him. "You're asking dangerous questions, Sarah, especially here."

His words sent a shiver through me. Was Santo implying that the killer really did lurk around here and that I could be next if I kept prying? The smart thing to do would be to leave, but the image of Kendra lying in the hospital bed, beaten and bloody, flashed across my mind. *Buck up, Sarah. Don't be scared off now.* "That makes it sound like there is something to find here, and that you know what it is," I countered. I leaned closer to him and gave him a serious look. "Santo, women are *dying*. If you know anything, please tell me so that we can help to stop it."

He sighed. "You don't know what you're getting into." I gave him an even scarier glare than I'd given Vaughn, and he held up his hands in surrender. "Fine, fine. I don't know much, but I'll tell you what I saw. Maybe you can get the information to someone who can help."

At that moment, Vaughn came back from the bar. I scooted over so he could sit down, which left me sitting between him and Santo. Best to keep them apart for the length of this conversation. Vaughn frowned but didn't say anything, setting my second Coke on the table in front of me.

"Just in case you get any ideas, if I have cops knocking on my door tomorrow, I didn't say anything." He stared at Vaughn over my head, then turned his attention to me again. "I've seen Kendra and Alissa here a few times before. They're both pretty, so I kept an eye out for them. Mostly, they hung out with the friends they'd come with." Santo smirked. "The last time Kendra was here, she volunteered for the show upstairs."

"Show?" I asked.

His grin was so predatory that it made me want to squirm in my seat. "The upstairs can get a little rowdy sometimes. Drugs, sex, stuff like that. When Kendra was there, it was an orgy."

I felt my cheeks warm again and glanced at the upstairs loft. Jen and Stella had gone up there. Would they be all right? "Okay," I said, trying to clear my head and think. "So one of the people who participated took an interest in her? Is that what you're saying?"

Santo nodded. "Yes, one of those tall, dark, and handsome fellows." He gave Vaughn a significant look. "Not like us, but more like the generous patrons that run Tombstone."

What did that mean? I glanced over at Vaughn. He grimaced, seeming to know what Santo was getting at. "Do you know who this guy is, the one who took an interest in Kendra?" I asked Santo. "If we can identify him, we can tell the police. Even if they don't know that you told us, they'd have to check him out."

Santo looked around warily. "No, I don't know who he is," he lied. It was written all over his face. He knew who the killer was. "Look, I can't tell you anything else." He stood and looked around the room nervously, his earlier confidence gone. "I need to get going. Other places to be, you see."

"Wait!"

"No," Santo interrupted. "I've already said too much." He smiled at me, regaining some of his former flippancy, and said, "Until next time, Sarah," then headed off toward the dance floor.

I leaned back into the sofa. "He knew more than he was saying. I'm certain of it." Vaughn was still sitting next to me, and when I looked over at him, he was staring at Santo's back as the man struck up a conversation with some women across the room. "What did he mean when he said 'not like us'?" I asked.

"Huh?" Vaughn blinked a couple of times as he turned to me. "Oh. That was just..." His brows furrowed. "How do I put this? Santo and I are kind of on the bottom of the food chain, so to speak. No one cares about what we say or do. Whoever he was referring to must have some sort of power or influence in Seattle. Not someone who can easily be ignored."

"He compared this person to the owners of Tombstone. Does this place really have any power or influence?" I asked, having my doubts. It just looked like a seedy club to me.

Vaughn laughed, but it was not a happy sound. "Do you know how many times this club has been busted for one illegal activity or another? It happens at least once a year. Why hasn't the city pulled its liquor license? Arrested the owner or shut it down?" He waved a hand at the room around us. "This place shouldn't be operating, but no one has dared to try and stop it. Can you guess why?"

A chill ran down my spine. "Power and influence."

"And money, which is a little of both. Bribes and donations can buy a lot of goodwill with politicians." He took a sip of his drink.

I sat there, mulling that over. If Vaughn was right, the killer was someone who was well positioned and would be hard to track down, especially if everyone was afraid to identify him. No wonder the police were having such a hard time. "He's definitely mixed up with the owners of Tombstone, if we believe what Santo told us," I said aloud just as the music changed again to another beat that I could feel all the way to my toes.

Vaughn stood and held out a hand to me. "We should check in with the others!" he shouted over the music.

Taking his hand, I let him pull me to my feet. Since there was no sense in wasting a soda, I grabbed my Coke, and we made our way over to the stairs. Looking up at them, I dubiously wondered what we would see there. Hopefully, there wasn't another orgy. On the other hand, given what we were investigating, an orgy would be the least of my concerns.

Just as we started climbing, I spotted Jen and Stella near the top, fully clothed and making their way toward us. Vaughn and I moved aside to let the people behind us through and waited as our friends descended.

Jen's expression was one of frustration. I opened my mouth to ask her what was wrong, but she waved away the question and mouthed "later." She might have actually spoken, but I couldn't hear her over the music. Jen motioned toward the door, and I nodded, following her and Stella. We retrieved our jackets from the coat check and left Tombstone. All in all, we'd been in there for less than thirty minutes.

Jen and Stella walked with us to Vaughn's car. Once we were far enough from the club, Jen said, "No one would talk to us. Every time we asked about Kendra, the person we were talking to would get up and leave," she growled. "Eventually, we gave up and decided to come find you guys." She shrugged her shoulders but didn't look like she was ready to give up. "Did either of you find out anything useful?"

Vaughn and I glanced at each other. "Yeah," I began. "But it wasn't much. We met a friend of Vaughn's who gave us some information."

"He is *not* my friend," Vaughn scowled.

"Fine. An acquaintance of yours, then," I corrected, slightly annoyed. "A guy named Santo. He told us that Kendra had been here the night of some orgy, and a guy had taken an interest in her." Stella flashed a triumphant grin, but Jen looked disheartened. I told them everything that Santo had said and what Vaughn had thought it meant.

"So, the killer is targeting women who he sleeps with at Tombstone, and because of his connections, everyone is too afraid to turn him in? He sounds like some sort of mobster," Stella said, tapping a finger to her chin in thought.

"Is there a mob presence in Seattle?" I asked, remembering tales of the mafia families in New York. I hadn't ever seen any mob activity there myself, but there were establishments I knew to stay away from.

Jen nodded. "The Colacurcio crime family."

"Who?" That name sounded familiar, but I couldn't place it.

"Well," Stella said, "they aren't around anymore. Frank Colacurcio owned a bunch of strip clubs that were being used as fronts for prostitution, as well as being known for racketeering and money laundering. He was trying to expand his business to Portland, and was even rumored to be in the middle of making a deal with the crime families on the east coast, but he never got that far. His operation was taken down over ten years ago or so, and Colacurcio died about a year later." She looked over her shoulder at the club. "You know, I think I read that one of those clubs that he owned was in this area. What if Tombstone was one of them?"

"That would explain part of its shady reputation," Vaughn said pensively. "I grew up outside of Portland, so I don't know too much about Colacurcio."

I followed the logic train. "Maybe the new owners didn't change the club's policy much, just legitimized it. As long as no one is paying for sex, it's not illegal. They could just charge more to get in the door, and as long as the customers are consenting adults, no crimes are being committed."

"There's definitely something strange going on there, though," Jen mused. "They've been busted a few times for other things; that much is well known."

"We should tell Will about this and let him deal with it," Vaughn said. We all stared at him, and he blushed. "Th-that was the deal, wasn't it? We find out what we can and tell the police?"

As much as I hated to admit it, Vaughn was right. The four of us were not equipped to deal with this on our own. "Yeah, we can let the police figure out what to do next."

"We haven't found out anything yet," Jen said. "There's no evidence for them to go on. So unless this Santo agrees to talk to the police *and* identify this mysterious well-connected man, it's all rumors."

"Jen, we are *not* cops," I said, trying to shut down any vigilante ideas she might be coming up with. "We're a bunch of teenagers and not equipped to investigate a murderer. We're more likely to become victims if we mess around in this too much."

Jen looked like she wanted to argue, but Stella placed a hand on her shoulder. "Sweetie, Sarah is right. This was never about finding the killer on our own. We don't have the experience or resources to try to track him down."

"It feels wrong to do nothing while women are murdered. There has to be some way we can help," she said, conviction in her voice.

"We can go to Will," Vaughn reasoned. "He's intimidating, but he takes his job seriously. He'll listen and follow up with what we tell him. I'm sure he can convince Santo to talk." He reached into his pocket and pulled out his phone. "If you want, I can call him and ask him to meet us now. There's a Denny's not too far from here, and it's open all night."

Jen ran a hand over her face. "Fine. I just feel we could do more."

"We are doing as much as we can," Stella said gently and wrapped her arms around Jen, followed by me and then Vaughn. Jen smiled in spite of herself, and we laughed. The group hug felt nice. Safe and warm despite the outside chill. It was something I hadn't felt in a long time.

CHAPTER 19

TO MY SURPRISE, Will bought us all dinner. It was more like an early breakfast, but we didn't complain. He'd answered Vaughn's call right away and had met us at Denny's an hour later. The fact that Vaughn had Will's personal number was even more suspicious than the cop being awake and willing to meet us at this hour, but when I asked about it, Vaughn shrugged it off apologetically. "He's a family friend," he'd said. It was obvious that there was more to it, but in my infinite patience and understanding, I let it go.

"So," Will began once he'd finished taking notes and the waitress refilled his cup of coffee, "you went to this club and asked around about Kendra, knowing that the killer might have been there looking for his next victim?" He looked around the table at each of us in turn and shook his head with a sigh. There was a weary smile on his face. In the soft light of the restaurant, Will looked much less imposing than he had before. The other three times I'd seen him, he'd been scary and intimidating, but now, sitting at the table and blowing on his steaming cup of coffee, he looked like a regular person. He chuckled. "I don't think I need to say how incredibly stupid that was. This isn't an episode of *Scooby-Doo*. If you get caught by the masked monster, he'll kill you."

Jen frowned like she wanted to argue with him, but Stella put a hand on her arm and addressed Will instead. "You know as well as we do that no one at Tombstone would have talked to the police. We knew the risks going into it, so there's no use lecturing us about it now."

Will crossed his arms over his chest, looking annoyed. They were huge, like a bodybuilder's. "Miss Ruiz, while I appreciate your willingness to help, please don't try something like this again. I don't want to see any of you get hurt by taking risks and sticking your collective noses where they don't belong." He glanced at his notepad. "Sarah, Vaughn. Did Santo give any indication as to this person's identity?"

"No," I said. "Just what I told you before, that this person was well connected like the owners of the club and not like him and Vaughn, whatever that means."

"That's not much to go on," Will said, running a hand through his hair. "I promise I'll look into it. As much as I hate to admit it, Miss Ruiz is right. The staff at Tombstone won't talk to us. I should be able to track down Santo, though, and see if he'll tell me what he wasn't willing to tell you." He closed the notebook and looked at us. "I have to ask you all to stop looking into these murders. It's dangerous for you to be going around asking these kinds of questions, and what's more, you could even be seen by the killer or scare him off. We want to catch him, not have him kill you to keep you quiet."

"Are you any closer to catching him, then?" Jen asked with a determined look on her face.

"I can't tell you that, but rest assured that we will catch him with time," he said firmly. "Thank you for the information." He stood, put his jacket on, and pulled a twenty-dollar bill out of his pocket and tossed it on the table. "The check is already paid for, but feel free to order something else if you want it. Miss Frost"—his blue eyes tracked to me—"I apologize if I frightened you the times we met before. The investigation has been frustrating, and I should have realized Olivia might have relatives over, considering the time of year." He nodded to us one more time in farewell and left.

"He didn't seem so bad this time around. At least he didn't threaten to arrest us," Jen grumbled.

"Do you think he's going to take us seriously?" I asked.

"He will," Vaughn answered me. "I don't know if he'll be able to get Santo to talk. That guy is as slimy as an eel."

"Are you going to tell us how you know him?" Stella asked as she waved down the server to get more pancakes. "This Santo guy sounds pretty sketchy, and he's about ten years older than us, right?"

"Yeah," I piped in. Then turning to Vaughn, I said, "Your expression said you wanted to murder him while he was talking to me."

Vaughn scratched at the back of his head, his mouth pinched into a thin line. "He's kind of a friend of a friend. I don't like him because he's a creep and an enormous tool, but because he runs in those sketchy circles, Marius keeps him around," he said.

"Who's Marius?" I had to think about why that name sounded familiar. "Wasn't that the person Kat mentioned when you two were arguing on the roof?" I didn't remind him that I'd technically been eavesdropping on that particular conversation.

Vaughn glanced at Jen, and she gave him a slight shake of her head. "I'm surprised Jen hasn't told you yet," he said after a moment. "I think I told you about being in the foster-care system when I was younger and that it was Carter who convinced my guardian to reconcile with me. Well, that was Marius. He continues to act like a foster parent. A really, really intense foster parent."

Jen snorted. "You mean he's a huge asshole."

He winced. "Yeah, he's also that." Vaughn looked down at his half-eaten sausages. "Even so, I'm grateful for all he's done for me."

"You shouldn't be so charitable, Vaughn," Stella began. "The man threw you out as soon as you turned eighteen!"

Vaughn sighed. "I know it seems harsh and unorthodox, but Marius thought he was doing what was best for—"

"Don't give me that crap," Jen hissed. "How can you *still* defend him? It's his fault that Kat has it in her head that you two belong together. It's sick how he manipulates the people he claims to care about."

"You and Stella know this Marius person too?" I interjected, trying to give Vaughn a break from Jen's anger.

"Well, I haven't met him," Stella said.

"I have." Jen looked at her cup of coffee. "Kat and I have been friends since middle school. Marius is her godfather. He never talks to me much, but I've seen how he acts around Kat and Vaughn. He treats her almost like a daughter, but whenever he looks at Vaughn, it's almost like he's disappointed with him. Kat gets anything she wants from him, but he can't be bothered to take care of his actual ward. And Kat doesn't even see it. But they both seem to do whatever he wants." Jen turned to Vaughn. "Right? It's so obvious how manipulative and controlling he is, but both of you just take it."

As Jen spoke, I observed Vaughn. He shifted uncomfortably in his seat and looked around the restaurant as if Marius would somehow hear us talking about him. I knew how that felt, having been in Vaughn's place. It made me angry to see him going through the same things I had with Brian.

"We've reconciled up to a point," Vaugh said, "but I haven't decided if I want to go back to him yet. To live with him, I mean." He looked into my eyes, and I could see the conflict in them. He was deciding between the person who was supposed to care for him and his freedom. "If I do go back, I have to live by his rules." He grimaced. "Later on, if I decide to leave on my own, that could hurt Kat's feelings."

"Vaughn, you need to do what's best for you, not for Kat. Putting yourself into a bad situation to avoid hurting someone's feelings will only make things worse." Jen took his hand in hers.

"That's what Carter said." Vaughn smiled and squeezed her hand. "I'll be all right. I just need to think about it some more."

"If you need help, let us know," Stella said. "I'm sure we can help you find a room to rent."

"Where are you staying now?" I asked. He'd mentioned this before, hadn't he? Something about Carter helping him out. Jen and Stella would already know the details, but I couldn't remember what he'd told me.

"Carter is letting me stay in one of his condos for now. It's between renters, so he told me I could live there for six months rent-free if I fixed the mess that the last tenant left behind. I've got a few more months there, and then I'll have to find a new place. There's no way I could afford the rent Carter wants on it. Before moving into the condo, I couch-surfed and lived in my car, like I mentioned before." He shrugged, a little embarrassed. "It'll be okay. I'm sure I can find a new apartment or a roommate before I have to move out."

Stella yawned. "You shouldn't have any trouble. There are always people looking for housemates." She glanced at her watch. "Geez, it's late. Are you about ready, Jen? I think I'm going to ask for those pancakes to-go."

Jen finished her coffee while Stella got a box for her order of pancakes. We left the twenty-dollar bill on the table and headed out to the cars. I hugged Jen and Stella goodnight, and Vaughn drove me home. The ride back wasn't anywhere near as awkward as it had been at the beginning of the night.

I thought about what Vaughn had told us about his life and his guardian, Marius. He must have had a hard childhood if the person who was supposed to be his guardian was so strict with Vaughn, but doting on his goddaughter. It seemed unfair. What about his parents? What had happened to them? He said before that he'd grown up outside Portland, but that might not mean with family. Then adding possible homelessness to his already troubled home life? What a mess. He was under a lot of pressure.

"You know," I said as he pulled up to the curb outside my house, "if you ever need someone to talk to about... about anything, you can call me. My dad died when I was a kid, so I know how messed up it can be at times."

He smiled, but it didn't reach his eyes. "Thanks, Sarah, but I doubt you want to hear about it. My personal life hasn't been what you would call stable, and you saw how upset Jen was about Marius. He may not be the best father figure to have around, but he's the only one I have. I don't know if I can turn my back on him like some of my friends want me to."

"You don't have to explain yourself to me, Vaughn," I said with a sigh. "We've all got our issues, but you don't have to face yours alone. I learned recently that ignoring your problems only makes them harder to face in the end. If you need a good listener, I'm here for you." *Just like how Carter was there to listen to me.*

Vaughn nodded, his expression thoughtful. We said goodnight, and I got out of his car and walked up the driveway to my house, careful not to slip on the fresh coating of snow and ice. The door creaked when I opened it, and I tried to be very quiet as I took off my shoes and jacket. There was no noise from her part of the house, so Aunt Liv must have already gone to bed. I crept up the stairs, planning on changing and going to bed myself.

"You're home late."

My heart nearly jumped out of my chest at the sudden shattering of silence. I missed a step and almost went tumbling down the stairs but caught the railing just in time. Breathing heavily, I looked around until my gaze fell on Aunt Liv sitting on my sofa.

"Don't do that!" I gasped as my heart pounded in my chest. "You scared me."

She ignored my comment. "Where have you been?" she asked. "You've never been out this late before, and you didn't text me."

Somehow, I didn't think Liv would be happy if she knew that I went to a shady club looking for clues about Kendra Thompson's assailant. Especially when she'd told me to stay out of it. "I was out with Jen and the others," I said evasively, climbing the rest of the stairs.

She looked me up and down, one eyebrow quirked. "You're dressed pretty nicely for just hanging out with friends, and you're wearing makeup. I haven't seen you wear much makeup since you moved here. Also, I thought Jen drove a Civic?"

Dammit. Liv was testing me. *Keep calm, Sarah. You were out having some fun with friends, that's all.* "Vaughn dropped me off. He's one of Jen's friends."

Her expression changed from suspicious to surprised, and her posture became more relaxed. "Oh, Vaughn, hmm? I see."

I wasn't sure what caused her reaction, but it was working in my favor. "Yeah, we just came from a late-night snack after hanging out in Capitol Hill." I put my purse on the table, trying to act natural. "Sorry, I should have let you know that I was going to be out this late."

"No, it's all right." All the tension had eased out of her voice, and she was smiling. "You don't have a curfew, Sarah. I'm just happy to see that you're trying to date again."

That took me off guard, and I stumbled, having to catch myself on the edge of the table. "What? I'm not dating him!"

"Sarah, I don't mind. I'm not your mom, and you're not a child. You don't have to hide it from me." She gave me a knowing smile, then stood and stretched. "I've seen this Vaughn guy around with Carter before. If I remember correctly, he's pretty good-looking, right?"

"It wasn't a date!" My face felt hot. This conversation had left all sanity behind. "We're just friends."

Liv nodded, the grin on her face telling me that she didn't believe me. "Of course," she said placatingly. "It wasn't a date. I understand."

She didn't, but I didn't push it. Better to think that I was out with Vaughn on some romantic double date than to find out what we'd actually been doing. It was my turn to keep secrets.

"Whatever," I said, avoiding her eyes. "Can I please go to sleep now?"

She made her way past me and to the stairs. "Oh, before I forget"—she turned around—"how is working for Carter? Is he treating you well?"

The question came as a shock. We had avoided talking about Carter ever since she'd found out that I was working for him. "It's good. Great, really. He pays me well, and he's a nice boss. I like him."

Liv leaned against the railing, one foot on the first step. "He's not asking too much of you? I know he can ride his assistants pretty hard. When he gets busy, he expects you to be there all the time. Some people can't handle it."

"No, it's fine so far. We haven't gotten close to one of his deadlines. That will be the real test. He knows I'll be back in school soon, so he's trying to schedule the hectic weeks for when I'll be on break. Right now, it's a lot of admin work and purchasing supplies." I thought about it. "When I started, he said I would be helping him on projects, which I'm excited about. Being able to learn from him is worth any amount of work."

Liv sighed heavily. "He's a good man." She said it as if it was a bad thing. "Well, goodnight then." Her feet thumped on the stairs as she descended. A few moments later, I heard the door to her room downstairs shut.

I let out the breath I'd been holding. That was a close one. If Aunt Liv had found out about Tombstone... Well, I didn't want to think about it. It looked like I'd gotten away with it this time.

As I washed my face and got ready for bed, another thought occurred to me. If Liv wasn't already suspicious, why had she been waiting for me? Could she have figured out that we'd been looking into Kendra's attack? But that shouldn't matter anymore. We were done with it.

CHAPTER 20

RAIN DRIZZLED LAZILY, the sky above covered in black and purple clouds. The moon was hidden behind them, but, somehow, I knew it was full. It was cold, and my breath fogged in front of me, but it didn't feel as biting as it had the last few weeks. The sounds of my footsteps echoed off the buildings around me, and I knew that, once again, I wasn't in my own body but seeing through the eyes of another person. I caught a glimpse of myself in the rain-slicked windows of empty cars and saw the familiar face of Aunt Liv.

She approached the doors of a large building, one of the structures downtown that almost qualified as a skyscraper. The glass was so heavily tinted that it was impossible to see what was hiding beyond. It showed Liv's reflection, a beautiful woman with long, dark hair, clad in a black-leather jacket and jeans. After scanning a card on the security sensor, the doors unlocked, and she went inside.

I expected a large lobby behind the glass, but there were just a few sofas and a small reception desk behind which there was a wall with a single black door. There weren't even any signs declaring what kind of business this was. No one was there, and the lights were off, but Liv strode over to the black door like she knew where she was going, scanned her card again, and went through.

Beyond was a long hallway filled with more identical-looking black doors. Liv went through another to her right and another, again and again, in a confusing order that blurred together. There were no desks or furniture, just more black doors. Eventually, she was looking down a staircase that disappeared into the darkness below. It was hard to believe that she was still in the same building.

"Have you heard?" asked a familiar voice from behind her.

"Why do you think I'm here?" she replied without turning to the speaker.

Will stepped next to her, gazing down into the darkness. "Two more women are missing. Whoever this is, they are out of control."

"What do you think the Nine will do?" she asked without emotion.

The Nine. I'd heard that name in another dream. What was it?

"What they always do," Will replied and started down the stairs, the darkness swallowing him whole.

Liv hesitated for only a moment, then followed behind him.

CHAPTER 21

"DID YOU WATCH THE NEWS TODAY?" Jen asked over her sandwich. We'd met for lunch in the International District at a small Vietnamese bakery that sold bánh mìs.

"Two more women went missing?" I guessed, remembering my dream. I hoped it was just that, a dream, and that Jen was talking about the Seahawks signing a new player or anything else.

"Yeah," she said, confirming my fears. Jen stared at her sandwich. She'd only taken a few bites out of it, but she wrapped it back up. "I'm going to go back to Tombstone today to see if there is anyone there early who will give me more information. Maybe we missed something when we were there."

I'd been taking a sip from my iced coffee and almost spit it all over the table. "Jen, you can't be serious," I sputtered. "I know you want to help, but there's nothing else we can do."

"We could talk to the employees," Jen said earnestly. "They must have noticed some details they don't want to tell the police."

"No one would talk to you, remember?" I could tell she wasn't listening. A cold fear gripped my insides. What would happen if she did go back?

Grabbing her hand, I made her look at me. "Jen, you have to promise me that you won't investigate this anymore. Let Will follow up on what we gave him. He knows what he's doing, unlike us." I glanced at my watch. Carter would need me back at the studio soon. "Don't be stupid, Jen. Promise me you won't go to Tombstone. Please."

The defiance in her eyes was apparent, and I knew she wanted to fight me on this. Before, I would have backed down and trusted Jen to keep herself safe, but a lot had changed in the past few weeks. On top of that, during the short time I'd been back and rekindled our friendship, I'd seen that Jen could be reckless, and I didn't want something to happen to her.

We stayed like that for more than a minute before Jen sighed. "Fine. I'll leave it to the police," she mumbled.

I felt the tension easing out of my shoulders as I relaxed, feeling like a weight had been lifted off my chest. If Jen promised not to go, I believed she wouldn't. I let go of her hand and sat back in my chair. "So," I said as I took another sip of my coffee, "it looks like you and Stella made up. You were pretty upset with her the night we went to the hospital."

A radiant smile blossomed over Jen's face. "Yeah, she's going to come over and meet my mom tonight. It's a little out of her comfort zone, but she's trying. We're going to have dinner together."

"That's great!" I said and meant it. "I like her, and I'm happy you two were able to work things out."

The tops of Jen's cheeks turned a rosy shade of pink. "She really is amazing. I love just being around her, and I think what we have could be more." She continued wrapping her bánh mì and put the sandwich in her bag. "Do you need me to give you a ride to the studio? Your lunch is about over, right?"

"No, it's not far." I eyed her. Her grin was fading, and she still looked troubled. "Jen, are you okay?"

"I'm fine, just nervous about tonight." She stood and put her jacket on, avoiding my eyes. "Mom wants me to get a few things at the store before I go home."

"Jen—"

"I said I'm fine, Sarah," she snapped, then sighed. "Sorry, I'm a little stressed out, to be honest, but I'll be all right. I'll text you tonight and let you know how it went."

She gave me a half-hearted wave as she left the bakery, and I watched her until she drove off in her car. Jen had seemed more and more agitated ever since our undercover op to Tombstone a few days ago. This was the second time she'd suggested going back to the club. Her attitude was worrying, and I hoped that she would keep her promise.

On the walk to the studio, I considered the relationship of the two newly missing women to the dream I'd had the night before. I'd never seen the building that Aunt Liv had gone into, but it had looked like it was somewhere in the city. It could have been a real place, but then what would that mean? It was just a dream, wasn't it? Even so, that didn't explain how my dream predicted that two more women would go missing. It was possible I'd heard the news from Aunt Liv's room in my sleep, and this was my mind incorporating it into what I dreamed about. Yeah, that had to be it.

.   .   .

"Sarah," Carter said, pointing to the painting he was working on. "Please fill these areas with the yellow paint I have out. I'll add more detail later, so don't worry too much about keeping it even, but try to stay in the lines."

I started, coming out of my thoughts. "Yes, of course." Picking up the spare apron that hung on a hook behind the easel, I grabbed a brush and the container of yellow paint Carter had indicated.

As I filled the areas Carter wanted painted in, I thought more about the building from my dream. Carter was also a muralist. If anyone knew the city's commercial districts well, he would. "Carter, is there a building in town with black windows, no signage, and a small front reception area?"

Carter pulled a beer from the refrigerator and took a long drink. "There are a lot of buildings like that downtown. Can you be more specific?"

"Well, past the reception area, there was a black door, and past that, a hallway full of doors." I tried to remember the details of my dream. "After going through a lot of doors, there's a staircase that leads down past where you can see, which is weird since basements here are rare."

There was a *clink* as Carter put down the bottle. When I looked up, he was watching me intently. "Where did you see this building? Did Liv take you to it?" He was so serious that I got the impression that I needed to be very careful with how I answered his questions.

"No, I haven't actually seen it before," I said, my eyes narrowing. "So there is a place like that in town."

Carter frowned. "Yes, but I'm surprised you would have any knowledge of it. How do you know about it, Sarah?" He persisted.

I wasn't sure what he would think if I told him about my

dream, but I trusted Carter, and maybe he could tell me a little bit more about what that place was. "It's going to sound really weird," I said, embarrassed. "But I saw it in a dream last night." I described the dream while Carter listened intently, his beer forgotten on the counter.

By the time I'd finished, he was sitting on the couch, his arms crossed and a thoughtful expression on his face. He didn't laugh at the absurdity of it all but was considering everything that I'd told him as if it actually happened. "You heard them talking about the missing women before you found out about it happening? It wasn't reported on the news until this morning."

"Well, I could have just heard the TV downstairs," I said.

He made a thoughtful sound and was silent for a few more seconds, thinking it over. "You should tell your aunt about this dream. She would be able to tell you what it means."

I smiled, a bitter taste in my mouth. "She already thinks I'm snooping around too much as it is. What if she thinks I'm lying and I spied on her?"

"For that to be true, you'd have to believe that the events in your dream were real and you were looking at the world through her eyes." He chuckled. "I can understand why you would be hesitant to talk to her about this. Livy can be a bit scary when she thinks you're out of line. Do you have any reason to think that is what really happened?"

Aunt Liv had been working late recently and getting home after I'd gone to bed, but that was no reason to think that I was somehow seeing what she was doing. I mumbled something noncommittal in response. I considered telling Carter about the two other dreams I'd had but ultimately decided not to. He accepted what I was telling him now, but if he found out that this was a recurring thing, he might call Liv himself. I'm sure he had her number.

"If you don't want to talk to your aunt, that's your choice, but I think you will need to eventually," he said. "Things like this don't just go away."

I studied his face, but his expression didn't tell me anything. Was he teasing me? He hadn't done so before, but there was a first time for everything. Why was he so sure that I would need to talk to Liv about my dreams? I had far too many questions and not enough answers. "Do you know anything about the two women who went missing?" I asked instead of dwelling on his mysterious comments.

"Just what was reported on the news this morning. Both women were in their mid-twenties and neither had made it home from their commutes. The police think they were taken around Green Lake." He sighed and stood from the couch, walked over to the floor-to-ceiling windows, and gazed at the street below, watching people going about their day. "It's the first time that more than one person has been taken by the killer at once."

I swallowed hard and asked the difficult question. "Have the police found their bodies?"

Carter looked pained. "No, not yet. The bodies usually show up a few days after the women go missing. They are still trying to find them."

We both knew that the chances of the police finding the women alive and catching the killer were slim. It was a grim thought, but there was the possibility that the information that Jen and I gave Will would help the police get to them in time. I could understand why Jen wanted to go back to Tombstone and investigate more. How many other people would need to disappear before the killer was caught?

Carter let the subject drop, and for the next few hours, we worked on the painting that he'd had me fill in with yellow before. I could tell he was trying to keep the conversation upbeat, keeping me focused and not dwelling on the missing women. He kept me painting for a while, directing me to change colors when necessary and even showing me how to do a few techniques. It was exhausting, but I learned a lot and wanted to try some of what he showed me on my own projects.

When I left for the day, even though it wasn't that late, it was dark, and I hurried over to the light-rail station. Many other people were walking across the stadium parking lot, so I wasn't alone as I climbed the steps that went over the tracks. I was in a much better mood than when I'd gotten back from lunch, so when my phone rang with a number that I didn't recognize, I answered with a peppy, "Hello! This is Sarah." Sometimes, I ended up with calls from Carter's clients since his answering service redirected calls to my phone.

"Sarah," came a voice that I knew. "This is Stella. Jen's mom gave me your phone number."

Why was Stella calling me? I didn't mind that she had my number, but it seemed strange that she would call me instead of Jen. "Oh, uh, hi." I checked my watch. She should be at Jen's house having dinner. "Are you okay? Did the dinner not go well?"

"Have you seen Jen today?" she asked, and her voice sounded scratchy, like she'd been crying. That was strange. Did they get into another fight?

"Yeah, I had lunch with her. Is she not home yet?" My stomach tensed. Did Jen go to Tombstone regardless of her promise?

"No, she was supposed to be home hours ago. None of

us can get ahold of her," she said, and I could hear the panic through the phone.

My entire body felt numb. "What are you saying?"

"The police called and told her mom that her car was abandoned on the street." Stella took a deep, shaking breath. "Sarah, Jen is missing."

CHAPTER 22

DETECTIVE REED NODDED as he closed his notebook, having written down my recollection of the conversation Jen and I had had at the bakery earlier that day. The detective was tall and muscular with gray hair that contrasted against his tanned skin. We were sitting at Aunt Liv's dining room table while Will stood in the kitchen, looking out the window by the breakfast nook. Liv sat on the couch in the living room, head back on the cushion and eyes closed.

"Thank you, Miss Frost." Reed reached into a pocket and pulled out a white business card with the Seattle PD logo on it. "If you can remember anything else that you think will help, please give me a call." He set it on the table and stood.

As he did, Liv's eyes snapped open, and she stood to let the detective out of the house.

Once they were in the front entryway, Will took Detective Reed's seat across from me. "How are you doing, kid?"

I shrugged, not trusting myself to say anything.

Will sighed. "I know it's tough for you right now, but

dwelling on what happened won't help you. Believe me, I know how you're feeling. "

"How could you possibly know how I'm feeling?!" I snapped. "It's my fault that Jen is gone! She all but told me she was going to go back to look for more clues. I could have stopped her." My eyes filled with tears and my vision blurred. "I should have stopped her..."

"Sarah, you shouldn't blame yourself for the choices that other people make." He crossed his arms. His expression was stern but not unkind. "You don't need me to tell you that investigating the killer to begin with was not a smart idea. You've heard that enough, and I can appreciate that you wanted to help. Unfortunately, Jennifer went beyond what help she could reasonably offer. You did try to stop her. It's not as if you could have locked her in a room to make sure she didn't do something stupid. This is not your fault."

I blinked the tears out of my eyes. I knew what Will was saying was true, that there was no way I could have stopped Jen short of kidnapping her myself, but that didn't change how I felt. My heart was telling me that I could have done more to prevent this from happening. We should have never gone to Tombstone in the first place. Why didn't I try harder to dissuade her from looking into the killings?

Will pushed away from the table. "I need to talk to your aunt about a few things before I head out. Don't be too hard on yourself, Sarah. We're doing everything we can to find her."

I watched him as he headed out the door to the apartment, closing it behind him. A moment later, I could hear Liv's and Will's low voices in the hall.

My shoulders slumped as I wrapped my arms around myself, unable to keep the tears back. Self-loathing washed over me, along with the feeling of helplessness that I hadn't felt since moving to Seattle. Jen was going to die, and it was all my fault.

A few minutes later, I heard the front door close, and Liv came back into the apartment. Her face was hard, and I could feel the anger emanating from her. There hadn't been a chance to tell her about Tombstone before the cops arrived, so she'd heard it for the first time while I'd been telling Detective Reed. She now knew that we had been looking into the killings and Kendra's attack, and she was furious.

"When were you going to tell me that you and your friends were snooping around?" she asked, and I could tell she was trying to keep her voice level. " I thought that after what happened at the hospital, you'd be smart enough to stay out of it."

"We just wanted to help." I could feel my own anger rising, muting my grief. Who was she to tell me not to get involved? "We knew that no one from Tombstone would talk to the police, so all we did was ask a few questions."

"I can't believe you'd be so reckless! You should know better than to get yourself into dangerous situations, Sarah." Liv closed her eyes and rubbed her temples with her fingers. "An investigation like this is nowhere for a bunch of teenagers to stick their noses. You and your friends should have let us handle it."

"Who is *us*? Why are you even a part of this, Aunt Liv? You're not a police officer, so I can't figure out why you're investigating these killings." I wanted to shout at her, but my guilt kept me from embracing my anger. A part of me felt it was only just that I was getting some form of punishment for my role in Jen's disappearance. "I know we shouldn't have done that, and it was foolish. I know I should have done more to dissuade Jen from taking further action, but you're doing the exact same thing. Why can you handle them any better than us? What are you not telling me?"

Liv crossed her arms. Her hands balled into fists, and her body was so tense she looked like she was on the verge of violence. I wouldn't put it past my aunt to punch a hole in the wall. "I can handle this because I know what I'm doing. You'd have no idea what to do if you *did* find the killer. Because let me tell you, he wouldn't wait around for the cops. You can't protect yourself or your friends."

I didn't back down and tried to keep my voice even. "What would *you* do if you caught him, Aunt Liv? It's not as if you can arrest him."

My words cooled her temper somewhat. She shook her head. "I can't tell you, Sarah. I promised your mother I would keep you out of this."

A red-hot feeling washed over me. How dare she—or my absentee mom—decide what was best for me without my input? Liv kept treating me like a child, and my anger erupted as I started shouting at her. "Keep me out of what?! What are you hiding from me?!"

Liv opened her mouth to respond, but a loud knocking came from the front entryway. She looked over her shoulder and frowned. "Did Will forget something?" she asked herself then walked out to see who was at the front door.

I followed her. "We're not done talking, Liv!"

"Sarah, I can't do this right now. We'll continue this later," she said as she reached for the doorknob.

There was another loud bang on the door, like a heavy object hitting it very hard. A deafening cracking sound resonated throughout the room, and I saw the solid oak of the door splinter as it was hit again from the other side. It sounded like someone was trying to break down the door.

Liv whipped around, her eyes wide. "Go! Out the back."

I couldn't tear my eyes off the door. "Wha—"

Another CRACK sounded, and pieces of wood flew inward, striking Liv in the back. She fell forward and rolled with the momentum. Turning and crouching in a low stance, like she was ready to attack, Liv called back to me, "Now, Sarah. Get out of here!" Before I could move, I saw a *thing* step into the hole where the front door had been.

It was some sort of large animal, as big as a bear, but more wolf-like, covered with black fur, with a canine muzzle and pointed ears. Pulling its entire body into the entryway, the beast had to slouch down so that its head would even fit inside. It's lips peeled back, revealing razor-sharp teeth as its reflective yellow eyes focused on Aunt Liv still crouched in front of it. A low growl resonated from its chest, and its eyes flicked over to me as I half-turned toward the back door, my legs freezing in place. The growl was like the rumble of an old truck, and I could feel the vibrations through my shoes.

"GO!" Liv shouted, and her voice broke the spell. I dashed toward the back door as the rumble behind me became a snarl, and Aunt Liv let out a cry, something hitting the floor hard, making the ground shake.

In my haste, I slipped on the hallway rug and fell. Before I could get to my feet again, the rug was yanked hard from behind me. I rolled over to see the wolf-like creature using its paws in a digging motion to pull the rug toward him, and me with it. I couldn't see Liv, with its huge form filling the entryway. I wanted to make sure she was okay, but my inner voice was screaming at me to get away from it.

I tried to get to my feet, but the wolf took the end of the rug in its mouth and shook it, sending me sprawling again. It yanked the rug—and me—closer, and I kicked at its face, trying to get away. Pushing myself toward the back door, all I could hope for was that its size would make it hard for it to squeeze down the hallway after me.

The wolf opened its mouth wide, drool dripping from its fangs onto a tongue as long as my arm. It took a step forward, and I kicked its open maw again, trying to push back at the same time, but one of my feet slipped and went into its mouth.

Before its jaws could snap shut, the wolf yelped in surprise as Liv's fingers worked their way between its teeth. With a cry of pain, she wrenched its wide jaws open and yanked the muzzle away from me. I pulled my leg out before the beast could shake Aunt Liv off, and pushed back from them, scooting across the floor and closer to the back door.

The wolf shook its head violently, throwing Liv off it and sending her colliding with the railing. It focused on me again, growling and stepping one giant, furry paw forward, its nails digging furrows in the wood planks. My back hit the door, and I scrambled for the doorknob, unable to tear my eyes off the wolf.

Aunt Liv stood, a small black gun in her hands. Without hesitation, she pulled the trigger, again and again, firing at the beast.

I'd heard the sound of gunfire before, but being in the same room with it was nothing like you see in movies or what I'd experienced in New York. The sounds I'd heard back home were an echoing in the distance. Up close, it was so much louder than I'd expected. By the time Liv had emptied her clip, my ears were ringing.

The back door flew open as my sweaty hands found purchase on the knob, sending me sprawling outside and onto the back patio. I caught a glimpse of Liv jumping on the animal's back, then I was on my feet and running through the grass. It was pitch black, and I looked around wildly, passing the old iron swing set I'd played on as a kid. I could see lights from the neighbor's house ahead and the dim illumination of the streetlights to my left.

My foot caught on a rock, and I tumbled forward, my face hitting the soft grass and patches of snow as the beast soared right over where my head had just been. I rolled over and looked up to see the glowing yellow eyes staring at me, reflecting the lights from the house. Its hot breath stirred my hair as I got to my knees, not daring to look away from it. I'd read somewhere that you didn't run from predators, and that could be the reason why it had chased me into the yard. Even so, every instinct told me to run, but my legs wouldn't move. It was like the night Brian had almost kidnapped me. No matter how much I wanted to get away from this beast, my body wouldn't comply.

I heard running footsteps on the patio behind me, and the thing growled again. Then there was a flash of light to my right and the sound of a gunshot again, much louder than the handgun blasts from before.

I reeled away from it, falling to my side and covering my ears. The wolf was no longer paying attention to me, its mass of black fur and shadows backing away with a whimper as Aunt Liv stepped up next to me. She held a shotgun with a short barrel pointed at the monster.

"Stay away from her!" Her voice was cold and flat as she pulled the trigger again, the gun exploding with a roar of noise that echoed through the night. The glow from the muzzle flash illuminated the giant wolf crouched only a few yards away, cowering from my aunt. Its eyes were full of hate and rage as it turned from us and ran across the yard, through the bushes lining the property, and out of sight.

Liv stared after the monster, something that looked thick and black in the darkness smeared across her left cheek. After a few seconds of searching with no sign of movement, she lowered the shotgun and knelt next to me. She reached out and took my arm, examining it. Only then did I notice that my hoodie was torn and my arm was bleeding. It must have happened when I tripped, but I didn't feel any pain.

"Are you all right?" she asked, looking me over for other injuries.

"What the hell was that?!" I screamed as I snatched my arm back from Liv. My voice sounded hysterical even to me, but I couldn't care less. A wild animal had attacked me! "How the hell were you able to pull it off of me?! It was huge! Like four hundred pounds huge!" I was shaking uncontrollably, adrenaline still pumping through my system as I got unsteadily to my feet.

"Sarah, I can explain—"

"No! I don't want to hear what you have to say." I clutched my head with my hands. "Y—you've been keeping secrets and lying to me since I got here, and now I've been attacked by some giant wolf in our home? How can you explain that?!"

Liv didn't say anything as she stood, her knees stained with mud, bits of grass, and snow. I could see her thinking hard, trying to say something that I would understand. Lies, it would only be lies.

I held my hands up. "Too late," I said and walked around to the front of the house.

"Where are you going?" Liv asked. She sounded angry, but I didn't turn around.

"The studio!" I shouted over my shoulder as I passed the Charger in the driveway. I could hear police sirens in the distance. Will and Detective Reed would be on their way back. "Maybe Carter will tell me what the hell is going on!"

I could hear Liv's footsteps behind me, but I sprinted down the street in the direction of the light-rail station. It wasn't the brightest idea since there was still ice and snow on the ground, but my sneakers didn't slip on the concrete. I wasn't concerned with how to get on the train. I'd taken to having a small wallet on me at all times with my light-rail card, ID, and some cash. It was a good thing too. I didn't think I'd be able to go back to the house for a while. I glanced over my shoulder to see if Aunt Liv was following me, but she was just standing on the sidewalk near a street-lamp, staring as I ran from her. It could have been a trick of the light, but I thought I caught the glisten of tears on her cheeks.

CHAPTER 23

FORTY-FIVE MINUTES LATER, I stood in front of the glass doors leading into the building that housed Carter's studio. Aunt Liv had not followed after me. I suspected that she had stayed behind to explain the sounds of gunfire to both the police and our neighbors. I wondered what she would tell them. "Sorry, officers, we were attacked by a giant wolf" didn't make any sense, especially now that I'd had some time on the train to calm down. The whole night had been a confusing blur of action, starting with the phone call from Stella, but whatever had attacked our house had nothing to do with that, right? It was just a coincidence.

Suuure. And maybe I'll win the lottery tomorrow and move to a city where serial killers and rabid wolves weren't on the loose.

But if it wasn't a coincidence, what did that mean? Each of the victims had been partially eaten by an animal. Well, I now knew what animal. One that size would be hard to control, so how was the killer doing it? And how had he found our house? Had he been parked on the street watching? I hadn't seen any unfamiliar cars on the street, but I hadn't been looking for one either, so I might have missed it.

The wind blew through my ripped hoodie and made me shiver. I hadn't thought to grab a jacket when I'd left, and my clothes didn't offer me much protection from the cold. There wasn't much I could do to clean up before heading inside. I wanted to talk to Carter about that wolf. He had to know something. Even so, with my entire life falling apart around me, I didn't want to find out that Carter had been keeping secrets from me too.

Using my reflection in the glass, I picked the grass and other debris out of my hair, then mustered my courage and fumbled the key card out of my pocket with fingers numb from the cold. Carter had mentioned he would be working late. I could see the studio lights were on from the street. He was here, and I was finally going to get some answers.

When I got off the elevator and opened the studio door, pop music played over the speakers. Carter was where I'd found him before, standing in front of the large canvas. I spotted his phone on the counter in the kitchen. He had no idea that I had been on my way up.

He turned when the door opened, and his mouth fell into an "Oh!" of surprise upon seeing me.

"Sarah? What are you doing here? Do you need a ride again?" He set down his brushes and wiped his hands off on his apron, then pulled it over his head and set it over the back of a chair. When he looked at me again, he froze, his eyes flicking from my face to my torn clothing. "Are you all right? What happened?"

I felt my eyes begin to water as he approached me, and my heart raced. "A giant *thing* attacked Liv's house," I said, my voice breathy and cracking. "Some sort of animal."

Carter ushered me into the sitting area and helped me

sit on the couch. "Stay here. I'll get the first-aid kit." He rushed to the kitchen and crouched, pulling a large plastic bin from a cabinet. "Are you in pain? I can give you something for that."

"No, it just feels a little sore." It was the truth. My arm didn't hurt, and there wasn't that much blood. The only thing I had to worry about was the wound getting infected from the dirt covering it.

He came back with the bin and a warm washcloth, sat next to me, and started cleaning my arm. "What happened? I thought you were heading home after work today."

He pushed up the sleeve of my hoodie without touching the wound, using the same gentle care that I'd expect in a hospital. I winced as he dabbed hydrogen peroxide on the cut. "What happened?" I repeated. "Oh, not too much," I said, my tone dry. "Liv's house was attacked by a giant wolf."

Carter froze mid-dab, and his eyes flicked up to my face. "A giant wolf?" he asked, his expression neutral. "What do you mean?"

I could feel the anger again as I blinked tears out of my eyes. My chest felt tight, and I tried to speak evenly, but my voice cracked. "I mean, a giant wolf broke down the front door to our house, destroyed the foyer, barreled past Liv, and tried to eat me. Liv was able to *pull* it away from me, even though I'm sure it weighed a couple hundred pounds, then she pulled a shotgun from I don't know where and drove it off." I took a deep breath, trying to calm down. "I know that there is something weird going on that has to do with Tombstone. And now Jen is missing. Do you know why any of this is happening?" At least I didn't shout it this time.

"What? Jen is missing?" he asked, his voice growing

agitated. I nodded, and his Adam's apple bobbed as he swallowed. Carter tried to resume bandaging my wound, but he seemed to lose focus for a minute. Then he shook his head, gave me a half-hearted smile, and repositioned my arm. I wanted to jerk it away from him as I'd done to Aunt Liv, but Carter hadn't lied to me. Yet. I gave him a moment to let him gather his thoughts. I could hear my heart pounding in my ears.

He wrapped the bandage around my arm and secured it, then sat back, eyes searching my face. "I need to make a phone call first, then I'll tell you what you want to know."

I nodded as he got to his feet and walked over to the kitchen, grabbing his phone off the counter. I took my own phone out of my pocket and checked it for messages. Nothing. I thought that was odd. I'd wanted to go somewhere and think, but it was unusual that Aunt Liv hadn't messaged me to make sure I had arrived safely. She would have been finished with the police by now.

While Carter was on the phone, I got up and went to the bathroom. I turned the light on and looked at myself in the mirror. The face that looked back at me was unrecognizable. There were still bits of grass and dead leaves in my hair, grass and dirt stains on my pants and face, and one arm of my hoodie was ripped beyond repair. It was a wonder that no one on the train reported me to security.

I washed my hands and face, then picked the rest of the debris I'd missed earlier out of my hair. My clothes were a mess, and I couldn't do anything about it at the moment, but I cleaned myself as best I could.

When I went back to the main room, Carter had finished his phone call and sat in the armchair across from the couch. He didn't move as I approached, looking to be deep in thought. He only looked up once I sat.

"Do you want something to drink?" he asked.

"No, thanks." I stared into his clear, blue eyes and asked the question that I'd been asking everyone since I'd moved here. "What is happening, Carter?"

He sighed and closed his eyes. "It's a long story, and it may sound unbelievable, but here it goes."

His eyes snapped open, and he sat straighter. "There is a world that you don't know about hidden under the surface of what you know society to be. Think of every fairy tale you've ever heard and understand that these tales came from somewhere, with a basis in reality. The truth is, these stories aren't just to scare children and teach lessons; a lot of them are close to actual accounts of supernatural beings that roam the earth and sometimes prey upon mankind."

I opened my mouth to speak, but Carter held up a hand. "I know what you are going to say. 'That's not real,' or 'those are made up,' but you saw firsthand one of those creatures inside your own home. Or do you think there are still wolves around in North America that weigh half a ton?" He shook his head. "I know it's hard to believe, even if you've seen it with your own eyes, but there are things that can't be explained by science or technology. There are people who can shift into animals like this, and most regular people know nothing about them."

"What are you saying?" I asked, and I could hear the panic in my voice. "That I was attacked by a *werewolf?* That's... that's insane, isn't it?"

Carter adjusted his glasses. "Yes, that's what I'm saying. Sarah, you *were* attacked by a werewolf. A creature of myth and legend that inhabits the world we live in."

I couldn't believe what he was saying. Was this some sort of trick? I looked into Carter's eyes, and deep down, I knew that he was telling me the truth, or what he thought was the truth, but I still couldn't accept it. "No," I said, shaking my head. "There must be some other explanation. There's no way there's some secret world right under the noses of everyone. If others were attacked like I was, it would be all over the news. We aren't that dumb. People would have noticed by now."

He smiled, but it was sad. "Your aunt wanted to keep you out of this life. As cliché as it sounds, you are better off not knowing, but neither of us has the right to make that choice for you. Now it's come crashing down at your door, and there's no way to avoid it.

"But to answer you, people have noticed. It is all over the news. The government has noticed us and is helping in the cover-up. A plane is taken out of the sky by a dragon? It crashed over the ocean, and there were no survivors. Children go missing in a small town that is close to a wendigo lair? They must have drowned swimming in the lake. A supernatural being attacking women and eating them in a big city like Seattle? No, it's some serial killer who is feeding the bodies to animals to cover up his tracks."

"You mean the killer that's been on the loose is a were-wolf?" My breath caught, and my eyes widened. I swallowed hard. "What do you mean by us?" I asked in a small voice.

Before he could answer, there was a knock at the door. I jumped, whipping my head around to stare at it, waiting for the door to be broken in as another giant wolf barreled through it.

Nothing happened, and I started breathing again. Carter placed a hand on my shoulder reassuringly and stood. "It's open!" he called across the room.

"Wait," I said. "Does all of this have anything to do with Jen's disappearance?"

Carter patted my shoulder again and said, "I really don't know, but we will do all we can to find her."

The knob turned, and it opened in a blur as Vaughn rushed inside. "Carter, is she all right?" he asked before he saw me. I stood from where I was seated. "Sarah!" he said, sounding relieved and taking full, determined strides across the room. His eyes fell on my bandaged arm. "Are you hurt?"

"It's just a scratch," I said as Kat followed Vaughn in through the door but hung back from us.

Another person walked in, a man who was unfamiliar to me. He was tall and muscular, with an angular face and jaw, a dark-brown complexion, and amber eyes. He wore a pair of jeans and a white dress shirt with the sleeves rolled up. This man strode into the room as if he owned the place and exuded an air of confidence that was almost palpable.

While Vaughn fussed over me, I glanced at Carter, and my boss seemed to shrink into himself, staring at the floor.

"Carter," the man said. His voice was a deep baritone. "Is this the girl?"

"Marius," Carter said softly. He still wouldn't look into the other man's eyes. "I didn't realize you were coming with them."

The man named Marius's eyes flashed with anger, and he sneered at Carter. "I asked you a question. Is this the girl?" he repeated.

My fists clenched at his tone. This was Carter's studio, not his. How dare he talk to Carter that way? "Hi, *girl* here!" I said with a wave of my uninjured arm, my voice laced with false cheer. "Who the hell are you?"

Carter and Vaughn both winced, and Kat's lips curled in a small smile. Those cold amber eyes tracked over to me, and I felt as if they were trying to suck me in. I held my ground, using my anger to fight the urge to look away from him. A small voice in the back of my head whispered that it would be better to submit to that gaze. I ignored it.

One side of Marius's mouth tugged into a smirk. "Brave," he mused. "Funny, I was told you were timid." Kat stopped smiling and glowered at me. I guess she must have been the one who'd told him that. "My name is Dr. Marius Corvis. You may call me Dr. Corvis."

"Okay, *Dr.* Corvis," I said, throwing as much contempt as I could into his name. "Why are you here?"

"Carter called me," he said, his voice even. If my tone bothered him, it didn't show. "He wants to make sure that you and your aunt are safe and asked for my help."

The thought of that giant black wolf took the edge off my anger. My hands started shaking, so I shoved them into my pockets. "We are safe. It ran off," I said, but even I heard the uncertainty in my voice. I looked into Vaughn's eyes. "Jen's missing," I said.

His breath caught, and he stared back at me, the white showing around his irises. He looked upset, but didn't say anything. Kat let out a long breath, glaring at me like this was somehow my fault. What was wrong with them?

I glanced over at Carter, but he wouldn't meet my eyes. "Why would he call you?" I asked the doctor. "What can you do?"

Marius smiled, and it looked more like something you would see on a shark. "I can help you a great deal, Miss Frost. I am one of the people with enough power in this world to make sure that you are safe from all the things that go bump in the night. I've brought two of my associates with me, and they will be assisting you from here on out."

I glanced at Vaughn and Kat. Vaughn looked at me

earnestly, while Kat looked like she didn't want to be here. Why would she have agreed to help me?

"No offense," I said, "but I was attacked by an enormous wolf. I doubt anyone here would be able to protect me from that unless you brought an entire armory of weapons."

The other man smiled even wider, and it sent shivers down my spine. "Human weapons won't be necessary," he said and looked at Carter. "Has she been filled in?"

Carter nodded but still wouldn't meet his eyes. "Yes, but she doesn't believe it yet." If he was talking about his supposed underworld of supernatural beings, he was right. I didn't believe in all of this crap.

"There's an easy way to fix that," Marius said and turned his gaze on Kat, his eyes calculating. "Show her."

Kat gave Marius a short, stiff nod and pulled her shirt over her head. She wasn't wearing anything underneath.

"Whoa!" I said in a panic, looking from Marius to Carter and to Vaughn in turn. "Kat, what are you doing?!"

She didn't answer me, continuing to kick off her shoes and undress until she was standing in the middle of Carter's studio, completely naked. She shivered and closed her eyes, throwing her head back. There was a moment of silence. No one moved, and I could feel the anticipation in the air as if something were going to happen to the naked woman standing in the middle of the room.

Then, Kat shuddered and doubled over, hair hanging around her face. Her eyes snapped open, and they had changed from the brown I'd seen before to a golden honey-like color. Her muscles seemed to move under her skin of their own accord, and she groaned in pain as the sickening sound of snapping bone echoed through the studio. As much as I wanted to, I was unable to tear my eyes away as her human body reformed itself into that of a four-legged creature. Her long, dark hair retracted as fur grew all over her body. Before I knew it, where one moment a teenage girl had stood, there was now a wolf with golden fur, shaking itself and stretching like a cat waking from a long nap.

The wolf that had attacked my house earlier that night had been as large as a grizzly, but the wolf before me was smaller, lither, and all-around more elegant. I took a few steps back, but I didn't feel the same fear that I'd felt at the house. Sure, my heart was pounding in my chest, and I was shocked, but this wolf was different from the one I'd seen before. She was dangerous in the way that a well-fed lioness was dangerous. There was the feeling that she could kill me if she wanted to, but she had no interest in hurting me for the time being. She lay on the concrete floor and crossed her front paws daintily, turning her head from me and looking at Marius.

When my eyes followed the wolf's, I was surprised to see that Marius was not looking at her but at me. He grinned as my eyes met his. "I'm impressed, Miss Frost. I've seen women older and tougher than you scream, run, or faint when witnessing one of our transformations." He gestured with one hand, and Kat stood, trotting over to me.

"Marius..." Carter began, but the other man held up a hand to silence him.

"Wolves can smell fear, Miss Frost. So try not to act scared," Marius said, amusement in his tone.

The bastard was having fun tormenting me. My anger returned and evaporated any fear I'd been feeling a moment before. I stood my ground as wolf Kat approached and sat in front of me, tilting her head one way and then another as if she were confused and was waiting for me to make the first move. Slowly, I raised my uninjured arm and held out my hand, fist closed. I didn't try to pet her. That seemed stupid even to me. The wolf before me was still the same Kat who hated me, but I let her sniff my hand before I dropped it to my side.

The wolf shuttered, and I watched as she transformed into a woman again, until she sat cross-legged on the hard floor, naked and staring at me, her eyes returning to their natural brown. Kat was frowning. "You smell different," she said.

"What?" I asked, not sure I'd heard her correctly.

"You smell different," she repeated. "Not like a normal person. I never noticed when I was human, but as a wolf, I can smell it, clear as day." She got to her feet and retrieved her clothes, dressing with a haste that signaled that she might not have been comfortable being naked in front of me.

Her words got Marius's attention. "What did it smell like, Katherine?" he asked, his expression serious.

Kat frowned in concentration, furrowing her brow and studying me. "It smells like a sort of subtle perfume. Kind of floral, but also metallic, though that could be the blood." Her eyes flicked to my injured arm and from there moved to the various grass and dirt stains that littered my clothing. She sneered, relishing her next words. "Though, I could be wrong. There are a lot of scents on her right now."

Was she saying that I smelled bad?

"It's magic that you smell," Marius said. "Sorcerers and wizards often have some sort of scent that can be linked back to their magic. You've never met one, so I'm not surprised you can't identify it." He looked me up and down in a way that made me feel even more self-conscious. "Though, this hardly qualifies."

"Wait. Now you're saying there are *wizards*?" I shook

my head to clear it and looked at Carter, exasperated. "You've gotta be kidding me. These things can't be real. What's next? Vampires?"

Carter and Vaughn exchanged a look. Marius and Kat had the same infuriating smug smirk on their faces.

"That's it," I said, throwing my arms into the air. "This is crazy. Vampires and werewolves and everything else. I must have hit my head too hard when getting out of the house. Let me guess. You're all werewolves and can transform like that?" I gestured at Kat and glared at each of them in turn. None of them said anything, and their silence told me that I was correct. "When were you going to tell me?" The question was directed mostly at Vaughn. His omission hurt the most. Carter, I could understand—he was my boss and didn't owe me anything—but I thought Vaughn wanted to be my friend.

He took a step closer to me, his green eyes full of concern. "Sarah—"

"I can't," I said, waving a hand to keep Vaughn back. It wasn't fear that I was feeling, at least, not exactly. The idea of him being able to turn into a wolf should have been scary, but after seeing Kat transform, the idea of Vaughn being able to do the same was more disconcerting than frightful. She had seemed more like a large, dangerous dog than a wild animal trying to kill me. I had no fear of Vaughn harming me.

But it was all too much to take in. So much had happened tonight. It was overwhelming to have my world turned so thoroughly upside down. "I need some time. Let me think about this." I turned from the four of them and fled down the hall that led to the spare rooms, closing the door with more force than necessary.

CHAPTER 24

WHEN I OPENED MY EYES, I was still lying on the futon that Carter kept in the spare room. I'd come in here to think about what Carter had told me and about Marius showing up, and about how Kat had turned into a wolf right in front of me. I must have fallen asleep. For one wild moment, I hoped with my entire being that it had been a bad dream and I was just waking up after a long night working with Carter. But when I moved, my arm twinged in pain from my injury, and the enormous wolf that attacked me at Liv's house came flooding back into my memories.

Had that thing really been a werewolf? Some sort of mythological beast that turned into a monster at the full moon? If so, that meant that it could turn back into a person and still be out there, unnoticed by the masses and waiting for me to return.

Before I was able to go down *that* rabbit hole, there was a knock at the door.

I debated telling whoever it was to go away, but that seemed counterproductive. After all, the killer was still out there, and he still had Jen. I was so angry at Carter, Vaughn, and Aunt Liv. As much as I wanted to scream and shout at them, I had to help Jen. So instead of taking out my fear and anger on whoever was at the door, I sat up and said, "Come in."

The door creaked open, revealing Vaughn, with his shoulder-length black hair and green eyes. He looked pale, even paler than usual, and kept his eyes on the ground. "Are you okay? You've been in here a while."

"Well, it's been a long night," I said waspishly. "What do you want?"

"I'm just here to talk, Sarah. I'm sure you have a lot of questions about... about everything." He tried to smile, but it was forced.

He was right. I did have a lot of questions. For all of this, I was owed some damn answers. "Fine," I said and crossed my arms.

Vaughn slid into the room and shut the door behind him, then sat next to me on the futon. "Everyone is worried about you, especially Carter."

I didn't trust myself to say anything to that. Of course, Carter had no obligation to tell me anything before now, but it still hurt that I'd been left in the dark about something so big. Liv had said before that she'd promised my mother she would keep me 'out of it.' Well, this must have been what she'd been talking about.

"How long has this been going on? I mean, how long have you been a ...wolf? Is that the right thing to call it? A werewolf?"

"You can call us werewolves, or shifters, or wolves. It doesn't matter. Though, I prefer wolf. We're classified as shifters, but it can help to be specific sometimes."

I blinked at him. "Are you saying there are other types of *werebeasts*?"

He chuckled. "There are. Ashley—Carter's receptionist —is a weretiger, but she's a rare case. Around here, it's mostly wolves."

"What—" I stopped mid-sentence. "No, that's not important right now. When were you going to tell me?"

It was Vaughn's turn to blink. "Tell you what?"

"Really?" I asked, my tone flat. When he didn't respond, I flung my arms out, maybe a bit more dramatically than necessary. "About all this craziness! You haven't even answered my original question."

He sighed. "It's not like I go around telling people about it. No one else knows, besides other wolves, I mean. You're the only normal who knows. Normal as in normal human," he said before I could ask the question. "Well, you and my family."

It made sense that something like that would be very personal. You don't see people turning into supernatural beings every day. "You don't have to tell me if you don't want to."

"It's okay, but in return, you have to go out and talk to Marius. He still needs to straighten a few things out."

I made a face and scrunched my nose. "Like what?" He flashed me a "please just do it" look, so I nodded. "Fine."

He offered a tired smile, then stared forward, getting a far-off look in his eyes. "I've been like this for a while. About eight years.

"When I was eleven, my father took my mother, my little sister, Vanessa, and me on a camping trip in the Olympic National Forest, which is across the Sound. I was always a sickly kid, so he thought the fresh air would do me some good. We were supposed to be there a week, and I was excited to go since I wasn't allowed to leave the house very often due to my condition. The first few days were great—

we had fun spending time together, and my dad tried to teach me how to fish, but I was terrible at it, of course."

He smiled at the memories, but it was somehow sad. "It was the best and worst week of my life. Around dusk on the fifth day, I went down to the river we were camping by to play in the water and try to fish. My dad was cooking dinner for us, and my mom was taking a nap with my sister, so I went by myself. It wasn't the smartest thing to do, but I didn't know any better. I was by the lake for about ten minutes when I noticed something moving through the trees, coming toward me. It was getting dark, so it was hard to see what it was, but it looked big. I'd never seen a bear before, so as stupid as it was, I stayed where I was standing and tried to get a look at what I thought was a black bear." The sad smile faded from his face, and his expression was flat. "It wasn't a black bear. It was an enormous wolf that was stalking me. I didn't even have time to scream before it attacked."

I covered my mouth with a hand. What a terrible thing to happen to a child.

"My dad had been coming to get me when I was attacked," he continued. "He happened to have his shotgun with him." He glanced over at me. "Normal bullets don't do any permanent damage to us shifters, but it hurts like hell, and it scared away the one that attacked me. My parents rushed me to the hospital, but my injuries were too severe. The doctors weren't sure I'd make it through the night."

"What happened?" I asked, transfixed.

"When I woke up the next day, I was full of energy and healing well. I felt better than I ever had in my entire life. Shifters are healthier than humans, and we don't get sick. After that day, all my medical conditions went away. It seemed like a miracle at the time."

"But it wasn't," I said.

"No," he said, and, this time, his smile was bitter. "It wasn't. The next full moon came three weeks after the camping trip. We don't have to change during the full moon like in the stories, but our emotions are tied to whatever magic controls the change. At the full moon, those emotions are closest to the surface. New wolves almost always change their first moon cycle, and I was no different. It's much longer and more painful the first few times than what you saw Kat do. My sister woke up in the middle of the night to see her brother transforming into a monster. Vanessa screamed, and my parents ran into our bedroom, where they found a wolf cub snarling in the corner."

"They pulled Vanessa out and locked me in there. Vanessa kept telling them that the wolf was actually her brother, but they didn't believe her. I don't remember what happened, but I found out later that they rushed her to the hospital and called animal control for the wolf in their house." Vaughn looked at me, and he had tears in his eyes. "You see, she'd tried to calm me down, and I'd bitten her." He turned away and leaned forward, head in his hands, face hidden behind a curtain of black hair. "I could have killed her, or... or *turned* her."

He paused, but I didn't say anything. What could I say to him that would make it better? Vaughn had been a child and couldn't control himself, but I was sure he'd been told that a thousand times. If he didn't believe it, what good would it do to tell him again?

It took him a moment to regain his composure. "By the time animal control arrived, they only found me, naked and passed out on the floor of a destroyed room. They assumed that the wolf escaped out of the window and that I'd been hiding under the bed. The next day, Marius was at our door."

I felt my eyebrows climb my forehead. "That's convenient."

He laughed. "Yeah, he has a few people in animal control who will let him know if they hear anything weird, and finding a wolf in a child's bedroom definitely qualifies. They contacted him as soon as they got the call."

"After that, you went to live with Marius? Your parents just gave you up?" I winced. I hadn't meant my words to sound so accusatory. Losing a parent had been devastating to me, and my mom wasn't the same after Dad died. I'd felt abandoned, but that would be nothing compared to my parents *giving* me away.

"You have to understand," he said defensively, "they weren't equipped to deal with a little boy who turned into a wolf once a month. They had Vanessa to worry about and keep safe, and having me living with them would complicate things. Some parents who don't know how to deal with their wolf kids lock them in cages near the full moon, not knowing they can shift at other times. How do you think that affects them? To be viewed as a monster that needs to be locked in a cage?"

I thought about it, then gave him a grudging nod. That would be even more traumatizing. "Okay, I can see how that would be bad," I admitted.

Vaughn stood and stretched. "That's my story. Are you ready to go back out there? I know it sucks to have to keep going after everything you've been through, but it's not a good idea to keep Marius waiting."

I sighed. This night was never going to end, but I'd agreed to do this. "Yeah, I guess." Vaughn reached out a hand to me, and I took it, letting him pull me to my feet.

When we re-entered the studio's main room, Marius and Carter were in the far corner, speaking too low for me to hear them. Kat was nowhere to be seen, and I was a little relieved about that. Kat and I didn't like each other much, and tonight, I'd seen her naked *and* watched her transform into a wolf. I wasn't quite ready for the level of awkwardness that that was sure to bring.

We paused in the kitchen, waiting for the others to finish their conversation. My eyes lingered on Marius. "Tell me about Marius," I said. "He seems to be in charge. I've read the teen paranormal romance books. Is he some sort of alpha?"

Vaughn's grin at my quip looked strained. "Yes. Marius is the leader of the Seattle area pack," he said under his breath. He stared at Marius, and I saw a mixture of respect and fear in his eyes. "Just like wild wolves, werewolves live in packs. It's kind of like living in an extended-family capacity. We all report to him every few days or so, and we all help each other out. If he needs us for any task, we are there, and in turn, he makes sure that we all have a roof over our heads and food to eat." Vaughn paused, then added, "As long as we do what he says, everything is fine."

The way he said it made it sound like he had gone against Marius a few times. Things were starting to fall in place, if that was possible with this fantastical story. Marius was Vaughn's guardian, but he'd kicked him out, which was why Vaughn had been homeless. I remembered the argument Vaughn and Kat had been having on the rooftop of Carter's studio. "What happens if you don't do what he says? He already discarded you once," I asked, watching Marius out of the corner of my eye. By the way he was smirking, I had a feeling he could hear us.

"Discipline," he said and looked away. "It's best to be

careful around him. He isn't a kind man. If he's offering you help, it's because he wants something from you or he thinks that you can repay the favor later."

"What could helping me do for him? I can't pay him or anything."

"I don't think it's you that he wants something from."

"Aunt Liv," I said. This had to do with my aunt's secrets. "What does he want from her?"

Vaughn glanced over at Carter. He and Marius were still having a quiet conversation. Even I could tell from here that Marius was leading the discussion. "That's a deep question. There's a lot of backstory that you're missing."

I narrowed my eyes. "Then fill me in. I'm tired of being left in the dark, Vaughn."

"Okay, okay." He held his hands up in surrender. "It can't really be helped at this point, but there's a lot to explain." He paused to think before starting again. "Olivia Frost—your aunt—works for an organization called the Syndicate of Nine. It's kind of like a United Nations of sorts. There are eight supernatural representatives plus one mortal, hence the 'nine.' They govern their respective factions and make policies regarding how their people interact with humans. They're responsible for keeping both their people and the people who live around them safe."

"Who is the *normal* person in the Syndicate? Is it some sort of government employee?" It would make sense if the government was involved in this. Hadn't Carter said they were before?

Vaughn nodded. "Yes, he works for the US government. That was part of the treaty that the government signed with the Syndicate when it was formed forty years ago or so. Before that, it was more like the old stories, humans against fairy-tale creatures. Mankind had to use whatever weapons they could to protect themselves, and supernaturals had to veil themselves even more than they do now. The Nine is headquartered in Seattle, but they have reach across the globe and work with other countries as well. As a result of the treaty, we can integrate into society and live normal lives, within limits."

"Limits," I mused. "Like not attacking people?"

He smiled. "Something like that. It's not so bad with wolves, but with other creatures, especially ones that feed on humans, it can get a little complicated."

One mythological creature that fed on humans in stories came to mind. "Vampires? Are those really, uh, real?"

"Yes," he said, sighing. "Though they are not like all the movies you're seen." He smirked. "And they don't sparkle."

I punched his arm without any force, and he laughed. "How does that work if they can't feed on humans? Do they raid the local blood banks?"

"That's actually not that far off of what they do." He looked like he was about to say more, but I cut him off.

"Aunt Liv," I said. "I need to know about Aunt Liv, not vampires or whatever else is out there. Why would that wolf have attacked the house?" I took a deep breath and asked the question I'd been dreading. "Does this tie into Jen's kidnapping?"

Vaughn's face looked stricken, and he swallowed hard. He cared for Jen. "As... As far as your aunt goes, she's sort of one of the Syndicate's enforcers. She handles the day-to-day minutia of supporting the supernatural community and helps settle disputes of territories between factions, investigates rumors of unauthorized supernatural activity, delivers notices, stuff like that, and if one of us commits a major crime, she hunts us."

"*What?*" I asked very quietly.

Vaughn swallowed hard. "If one of us reverts to killing humans, she is one of the people who will hunt us down and take us out. She's not the only one, but she's one of the best." He looked into my eyes, and I could see the fear there. I remembered our rooftop conversation from a few weeks ago. *Is your aunt nice? I've heard a lot about her, so I was just wondering...*

If what Vaughn was saying was true, my aunt was the supernatural world's boogeyman. "Was the wolf after me or Aunt Liv?"

"That's the million-dollar question." Marius's deep voice came from right next to me, making me jump. I whipped around, and he was standing a few feet from me, staring with those amber eyes. Carter was standing a little way away from us. When had they finished talking? "Who was the wolf more focused on?" he asked.

I felt the bottom drop out of my stomach. "*Me*," my voice was barely more than a whisper. "It attacked *me*. It chased *me*." I blinked tears out of my eyes. "Why?"

"You and your friends have been snooping around," he said, his voice harsh. "Did you think no one would notice? If I had to guess, you were the one who was supposed to be taken. When the vampire went to your house to take you, he—or she—found that you were a close relative of the infamous hunter who is an expert at killing its kind. So it went for your friend and sent its fiercest wolf to take care of you. You were lucky that Olivia was home when it arrived."

"N-no. That can't be true. How would they know who we are?" I blinked, absorbing what Marius had said. "The serial killer from the news is a vampire? And how long has my aunt been this 'infamous hunter'?" It seemed hard to believe that Aunt Liv—*my* Aunt Liv—was this person that these people all seemed to fear.

"I am not here to talk about your relationship with the hunter. As for the vampire, it is just a theory." Marius sighed, but his expression didn't change. "But it seems sound. They saw you asking around at Tombstone or got to the person you talked to. There would be no reason to try to kill you otherwise. It would enrage your aunt and force her to take more drastic measures to hunt it. Why would it risk that?" He leaned into me, forcing me to take a step back. He was only a few inches from my face, and I could smell his cologne. "You must have seen something that he's afraid of."

I racked my brain. The killer must have been at Tombstone when we were there and followed me home. How else would he have known where I lived? If he'd watched the house after that, he would have seen Aunt Liv. If she was as scary and infamous as Vaughn made her out to be, then the killer would have known who she was and decided that I was too big a risk to let live. It felt like something was stuck in my throat as I reached the natural conclusion. If the killer couldn't target me himself, he targeted one of the people I was with. Jen, who was his type anyway and didn't have a badass aunt looking after her. Jen, who was already a little reckless and didn't want to leave the investigation to the police, must have gone back to Tombstone.

"It's my fault," I whispered. "It's my fault Jen was taken."

"No—" Vaughn said, but Marius's glare silenced him.

Marius leaned back from me, satisfied with the conclusion I'd come to. "There are consequences to all of our actions."

"It's my fault," I said again, and I started shaking. "H-how can I fix this? There must be some way to find Jen. There has to be." I stared into Marius's eyes, pleading with him. "Tell me what I can do."

"There is nothing you can do, *human*," Marius said the word like a slur. "You've already caused more trouble than you're worth. Go home. Your aunt can protect you and get you somewhere safe."

It felt like a slap in the face. "But I want to help," I said, but my voice sounded meek, even to my ears.

"You *can't*," he said with finality. "You're weak. Only one of us can fight against this threat." Marius turned from me and said to Carter, "I already have some of my wolves looking for the one who attacked their home. It was no one in my pack, of course, but there are few lone wolves in the area, so we should be able to find him without much difficulty." He glanced over at Vaughn. "You and Katherine will take Miss Frost home. Do not leave until she is safely back with her aunt."

Vaughn nodded, and Marius walked briskly to the door, leaving us all standing there as he closed it behind him.

Carter gave it a minute before clearing his throat. He looked tired. "Are you two all right?" he asked Vaughn and me.

I tried to keep my voice steady. "Yeah, I think so." I was so frustrated at the situation, and even more so that there was little I could do to help. My anger was mostly because I knew that Marius was right, that the reason Jen was taken was because the killer couldn't get to me. That made it my fault.

"Marius can be a little... intense," Carter said with a shiver. "He's very good at what he does. Don't take what he says to heart. Running the pack, he has to be hard on those around him."

I glared at Carter, realizing that part of my anger and frustration was directed at him. "He acted like you were dirt beneath his shoes. How could you let him treat you like that?" I asked, the heat creeping back into my voice.

Carter looked away. "Marius runs the pack in Seattle. I used to be in it, but I left. When he mentioned that there weren't many lone wolves in Seattle, he included me in that. I don't *have* to do what he says anymore, but I'm also not under his protection. It works best to let him run the show until he leaves. It's just easier." As if he knew I was going to ask why he left Marius's pack, Carter added, "I don't want to talk about this. Let's focus on getting you home, shall we?"

"I drove here with Kat," Vaughn cut in before I could reply. "We'll take you home."

The thought of doing what Marius had told me to do made me want to throw up, but I didn't see any other options. "Fine," I growled.

It took ten minutes for us to find out where Kat had run off to. She'd walked to a convenience store nearby and bought a few energy drinks and snacks. Vaughn had explained to me that changing into a wolf and back again took a lot of energy. Vaughn and Kat sat in the front of his car while I slid into the back and munched on the sour cream and onion chips Kat had gotten for me. I didn't like the thought of going home and confronting Aunt Liv after the fight we'd had, but I wasn't getting a choice in the matter.

Since this was close to the Industrial District, there wasn't a lot of traffic at this time of night. Sure, there were some people at the restaurants around the studio, but people didn't live in this area, so the streets were pretty quiet.

It had been a difficult night for all of us, so we didn't talk much as Vaughn drove, the only sound being the crunching of chips as I ate. It was awkward as hell.

"So," I began, breaking the silence, "you said I smelled like magic before. Why do I smell like magic?"

Kat glanced at me. She may have gotten me snacks, but that didn't mean we were friends. There was a good chance Marius had ordered her to do it. "Why are you asking *me*?" she asked, sulking. "You're the one who smells of it. Maybe you're a mageling." I must have looked confused because she continued without prompting. "A mageling is an untrained magic-user or someone who is just coming into their powers. It may not be from you, though. Your aunt is said to have magic that makes her as strong as one of us."

I remembered how she pulled back the maw of the giant wolf. "I guess. How else would she be able to be the boogeyman?"

Vaughn stifled a laugh, and Kat frowned at me. Her eyes narrowed. "For someone who just found out their entire world is a sham, you're taking this in stride."

"If I stopped to think about it for any length of time, I'd be huddled in a corner crying and no good to anyone." I sighed. "There'll be time to have a breakdown later. Right now, I need to try to remember what I saw at Tombstone that makes me so interesting to the killer."

"Do you think you saw something?" Vaughn asked, his eyes focused on the road. "I was with you the entire time, and I didn't see anything out of the ordinary."

"You were busy having a glaring match with Santo," I retorted. "Besides, you *weren't* with me the entire time. You went to the bar twice to get drinks." I leaned back into the seat and thought. There was nothing out of the ordinary that I'd noticed, though it was hard to say what had been ordinary there. I growled in frustration. "If there was some detail at the club that the killer thought I saw, I didn't pick it out from the background. I have no idea what it could be."

Vaughn and Kat glanced at each other, and there was the impression that they were having a silent conversation.

"What?" I asked, exasperated. "That is so unfair."

That brought a chuckle from Vaughn. "Oh, I just thought we could go back to Tombstone and figure out what the killer thinks you saw. With us there, it wouldn't be so dangerous."

"And *I* think that is a monumentally stupid idea, and we are *not* doing that." Kat scowled. "I don't want to cross Marius or the hunter—your aunt. It wouldn't end well for us."

"Going to Tombstone is what Jen wanted to do, and look what happened," I said softly, and we all fell silent again.

Vaughn turned onto my street, and I spotted my house. It looked the same as it always had from here. You wouldn't even know that something had happened there tonight. True, the door was gone, but other than that, the house looked normal as we pulled up to the curb. Liv's Charger was in the driveway, but none of the lights were on.

"We'll follow you inside and inform your aunt of Marius's instructions," Kat said as we unbuckled our seat belts.

Vaughn gave me a brief smile as we got out of the car. He probably intended it to be comforting, but he just looked sickly to me. Tonight was wearing on him as well.

As I climbed the stairs to where the front door should have been, I felt my stomach turn. It was pitch black inside, and I fumbled for a light switch, flicking it on. The hallway floor that was once polished oak was now torn to shreds.

Furrows from claws covered every surface that hadn't been completely ripped apart. The front door lay in two pieces, discarded at the bottom of the stairs. I knew that there had been a lot of damage when the wolf attacked the house, but I hadn't realized it had been this much.

The destruction continued all the way to the back door, left wide open, which seemed strange to me. Why wouldn't Aunt Liv have closed it after I'd run off?

I took a tentative step into the house, and then another once I'd found the floor would hold my weight.

It was then that I noticed the door to Liv's part of the house was open and that the apartment within was destroyed.

CHAPTER 25

I STOOD in the middle of the doorway, taking in the ruins of my childhood home. Everything was in tatters. The couch and the paintings on the walls, the kitchen table, and the carpet—all of it was destroyed. The TV lay in a broken heap next to the stand, looking as if a large object had crashed into it. There was a moment of silence from behind me, then Vaughn and Kat flowed around me like water around a rock. They moved like shadows through the apartment, Vaughn going to check the kitchen as Kat went down the hall to the bedrooms.

The wolf that had attacked earlier had only been in the hallway before it chased me out the back door. It had never gone into the living area downstairs or any of the other rooms, which meant that something else had been in here since I'd been gone. I willed my legs to move and stepped over to the staircase, looking up. The damaged door was blocking it, but the stairs looked to be intact and undamaged. Whatever had happened had been confined to the downstairs.

I felt numb. As if the events that had already happened

this night hadn't been enough, now my home had been ransacked and my aunt was nowhere to be found. Was she hurt? Could she even still be here? I took a step further into the hallway but felt my constitution waver. What if Liv had been killed?

"No one's here!" Kat called from one of the bedrooms. "There is some blood, but not enough to come from a serious injury."

Relief washed over me, and I let out a deep breath. Maybe Liv was okay.

Kat came back down the hall as Vaughn came out of the kitchen. "There's no one here," Kat said again.

"She should be here," I whispered.

"Could she have gone to look for you?" Vaughn asked.

I shook my head. "No. I'd told her I was going to the studio. She knew where I was. If she'd left to look for me, why would the house be wrecked? And why would her car still be in the driveway? What could have happened here?"

Vaughn was quiet as Kat walked down the hall and toward us. "It had to be some sort of fight," she said. "Your aunt's scent is on everything, so I can tell that the blood isn't hers." Kat motioned for me to follow her. "You need to see this."

I stepped forward automatically, not knowing what I was doing. I was shocked at the destruction, but not as much as I was when Kat showed me Liv's room.

Aunt Liv had moved into the master bedroom once my grandparents had left. I'd been in it a few times since I'd moved in, but I didn't hang out in here often. It had been stylish and modern-looking, with a king-sized bed as its centerpiece. The bedroom that I was standing in now had been given the same treatment as the rest of the first floor. The dresser looked like it had been hit by a car and pieces of it lay all over, along with its contents. The shattered mirror lay on its side with pieces of glass flung as far as the bed, which had been thrown into a corner, the frame broken and the mattress ripped.

The room's newest feature drew my attention. Part of the far wall had been blown outward, and cold air was blowing in from outside. The hole was jagged, with bits of drywall and siding hanging on by thin pieces of scrap. One corner was stained a dark red. That was the part that Kat was examining.

I sank to my knees, glass crunching beneath me. "What happened...?" I trailed off. There weren't any gouge marks in here like in the hallway, but the wolves could turn back into people after all.

Kat wrinkled her nose and repeated her earlier words. "The blood isn't hers, but I do smell that there were two other people here. So it must be one of theirs." She inhaled, nostrils flaring. "The room is also full of that thing I scented on you earlier." She meant magic. "But it's different. I think it's tied to the hunter's scent."

"What does that mean? Is my aunt a wizard?" My voice sounded steady as I spoke, which surprised me. I was feeling anything but calm.

"Something like that," Kat said, her voice serious. She turned toward me. She was holding her phone in her hand and frowning at it. "We should see if Vaughn found anything."

We went to find him in the kitchen. He hadn't found anything to help us. "I smell gunpowder."

"Liv used two guns tonight. Some sort of short-barreled shotgun and a handgun. It was the first time I'd seen her ever use a gun." My voice sounded hollow. *Focus, Sarah.*

Losing control won't get you anywhere. "What do we do now?"

"We need to get back to Marius and let him know what happened," Kat said. "I already tried calling him, but his phone is off. He must be out looking for the rogue wolf." She looked at me. "You should stay here until we sort this out."

"We can't leave her here," Vaughn argued. "Marius made it our responsibility to bring her to her aunt. Well, Olivia isn't here, so we have to keep her safe until we can find her."

A sudden look of rage crossed Kat's face. "You just want to spend more time with her!" she spat. "Marius agrees that we should be together. Not you and this!" She gestured at me. Did I not even merit a name?

It was Vaughn's turn to get angry. "She's my friend, Kat. Like you. Like Jen." I saw the heat die from Kat's face at the mention of Jen's name. "Besides," Vaughn continued, "we are *not* an item, and we *never* will be. So stop trying to control who I talk to and befriend. You're only pushing me further away."

Ouch. Even though I already knew how they both felt, thanks to being filled in by Jen, it still hurt to hear Kat being rejected like that. She stood in shocked silence.

I wanted to slap both of them. We didn't have time for this. "Hey," I said, trying to get their attention, "we should get out of the wrecked house before whatever did this comes back. Or, you know, the police get here. I'm sure one of the neighbors has called them by now. This couldn't have been quiet."

Kat glared at me, and I could see the anger and hurt in her eyes. "Fine," she hissed and stomped out of the living room and into the hall.

Vaughn watched her go, and I winced at the sound of my family's shattered lives crunching beneath her feet. Vaughn looked just as hurt as she did. It must have really hurt him to do that to her. There were a few awkward moments before he said, "I'm sorry, Sarah. I didn't mean for you to get dragged into that."

"It's not your fault," I said.

"No... but that doesn't mean I'm not partially responsible for how she's treating you." He let out a long sigh as if he'd aged ten years. "I should have been more firm with her before now. Kat is used to getting whatever she wants, so it's tough to say no to her since Marius will do whatever she asks of him anyway, but she's like a sister to me. I love her like family, but I don't feel the same way that she does."

I put a hand on Vaughn's shoulder. "Vaughn, you don't have to explain yourself to me. I'm not adept at navigating relationship waters myself." I bit my bottom lip, considering if I should say more. To hell with it. Vaughn had confided in me earlier; I could return the favor. "I know a little about not being able to stick up for yourself in an unbalanced relationship. I moved here because my ex tried to kidnap me."

Vaughn blinked. "*What?*"

It was hard not to smile. Compared to everything that had happened tonight, all the events with Brian felt insignificant in the grand scheme of things. It was almost funny to me that only a few weeks ago, I'd been dreading talking to anyone about it. It's amazing how a life-or-death situation can put things in perspective. "Tell you what. If we get through tonight, I'll tell you all about it."

Kat was waiting for us outside by Vaughn's car. She leaned against it with her arms crossed over her chest, looking like a pouting teenager, which she was. She was very serious for being the same age as me. When we approached, she threw me a sullen look and got in without a word.

Great. One of my protectors wanted to murder me.

We got into the car, and Vaughn pulled away from the house. "Don't worry too much, Sarah. Your aunt might have gotten away. She could even be waiting for us at the studio."

While he talked, I pulled out my cell phone and tried calling Aunt Liv. It went straight to voicemail. "Dammit," I muttered. I sent her a text asking where she was. Maybe Vaughn was right, and she would be waiting for us. But if that was the case, why was her phone off? Had it been destroyed in the fight?

Out of the corner of my eye, I saw a dark shape move. I turned to look out the window just in time to see a large truck with its headlights off coming straight at us. "Vaughn!" I yelled as the truck collided with us. I grabbed onto the back of Vaughn's seat as the truck backed up then slammed into the car again, making it spin. Vaughn tried to regain control, but there was another hard hit on the trunk, and the deafening sound of cracking and crunching metal as the driver's side smashed into a streetlamp, sending safety glass flying.

Vaughn swore as his car stalled, and he tried desperately to start it again. The truck that had hit us backed up to ram us again. I peered at the windshield, but it was too dark to see who was behind the wheel. The engine of Vaughn's car turned over, and we jerked forward just as the truck rushed at us, missing by less than a foot.

"What the hell?!" I looked out the cracked rear window to see the truck that had tried to kill us crumpled around the lamppost. The driver-side door opened, and a man got out, dressed in sweatpants and a T-shirt. He dashed out of the light and disappeared into the darkness of the night.

"He must have followed us from the house," Kat said as she pulled her shirt over her head. "If he's a shifter, he'll be able to catch up with us."

"If we can get to the highway, he won't be able to follow," Vaughn said as we turned onto Tenth Avenue. We were lucky it was so late and that there were no other cars because, with the way Vaughn was swerving, he would have hit anything on the road.

I was still turned around in my seat, watching out the rear window, when I saw movement in the shadows behind us. "I don't think we have that long."

Vaughn swore again and pressed on the gas, making the car accelerate and pushing me back into the seat. The figure moving on the street grew distant, and Vaughn turned another corner.

"We can't keep this pace," Kat said. "We're bound to hit some traffic soon."

"I know," Vaughn growled. "Let me get to First Avenue, and we'll ditch the car. It's pretty much a straight shot to the studio from there."

We drove in a tense silence as I kept watch out the back. Kat rolled down her window and stuck her head out, her long, brown hair flowing in the wind. She watched the road behind us as well. It seemed dangerous to me, but I didn't question it. For all I knew, she could withstand being struck by something outside of a moving car much better than a normal person.

After a few minutes with no sign of our pursuer, Vaughn slowed and pulled into an apartment building's parking lot. It was packed with vehicles, but he found a spot and squeezed in. "He'll have a tough time finding the car in here. There will be too many scents around from everyone else living here."

His explanation must have been for my benefit, as Kat didn't react to what he'd said.

"What do we do now?" I could hear the panic in my voice.

"*You* stay by the car," Kat growled. "You can hide while we take care of him."

"And be a sitting duck?" I asked, my voice rising more and more into hysteria. "No way!"

"Sarah's right; we can't leave her here," Vaughn said to Kat, then to me, "I turn into a white wolf. There could be other things besides that black wolf out there, so remember what we look like. Stay close to us, but don't get in the way. We're still a few miles from the studio, but if we hurry, there's a chance we can stay ahead of whatever it is." He had to shove his shoulder into the door to get it to open. It popped open with the crack of snapping metal.

Kat scoffed and opened her own door. "There's no way *she* will be able to stay ahead of whoever it is."

"Stop it, Kat. This is bigger than our relationship issues," Vaughn said as he got out of the car and pulled his shirt off. "Marius wanted us to protect her, so that is what we are doing."

I shouldn't have felt embarrassed that they were undressing in front of me; I'd seen them both naked, after all, but I still did. "I can keep up," I said, averting my eyes and slipping out of the back seat. Fortunately, my door was undamaged and I was able to get out.

I gave it to a count of twenty and looked up to see that where Kat and Vaughn had just been standing were two wolves, one the golden color Kat turned into earlier and the other with snowy white fur. It was odd, them standing there in the parking lot, surrounded by cars and asphalt. They looked like they belonged on the set of some fantasy movie filmed in Europe or New Zealand, not in the concrete jungle that was modern civilization. Though, to be fair, the natural forests surrounding Seattle did have that same otherworldly feel to them.

What had I gotten myself into?

While I pondered that thought, the white wolf nudged me forward, jarring me back into the present. Right, someone was trying to kill us. I would question my life choices later.

I followed the wolves out of the parking lot and onto the street. They trotted briskly ahead of me as I ran to keep up. They matched my pace, and we made our way down First Avenue. If anyone saw us, maybe they would think I was walking my dogs. My huge two-hundred-plus-pound dogs.

We'd been running for a few minutes when Kat suddenly looked over her shoulder and let out a low growl. The white wolf pinned his ears back and slowed so that he was trotting next to me. Kat looked around and made a sharp left into the parking lot of a construction site with a chain-link fence around the work area. Caution signs were posted all around, and the advertisements of various companies blocked the view of the area from the outside.

There were always new buildings under construction in this part of town. Seattle was over one hundred and fifty years old, so older buildings got torn down to make room for new high-rises. In a place as crowded as greater Seattle, real estate moguls knew that rental housing was the quickest way to make a return on their investment. Thus, new construction was on just about every street downtown.

Vaughn nudged me with his side, and I instinctively wrapped my fingers into his fur and let him pull me forward. The three of us slipped through a crack in the gate and dashed into the construction site. I hopped over tools and metal building materials, the golden wolf in front of me leading the way and the white wolf at my side keeping me steady.

There was the scraping of metal on concrete behind us, and I glanced over my shoulder to see the fence shudder as it was moved aside, letting in something much bigger than the other two wolves. The memory of the giant black wolf spurred me forward. I ran as hard as I could through the construction site, Vaughn still by my side. My heart pounded like it was going to burst out of my chest. All that I could see were piles of materials and scaffolding, no real place to hide. Kat whipped around, circling behind us, and Vaughn moved me forward and out of the way. A snarl of challenge rose from the golden wolf's chest, and another much deeper growl from the darkness answered it.

At the sound, Vaughn stopped pacing and looked around, lips peeled back from his fangs as he tried to pinpoint whatever was following us. Kat sniffed the air and stared intently at the chain-link fence that separated us from the street beyond. We were standing in the middle of the metal skeleton that would become the first floor of a new high-rise apartment building. Construction had been paused because of the weather, with fresh snow dusting the site. I could hear my heart pounding in my chest as I waited for something to happen.

The shadows moved to my left, and in a blur of motion, the black-furred wolf hurled itself at me from the darkness, fangs and claws flashing.

The white wolf threw his shoulder into me and sent me sprawling, moving me out of the other wolf's trajectory. It soared over where I'd been. Vaughn darted out of the way in a flash and snapped at the attacker's legs, but missed.

There was a blur of golden fur, and Kat dashed at the

wolf, slamming her smaller body into one of its legs as it landed and throwing the much larger creature off balance. She fled before it could turn and snap its maw at her, and Vaughn rushed in from the other side. When it turned to him, Vaughn retreated and Kat came in, ripping at its unguarded side with her fangs.

The giant wolf leapt at Kat, but the smaller wolf dodged him, dancing out of its reach and allowing Vaughn to come in at it from the other side again. They worked together as a team, and it was enraging the other wolf.

They fought like that for what felt like hours, but must have only been minutes. While their hits connected with the giant wolf, they couldn't do much damage. It had more mass than the two of them, and they barely kept themselves from being impaled by those fangs. The black wolf was getting faster as its rage grew, and even I could see that the misses were getting closer. Eventually, it would get one of them.

Vaughn darted in, going for the wolf's neck, but the larger wolf was waiting for him. This time, it let the golden wolf land a strike on its side, ignoring her and keeping its attention on Vaughn, who had to retreat, dashing to the side to avoid the beast's teeth.

He'd been too close. As Vaughn leapt back, the wolf caught his right back leg in its jaws and slammed him to the ground. Kat let out a snarl of rage and pounced onto the wolf's back, using her claws and fangs to tear into it.

Blood spattered the ground, and the wolf yelped in pain, letting go of Vaughn and thrashing around to get Kat off of its back, trying to catch her as she fell.

Kat had thought ahead. She used the momentum of its first shake to leap off the beast, propelling her forward. She skidded to a stop in the gravel about ten feet away, growling as she flipped around to face it. They circled each other, snapping their jaws.

While Kat held the black wolf's attention, Vaughn limped away, trying to regain his bearings. The wolf turned as if it would go for Vaughn, making Kat charge it in desperation, but it had been a ploy. The beast whirled around to meet her with lightning speed. It was so much larger than Kat that it already had its maw around her neck by the time she realized her mistake. The golden wolf let out a high-pitched whine followed shortly by a popping sound, and Kat went limp.

With a howl of anguish, Vaughn leapt at the beast, knocking Kat out of its mouth and raking at its eyes with his claws. The giant wolf yelped in pain and snapped those huge teeth down on Vaughn's injured leg, shaking its head and flinging Vaughn around like a ragdoll.

I looked around desperately. There had to be something that I could do to help them. I spotted a metal pipe a few steps away and dashed over to grab it. The metal was freezing cold, to the point that it hurt to touch, but I raised it over my shoulder like a baseball bat. Then, with my own growl of rage and fear, I took a few running steps to where the giant wolf now had the white wolf pinned, and with a rush of strength that made my head spin, I swung the pipe with everything I had at the wolf's ankle.

There was a loud CRACK, and the wolf reared away from Vaughn, howling in agony.

I dropped the pipe and scrambled away from the beast as it whipped around and snapped its jaws at me, missing by mere inches. Now, it focused its attention solely on me as I backed away.

In the time that I'd distracted the wolf, Vaughn had been able to wiggle from beneath it and get out of the range of its claws. Stumbling a little, he retreated further and changed back into a man.

I didn't dare turn and run from the wolf. There was no doubt that it would catch me and rip me to shreds in moments. Regardless, I was now shaking so hard with fear that I wouldn't have been able to get far. If I could keep it focused on me long enough for Vaughn and Kat to recover, we could still have a chance.

The snarl it let out shook me to my core, and I had to dig deep into my gut to find the courage to hold my ground and not flee in terror as it stalked toward me, ignoring the other wolves.

Kat rolled over, grunting, and I felt my heart speed up. I let out a mental sigh of relief. I was sure the black wolf had killed her, but I guessed she was going to be okay. Perhaps she wasn't as injured as I'd thought. A low, rumbling sound brought my attention back to the wolf in front of me. All its muscles tensed to pounce, and I knew I was out of time.

Not seeing another choice, I turned and ran from the wolf and toward Kat. If she was conscious, there was a chance that she was waiting for a good opportunity to attack. Maybe I could distract it long enough for her to do some damage. There was a crashing sound behind me, and I thought for sure that I was done for, but I made it to Kat. She got to her feet, her tail flicking in jerky, agitated motions. She watched me pass, and I risked a look over my shoulder.

The big wolf thrashed around on the ground in front of Vaughn, and he had ahold of the leg that I'd hit with the pipe. It snapped at Vaughn, and he let the limb go, managing to avoid getting his own leg bitten off.

As it tried to take a chunk out of a very human and

naked Vaughn, Kat went back on the offensive. Seeing an opening, the golden-furred wolf bounded forward and raked her front claws down the beast's left side, then brought her fangs down on its tail. Forced to turn back to Kat, it gave Vaughn a chance to grab the pipe that I'd dropped. He raised the pipe like a club, and as Kat jumped away, Vaughn brought the pipe down on the beast's skull with a sickening CRUNCH. The wolf collapsed to the ground.

I could see its chest rising and falling as it breathed. It was still alive, even though Vaughn had all but flattened its skull. He crouched near the beast, still holding the metal pipe, his dark curtain of hair hiding his face. Blood was dripping from where the wolf had caught him.

"Are you all right?" I asked, taking a step forward.

Vaughn held up a hand, and I froze. With a deep breath, he raised the pipe again and hit the beast in the head a second time. The enormous wolf's unconscious body jerked, but other than that, it didn't react. Vaughn let out a long breath and looked over at me, his eyes wide and terrified. "I just needed to make sure he wouldn't wake up for a while."

Kat limped over, nuzzling her face against Vaughn's uninjured leg. Vaughn patted her and smiled, dropping the pipe to the ground again with a loud clank. They backed away from the beast, and Vaughn waved me over.

As I approached them, Kat turned back into a human and sat on the ground. "Ah!" she hissed in pain. "I think my shoulder is dislocated."

Vaughn knelt and took her wrist, then with a gasp of pain from Kat and another popping sound that I never wanted to hear again in my entire life, put her shoulder back in its socket. "Are you going to be able to walk?" he asked her, and it took me a second to realize he meant when she was on four legs.

"Yeah," Kat said as she took several deep breaths, trying to recover. "We should get out of here before he wakes up." She glanced over at the large wolf, then down to her naked form. "It's best if we change back to wolves."

Right, because running around in downtown Seattle with two naked teenagers was sure to draw attention. Or get us arrested.

I nodded and waited while they changed back into wolves. Then we made our way out of the construction site and toward the studio.

CHAPTER 26

BY THE TIME we got back to the studio, I was exhausted, and my arm was aching more than ever. The other wolf had roughed up Vaughn and Kat, but somehow, we were all in one piece. Carter was still there and was so shocked by our entrance that he dropped his phone as he leapt up from the couch and rushed over to us. "What happened?"

"We were attacked on the way back," I said as Kat and Vaughn trotted past me in wolf form. "First by a truck that tried to run us off the road, and then by that wolf I told you about." I looked down at myself and noted that I was even dirtier than before. The cut on my arm had reopened, and the bandage that Carter had placed earlier was soaked through with blood. "Do you think you could bandage my arm again?"

"Of course," he said as he led me over to the couch. The first-aid kit was still where he'd left it. While he was tending to my wound for the second time that night, Vaughn and Kat transformed back into humans.

"Did Aunt Liv come by here? Has she called you at

all?" I bit my bottom lip, instinct telling me I knew the answer already but hoping I was wrong.

"No, I haven't heard from her. Is she not answering her phone?" He cursed when I shook my head. "That's not good," he said, running a hand through his hair, then glanced over at Kat. "What about Marius? Have you been able to get ahold of him or the rest of your pack?"

"No, they're not answering either," Kat said, stretching her arms over her head and shaking out her hair. "Do you have some extra clothes, Carter?"

"Yes, I have a few," he said, motioning for her to follow him. He took her down the hall.

Vaughn sat on the floor next to the couch and pulled the first-aid kit over to him. He started cleaning the wound on his leg.

He was still naked, and, even though I'd seen it before, I still wasn't comfortable with that. I angled myself to where I could just see his head and shoulders over the arm of the couch. "Are you okay?" I asked. "It looked like that wolf took a chunk out of you."

"It hurts a lot," he said with a wince. "But we heal faster than normal humans, so I'll be fine in a few hours."

"Wow, really?"

He grinned at me. "With all the shit that comes with this curse, there are a few benefits too. Healing is one of them." He winced again and looked at me with a sheepish expression. "Do you think you could help me? This isn't as easy as it looks."

I took a deep breath and steeled myself for what I was about to see, then stood to help Vaughn. Trying to keep myself detached and focused on what I was doing, I knelt and helped him clean and bandage his wound. This was the first time I'd played nurse like this, so he instructed me as I spread the ointment over the wound and wrapped it with gauze. Vaughn kept his hands over his private areas for my benefit.

"That should be good," he said as I taped the gauze in place and sat on my heels.

I stole a glance over at him. Vaughn was bruised and dirty, but whole. There were a few minor cuts and scrapes on his hands and arms, but I was surprised by how little damage he'd taken during the fight. He was also muscular, very muscular. I looked away.

"Do you think that wolf will be after us again?" I asked.

Vaughn frowned. "I don't think so, at least not tonight. I hit it as hard as I could and, not to brag, but I'm pretty sure I fractured its skull. Even as a shifter, it wouldn't be able to get up and walk that off. It'll be out for a few days at least. Marius will find it by then."

"What will Marius do?"

He was silent for a moment. "This wolf has been aiding a supernatural serial killer and attacked a hunter and her family in their own home. There is only one option open to Marius. He'll have to execute it."

I felt a chill run down my spine. Marius had seemed unconcerned and arrogant when I'd met him. I knew he was dangerous, but if he could take out that beast by himself, dangerous didn't even begin to scratch the surface.

Carter and Kat came back from the bedrooms, the former carrying a bundle of clothes in his arms. "I've got a change of clothes for each of you. Sarah, you'll have to keep on your jeans, but this sweater should fit you." He tossed me a black knitted sweater and knelt beside me. "That looks pretty good," he said, examining the work I'd done on Vaughn's leg.

"He walked me through it," I said, taking off my ripped

hoodie and pulling on the sweater. Kat was hanging by the kitchen, glowering. At me. She was dressed in a T-shirt and a pair of sweatpants that looked a few sizes too big for her.

We had to get past this ridiculous feud between us, and I was going to put an end to it. I needed her help to find Liv. I clenched my teeth, got to my feet, and walked over to Kat. She eyed me as I stopped in front of her.

"Thank you, Kat," I said with as much sincerity as I could muster. "If it wasn't for you, I'd be dead now. You and Vaughn saved my life, and I'm grateful. I know you don't like me, but I hope that we can be friends someday." I held my hand out to her.

She stared at me, not saying a word. I thought she was going to leave me there looking stupid with my hand held out, but after a moment, her lips curled in a small smile and she took my hand, shaking it. "We'll see," she said, squeezing a little harder than was necessary. Kat and I had our differences, but after tonight, I trusted her with my life. I think she understood that too.

"Sarah," Carter said, getting my attention. "I need to talk to you. Can you come with me for a few minutes?" He walked over to the stairs that led to the roof, and I followed him. Was I in trouble? Should we not have come here?

Once we were outside with the door closed behind us, Carter walked over to the railing, looked out over the city, and motioned for me to join him. The earlier clouds had cleared, and the roof was lightly dusted with snow that glittered in the moonlight. The sweater he'd given me was thick and warm, much warmer than my hoodie had been, so I only felt the cold breeze through the new rips in my jeans. I leaned on the railing and watched him. He gazed at the full moon, a strange look in his eyes, and it struck me that he looked pale and tired. He was all by himself and not part of

Marius's pack. That meant that he didn't have anyone to watch his back or protect his friends. He must have been so worried about Liv and all of us.

"Are you all right?" I asked, unsure of what else to say.

He smiled, but it was strained. "No, not even in the slightest, but I'm not the one you should be worried about."

I looked down at the street. There was no traffic in this part of town. How late was it? One, two in the morning? "Aunt Liv," I whispered.

"Yes," he said, and his voice was rough. He turned to me, and the look in his eyes was so fierce I almost took a step back from him. "There is no way she wouldn't have come to find you after talking to the police. She would have been here hours ago, even if your house was attacked again. Livy would have come to find you."

"What are you saying?" I said, and my voice sounded far away.

"That she can't come and look for you. That someone is keeping her from doing so. From what Katherine told me while we were looking for clothes, it sounds like Liv was taken from the house by force." I saw his pupils contract and could feel the anger emanating from him.

I could feel my legs shaking, even though I wasn't cold. "Why?" Tears filled my eyes, and I fought to keep them there. "First Jen and now Aunt Liv. Why would they take her too?" I was losing everyone I cared about.

"I don't know, but I think we might be able to get to her in time." He closed his eyes for a long moment, and when he opened them again, they looked calmer. "You may have the ability to find Livy. Kat said she smelled magic on you before. What if that was not Livy's magic, but yours."

"I don't understand," I said. "How could it have been my magic? I can't cast spells or anything. I've never mysteriously done something I can't explain. I mean, I've gotten into my fair share of trouble, but most of that was my own fault."

Carter waved a hand. "Magic doesn't work like that." He paused and blinked. "Or it does, depending on who you are."

"What?" Now I was even more confused.

He sighed. "It's hard to explain, but in the interest of expediency, I will tell you that some members of your family have the ability to use magic. Your father did, and so does Livy."

"Dad could use magic?" I asked, incredulous. "Why has no one ever told me?"

He shrugged. "I don't know anything about that, but we don't have time to waste, Sarah. Livy's ability is weak, but you may have inherited some of it from your father. We can use that to find her. I need to know if you've had anything strange happen to you, anything at all. Any more of those dreams like the one you had of your aunt in that building?"

I thought hard about the three dreams where I seemed to inhabit the bodies of different women. One detail stood out to me. Hadn't Grandma and Liv both mentioned the 'Nine' in them?

"I've been having these dreams since I've been living here. Three times, but the 'Nine' was mentioned in two of them." I told Carter about those dreams that I'd had with my grandparents, the woman named Ava, and Aunt Liv.

"Sarah," he said once I'd finished, his face serious, "I don't think these were dreams at all. It sounds to me like your abilities have been manifesting since you moved here. These were visions."

"Visions?"

"I think these events really happened. Livy has a cousin

in London who works for the Syndicate in Europe. You were seeing through the eyes of women in your family who have—or had—magical abilities." He gazed out over the city. "Your aunt told me about some of what she can do. She didn't mention visions, but magic like this is not a precise science. Abilities can manifest differently, depending on the person. I'm not a mage, so I just know general information. The best source would be another magic user, and given the circumstances, someone from the Syndicate will want to speak with you about it once this is all over."

I had to think about that. The dreams had seemed a little off at the time, but I had seen that building Aunt Liv had gone to, and Carter had confirmed that it did exist. If that was the case, were these dreams memories of people in my family? Or could they have been in real-time? How would this help Aunt Liv?

"Listen, Sarah," Carter said, looking at me again. I knew that look. He was making a difficult decision in his head. "I'm going to tell you something that is going to rip your world apart," he said. "But you can't lose yourself in it, not tonight. I wouldn't tell you this under normal circumstances since it wasn't my decision to keep this from you, but I think you can help your aunt if she was taken by the killer. You, Sarah, can save her life. So I need you to focus and fight through the pain. Can you do that?"

I swallowed hard and nodded, gripping the railing tightly. So much had already happened tonight, and I had trouble believing that anything else could surprise me, but Carter's voice sounded serious. No matter what he told me, I would overcome it to help Aunt Liv.

"Your father did not die in a car accident," he said, his voice flat and emotionless. "He was murdered."

My thoughts ground to a halt. Whatever I'd assumed Carter would say, it wasn't that. "He was *what?*"

"David Frost was murdered. Not only that, but his murder was later covered up by the Syndicate so that it looked like a car accident. Shifters and other supernatural beings usually stick to their own kind. When one of us is killed, there aren't many humans we are close to, so there is no need to stage a death as anything other than what it is. But mages and other people like you live with one foot in the human world and one in ours. When those with abilities like that of your family get killed, the Syndicate will present a rational death for the world to see, one that is believable for the mortal authorities. Dave was my friend, so I know what really happened to him." He paused to give me a chance to take in what he'd told me, his brows furrowed in worry.

"Does my mother know?" I asked in a whisper, still in shock at what I was hearing.

His features grew hard. "Yes. She was the one who decided not to tell you. Your grandparents disagreed with it, but you're her daughter, so they respected her wishes and allowed her to take you away from the rest of your family here. The Syndicate paid handsomely for you and your mother's new lives, as they do for the families of those who die working for them."

Hot anger roiled within me. "Mom knew, and she didn't tell me? She knew Dad was *murdered*, and she didn't tell me?!" I shouted, my voice echoing off of the buildings and empty streets. How could she have kept this from me all my life? How could she have *lied* to me?

"Sarah!" he said sharply. "You have to focus. Dave was killed because of his abilities. The same abilities that I think you might possess."

His tone cut through my emotions. I unclenched my fists and took a few deep breaths to calm myself, then nodded for him to continue.

"Your father had a few abilities that he could use. As far as I know, the magic in your family isn't that strong, but it's been honed so that they can get all they can out of it. They use it to enhance their bodies so they can fight a supernatural like me and come out alive. Livy, your grandmother, and their relatives in Europe use it, too, and that's why I think you saw those visions. Somehow, your magic is different from theirs, but you're connected to those people in your family who can use it. In what you thought was a dream, you saw through Livy's eyes because of your power. There was no other way you could have known what she was seeing."

It clicked. "You're saying that I could somehow use that ability to connect with Liv again and see where she is." I looked out over the buildings toward Puget Sound. Slivers of moonlight reflected off the dark seawater. "For Liv, I'm going to set aside the fact that my entire family has been lying to me all my life." The words tasted bitter on my tongue, but I pushed through it. I could rage to my heart's content later. "How do I activate this ability? Is it an incantation? Do I have to sacrifice a goat?"

"That's the part I'm not sure about. Livy channels her magic through the tattoos on her back, but what you can do is different." His brow furrowed, and he chewed on the fingernail of his right thumb as he thought.

Tattoos? I'd never seen a mark on Liv. "What do I need to do?" I asked in desperation. If there was a chance that I could help Liv, there really was no choice. She was family, and I would not allow her to suffer. I wouldn't let what happened to my father happen to her.

"Well, you were asleep when you had these visions, and I think that is the answer. Not with you sleeping," Carter said when he saw the look on my face. "Just being in that frame of mind. I want you to meditate. Clear your mind and focus on your objective. Focus on Livy."

"Do you think that will work?" I asked, and there was doubt in my voice. Thinking those visions were just dreams, I hadn't tried to bring one on.

"I do," he said with much more confidence than I felt. "I've been around a few mages before, and they've told me that focus and will are at the core of all magical ability. A lot of apprentices start off with meditation exercises, so I think we should start there."

I knew nothing about magic, so I would have to take Carter's word for it. "Okay," I said, looking around, not sure what to do.

"Let's go inside. You can use the spare room to meditate while we get in contact with the Syndicate. If we can get some help, it will go a long way toward finding Livy and getting her back."

We went inside. Vaughn had dressed and was passed out on the couch, and Kat was in the kitchen, cooking something with a lot of garlic. She looked at us as the door to the roof closed and pulled some plates out of a cupboard.

"Here," she said, sliding over the two plates as we approached the kitchen. "It's just eggs and garlic toast, but we've been running around all night, and I thought food would be good for us."

"Thanks," I said and sat on one of the kitchen island's stools. With all the excitement of the past few hours, I hadn't even stopped to think about food. I watched Kat as she cleaned the pan she'd used. Her cheeks were pink.

Carter pulled a few sodas from the refrigerator and

passed one to Kat and me. "Good thinking, Katherine," he said with his charming smile back in place. How did he do that so well when I knew how much he must have been hurting? "Any word yet?"

She shook her head. "I still can't get ahold of anyone in the pack. Even my parents aren't answering their phones. Marius must have taken everyone with him."

That made me wonder how many people Marius had at his command. There could have been a dozen or a hundred werewolves running around Seattle for all I knew.

"Your parents are wolves too?" I asked without thinking. Both Kat and Carter looked at me. "Sorry," I mumbled and shoved toast in my mouth to keep it from saying anything else stupid.

"Yes," Kat said curtly to me, then went back to her conversation with Carter. "What should we do? Without the hunter," she said, "we don't stand a chance of warding off the vampires' attacks forever. She'll need to go somewhere she can be protected."

I almost choked on the toast. Was Kat talking about putting me into some sort of witness protection? Maybe it was the exhaustion clouding my thoughts, but I didn't want to move again. I'd just gotten to Seattle.

"I have a plan," Carter said. "We're going to use Sarah's magical ability to find her aunt. Once we know where she is, we can get the Syndicate to back us up in extracting her and taking out the one responsible for all of this."

"Do you think that will work?" Kat asked, eyeing me. I knew she was doubting that I had any ability to help. My first instinct was to stick my tongue out at her, but I was trying to mend our bridge, not burn it down. I continued chewing on my toast with dignity.

"Yes, I do," Carter said to her. He looked at me. "Sarah,

why don't you make yourself comfortable in the spare room so that you can focus? Don't worry about us. I'll make arrangements for some backup. Just find where Livy is, all right? With any luck, we'll be able to get to her in time."

I suddenly wasn't hungry anymore and pushed the plate away from me, the food half-eaten. It was all on me to find Liv so that she could be rescued. If I couldn't do it, there was a good chance that my aunt and my best friend would both be murdered, like my father. No freaking pressure or anything.

Carter put a hand on my shoulder. "It will be okay, Sarah. Clear your mind and focus on Livy. If you can't bring on any visions, we'll figure out another way to find her."

I wasn't sure how we would do that, but I nodded and stood, and tentatively made my way to the spare room. There were no other options; I had to do this. For Aunt Liv.

CHAPTER 27

FOCUS. I told myself as I sat cross-legged on the futon, staring at the blank white wall. I'd shut the door to the spare bedroom, closing off the sounds of talking from the studio beyond. I tried to think about my visions, but what Carter had told me about my father's death kept getting in the way. Through all of this, I was angry that something so important had been kept from me. Dad had passed away eleven years ago. Was my mom ever planning to tell me the truth about what had happened to him? Or was that part of the "I promised your mother that I would keep you out of this" that Liv had told me about?

FOCUS! There would be time for these questions later. Right now, if I didn't want to lose Aunt Liv, too, everything else had to be put aside. I let out a deep breath. I'd never done meditation before, but I had done a yoga class or two with my mom. Using what I remembered, I breathed in and out in deep, even breaths, concentrating on the movement of my chest and muscles.

I brought Aunt Liv's face to the front of my mind. How she smiled when she'd first seen me at the airport and how

I'd felt both excited and upset about my situation. I thought about that first dinner in our home, when I found out she'd signed me up for figure-drawing sessions without asking me, and how she'd waited for me to get home when we'd gone to Tombstone. Tears stung my eyes. She was like my big sister rather than my aunt. I loved her so much that it would tear me apart to lose her. Liv was there for me whenever I needed her, but this time, she needed me. I had to find her before it was too late.

With some difficulty, I reined in my emotions. I tried to picture Liv how she'd looked earlier that night, standing outside with the shotgun in her hands, firing at the black-furred beast in front of me. Even if they had her, she would be out there fighting. She wouldn't give up. I closed my eyes, letting myself drift for a while. There was no way to tell how much time was passing, but the seconds felt like they were crawling by.

The smell of gasoline filled my nose.

It felt like my body was on fire with incandescent rage. I've never felt anger in the magnitude of what I was feeling now. Knowing that it was not my own did little to ease that storm. I tried to focus past the emotions and, after a few moments, was able to feel other things. Everything was pitch black. There was pain in my side and left leg, the pinch of rope binding my arms behind my back and my legs together, and the feeling of the cloth gag that was in my mouth. There was a hard surface under me, and as Aunt Liv rolled over, I realized that I could hear tires crunching on gravel and the sound of an engine. She had to be in a moving vehicle.

The brakes squealed, and the movement stopped, with

the engine turning off a moment later. Footsteps sounded from outside, and, with a click, dim light flooded the area around Liv as the lid of the trunk popped open. A man stood outside, looking at her, silhouetted by the streetlights above him.

I felt the hot rage surge through Liv as her body bucked, trying to move, but she was only able to struggle against her bonds and glare at her captor.

The man smirked. "That rope is made out of mermaid's hair. Not even you could break free of it, Hunter." He reached in and grabbed a fistful of Liv's hair, pulling her head back so that her neck was exposed. He leaned in close, putting his nose on the skin there and inhaling. Her skin crawled as he spoke, and she struggled even harder. "You're lucky I've already eaten tonight, but I've got other plans for you." He pulled back, and I felt a sharp pain in Liv's thigh, the feeling of something piercing skin. The man let go of her hair, a syringe in his other hand. Icy fear replaced the rage inside my aunt. "Get her inside and set up the ritual."

A larger man stepped forward. As they pulled Liv out of the trunk, I caught a glimpse of a gravel parking lot and an industrial-looking area by the water. There was a bridge and big cranes for large shipping containers across the street. The larger man threw my aunt over his shoulder and carried her up a few steps and through a heavy steel door. Liv didn't struggle, and I fought through her drowsiness to take in every detail that I could. Whatever that man had injected her with was beginning to take effect.

The inside of the warehouse was big enough that it was hard to see the ceiling in the dim illumination. Still, from what I could see from Liv's perspective, it housed labyrinth-like rows of storage containers in various colors, like those you see at a shipyard. I noted that Liv's limbs had a tingling sensation, which meant they were about to go numb. The man carrying her went around a few corners, and the world began to drift into darkness as Liv started to lose consciousness.

They came to an area lit by candles, and it took me a minute to figure out what Liv was seeing. A large circle was drawn on the floor in black paint, candles set in intervals around the circle. The larger man placed Liv in the center of the ring, and as she struggled against the poison in her veins to move, he pulled his fist back and brought it down hard on the side of her head.

My eyes snapped open, ears still ringing from the blow that Liv had taken. The pain was gone. All I could feel was the dull ache in my arm from my newly bandaged, clean cut. I jumped to my feet and threw the door of the spare room open. I knew where the killer had taken Aunt Liv.

When I dashed into the studio area, panic-driven and on the verge of a genuine breakdown, there was a person who hadn't been here before. Will, the cop working with my aunt, was sitting at the kitchen island, reading on his phone. He looked up when I entered the room.

"What are you doing here?" I asked with more accusation in my voice than the situation required.

Will smirked. "Carter called me. He thinks that you all need some backup from someone who is used to dealing with monsters. He seems to be under the impression that the four of you are going on some kind of rescue mission." His eyes flicked over to Carter, who was leaning against the wall a few feet from Will. "That's not how this works, Godfrey. None of you are members of the Syndicate, and we don't work with amateurs."

"Marius isn't answering his phone," Carter said, and he showed much more confidence when he spoke to Will than when he spoke to Marius. "The Nine have their people looking for her, but we don't have a lot of time. How long do you think she will last with the enemy?"

They glared at each other, neither one of them backing down.

Vaughn popped his head over the couch. He glanced at Will and Carter, at Kat sitting on the stairs that went to the roof, then back at me. "Did you find anything out, Sarah?"

Everyone's gaze turned back to me, and the panic rose again. "Yes," I said, hugging myself with my arms. "I saw her being taken to a warehouse on the water, right by the West Seattle bridge. I don't know which one it was, but I would recognize it if I saw it. "

"Absolutely not," Will growled. "This isn't a game, Sarah. You're not a wolf or some other supernatural. You're not some sort of vampire hunter. You're a normal person. If you go into this, you will die."

I felt my anger rising at his words. This was *my* aunt. I wasn't going to let something happen to her. "If it wasn't for me, you'd have no idea where to find her. I can help! I was able to see through her eyes and can guide you to where she is. There are a bunch of warehouses on the waterfront that all look similar. I can tell you which one it is, but I'll need to see it for myself to be sure." I knew I sounded like some petulant child, but I didn't care. We didn't have time to waste raiding the wrong warehouse, so I was going, and there was nothing Will could do to stop me.

Will slammed his fist on the counter in anger, and I remembered what Vaughn had said about their emotions being closer to the surface during the full moon. He pulled his arm back, and the granite was cracked where his fist had connected. I heard Carter *tsk* in annoyance as Will stood.

"If you're done destroying my property, we should get going. We don't have time to waste."

Will glared at me, ignoring Carter. The look reminded me of the first time I'd seen him talking to Liv. "I don't think you understand, Miss Frost. You can't stop these people. If they see you, they will kill you. Our mission is to find your aunt, and we don't have time to babysit you."

Carter cleared his throat loudly, and Will let out a groan before turning his head to look at him. "What, Godfrey?"

"Think clearly about this, Will. It will be faster to find Livy if we have Sarah there directing us to the right place." He looked over at Vaughn, who was still peering at us from over the couch. "Vaughn is injured, so he can come along and stay with Sarah and keep her safe. Like it or not, we will need her help to get there in time."

Will rubbed his temples with his fingers. "Fucking civilians," he muttered under his breath. He met my eyes. "You are not my responsibility, you hear me? You do what I say when I say it. If I say run, you run. If I say leave us behind, you better fucking do it. Got it?"

I nodded and stared into his eyes, willing myself not to let him see the fear I was feeling.

He watched me for another moment, then sighed. "I can't believe I'm agreeing to this. Okay." He pulled his keys out of his pocket, turned, and strode to the door, the rest of us following behind him.

"I was able to track down Santo and got him to talk," Will said over his shoulder. "The vampire in question goes by the name of Calem. He moved here a few months ago from Chicago, where there was another string of murders he was never suspected of committing, but they conveniently stopped after he moved."

"Santo wouldn't say anything to us," Vaughn said as we followed Will into the elevator. We exchanged a look. Santo wouldn't have talked to the police willingly.

Will smirked. "Oh, I can be convincing. All *you* need to know is that this vampire may be unstable. Calem hasn't checked in with the local cabal for some time, and they think he's been having some issues adjusting."

"A cabal is a group of vampires," Kat said before I could ask. "It's like a pack of wolves, but you know, vampires."

Will scowled. "The cabal is supposed to keep new vamps in check and prevent something like this from happening."

"Wait," I began as my thoughts started adding up. I eyed Vaughn. "When Santo mentioned the proprietors of Tombstone, he meant vampires?"

Vaughn nodded.

"When he said, 'like us,' he meant werewolves?" I scowled.

The elevator doors opened to the lobby. "Don't be too mad at the kid," Will said as we headed for the front doors. "He's not supposed to tell anyone. Let's just focus on surviving the night. Then you can ask all the questions you want."

The Industrial District wasn't far from the studio. Within minutes of piling into Will's Camry, we were heading down East Marginal Way, following the waterway. Will drove the car slowly down the street. There weren't any people out right now, but we passed a few collections of tents hidden away on the sides of buildings. I couldn't imagine sleeping outside with how cold it was. As we got closer to the bridge, the tents and recreational vehicles that showed signs of being lived in dwindled to none. It seemed weird to me, as the homeless population in Seattle was high, and just about every street had at least a few people living on it.

Will pulled into a parking lot by the pier and parked behind a small building. The lot was empty. Looking around, he said, "It seems like we're in the right place. There is no one on the street here."

"Why is that?" I asked. "There's usually at least one person sleeping in their car."

"It's because the vampire's lair is so close. Missing transients won't go reported for weeks, if at all. The others will know to avoid an area if people keep disappearing off the street. It could mean that more have been killed by the vampire, but it would be impossible to tell how many since most people camping out here aren't registered anywhere. Most of the time, their families don't even know where they are, and some have been homeless for years." He shook his head. "It could also mean that there is more than one vampire, and they are feeding on a lot of people. I can get help from the Syndicate, but..." He trailed off. I knew why. If we waited for backup, Liv would be dead before we could get to her.

"Which building is it?" Will asked with a glance over his shoulder at me.

Vaughn leaned back so that I could peer out the window. I could see part of the street beyond the metal container we'd parked behind, which gave us some cover. I scanned over the buildings until my eyes fell on the large warehouse identical to the one from my vision. A billboard sign was attached to the roof, but it was too faded to make out the words anymore. "There," I said, pointing. "The one with the sign above it."

Will nodded and opened the car door. Everyone followed his lead. "The front doors will be guarded, and there's a chance that they've seen my car. Hopefully, they think it's someone parking here to do their business and leave." He narrowed his eyes, staring at the warehouse. "There should be a loading bay around the back of the building, and there's a good chance that it won't be watched as closely. We should be able to slip in through there." Will glanced at Vaughn and me. "You two stay here, where she will be out of the way."

"No," Vaughn said, staring Will down. "We might need her again, or you could need me to jump in. We'll follow in behind you at a safe distance. I'll protect Sarah."

I doubted I would be able to get to a state of calm where I would get more visions in the warehouse, but I also didn't want to stay in the car, so I kept that piece of information to myself.

Vaughn and Will glared at each other for a few long moments. Carter crossed his arms and frowned but didn't say anything. Kat seemed disinterested.

After a minute, Will sighed. He looked frustrated. "So be it. We don't have time to argue. If she gets killed, it's your fault." He took off his jacket and tossed it in the car, then unbuttoned his shirt.

My breath caught in my throat. In all that was happening, I hadn't stopped to think about why Carter had called Will. He worked with Liv, but he must also be a supernatural. "Are you a wolf too?" I asked, feeling dumb that it took me this long to figure it out.

In response, he smirked at me and tossed his shirt in the car to go with his jacket. Will was very muscular, even more so than Vaughn, and it was even more apparent with his shirt off. I tried not to stare, but no direction was safe to look in since Carter, Kat, and Vaughn had started taking their clothes off as well. My face felt hot as I looked away from the undressing people and up at the moon. It was bright in the sky even though clouds drifted in front of it.

When I looked back at my companions, four wolves stood in their place. There were the white and golden-furred wolves that I knew were Vaughn and Kat, along with two new wolves. One was lithe with red and gold coloring similar to Kat and another larger and gray. The gray one had a scar down the side of his face that was visible even in the moonlight. That must have been Will.

Vaughn padded over to me and sat, staring up at me and tilting his head to one side. I looked at his leg. The wound from earlier was stark against his white fur, but it had already scabbed over and looked days old. By morning, it would probably be gone. Vaughn tilted his head the other way, and I could almost hear him saying, "Are you ready?"

I let out a deep breath and willed my pounding heart to slow. "Let's do this."

CHAPTER 28

I FOLLOWED the wolves around the back of the warehouse, dashing from shadow to shadow and attempting to be as quiet and quick as possible. Vaughn stayed by my side while the other three ran ahead. Just as Will had said, there was a loading area on the far side of the warehouse with four bays. They were all closed, but stairs were leading to a door next to them. There was no telling what was on the other side of it, but as we approached it, Will shifted back into a man and crouched next to the door. He listened for a moment, then crept back down the stairs.

"I didn't hear anything," he whispered. "Sarah, stay back for a moment. I'm going to rip the door down. There could be a trap, but we're going to do it anyway." Will transformed into a wolf again, and I backed away from the stairs, far enough to be out of easy range, or at least I thought it was far enough. Did supernatural strength also mean unnatural speed?

The wolf Will let out a low *huff*, then, in one swift movement, rose onto his hind legs and dragged his front claws down the door. With the ear-splitting sound of scraping and crunching metal, the door tore open under his paws. The wolf jerked back, and the door came with him, ripping free of the hinges that held it in place.

As if on cue, the red-furred Carter dashed up the steps and into the dark warehouse so fast that he was a blur. A second later, Kat followed Carter. Her golden fur was glistening in the moonlight. Will glanced at me, meeting my eyes. I knew that he wanted me to stay outside. I shook my head, and he lowered his head in seeming irritation, then turned and leapt into the darkness after the other wolves.

Vaughn and I followed after them, and I peered into the dark warehouse. From where I stood, it was all dark shadows. I wasn't as ready to run in like the wolves had been. They could protect themselves, but I was powerless against these monsters. Vaughn pressed his shoulder against my leg, and I looked down at him, giving him a strained smile. "Now or never, right?" I stepped forward into the blackness to find my aunt.

I pulled out my phone with shaking hands and turned the flashlight app on. It was nowhere near as bright as an actual flashlight, but it was better than nothing. At least I could see where we were. The light illuminated a small area in front of me, casting everything outside its radius into deep shadow. The white wolf stood out like a ghost in that blackness, and I noticed more about my surroundings than I had in the vision of Aunt Liv. She had been focusing on what the people around her had been doing, and I had been in too much of a panic to find her to have recognized subtle details.

The warehouse was damp, smelling of mildew and rusted metal, with a concrete floor that was dark with water and dirt. The area around me was lined with more large, metal shipping containers, forming corridors in the otherwise pitch-black warehouse. The containers were stacked two high on each side, forming walls almost twenty feet tall. I knew that the wolves and other supernatural beings were in here with me, but it was so quiet that it felt like Vaughn and I were alone.

My shoes scuffed the ground as we started forward, while the white wolf by my side made no sound. I couldn't stop thinking that I was in a horror movie and had an almost uncontrollable urge to turn around and make my way out the door, but I forced myself to press forward instead. Helping Aunt Liv gave me enough courage to overcome my fear.

We turned corner after corner, meeting only the same faded paint and rust-coated walls from before. It occurred to me that these corridors were set up in a way to lure us into an ambush of some sort, but we didn't have any other options. The wolves may have been able to jump and dart around, but there was no way regular old me would be able to scale the walls. Besides, I wasn't sure if I was up to date on my tetanus shot.

The silence was shattered by an echoing snarl from somewhere in front of us. I couldn't tell if it had come from further along the corridor or somewhere over the metal walls, but Vaughn nudged me with his shoulder, and I jogged behind him as he ran ahead.

Banging sounds came from around us, sounding like they were coming either from the other side of the containers—or from inside. My mind treated me to a horrifying image of hands beating the walls from inside the containers, bodies packed together, clawing to get out like some zombie-apocalypse movie scene.

I gasped for breath as we ran, the sounds of clanging metal getting closer. The container above and to the right shuttered as we passed below it. With a deafening crash, the container fell from its perch, knocking the next one over as it fell to the ground. I dashed forward with the white wolf, running as hard as I could. The container missed us by a few feet.

"What the hell?!" I gasped out, clutching at a stitch in my side. My bandaged arm had begun to hurt. The wound had torn open again. Vaughn's head was on a swivel, his eyes darting around, ears flicking back and forth as if he could hear movement around us. All I heard was a ringing in my ears.

I waved my makeshift flashlight around, looking for what might have caused the container to fall, but the phone's weak beam was only able to show the first few feet in front of me in any great detail. Vaughn's lips peeled back from his fangs in a silent snarl as he saw things moving in the dark that I could not. I backed up, staring wide-eyed at phantom shapes around us. If only we could find a light switch.

Vaughn suddenly rammed his shoulder into my side, making me stumble forward as something hit the floor right where I'd been standing. I whirled around, shining my phone's light on the shadowy figure of a man straightening from a crouched position. With a chill, I recognized him from my vision. He was the large man who had carried Liv into the warehouse and then hit her with those giant fists when she'd struggled. The white wolf snarled at him, and the man grinned, showing elongated, sharp canines.

"Well, well, well," he said with a voice like dry leaves scraping over concrete. "I'm surprised you survived. Spike doesn't usually let his prey get away." Spike must have been that primeval black wolf that attacked Vaughn, Kat, and me. "But if you're standing here, I guess old Spikey is done for."

He had a slight accent that I knew well from the east coast, pronouncing the vowels off his upper teeth. It reminded me of films from the 1930s with speakeasies and vintage cars.

"Where is she?" I heard myself whisper.

The vampire's smile grew wider. "The little mouse has got some backbone, hmm?" There was a blur of movement, and Vaughn lunged, teeth flashing and finding purchase in what a second ago had been empty air and now was the big man's forearm. The vampire cursed and wrenched his arm back, but Vaughn held on tight, ripping the flesh from his arm before letting go.

"Fucking wolf!" he growled as he took a step back. The wound was deep, but it didn't bleed.

Vaughn backed away as well, keeping himself between the vampire and me. My back was against one of the containers, and I looked down the next corridor but could only see a few feet into the darkness. One of Vaughn's ears flicked in the direction leading away from the vampire, and I thought I knew what he was trying to communicate. When he made an opening, he wanted me to run.

The vampire laughed like his injured arm was the most hilarious thing in the world. "You won't get to her in time." He looked into my eyes, and I felt a falling sensation in my stomach. "You'll make a good snack for our newest—"

The white wolf gave no warning and leapt at the vampire before he could finish his sentence, teeth and claws bared. Without a second thought, I took off, dashing around the next storage container and running as fast as I could through the corridor and away from the snarling and yelling behind me. My heart was pounding in my ears, and all I could think of was getting to Aunt Liv before the vampire killed her.

As my feet thumped against the wet concrete, I could

hear other sounds that got louder with each step. Shouting, growling, whimpers, and the unmistakable noise of dense objects hitting the metal shipping crates with enough force to cause them to scrape along the floor.

How many men had I seen in my vision? Two or three? Were they all vampires? How many more were there that I hadn't noticed? If they could all move as fast as the last one, I didn't know how we would be able to pull this off. Liv's face flashed in my mind, teeth gritting as she pulled open the jaws of the giant black wolf that the vampire had named Spike. No regular person could have done that. If I could get to Liv and free her, maybe we would have a chance.

I heard the sound of running feet beside and above me, and looked up at the storage containers to my right. There was a shadow moving on top of them, keeping pace with my frantic steps. Was it one of the wolves, or was it an enemy? My heart pounded in my chest as I tried to speed up. I wouldn't be able to keep running for much longer. As fast as I'd seen the last vampire move, I knew there was little hope of outrunning it.

My breath came hard as the stitch in my side flared into real pain, and I slowed, putting one arm on the wall beside me as I tried not to throw up. I cursed myself for not keeping up with cardio, but I'd never been much of a runner. I listened hard, trying to hear the footsteps of whatever was following me, but I didn't hear anything over my breathing. My throat burned, and between that and my side, it was hard to concentrate on what was happening around me. If it was a vampire, it must have caught up. There was no way I would be able to get away from it like this. I was a sitting duck in a den full of monsters.

Out of the corner of my eye, I saw a shadow move, and I stumbled back in panic, tripping over my feet and tumbling to the ground. My phone skidded away from me, and a large paw stepped on it, stopping it from going farther. My first thought was, *No! My screen!* Followed by *I'm so dead.* It's a good thing I have my priorities straight.

The golden wolf huffed in annoyance as I stared at her. I scrambled to my feet. "Kat?" I asked, eyeing her.

I swear to God that she rolled her eyes at me. As a wolf. Rolling her eyes. It was like she was saying *Yes, stupid.*

"Where are the others?" I leaned down to grab my phone. She withdrew her paw from it. The screen wasn't scratched too badly, but I'd need a new case.

Kat flicked her head at the darkness, and I thought I understood. Will and Carter were still out there, fighting. I could hear snarls and yells in the distance, but these stupid containers made it hard to figure out how far those voices were. I hated this warehouse.

"Vaughn is back there, fighting a vampire," I said, trying to catch my breath. "Have you found Aunt Liv yet?" The wolf shook her head. "Can Vaughn handle the vampire on his own?"

Kat hesitated before dipping her head in a nod. I bit my bottom lip. "I need to find Liv. We need to get her and Jen out of here."

The wolf gazed into the darkness behind me, then turned her attention to me, watching me to see what I would do.

"He'll be okay," I whispered, more to convince myself than Kat. With another look behind me, I continued down the corridor, jogging this time, now with the golden-furred wolf by my side.

"How big is this stupid warehouse?" I muttered as we turned yet another corner a minute later. "It's a freaking maze."

Kat huffed next to me and looked up at the containers, then back at me.

"No, I can't climb those." I pointed at my chest. "Regular human. Remember?" There was a scuffling sound ahead of us, and both of us looked down the corridor, the wolf's ears pinned back.

The vampire came out of nowhere. One second, I was looking around, thinking of where to go, Kat at my side, and the next, a face that was contorted with rage and full of fangs rushed into my small beam of light. Kat moved quicker than lightning, barreling claws-first into the thing's chest, keeping its snapping jaws away from me.

I withdrew a few quick steps until my back hit the wall of one of the containers. Kat kept the vampire away from me. She lunged at it with claws and teeth as it tried to move forward. This vampire didn't take the time to talk, but it looked much less human than the last one had. It was too far gone for that.

This vampire was female. Long, stringy black hair fell over her shoulders. She looked like she'd been wearing a cocktail dress at one point, but it was so ripped and dirty, it was surprising the garment was still clinging to her body. She didn't speak as the other one had. Instead, she stared at me, barely taking notice of the wolf keeping her at bay. Her eyes were different from those of the last vampire that I'd seen. They were glowing in the darkness, a red the color of hot coals.

Kat lunged forward, and the vampire turned from me to meet the wolf, but as she had with the black-furred Spike, Kat danced out of her reach before she could grab her. The wolf threw a look over her shoulder at me, and my feet spurred into movement. Kat faced off against the vampire as I ran again. I felt guilty for leaving her there to deal with the monster by herself, but what else could I do? I was only a human.

I had no idea how many enemies we had. Kat must have been helping Will and Carter before she came looking for me. Would there be more up ahead? I knew there was at least one, the one who had been kidnapping women all over the city for the past few months. Calem. He was still here, and he had Jen and Liv.

There was a dim glow of light coming from around the next corner, and I dashed toward it. Using the part of my mind that was still capable of rational thinking, I knew it could be a trap since, as far as I could tell, the vampires and wolves didn't need light to see, just us humans. Maybe Aunt Liv had gotten out somehow? Or it could have been where they were keeping Jen and the other women.

I emerged into a more open area, surrounded on three sides by more containers. I could just make out what looked more like a wall, and not another metal container, most likely for the offices that would have been here when the warehouse was being used for its intended purpose. I couldn't see any doors that might lead to the offices because it was partially blocked by shipping containers. The space wasn't large, but it was at least as big as my living room at the house.

My light showed me an area that was clean compared to the rest of the warehouse. All of the dirt and grime had been scrubbed off the floors, and in the middle was a circle painted on the ground. It was a suspicious dark-red color, not black like I'd thought in my vision. All around the outside of it, were painted letters from a language I didn't recognize. Candles were lit and placed at the top, bottom, left, and right, like the points of a compass. In the middle of the circle was a mass of red flesh that I didn't want to look at too closely. Wax dripped down the sides of the candles, but they looked like they hadn't been lit for long. We must have interrupted the vampire in the middle of whatever he'd been doing.

Next to the circle was a woman sitting on the concrete, leaning against the wall with her hands and feet bound by a silvery rope. She stared at me as I came into the light of the candles, her eyes wide in surprise. She looked as she had earlier tonight, if only a little more roughed up.

"Liv!" I cried at the sight of her and ran over. There was no one else around. She was gagged, and it took my shaking fingers a few tries to undo the tight knots. Some of her hair came out with the tangled gag.

"What the hell are you doing here?!" she gasped when I finally got the gag off.

"Saving your ass," I said as I moved to the silver rope binding her limbs together. "I came with Will, Carter, Kat, and Vaughn."

"Where are they?" she asked, scanning the darkness as I worked. Aunt Liv was special, so it was possible that she could see better than I could, but her eyes didn't focus on anything.

"Somewhere out there, keeping the vampires distracted," I growled in frustration. "I can't get this stupid rope to give!"

"If you have a steel knife, it will cut right through it," she said, sounding much calmer than I felt. "Or anything with iron."

"Right, because they totally gave me a weapon," I replied with as much sarcasm as I could muster. If I acted like everything was normal, maybe we would get out of this alive. "Hold on, I've almost got it." My fingers were starting to hurt from trying to dig my nails between the fibers, but it was loosening. If this was mermaid hair, it was incredibly strong. "Ah!" I exclaimed as I got my thumb into the knot and pulled it free.

Liv shook her hands and rubbed her wrists as I moved to work on the bindings around her legs. "Did Will figure it out? Why did he bring you with him?" This last question sounded angry.

"Actually, I'm the one who found you, Aunt Liv. I've been having these weird visions since I moved here, but I can explain it to you after we get out of here. Bringing me along was part of the deal, and it's a good thing I'm here since everyone else is busy." I worked on the knot on the other rope, and it loosened enough for Liv to slip her legs out of it. Now that it was no longer binding my aunt, I examined the rope in amazement. Each strand was fluid in my hands and lighter than air, glowing like starlight.

"Hey," Liv said sharply, drawing my attention back to her. "We don't have time for that right now." She got to her feet.

I pocketed the mermaid-hair rope and stood as well. I could hear the sounds of my allies somewhere in the distance. "What do we do now?"

Liv's lips stretched into a grim smile. "What else? We fight."

CHAPTER 29

"FIGHT?" I asked, my voice high. "Are you insane? The others have teeth and claws and stuff. We don't have anything."

Without saying a word, Liv reached into her jacket and pulled a gun from a shoulder holster. The same handgun I'd seen her pull at the house. I felt my mouth drop open. How the hell did she still have that and why would the vampires let her keep it?

Liv held it out to me. She looked me dead in the eyes, strangling my protest that I didn't know how to use a gun before it left my throat.

"Point. Pull," she said, then touched her finger to the gun's sights. "Use that to aim and try not to hit any of your friends. There are six bullets left. Keep your fingers out of the way of the slide." She showed me how to hold the gun and pushed it at me, forcing me to take it.

The gun felt huge and heavy in my hands. It was much bigger than I thought it would be. How did she expect me to use this? "Point. Pull," I repeated to myself. "And hopefully hit something." I looked at my aunt. She didn't have anything else in her hands. "What are you going to do?" I asked. "If I have your gun, you'll be weaponless."

With a grim smile, Liv reached into her jacket and pulled out a small cylindrical tube the size of a soda bottle with a handle. She flicked her arm, and I heard a soft snapping sound as whatever it was extended into one of those long sticks with handles that you see in martial-arts movies. From what I remembered, it's called a tonfa. In the dim light, I could barely make out the intricate carvings running the entire length of the weapon. Liv whispered a word that I couldn't make out but made my ears ring. The carvings shone with ethereal blue light, forming the ghostly shape of a blade that fit over the tonfa.

She flexed the fingers of her other hand, whispered another word that made my mind swirl, and the ring that was on her middle finger glowed with the same blue light, forming a transparent, spiked gauntlet. "Mundane weapons like my pistol don't do much damage to vampires, but it should sting enough to give the others a chance to jump in. Don't worry. I have my own weapons that the vampires were too stupid to look for."

My mouth must have been hanging open because Liv took one look at my face and smiled for real. "Let's get through this. Then we'll talk. Stay out of the way, but don't go wandering off," she said and dashed off into the darkness.

I ran after her, keeping her in my sight but staying far enough behind that she was little more than a shadow in the dim light of my phone. I hoped the battery would last until this was all over.

Liv moved through the corridors, and she didn't look around as much as I did. While I'd found the passages dizzying in my vision, there had been no alternate hallways to go down, so this must have been a straight shot to the front doors.

I was right. Within a few minutes, we were looking at the doors that led out to the parking lot. The heavy doors were chained from the inside. Not only that, but a crowbar was shoved into the handles and twisted together. These doors were larger and thicker than the back door that we had come in. It would have been much more difficult, and louder, if Will had tried to claw through these to gain entry. He would have gotten through eventually, but it would have taken precious time. The vampires must have been expecting us to show up, and if we had used the front door, it would have been a massacre.

Liv looked around, then hit a switch on the wall. There was a clicking sound as the warehouse lights turned on one by one, illuminating the entire area. Most of the bulbs were burned out, but enough of them worked that it made my pitiful light obsolete. I turned it off and put my phone in my pocket.

"I can't believe that worked. The owner must still be paying for the electricity," Liv said, mostly to herself. She motioned for me to follow her down a corridor and in the direction of the sounds of fighting, growling, and snapping.

"Why did you go for the light switch?" I was thankful for the light. It made this feel less like a horror movie, but why had she gone for light instead of helping the wolves?

"It's for us," she said softly, moving with quick, measured steps on the concrete floors, keeping the sound of her movement to a minimum. I didn't know why she was bothering. I was making plenty of noise for both of us. "Turning on the lights doesn't help them at all, but we don't have night vision. It gives humans an advantage, and I'll take what I can get." She looked around, planning what we were going to do. "Okay," she whispered. "We are going to find Jen and get out of here. That way, I can give Will the signal that I'm okay, and they can just leave. My people can take care of it from there."

"You mean the Syndicate?" I asked.

She glanced at me, her expression sharp. "How do you —?" She shook her head. "No, that's not important right now. We need to go back to the clearing. I think the offices are there, and I have to believe that's where Jen and the other women are. Follow me, and stay quiet."

We moved back into the depths of the warehouse, and this time, she moved with careful slowness, looking around corners before waving that it was safe for me to follow. I tried to ask her what she was doing since she hadn't cared about the noise before, but she glared at me and cupped a hand to her ear.

I didn't hear anything. Then it clicked. Where were the sounds of growling and banging that I'd heard earlier? My stomach lurched. Had the wolves been killed while I was rescuing Liv?

We wove through the maze of metal and rust. Even though we were still in danger and unsure of what had happened to our allies, it was an enormous relief to have Liv back. Now, we just had to find Jen and get out of here. *One person rescued, one to go.*

When the dim glow of the candles was around the corner, Liv held out a hand to stop me and pressed one finger to her lips. I listened. After a moment, I could hear what she must have: the sound of footsteps.

We crouched behind the edge of the container. A few seconds later, a large man came jogging from a corridor on the other side of the clearing. He looked even bigger and more menacing in the light. The area around the circle was empty now. He cursed and looked around wildly, then walked around the circle, being careful not to disturb the candles, to where Liv had been tied up.

I could see the muscles on Liv's back tense as she watched the man, like a cat focusing on its prey. He paced around the clearing in agitation. When he had his back to where we were crouched, she moved.

One second, she was in front of me, and the next, she was dashing across the open space, closing the distance with the vampire in the blink of an eye.

He must have sensed her coming because he dodged at the last second and turned to meet her charge. I watched as the fingernails of one hand elongated, and he used them like a spear as Liv rushed him.

Before I could shout a warning to her, my aunt changed course at warp speed, sidestepping the jabbing nails and smashing her glowing gauntlet into the vampire's face. There was an audible crunching sound and grunt of pain, then the man staggered backward, thick, black blood streaming from his now flattened nose. The fact this vampire bled while the other one had not barely registered. I was pretty sure that if Liv had hit *me* like that, I would have been unconscious on the ground, but the vampire only took a few steps to steady himself.

"Bitch!" he hissed through the blood. He swiped his razor-sharp nails blindly at her, but Liv had already backed out of his reach. His feet sent candles tumbling, and he swore again, looking down at them.

Liv took the opportunity to slash with her blade, cutting through his shirt with a zapping sound and a spray of that dark blood, obscuring the circle and extinguishing more of the candles as he toppled to the floor.

The flames on the ones that were still lit flared as blood

speckled the circle and whatever had been inside of it. The lines drawn on the concrete stood out, more distinct than they had been a second earlier. Liv paused, noticing the candles for the first time. With a look of realization that I didn't understand, she left the writhing vampire on the floor to kick the remaining lit candles away from the circle. As she did so, the sharpness of the paint against the concrete faded. I shook my head to clear it, and when I looked back, the paint looked normal again.

Once Liv had extinguished all the candles, she approached the vampire on the ground with a calmness that was eerie. The tonfa must have cut deeper than I thought it had if he hadn't been able to get up when Liv's attention hadn't been on him. She rested the tip of the ethereal blade on his chest, and a low noise not unlike the hum of electricity permeated the small area. Feeling that it was safe to come out of my hiding spot now, I took a few steps into the clearing.

"Who is Calem working for?" she hissed, eyes on the vampire. "There's no way he's smart enough to do this all on his own. There has to be someone pulling the strings. If you can tell me who that is and help me bring Calem in, I'll ask the council to be lenient with you."

He stared at her, his hate and loathing plain on his face. "Go fuck yourself," he spat at her.

"Have it your way," she said, her voice icy, and she drove her blade into the vampire's chest.

There was the acrid smell of burning flesh as the blade ran him through the heart, making my stomach turn. The vampire convulsed once, then was still. Liv pulled the blade out and muttered "stubborn fool" before glancing over at me. "We should find the others."

The scream of crashing metal cut off her words, and Liv

bolted in my direction, grabbing me and pulling me out of the way as a door from one of the metal containers crashed to the floor. The door slid across the concrete until it smashed into the side of another container, blocking the way that we'd come from.

"What the hell was that?!" I shouted as Liv tried to locate what had thrown the door.

On top of one stack of containers stood a tall man with blond hair that came to his shoulders. I hadn't been able to see him very well in my vision, but in the harsh fluorescent light, I realized that I had seen him before. He'd been the one that I'd locked eyes with from across the room at Tombstone when we'd been questioning Santo.

The vampire glared down at us and leapt the twenty or so feet to the floor, landing lightly on his feet. The left side of his face was stained with blood from a gash on his cheek, but the cut didn't look deep. It was just a scratch.

"So it's come to this," he growled.

"Get back," Liv said to me as the vampire slowly closed the distance between us. "Get over to the corridor you came in from so that you can run if you need to."

"But," I began, unable to tear my eyes from the man approaching us, "what about the wolves? Where are they?"

"Where indeed?" the vampire said with a smile, showing his fangs. He paused a dozen feet from us. "I don't hear the sounds of battle anymore. The wolves haven't come to your aid yet. Which means they are already dead."

"Where have you been during all this, Calem?" Liv shot back. "Why would you leave your lackeys to deal with an infiltration that could expose you to the Syndicate?"

He grinned even wider, and it was a twisted, inhuman thing. "I've been entertaining my guests."

At his words, my fear evaporated. "Where is Jen?! What have you done to her?!"

The vampire tilted his head to one side like a bird that had heard an interesting noise. "Jen? Which girl is that?"

"Sarah!" Liv hissed, shoving me with an arm. "I said *get back!*"

Grinding my teeth, I retreated as far as I could, giving them space to prowl around each other. I was furious that the man who had kidnapped my friend had no idea who she was, but me yelling at him wasn't going to help us find Jen. I raised the gun that Liv had given me in shaking hands. The vampire I'd seen in my vision watched Liv warily, forgetting that I was there. She matched him, step for step. Liv must have really been someone that the supernaturals feared if this guy, who'd already kidnapped her and tied her up, was still being cautious.

They circled each other slowly in the confined space, around the circle on the floor. He didn't make a move to get closer to her, but he was angry, his face looking less and less human with each passing second. He started to look more and more like that feral vampire that had attacked me earlier.

I could see Liv's jaw flexing as she clenched her teeth. She was beyond angry, but when she spoke, her voice was calm. "It doesn't have to be like this, Calem. You can still surrender and let me take you in. You've hurt many people, and the humans are scared. Even if you can take me down, another hunter will take my place. Eventually, you'll be caught. We don't have to fight."

"It would have been easier for you if you'd laid down and died, Hunter." His eyes flicked to me, and I took an involuntary step away. "If we'd been able to complete the ritual, I would have left your family alone, but after I'm finished with you, that girl will die as well."

Liv scoffed. "Don't make me laugh. You already tried to kill her once. And you failed, as you may recall. Even if you were able to achieve whatever it is you're planning, she's seen your face, so you'd have to hunt her down anyway. She can identify you to the Syndicate, and they'll force your maker to turn on you. If you give up now, it will make it easier for everyone."

The blond vampire scowled. "And face your justice? They would have me imprisoned and starved before they kill me. Once I deal with you, I can leave the country and go into hiding. In a hundred years, they'll have forgotten all about a few human deaths and welcome me with open arms."

Liv still watched him carefully, mimicking his movements and not letting him get too close to where I was standing. "What I don't get is why you didn't run when the girls found you at Tombstone. Why attack me? No one would have known you'd left. You had to know that by going after me, there was a chance you'd get caught. It seems like an incredibly foolish risk."

At her words, the vampire's face fell into an expression that could only have been confusion. He opened his mouth to speak, but no words came out. That even made my aunt pause. He looked terrified. "Why, why, why?" he whispered under his breath. "It doesn't make sense. I had to do it. He wouldn't let me go, but I can't tell, can't tell." He raked his nails down his face as he spoke, leaving bloody lines that oozed. The switch from his wary confidence to the wide-eyed, deranged man in front of us was so abrupt that I lowered the gun and looked to Liv for some indication of what to do.

She kept a wary eye on the vampire but didn't let her guard down. "Why don't you just calm down and get on the floor? I can take you to people who can help you if you let me. I can't promise that they'll be gentle, but they will be fair."

"No, no, no!" he raved. "They can never find out, never! If they suspect you, kill them. If you can't get away, DIE!" he screamed. Without warning, the vampire charged at her across the circle, screaming incoherently with rage.

Liv brought her blade up in a block as he swung his arm at her. His clawed hands scraped against the tonfa, unable to find purchase. The other arm came in, and she ducked, using her fist to uppercut him in the jaw with the gauntlet. He staggered back from the force of the blow. Liv pressed her advantage, swinging the tonfa at his neck, going for a killing blow—so quickly that it looked like a blur. He leaned back and the blade missed him by inches. When the tonfa cleared him, he straightened, raking the claws of one of his hands at Liv's eyes.

She moved to the right, claws flashing past her face. Just as swiftly, she grabbed him by the throat with the gauntlet. With the tensing of muscles and a force of strength that seemed impossible, she drove the monster to the floor, smashing him into the concrete. The arm holding the tonfa rose past her head, preparing to strike with the extended part of the ethereal blade and end the fight, but the vampire slammed his knee into her side, causing her to cry out in pain. He brought a fist into her stomach, sending her flying ten feet into the air as the tonfa spun away from her. The blade flickered for a second, then disappeared, leaving only the rune-carved wood in its place.

Like a cat, Liv landed on her feet just in time to block the vampire's fangs with her forearm. The fangs pierced the leather of her jacket and sank an inch into skin and muscle. She screamed in pain, blood dripping from her forearm to the floor.

"Liv!" I yelled, trying to aim with the gun. Before I could do anything, she swung the gauntlet hard into the side of the monster's head once, twice, three times before he released her in a scream of agony, holding his head as she rolled away from him and closer to the discarded tonfa.

The vampire pulled his hands away from his face. Blood ran from his right ear, where Liv had hit him with the gauntlet. He whipped his head around to where she was reaching for the tonfa, eyes narrowed, and bounded forward, grabbing one of Liv's legs, yanking her away from the weapon.

She cursed and rolled onto her back, kicking at the claws holding her as he dragged her closer. His jaws snapped at her as a well-aimed kick connected with his neck, keeping the fangs away.

A howl shook me to my core. It echoed around the room, and if not for the gun I was holding, I would have covered my ears and cowered in a corner. Over one of the containers came the gray-furred wolf, muzzle and paws stained red with blood. Will.

The vampire let go of Liv and jumped out of the way as the wolf dropped to the floor, crouching over my aunt. A growl rumbled deep in the wolf's chest, and Liv wiggled out from under him, going for the tonfa again. The vampire kept his distance, hissing like some large cat as the wolf guarded Liv as she re-armed herself. The runes on the lacquered wood sparked to life, and the blade returned as she recalled the magic to it.

"Took you long enough," Liv said, a grin stretching

across her face. Will huffed out a breath at her, and the two of them faced the vampire together.

Liv gripped her tonfa in one hand. The gauntlet flicked out of existence, leaving just her fist in its place, the sleeve of her jacket ripped and mangled as blood still dripped from it to the floor. Will pulled his teeth back from his fangs, snarling at Calem as the vampire blinked rapidly at him.

"Alive?" the vampire whispered as if he was talking to himself. "Are all the others dead then?" His expression contorted into one of rage. "No! I will not be beaten by the likes of you!" he shouted and charged at the wolf.

Liv and Will darted in opposite directions. Calem went after Will, grasping at the wolf with his hands, but Will slipped out of his clutches, leading the vampire to the other side of the open space while Liv rushed to meet them.

Will turned abruptly to face Calem. Together, the wolf and Liv attacked, Will raking his claws on one side while Liv slashed with her blade on the other.

The double attack had been unexpected, and the vampire fell back from the onslaught, leaping high into the air and digging one hand into the metal container above them. He used the purchase he had to propel himself upward and onto the top of the container, looking down at us. Light from the flood lights above outlined his form, his chest rising and falling from exertion. I didn't know vampires could get tired. Then again, everything I knew about them had been from movies.

I glanced over at my aunt and the wolf. Liv didn't look so good. Her arm was still bleeding, and she, too, breathed heavily. Her expression was one of agony with each breath, but she stood her ground. Even with her injuries, she'd moved faster than anything I'd ever seen before. Carter had mentioned that Liv used her magic in a different way than I did. Was this what he meant? Was her magic the reason why Liv, who was just as human as I was, could hold her own against a vampire and a werewolf in the same night? Maybe she was the one who'd blown a hole through the house.

When I glanced back, Calem was still on top of the container. Hope surged in my chest. He could leave, run from Liv and Will, and this fight would be over. He was outnumbered and could just cut his losses.

He took a step forward, pushing off the edge and falling with unnatural speed, aimed straight at my aunt.

She was unable to dodge in time as he planted a foot into her chest, knocking the wind out of her and sending Liv skidding across the floor. The vampire pounced, raising one arm to smash his fist into her head. If he connected, the blow would kill her.

"No!" I shouted, but I needn't have worried. Liv rolled out of the way as the fist came down and cracked the concrete where her head had been a moment before.

Liv jumped out of the way as Will dashed in. It reminded me of how Vaughn and Kat fought together, but Liv and the gray wolf did it better. Compared to the two in front of me, the younger wolves were amateurs. My aunt's hands moved so fast that they were almost a blur, making her glowing blade look like one of those long-exposure photos of fireflies in the summer, where the light was just one long, continuous line.

Liv's blade connected with the vampire as she retreated, the ethereal weapon making the sound of a bug zapper when some hapless insect wanders into it. He screeched in agony as her blade both cut and seared his flesh.

Will dodged one of Calem's outstretched hands, then clamped his fangs onto the vampire's other arm as he ran past, dragging the creature back and, with the momentum, throwing him into the side of one of the shipping containers with a loud *crunch*.

The wolf staggered to one side, and I only then noticed that he hadn't quite dodged the vampire's claws. The fur on his left side was stained red in a long line going all the way to his flanks. He panted, tongue lolling out of his mouth even as the vampire pulled himself out of the dent in the metal surrounding him. What surprised me most was that even with the force of impact and the beating he'd already taken, Calem looked like he had just a few scratches.

It was then that I realized the longer they fought the vampire, the less likely their chances of winning were. It wasn't that they couldn't match the vampire in speed or strength. The two of them together appeared to be able to hold their own, but Liv was human, and she would eventually get tired and make a mistake. Both Liv and Will were injured, but aside from the minor blows that the pair had landed, the monster they were fighting was still whole. Where were the other wolves? We needed them to turn the tables to our advantage.

I looked down at the gun I gripped in my hands, white-knuckled from the intensity with which I was grasping it. It was a crazy notion. Aside from never having shot a gun before, that thing moved so fast it was hard to see, and he would be impossible to hit. But I needed to do something, didn't I? I couldn't let the vampire kill Liv and Will while I stood there and did nothing. Right now, the monster was ignoring me, so it was the perfect opportunity.

My hands were shaking as I pointed the gun again, but I tried my best to aim while they were dashing about in blurs of motion. I breathed deeply in an attempt to calm my nerves. There would only be one chance to get this right.

One bullet wouldn't kill him, but maybe I could give Will and Liv an opening and distract their opponent for a few precious moments.

Seconds seemed like days as I waited for the perfect opening, praying that I could hit the thing, praying that I would not hit Liv or Will and make things worse.

Will pulled back as Liv rushed forward, slashing with the tonfa, but her injuries had caught up with her. The vampire fended her off with apparent ease and pushed her back. She tumbled backward and out of his reach to catch her breath, guarded by Will's fangs. Liv rolled into a crouch, and the vampire tensed to press his advantage, grinning and knowing that he was close to winning this fight.

I pulled the trigger.

A CRACK as loud as thunder rang through the warehouse, and the vampire jerked to one side, blood blossoming on the pale skin of his shoulder. His head snapped in my direction, and his attention focused on me, his mouth in a snarl of fury so that I could see his blood-covered fangs even from this distance. My ears were ringing from the gunshot that hadn't done anything but annoy the monster in front of me.

As his eyes met mine, I felt like I was falling forward. Everything else faded away except for his eyes. There was no way that I could have seen their color from where I was standing, but somehow, I knew they were the color of a summer sky. Somewhere in the distance, I heard the gun clatter to the floor, but it was unimportant under the gaze of those eyes.

His attention was only on me for a few seconds, but that had been the point, after all.

In the moment of my distraction, Will and Liv pounced

on the vampire, the wolf's claws raking at the thing's midsection while Liv's bladed tonfa swung at his head.

The ethereal blade cut through the vampire's neck, separating it from his shoulders and sending his head toppling to the floor. The body flailed around for a second, then dropped lifelessly to the floor, blood oozing from the place where his head had been.

CHAPTER 30

THE SNARLING and growling of battle died as suddenly as the vampire did.

I felt my stomach lurch, and quickly turned away from Calem's decapitated head, breathing through my nose. Throwing up wasn't going to do any good in this situation. People were decapitated in movies and in video games, but it was different seeing it myself. To make matters worse, I'd had a hand in bringing about this person's death. There were going to be years of therapy in my future.

Trying to focus on something, anything else, I thought I saw movement down the corridor that led to the back door. I squinted, and the shadows resolved themselves into the forms of two wolves, one with snowy white fur and one with honey-gold fur.

Vaughn and Kat looked mostly uninjured, though Vaughn's muzzle was stained a dark brownish-red. Their fur was ruffled in places, and Vaughn still limped, but they looked to be okay, which was a relief. I was so grateful to see them that I heedlessly rushed over to them.

There was an angry shout from my aunt behind me, but

I didn't care. I fell to my knees in front of the wolves and wrapped my arms around them as tears welled in my eyes. "You're all right!" I said through my sniffling. "I was so scared that they'd killed you both."

The white wolf leaned into me, but the other stayed stock still, in shock. We'd had our differences, but with everything that was happening around us, I was glad that Kat was alive. After a few moments, Kat huffed out a sigh, and I felt her muscles relax.

There was a sound behind them, and I looked up to see the red-furred form of Carter coming from the direction that Vaughn and Kat had, looking worse for wear. Even from a distance, it was plain that his fur was sticky with blood, the same dark stains matting the fur on his legs. He was limping, keeping weight off his back right leg. When our eyes met, his ears perked up, and he padded over to us.

I sat on my heels, releasing the other two wolves. When he got within arm's length, Carter lay on the floor, watching me out of the corner of his eye.

Vaughn sniffed at the blood on his paws as I scooted closer to Carter. He didn't move as I reached out and ran my hands through his fur, looking for injuries. I couldn't find any cuts, but when I touched his back leg, a low growl rumbled in his chest. *Right, don't touch that.*

After I checked him, he got to his feet again and walked past me over to Liv. She was sitting on the concrete near the body. She or Will had moved the vampire's head out of sight, and I was relieved that I couldn't see it. Carter stopped in front of her, tilting his head to one side as he watched her face.

Liv narrowed her eyes as she watched him but shook her head in exasperation. "You idiot. Why'd you bring those kids?" she asked, annoyance touching her voice. A moment later, she patted the top of his head with the hand of her uninjured arm. "Thanks for coming for me. I'm not sure I could have gotten out of this one."

Carter's mouth dropped open in a dog-like grin.

Liv met my eyes and motioned for me to come closer. I jogged over to my aunt and knelt next to her. "You should go look for any signs of Jen and the other women. I wouldn't ask you to do this, but I'm not in any condition to help you search," she said. "Take Carter and Will with you and call for help if you need it. These two kids should be enough to protect me. If each of them took out one vamp, I don't think there are any left, but it's better to play it safe for now." She glanced past me. "Do me a favor and bring me my gun. I just need to rest a little."

At Liv's words, Carter trotted over to me. The red and gold wolf was still favoring his back leg, but that didn't seem to slow him down. Will had a long bloody line, matted in his gray fur on one side where the vampire had grazed him, but he wasn't showing any sign that he was in pain. If Liv thought that they had a better chance of protecting me, even like this, she was probably right.

We'd run almost the entire length of the warehouse in our various fights with the vampires, so the only place they might be was in the offices, but we had to find a way in.

I retrieved Liv's gun and took it to her. Following the wolves, I climbed over the mutilated container door that the vampire had thrown, and we made our way past the now-extinguished candles and headed toward the back wall.

Carter sniffed around and let out a low whine, bringing my attention to a three-foot gap between the container next to us and the wall. He gave me a look that told me to follow him, then disappeared behind the container. I stepped over and glanced around the corner, surprised to see a narrow walkway that we could fit through.

I followed Carter down the narrow opening, Will a few steps behind me.

The end of the narrow passageway opened into a genuine hallway, with walls that looked like they had once been white but were now stained with red and brown smudges. I didn't want to think too much about what those stains were. There were three doors, the two closest to me wide open. These had to be the offices that we were looking for. I glanced at Will, then strode over to the first open door, trusting that the werewolf's reflexes would keep me safe. Unlike the lights Liv had turned on by the front door, these lights didn't turn on when I flipped the switch on the wall. My only choice was to pull my phone out and use its flashlight again. With the wolves at my side, I peered into the first room.

The room was small but less filthy than I'd been expecting. A few bare mattresses were laid on the floor, and a desk with a broken leg was pushed against the far wall. A monitor with a cracked screen lay on its side by the desk, and I would bet anything there was an old computer hidden somewhere in that mess of broken wood. There was no sign of anyone in the room, but I hadn't expected there to be. If you're trying to keep someone from escaping, you don't leave the door wide open.

In the next room, there were piles and piles of trash bags. Will trotted into the room, sniffing around, while Carter stayed by my side. Despite appearances, it didn't smell like this room was full of garbage. Will pawed at one of the bags, tearing it open with a claw. A few items fell out, and I shined my flashlight on torn clothes, fast-food wrappers, a wallet, keys, and a cellphone. I picked my way through the garbage to where Will was and leaned down to pick up the items, examining each in turn.

My breath caught in my throat. These were Jen's belongings.

I hurriedly put the keys, wallet, and phone in my pants pockets and looked around at all the trash bags, reminding me of the night Vaughn and I had seen Will in the alley by the bar and the lumps of red flesh on the ground. My hands were shaking. "Is she in here?" I whispered, fear gripping my chest.

The wolf shook his head, and I let out the breath I'd been holding.

"Okay," I said, trying to calm down. "One more room to check."

Carter sniffed at the closed door to the last office. His lips pulled back from his teeth, and a growl bubbled from his chest, but when I reached for the doorknob, he didn't stop me. I turned it and pushed, but was only able to open the door a crack before it stopped, as though too rusted to open. But it was enough to be assaulted by the sickening smell of sewer mixed with something rotten flooding my senses, and I almost gagged. I covered my mouth with the sleeve of my sweater and shoved my hip against the door. The hinges screeched in protest, but after a few more shoves, it finally gave, and the wolves and I stepped cautiously inside.

The room was pitch black, but I could hear sniffling coming from somewhere in the dark space. I raised my phone to see if I could catch anything in the flashlight's beam. The room was covered in more trash and other refuse. Some I was sure was dried blood, and some I didn't want to know what it was, but could guess from the sewer smell. There were indistinct shapes covered by blankets and trash bags, and I caught a glimpse of a few flies feasting on the discarded remains of what I hoped was old food. The dim light fell upon two bloody masses, and then my heart nearly stopped as I spotted a figure huddled in the corner of the room, shoulders shaking as if the person were crying. I took a few steps closer and saw a bowed head sporting a pixie cut.

"Jen!" I shouted and ran forward. I didn't get far before both Carter and Will cut me off, both growling softly.

"What are you doing?" I asked, more than a little irritated. It was Jen! She was alive! "Get out of the way! I need to make sure she's okay."

They didn't move, and when I tried to move around them, they blocked my path again, showing their white fangs in a silent warning. I didn't know why they were doing this, but it made me angry. I tried to push past them, but Will shoulder-checked me so hard I almost fell, which would have been a bad idea in this filthy room.

There was the sound of running footsteps, and I heard Aunt Liv's voice call out, "Did you find her?!" And then she was behind me, swearing under her breath. Vaughn and Kat followed her in, still in wolf form.

"They won't let me through!" I shouted, pointing at the wolves, who stared at me expressionless.

"Sarah," Liv said, and her voice was pained. "You should leave the room."

"What?! It's Jen! She's alive and needs help!"

Aunt Liv put a hand on my shoulder. I glanced at her, but she was staring at Jen. I followed Liv's gaze. Jen was still sobbing. "Jen," Liv said, her tone gentle, "look at me, please."

It struck me how off that request was. After everything that Jen must have been through tonight, being kidnapped and put in here, and whatever else that vampire did to her, why was Liv asking her to look at us instead of helping her?

Whatever I was going to say died in my throat as Jen, obeying Aunt Liv, slowly raised her head, peering at us through the shadows.

Jen's eyes were two red-hot pinpricks in the darkness, glowing like smoldering coals in a dying fire.

She turned that glowing gaze on me, and my legs froze. The room tunneled, and everything fell away. All sound was muffled as if I were hearing things underwater. All I could see were Jen's eyes.

Someone shoved my shoulder hard, and I stumbled. It was like a spell had broken. All the sounds, sights, and smells of where I was came flooding back into my senses. I shook my head to clear it. "What *just happened?*"

"It's their gaze," Aunt Liv said.

"What are you talking about?" I didn't understand what she was saying. It was just Jen sitting over there, nobody else.

She ignored me. "Carter? Can you do it? I don't think it's safe for us."

"Do what?!" I shouted, getting angry. "We need to help her now!"

"No, Sarah," Liv said coldly, cutting me off. "You and I can't help her." She looked at me, and I could see the rage boiling underneath the cold expression. "Jen has been *changed.*"

And just like that, it clicked. There was a moment of stunned silence, and then I felt hot tears rolling down my cheeks. "No," I whispered. In a flash of insight, the two lumps of bloody flesh next to Jen made sense, and I felt my stomach turn over again. They had said that two other women had gone missing.

While we'd been talking, Carter had shifted back to his human form. He stepped around the refuse on the floor on soundless feet and approached Jen. She cringed away from him, but he knelt next to her, muttering words too soft for me to hear.

After a few moments, Jen's posture relaxed, and she nodded, closing her eyes. Carter reached out and took her into his arms, lifting her like a child and standing.

"It hurts, it *hurts!*" Jen sobbed as Carter carried her across the room. "I didn't mean to hurt those women, but I couldn't stop myself. I couldn't. It's my fault that they're... that they're..."

"Shhh," Carter shushed her and pulled her close to his body. He didn't limp, though the stiff way he walked told me his leg still pained him. "It will be okay, Jennifer. Just relax. You're safe now." He crossed the room to us, keeping Jen's head away from us.

Liv took off her jacket and handed it to Carter, leaving her in just a tank top. He somewhat awkwardly wrapped it around Jen in her torn and bloody clothes.

"Will and I will head out first," Carter said to Liv as he passed. "I don't think there are any more enemies here." He gazed down at Jen, who'd buried her face in his chest. She was still shaking. "We need to get her away from here." He left the office without waiting for my aunt to respond. Will, who remained in his wolf form, trailed behind him. He glanced back at us, giving Vaughn and Kat a sharp nod of his head before departing, then they fell in behind them.

I watched them go, feeling numb. How could I have let this happen to my friend? It was my family—and me in particular—who had dragged her into this mess.

"We should follow them out," Liv said, putting an arm

around my shoulders. She smiled at me. "Do you mind? I'm having a little difficulty walking."

We made our way back down the corridors and toward the door at the back of the building, the way the others had gone. When we got to the fallen container from the first vampire Vaughn and I had encountered, I helped Liv climb over it. It took all my willpower not to stare at the dark-red stain on the floor near it, and I was relieved once it was out of sight.

"Why didn't you tell me about Dad having powers?" I heard myself ask. "It would have been really awkward if I'd just started using magic in class one day." *Why didn't you tell me he was murdered?* I thought, but I knew if I said it out loud, I wouldn't be able to keep it together. Jen still needed my help.

Liv looked away from me. "We didn't think you had inherited our family's gifts. Your mom knew what signs to look for, and we had you every summer until you were fifteen. Under normal circumstances, if talent with the art is there, it shows up during the beginning of puberty, as early as eleven and as late as fourteen. When you'd shown no inclination at all, we'd thought the ability had skipped you."

I felt put off by that. "You sent me away to go live with Mom because I wasn't the same as the rest of the family?" I shot back, annoyed. "Do you know how often I was left on my own?"

"Sarah," Liv said, her voice soft. "You don't understand how rare magic is. Only a few hundred people in the entire country can use it. For a family to have three generations in a row who can use it for more than party tricks is practically unheard of. We were hoping that you could have a normal life away from the dangers of all this. But here we are." Liv smiled, but the expression was bitter.

When we came out the back door of the warehouse and into the brisk night air, Will's Camry was waiting for us a few feet from the door, and Will was sitting in the driver's seat, fully clothed. Carter was in the back seat, holding the weeping Jen in his arms.

"I'll take her to headquarters," Will said out the window, mainly to Liv, but he glanced at me. "They will be able to take care of her there. There's a procedure for new vampires." He tried to give me what he must have thought would be a reassuring smile, but it looked tired. "They will help her come to terms with what has been done to her and ease her into her new life."

I nodded, feeling numb.

"Marius is coming to pick you all up," he continued with a smirk that was definitely not intended for me. "You kids better get your clothes." Will popped the trunk and got out of the car.

Out of the corner of my eye, I saw Liv grimace. "Ugh, I hate dealing with that asshole."

One side of Will's mouth tipped up. "I've got an extra sweater. You look cold."

Liv took the sweater from Will with a resigned sigh as he closed the trunk, watching him get into the car and drive off. Vaughn and Kat had transformed back into humans and started dressing as she turned to me.

"I can't believe you're here," she hissed, pulling on the dark-blue sweater that was a few sizes too big for her. "What possessed you to come to this warehouse, of all places, to look for me?" Liv was angry, but not as mad as she'd been the night at the hospital when I'd talked to Kendra. "That was really stupid, Sarah. You could have been killed a hundred times over in there, even with the wolves to help you." There were tears in her eyes. I'd never seen her cry before, not even at Dad's funeral.

"We wouldn't have found you without her," Vaughn said from behind me, and I could feel his presence there. "She was the one who was able to guide us here."

"Yes," came Kat's voice, although grudgingly. "We wouldn't have reached you before whatever they had planned for you, Hunter."

"Aunt Liv, I'm not completely incompetent. You won't see me arguing with the fact that this is all a bit over my head, but there was no way I was going to sit by and let you be murdered." I stared at her, blinking back my own tears and trying not to think of Jen's new smoldering red eyes. "I won't lose anyone else, not if there's something I can do about it."

Liv frowned at each of us in turn, then swore under her breath and sighed. "You shouldn't have come to Seattle."

Before I could say anything to that, headlights appeared down the street, coming toward us. We watched as one of those giant black SUVs that could seat an entire soccer team and still have room for more pulled into the parking lot and drove up to where we were standing. The car stopped, and the front passenger window rolled down, revealing the angular face of Marius in the driver's seat.

"Miss Frost," he said cordially to my aunt, "I hear you need a ride."

Liv groaned. "Save it, Corvis. I'm assuming Will already told you what happened."

Marius pursed his lips and nodded. "That, and that you need to go to Syndicate HQ so that they can clean up this mess." His eyes flicked to the warehouse. "Though if you want, I can have my wolves do it for you. They would be much quicker than the Syndicate's people could manage, and likely beat the normal authorities as well. That"—he gestured at the door that Will had mutilated—"is bound to get some attention if a police car cruises by."

Liv looked like she wanted to argue but took a deep breath and closed her eyes. When she opened them again, her expression looked as if she'd swallowed something bitter. "Fine," she spat. "What will it cost me?"

He grinned at her, and it looked predatory. "I'll bill it to the Syndicate."

There was the *click* of the doors unlocking, and we all climbed into the SUV.

I could see Liv watching Marius, but he showed no emotion. Instead, he asked Vaughn and Kat if they were all right, and they said that they were.

"Kat and I should go to the studio," Vaughn said as he buckled his seatbelt. "It's the closest spot. Pack HQ is in Bellevue, so it's the opposite direction of where you're headed."

Liv shook her head. Her eyes flicked to Marius. "They need to come with us to the Syndicate. They'll want to ask them questions and piece together all the events from tonight," Liv said as she glanced back at me, smiling at the look on my face. "Don't worry. I just need to tell my superiors what happened. If Corvis is playing bodyguard, we'll be fine."

Marius didn't say anything, but I could see his smirk from the back seat.

"You should go to the hospital," I said to Aunt Liv, looking at her injured arm and bruised neck. "They were pretty rough with you, and I didn't even see what happened at the house. Who knows what kinds of injuries you have?"

"Yeah," she said with a sigh. "I don't want to, but I think one of my ribs might be broken. It hurts to breathe, but I need to report in first. We can go after that, and I'll talk to Carter about letting you stay at the studio for a little while. You should be safe with him."

"My wolves will be patrolling the area, just in case anything tries to come after you again," Marius said as he pulled out of the parking lot and onto the road. "If you need anything, they'll be close by. Carter won't like it, but he'll bear it." He sounded amused, and it pissed me off.

"Why do you treat Carter like that?" I asked before I could think better of it. "He's a wolf, too, right? He's part of your pack, or used to be, so why do you treat him like he's little more than a bug beneath your shoe?"

There was a ringing silence at my questions. The only sound to be heard was the engine and the whisper of the road beneath the tires. I was too numb and angry to be scared of Marius. He wasn't even close to the biggest, baddest thing I'd seen tonight.

Liv turned to me and opened her mouth to speak, but Marius interrupted her.

"He's not a member of my pack, Miss Frost. He and Will are both lone wolves that I *allow* to live in my territory." I saw his dark eyes watching me in the rearview mirror. I stared right back at him. "Years ago, Carter did run with us, but he struck out on his own. Many other alphas would kill a wolf that tried to leave, but I find that it's more useful to have an ally I can call on whenever I find need of it."

"So you left him alive because he could be useful?" I could feel Vaughn's and Kat's eyes on me, begging me to stop, but I ignored them.

The alpha chuckled. "My position requires absolute authority and respect. If I appear weak, other monsters move in, and the people of this city suffer." The leather wrapping the steering creaked under his grip. "Any challenge to that authority, no matter how benign, is unacceptable. Carter understands that, and, thus, he shows subservience in my presence. *As is his place.*"

My face felt hot as my temper rose. I wanted to argue with him more, but Vaughn's hand took mine, and he squeezed my fingers. I pulled my eyes away from Marius's and counted to ten in my head. Even if he needed to show his dominance to protect his pack and the city, he didn't need to be such an asshole about it. After a few seconds, I let out a long breath and flashed Vaughn a weak smile. I'd have to let this go for now.

A few minutes later, Marius pulled the SUV up to the big, dark building that I'd seen in my dream. It was still ominous-looking, rising at least twenty stories in all black glass. Some people may have thought it looked modern and sleek, but I thought it looked foreboding, like a burned tree in the middle of a thriving forest. Maybe it was because of what I knew it housed that my perception of it had changed. It was more than just a building to me. It was the symbol of the secrets and lies that had slowly crept into my life since moving here.

The SUV turned into the entrance of a parking garage next to the building, leading down and under the structures next to it. Lights flickered on as the car approached, no doubt their sensors identifying the vehicle's movement in the depths. I glanced at the clock on the dashboard. 3:45. It had been an exhausting night.

There were three other cars parked in the garage. Will's Camry was in a spot next to an elevator, and next to it, there was a late-model Mercedes and a silver Audi.

I glanced over at Vaughn, but he shrugged. He didn't know who else was here either. Will had brought Jen to this building, but the question on my mind was whether she was within the actual structure above us or down that dark stair-case I'd seen in my dream.

We all followed Liv out of the SUV and took the elevator down to B5, which I assumed meant basement five. Were there really five basement floors? I hadn't heard of any other building like that in Seattle.

When the elevator doors opened, we stepped into a large antechamber. The walls were whitewashed and pristine, adorned with paintings that looked vaguely familiar, like I'd seen them hanging in museums. The room was well lit, and I saw a set of large double doors on the far wall. Will was there, off to the side of the doors, talking to two well-dressed men.

The man on the left was tall, at least six feet or more, with olive skin and short, black hair that was slicked back stylishly. He was dressed in a dark-gray suit that looked like it cost more than Will's car. He had the appearance and bearing of the kind of man that my mother would meet with for work. A person with more money than he knew what to do with.

The tall man caught me looking at him, and he smiled at me, showing the barest tip of his fangs.

"Vampire!" I hissed and jumped backward, tripping over my own feet.

Vaughn caught my arm and helped steady me. "It's okay, Sarah. He's one of us." He gave the vampire a nod of his head. "Councilman," he said, his tone conveying respect.

"Forgive me for scaring you." The vampire's voice was deep and velvety, with the hint of a British accent. "My name is Richard Crawford. I'm a sitting member of the Syndicate of Nine."

The other man was a few inches shorter than Richard Crawford and not quite as suave-looking, but he, too, was wearing an expensive suit. He had dirty-blond hair and looked to be in his early thirties. His face wasn't kind, and he didn't even attempt to greet us as Crawford had. He watched Kat, Vaughn, and me with suspicion, like we had had some influence on the night's events.

Crawford glanced over at his companion, but when the man said nothing, he sighed and said, "This is Eric Cross. He's also a sitting member of the Nine."

"What kind of supernatural are you?" I asked wearily.

Cross scowled. It didn't fit on his face, which looked like it should be in a men's shaving commercial. "I am a human, young lady," he said in a supercilious tone.

Will interceded before I could snap at him. "These three"—he gave a sweeping motion at Kat, Vaughn, and me —"assisted us in taking down Calem, the rogue vampire that has been terrorizing the city the past few months. They need to be debriefed."

Eric Cross sighed. His stern expression faded, and he looked weary. "You brought kids with you?" It annoyed me that he called us kids, but I ignored it for now.

Will raised his eyebrows. "Councilman, I had a source who could take me to where Olivia was being held. If I'd waited for backup, she would have been dead by the time we got there. I didn't know how many rogue vampires were at the location. Three wolves and one gifted human were all I had to work with."

I eyed Will. He hadn't wanted me to go with them in the first place, but now he made it sound like it was his plan all along. If he got a promotion out of this, I was going to kick him. Will didn't meet my gaze, but I thought I saw the corner of his mouth lift in a slight smirk. *Ass.*

After considering Will's words, the man I assumed was the government liaison nodded once and gestured for us to follow them. Cross swiped a key card on a panel next to the doors. Then, with an audible *click*, the doors swung inward to reveal a large room. It looked similar to how I imagined the city council chambers would, except that instead of the council podiums facing out into the greater space, they were in the shape of a horseshoe. I counted nine seats, confirming that this must be a meeting room for the Syndicate of Nine. Any other number wouldn't have made sense. They were called the "Nine," after all.

Crawford placed his hand on my shoulder as I passed. "I've put Jennifer somewhere nice and quiet where she can rest." He squeezed my shoulder in what he must have thought was a comforting manner, then dropped his hand. "Don't worry too much about your friend. I'll take good care of her."

Emotions flooded me to the point that my heart ached. If he could help Jen, then this man was more compassionate than any vampires I'd met tonight. My best friend was one of them now, so they couldn't all be bad, right? Just because she'd been kidnapped and changed into something other than human against her will didn't change that we were still best friends. She was still Jen. Nothing would keep me from doing everything I could to make sure she came out of this all right.

I didn't know what to say to him, so I nodded my head and followed the others into the meeting chambers.

CHAPTER 31

AUNT LIV WAS in the hospital for a few days. Besides her arm being damaged from the vampire's fangs, she also had a fractured rib, but the doctors assured us that she was going to make a full recovery. She told them it had been a dog bite, and they wanted to run a bunch of tests. I couldn't live at the house with the state it was in, so Carter let me stay in the spare room at the studio. He stayed there, too, making an excuse that he had a lot of work to do so it would be easier for him to sleep there, but I knew it was really to watch over me. I didn't mind. Carter was good company, and working longer hours with him distracted me from everything else that was going on.

The morning after our adventure, I saw on the news that the warehouse Liv and Jen had been imprisoned in had burned to the ground. Apparently, the containers inside had not been empty, and the contents, whatever they were, had been quite flammable. Not many people visited that area of town at night, so by the time the authorities were called in, all they could do was contain the blaze. They suspected it was arson, but since the company that owned the building was in another country, the police were having a hard time questioning them.

No bodies were found, so whatever Marius's pack had done, they'd removed all evidence of our fight with the vampires.

Marius was not happy with Vaughn and Kat for going to take down the vampires with two lone wolves, but he was lenient with them since they received accolades from the Syndicate of Nine. The Syndicate commended them for their help in defeating the vampire that had been murdering women. I suspected that Will had something to do with getting them into Marius's good graces. I guess he wasn't such a bad guy after all.

I was supposed to go back to high school in mid-January, but Liv was able to pull a couple of strings with the superintendent of the school district. We received permission for me to go back in February, once everything was settled and the house was repaired.

A week after Liv was released from the hospital and we'd gotten the house livable enough to stay there, she gave me a necklace with a silver pendant and a card with an address on it. "Go there on Wednesday at eleven for brunch. Jen will be waiting for you." I hadn't seen Jen since that night at the warehouse. Liv pointed at the necklace. "The Archmage gave me that amulet. Wear it when you go to see Jen. Do not take it off while she is around. Do you understand?"

I nodded and put the card and the necklace in my pocket, then helped Liv finish taping plastic sheeting over the large hole in her bedroom wall. She was staying in one of the other bedrooms while repairs continued throughout the house.

On Wednesday, I went to the small café in Belltown at

eleven. It was overcast, and I found Jen sitting in the shade of the awning that covered the patio. She wore a turtleneck sweater that covered her skin from the neck down, gloves, and those oversized sunglasses that you see celebrities wearing in fashion magazines. Yet, she didn't look out of place. On the contrary, she blended in well with the winter jackets that most people were sporting. I slid into the chair across from her and laid both my hands on the table.

Jen reached out and gripped them hard, just shy of painful. I could see the cracks forming in her calm demeanor.

"How are you doing?" I asked. "Are you adjusting?"

"Yeah," she said with a small smile. Jen took off her sunglasses and set them on the table. There were large bags under her eyes, and she looked paler than usual, but her eyes were normal. Not the smoldering coals they'd been the last time I'd seen her. It didn't feel like I was falling either. They were Jen's eyes. "It's difficult not being able to see my mom or friends, but I'm working on my control. As far as they know, I'm still missing. Richard said I could contact them soon, but to give it a little while. Only you, Vaughn, and Kat know the truth about my... condition." She chuckled bitterly. "I never ever knew they were werewolves. I've known Kat for years, and she never told me."

"What's it like?" I asked, unable to help myself. "Sorry, I don't mean to intrude. If it's too painful—"

Jen shook her head. "No, it's fine. Actually, it would be nice to talk about it. Everything is so new for me." She sighed. "It's not like what you see in movies. I don't have some insatiable bloodlust, and I don't burn when exposed to sunlight. However, Richard told me that sunlight can kill us if we're out in it for too long, so no beach trips for me anytime soon. Richard is the Syndicate member who is taking care of me for now," she explained. "Being awake during the day is like having a nasty hangover. I'm tired, sore, and I want to sleep, which is what most of us do. In the daylight, our senses are dulled, and we don't have supernatural strength, so we are vulnerable.

"I do drink blood, and everyone around me smells different than they did before, but, well, it's hard to explain." She paused, and I could see her thinking over her words. "It's like when you smell food, and even though you're not hungry, you think to yourself, 'I could eat.' I feel that way whenever I'm around normal people. Richard keeps me full, so it's not like I'm going to lose control while I'm in public, but it's tough to even be around people, at least for now. He tells me that I'll get used to it in a few years."

Jen seemed so dejected that it was all I could do not to get up and give her a hug. I reached out and took her hand again. "You'll get through this," I said. "I'll be here to help you." I squeezed. I tried to keep my voice steady. "And... and I'm sorry. I'm so sorry about all of this. The vampire was trying to get to me, but it couldn't directly, so it went after you. It's all my fault."

Jen's eyes jerked up to mine. "What are you talking about?"

"It wanted me," I said, lowering my voice as a couple took seats at a table across the patio. "But Liv was there, always protecting me, so he went after you instead." I closed my eyes and turned my head away from her, ashamed of my confession. "If it could have gotten to me, it would have never come after you. I should have stayed close to you, ensured that you were safe, and weren't doing anything reckless. I should have stopped you from going to Tombstone."

"Sarah—"

"It's all my fault, Jen. You might not forgive me, but you need to know that I'm sorry for everything. I'm sorry that I let this happen to—"

"Sarah, will you listen to me?" Jen said, her voice so sharp it made me look at her. She was scowling. "Who told you that? Who told you that it was your fault?"

"Marius figured it out. He arrived at Carter's studio and explained how stupid we'd all been and how the vampire had been after me." I shook my head. "It should have been me taken, not you, Jen."

"Marius," she began, her scowl deepening, "is an asshole. Calem—they told me that was the vampire's name. He wasn't after you at first. He was coming for me."

I stared blankly. "Then why did his wolf attack my house?"

Jen looked at her hands. "When he took me to that warehouse, he tied me up and talked to me. I think Calem got off on bragging about how he picked me. He'd seen me at Tombstone, asking around about Kendra. I never spoke to him while we were there, but I remember seeing him in the upstairs loft. He... he..." She took a deep breath to collect herself. "He tortured me into telling him who was there with me. He already knew about Stella since she was with me upstairs, but he made me tell him about you and Vaughn too." She was on the verge of tears, and her bottom lip trembled. I wanted to tell her to stop, that it wasn't her fault, but I wanted to hear the rest of it.

"When he heard Vaughn's name, he was shocked. Not shocked like he knew him, but more like he knew *of* him, and he was agitated. He kept muttering about covering his tracks. Then, when I told him your name, he flipped out. I didn't understand it at the time, but I know now." She looked at me. "Everyone is afraid of Liv. She made a name for herself wiping out an entire brood of fifteen vampires in one night in Portland a few years back. That's why he wanted to sucker punch her at her home, with you there. He wanted to catch her off guard, and there was something he wanted from her, but I don't know what that was. There was someone else, someone telling him what to do, but I never saw who it was."

I thought back to what the vampire had been saying before he died. *I had to do it. He wouldn't let me go, but I can't tell.* Who had he been talking about? At the time, I'd thought he'd been raving because Aunt Liv had been about to fight him, but, now, I wondered if there was something else going on. With Calem and his cronies dead, there was no way to find out if there was an even bigger plot.

Jen wiped a tear that had escaped with the back of her hand. It wasn't the color of blood or anything. It was just a normal tear. "You see," Jen said, voice breaking. "It was my fault that he went after you, not the other way around."

"It's not your fault," I said, heat creeping into my voice. How dare that bastard hurt my friend? How dare he lay one finger on her? If he wasn't already dead, I'd kill him again. And how dare Marius manipulate the truth to manipulate me. "You're right. Marius is a huge asshole."

She choked on a laugh. "I always thought he was. This proves it." She took a deep breath, then flinched. She stared at me, her eyes wide. "Sarah," she said, her voice soft. "I just noticed that you don't smell like anything. How is that possible?" Jen's eyes moved over to the couple across the patio. "I can smell them, but I can't smell you."

I pulled the amulet that Aunt Liv had given me out of my shirt. "Liv gave this to me. She said it would make it safe to be around you."

She blinked rapidly, and I knew she was holding back tears. "You don't smell like food or anything else." Jen looked down at her hands again and then back to my face. "C-could you get one of those for Stella and my mom? I haven't been able to see them at all since this happened."

I scooted my chair next to hers and wrapped an arm around her shoulders. "Yes, of course."

Jen laid her head on my shoulder and cried.

A Syndicate mage named Lisa Nguyen came to test my magical abilities. She had me take what she called the "standard test." Lisa laid a metal cube, a blank piece of paper, and a polished wooden stick that I recognized as a wand, thanks to pop culture, on the table. I imitated motions and spells that I'd seen in movies and was surprised to see that some of them actually worked. From what she'd told me, all the items could do something, but I could only get the wand to work.

"It's all right," she said, and she put the items in her bag. "There hasn't been anyone who has been able to activate all three items on the first try in over five hundred years. Just being able to use one well means you have a lot of potential. We should have you start training right away."

"Do I need to go choose my wand and pack my things to go to some magic college in the countryside?" I was only half-joking.

The mage laughed. "No, no. The wand worked for you the way it did because you believed that was how it *should* work. Magic helps us shape reality around our will." She picked up the cube and held it in her hand. Before my eyes, intricate little carvings emerged from the surface of the metal, churning and moving until the shapes formed a flower on it. The metal moved around it, and the shape changed to that of a budding blossom. "With practice, this would be easy for you to do. These items are tools to channel your magic, the same way that a wire channels electricity. While you don't need devices to work your will on the world around you, they help you get the desired effect, especially at the beginning of your journey." The cube returned to its original shape, and she set it on the table.

"You have the potential to become a fully-fledged Syndicate mage. According to your family records, it would be the first time in over a century that anyone in your family could achieve such power." Lisa smiled as she raised the wand, a fond look on her face. "Your aunt and father had a hard time getting this to spark."

"You tested them too?" I asked.

"Oh yes. I have jurisdiction over the testing in Washington and Oregon. Most children start showing an affinity for magic once they hit puberty, so you're a bit of a late bloomer, but don't worry," she added quickly. "That doesn't mean you are any less talented. Magical ability is so varied that it's hard to standardize the testing, but this seems to work well." She smiled at me, and it reminded me of an old '60s TV show where the housewife would smile while telling you how great the vacuum cleaner was.

I was silent for a moment. "To tell you the truth, I'm not sure that this is something that I want to do. My aunt was almost killed because of what she can do, and you're saying that my abilities are stronger? Those powers that the rogue vampire used were evil. I'm not sure that I want any part of that."

Lisa chuckled at my words. "I don't think you quite understand how magic works yet, Sarah." When I didn't say anything, she continued. "Let me put it this way. A sharp blade in the hands of an enemy is a deadly weapon. In the hands of a friend, it's a great defense, and in the hands of a surgeon, it allows them to heal. Magic is like that blade. Your power isn't inherently good or evil. Like any other tool, it's how you choose to use it that gives it intent.

"Your aunt uses her abilities not only to enhance her own body, but to use that enhancement to help protect the normal humans who would get hurt if another supernatural being were to target them. It's how you use the magic that gives it meaning." Lisa smiled at me and put the three testing items away and packed away her notes. She stood and put a hand on my shoulder. "Think it over. If what you want is to learn to control it so that it doesn't hurt anyone, we can do that, but I think you should give yourself a chance to nurture your abilities and see what you can become with its aid." She squeezed lightly, then let go and saw herself out the front door.

"What are you going to do?" Vaughn asked when I told him about the test. He and Kat had picked me up from the house in Vaughn's new car, and we were on the way to see a movie.

"I don't know," I said from the back seat. "I'm not sure if I want to learn magic after everything that's happened, but on the other hand, it's not like I can close my eyes and pretend all this doesn't exist. There's a chance someone could come after us again since Liv is still working for the Syndicate. They said they were going to give us some extra protection, but you never know."

"It would be good if you could defend yourself," Kat said with a small smile. Ever since the night we rescued Aunt Liv, she had been much friendlier to me.

"Ha ha," I said, my voice flat. "You think I should do it?"

"Absolutely," she said, then thought about it. "I can buy you a pointy hat and a staff."

We all had a good laugh at that. "How are the renovations on the house going?" Vaughn asked. "Are they going to be finished soon?"

"It would be nice if they were," I said as we turned into the parking lot. "Liv's been cooking upstairs since the downstairs kitchen is trashed, and she doesn't always clean up after herself right away. I like having my own space."

"I'm sure Carter would let you stay in the studio for longer if you want," Vaughn said as we got out of the car and walked to the theater. "Knowing him, he'd be happy to let you stay there."

I shook my head. "Nah, there's too much stuff I need to do around the house. Besides, Liv is there now in case anything happens. She's almost recovered. That's one good thing about her magic being used to augment her body." We went into the theatre. It was crowded, but we had a good time.

I called Lisa the next day and scheduled my first appointment. If I was going to have to learn how to control my magic anyway, I might as well learn how to use it. There was always the possibility that it could come in handy one day.

When I told Liv about my decision, she wasn't happy or angry. She pursed her lips and said, "Your mom isn't going to like it. She kept you away from here for so long because she wanted to keep you out of this life, the life that killed Dave."

I was quiet for a moment, sitting on the new couch, on

the opposite end from Liv, staring at where the TV once was. We hadn't gotten a new one yet. "Dad was like you, wasn't he? They called you a hunter, Kat and Marius."

"That's not really what I do. I'm more of a liaison of sorts, but I'm trained to defend myself and to hunt down rogue supernaturals when they start preying on people. I guess that's where the name comes from." She sighed. "Yes, he was like me, but better. He went beyond hunting rogues that went out of control. He knew how to get people to listen to him."

She looked down at her hands. "Dave went missing one night. I knew something was wrong when he didn't come home, but no one I called at the Syndicate would tell me what happened. We didn't find out until the next morning that he'd been attacked by a wolf that he had been tracking." Liv gazed up at me, eyes shining. "What's worse, is that we never found the killer. That's what scared your mom so much, that if even Dave could be killed like that, how could the Syndicate of Nine protect her family? Supernaturals are everywhere, but those of us who work for the Syndicate are only well known in our area, so she fled to the other side of the country."

"She abandoned her family," I said without any heat.

"No, she did what she thought best. I can't blame her for wanting to shelter you from all this." She scooted over to me and laid her head on my shoulder. "But I have to say, I'm glad you came back. If you hadn't been here, I'd be dead."

My eyes stung, and I blinked tears out of them. "Don't say that," I said, and I had to clear my throat before I continued. "I can't lose you too."

"You won't," she assured me. "Are you sure you want to do this? You can't unlearn this stuff once you know it."

"Yes," I said.

It was settled. I could tell that Liv wanted to argue more, but, for once, she let it go. She finally trusted me to make my own choices.

I'm not 100 percent better yet, but in light of the events of the past few weeks, I'm doing okay. My problems with Brian and my reasons for moving to Seattle are still there. Mom is absent, and I'm trying to find a happy medium between my anxieties and pressing the reset button on my life.

Now, I have new nightmares that wake me up in the middle of the night in a cold sweat. Dealing with everything is a lot of work, but it gets easier every day. Even with what I've gone through, I have a feeling that I've barely had a glimpse into the world that lives just under the surface of our reality. There is the constant feeling that the worst is yet to come and that I can do little to stop it, but at least I don't have to face it alone.

Vivian Bricker has been writing fantasy stories since she was old enough to pick up a book. She lives near Denver, Colorado with her husband and two Shiba Inus, and has a degree in business administration. Free time is hard to come by, but when she has a few extra hours, she likes to paint, practice archery, and run tabletop roleplaying games.

Twitter/X: @VBrickerAuthor
Website: brickerandnobles.com

www.ingramcontent.com/pod-product-compliance
Lightning Source LLC
Chambersburg PA
CBHW022007310726
48972CB00006B/1558